# A
# Sisterhood
# of Heroes

## A Sister is so Much More Than a Sister

Bob Boze
Casey Fae Hewson
April 2022

## Table of Contents

# Chapter 1 – Another Day

Teagan watched as they loaded the badly banged up accident victim into the back of her helicopter. A second later the strong smell of alcohol drifted into the cockpit. "Yup, definitely a DUI!" she mumbled inside her helmet as she tried to wave the alcohol cloud out the back door.

Late twenties. Thirty at most. The guy's right arm was in a sling, his face had several cuts and bruises, plus she was quite sure his nose was broken. Too bad. He looked to be quite handsome. Or at least had been, until he decided to do some facial reconstruction on himself.

Before the stretcher was halfway in, Aoife climbed in, blocking Teagan's view as she guided the front of the stretcher into the bottom rack of the stretcher shelves.

"Effa, you need help?" Teagan asked.

Once the front of the stretcher was stable on the rack, Aoife looked over at Teagan and shook her head. Teagan could see her smile through the tinted face mask of her helmet. *Good, at least he's not critical.* She knew Aoife would never smile unless he looked a lot worse than he was, which was often the case with drunk drivers.

On the other end of the stretcher was Erin, who guided the back of it onto the shelf, then locked it in place; making sure the green 'lock light' came on. The two of them were a well-coordinated team and Teagan was glad it was two of her sisters working with her. They, and their other two sisters had all become first responders, in one form or another. Even the sixth, Baby Fae, was off getting her commercial pilots license so she could become an air tanker pilot with Cal Fire. They all lived together, had studied together, practiced, and quizzed each other all through school and even into their rookie training.

"You coming with us?" Aoife asked Erin.

"Can't... they need my help checking the two girls this asshole ran into. You all set?" Nodding, they both turned and gave a thumbs up to Teagan, who already had her hand on the throttle and collective. Aoife strapped in while Erin jumped out, slid the door closed, rapped on the side of the chopper twice then bent over and ran till she was clear of the rotors.

As soon as she knew Erin was clear, Teagan turned the throttle and brought the main rotor up to flight speed. After scanning the instruments to make sure the fuel controller was holding the rotor's speed steady, she eased the collective up. Checking outside, she listened as the rotor's blades dug into the air and the helicopter started to lift off.

Another glance at the instruments and everything looked normal. But suddenly she had a bad feeling; something wasn't right. A second later she lost yaw control. Now, some twenty feet off the ground, she'd already started to ease the collective back down just as she heard Aoife, who had also been watching and listening intently, shout "Abort! Abort!" in the headset.

Descending quickly, the tail came around to the right, the skids bit into the dirt below them and Teagan fought to keep the chopper upright.

The skids digging into the dirt probably had more to do with getting control of the chopper then Teagan did. As soon as it came to a stop, she started shutting things down and turned to Aoife. "Call home and tell them we need another bird out here."

"Got it," Aoife answered. "Mercy Air Base, this is Air Three."

The door slid open and Erin stuck her head in. "You guys okay?"

Teagan and Aoife gave her a thumbs up and Aoife went back to her call for backup as "Go ahead three," came over the radio.

"Uh, our bird died. We need another bird for transport and a retrieval crew to get this one back."

"Is it flyable?"

"Only if it's on the back of a flatbed."

"Got it. Air Two's ready to lift off and should be to you in less than fifteen. Tell Teagan to wait for the retrieval crew so she can tell them what happened."

Teagan came on the radio. "It crapped out is what happened. The good news… we were only twenty feet in the air when the tail rotor quit and I lost yaw control."

"Okay, well tell the retrieval crew that when they get there and hitch a ride back with them."

"What's the penalty for accidently having it fall off the truck on the way back?" she kidded.

"Uh… that's the EC 130 so it's only about $2.4 million new. Your great, great, great grandkids should have it paid off before they retire. I suggest you hug it and don't let go till you and it are back in the hanger."

"Who the hell bought this thing? It's got next to no power compared to the 145s and it's definitely a male because it whines and goes into nap mode at least once a week." She couldn't help but hear the chuckles that came back but didn't know if it was Aoife, the dispatcher or both.

"I'll personally buy you a beer when you get back," the dispatcher told her.

"Oh, thanks. That'll make up for our near death experience… speaking of which, Aoife and I need a panty allowance since we soiled the ones we've got on."

This time it was definitely the dispatcher chuckling. "I'm not going anywhere near that line. Fly safe in your flatbed ride back."

***

Aoife looked down and the eyes of the guy on the stretcher were open and he was smiling. He stared at her name tag. "A… O… Fee… Do you always have this much fun on a body pickup?" the guy asked.

She locked him in a death stare. "My name is 'Effa' and this is our small bird. Usually a guy your size overloads it so, we probably wouldn't have made the hospital anyway."

"Funny," he said and tried to sit up. That resulted in a loud scream, then him passing out when he leaned on his damaged arm.

"What did you do to him?" Teagan asked.

"Nothing… yet," Aoife answered, adding an evil grin. A minute later he moaned and his eyes opened again. Pretending she didn't hear or see him wake up, she looked at her watch. They still had a few minutes left before Air Two arrived.

"Hey, Teag…" she said. "Who's driving Air Two?"

"Not sure. Why?"

"I was thinking. Since this guy's out, we could dump him in the bay on the way to the hospital and get a little live water rescue practice in."

"Hey! Great idea!"

"Um, excuse me… you can't just throw me into the water," he said. "Besides I can't swim."

9

Aoife looked down at him. "OMG. That's even better. We need to qualify with non-swimmers. How are you at flailing around while we try to get to you?"

"You… you're… sick."

"Yeah, the last guy said that too."

Just then the crew from Air Two stuck their heads in the doorway. "He ready to go?"

"I… I … I don't want her" – he poked his finger at Aoife – "coming with us!"

The Air Nurse from Air Two whispered loudly, "You let him hear what we do with DUIs?" She winked at Aoife and added, "Crap! I'm never going to get my Water Rescue Merit Badge!"

Suddenly the guy realized it was his being drunk that they were all reacting to. After they unlocked his stretcher and started to slide it out, he reached over and placed his hand on Aoife's arm. "Wait," he said. "Look, I'm sorry. I shouldn't have been driving. It was stupid… I know that now."

Aoife still had her helmet on but he could imagine her rolling her eyes. "You're apologizing to the wrong people. You need to tell that to the two girls you nearly killed. If it hadn't been for the fast reactions of the one driving, and her guessing the right way to turn to avoid you, they'd both be dead now."

"I… I…"

"Save it," she told him. The Air Two crew pulled him the rest of the way out, carried him over to their helicopter, slid him in and closed the door.

"Are you okay Eff?" Teagan asked.

"Yeah. I'm just so tired of collecting mangled bodies and listening to the person who mangled them say, 'I'm so, so sorry,' only to pull them, and more bodies out of another wreck a week later."

Teagan pulled her helmet off and smiled at her. "Erin and the others have things under control, plus it looks like the two girls came out okay. Ride back with us and I'll split the beer the dispatcher's going to buy us with you."

"Oh wow! How generous of you! You just want help holding 'Mr.-can't-keep-his-tail-rotor-up' so he doesn't fall off the truck and saddle our next three generations into slave-a-tude with Mercy Air."

"Slave-a-tude? Is that even a word?" Teagan asked trying to choke down a laugh.

"It will be after our second beer. Come on goofball, I'll woo the dispatcher while you rake through his wallet… oh, and better get enough so Erin can join us."

"I can't believe you just called me goofball! What are we… ten again?"

Wrapping her arm around Teagan's shoulders, Aoife walked them to the flatbed truck that their EC 130 was being winched onto. "We'll always be ten. Those years on the ranch will always be the best years of our lives." She paused, "And you'll always be a goofball."

***

The flatbed pulled out onto the road, the EC 130 wobbling on the back and laughter from some silly story about their growing up on the ranch streaming out the truck's back window.

Aoife and Teagan walked into 57 Degrees, waved at the owners, then headed for the bar height table permanently reserved for them by the back window.

Carol, the waitress, came over. "Tough day? You're both still in uniform, that usually means you came right from an accident. You both okay?"

They each hugged her before pulling out stools. "Actually, an easy day. That's why we're ahead of the rest. Only four transports to other hospitals and an organ run," Teagan told her.

"I take it that means the other three will be here shortly?" Carol asked, already knowing the answer. "I assume you brought a change of clothes as usual, so the back room's open if you want to go change."

"Think the others will be able to find the table?" Aoife asked, adding a chuckle.

"I think so… since you all practically live here." Just then they turned to watch the British Airways daily flight to Heathrow chew its way into the sky. "Different day, same table, same flights and us wishing we were on them," Carol said. "Be right back… go change."

A few minutes after they disappeared into the back room, Erin, Bridget and Kiera came through the back door. Carol, with Aoife and Teagan's drinks on her tray, intercepted them as they all headed for their table.

Before anyone could get settled, Aoife and Teagan came out of the back room, threw the hangers with their flight suits over the back of an empty chair and sat down. "And… where were you two? You were supposed to hold our table down. If it weren't for Carol, we'd be sitting on the steps in the parking lot," Bridget said.

Teagan looked at Aoife and the others, then turned and scanned the almost empty back area. Turning back to Bridget she stepped into her, kissed her on the cheek and told her, "Your reserved table is across the alley in the Enterprise Rent-A-Car lobby. It's the one that says, 'Reserved for Critter Control.' There's a space next to it that says, 'Set your traps here.'"

The rest were giggling when the last sister Fae, came through the door and made her way to the table. Conversation stopped and Keira asked, "What are you doing here?"

"My plane broke so I've got the next two days off."

"Aww, what did you do… break one of the training wheels on landing?" Teagan asked.

Fae scrunched up her face and gave them all a death glare. "Ha ha. Very funny! You know… I'm so glad I didn't have to grow up with the rest of you goofballs."

A second later she was surrounded by five of her sisters, the center of a giant hug.

***

Carol brought drinks for the last four sisters and they insisted her boss let her join them or they would never return to 57 Degrees; well at least till tomorrow.

Poorly timed with a conversation lull, Aoife let out an "Oh shit!" Everybody followed her eyes to a guy, obviously headed for their table.

"Hey, isn't that the guy that broke our whirlybird before we could get him to the hospital," Teagan asked Aoife.

"Yup, that's him," she answered, giving him a 'what the hell do you want' glare as he stepped up next to Aoife.

"That look tells me you're not happy to see me so I'll make this quick." Before he could launch into the speech he'd practiced,

13

he and Teagan locked eyes and he suddenly forgot why he was there.

The same feeling rushed through Teagan, soaking her lower girly parts like a fire hose had been turned on. *Damn, damn, damn, he cleaned up well.*

Aoife and the rest of them watched as the two of them stared at each other. Finally, Fae spoke up. "I know I'm the baby here but I'm pretty sure I know what that look means and I think Carol needs to find them a table off by themselves. Like maybe in the back room… the one with the lock on the door?"

Teagan was first to break out of their trance. She picked up her glass, walked around the table and took him by the hand. "Come with me before my sisters eat you." His eyes went wide and she added, "I'd not say a word if I was you." Then she turned to the table, "Back off! He's mine and anyone who touches him is going to need a ride in my whirlybird… Got it?"

Everyone nodded, Erin made cat claws, while Kiera made a cross with her fingers to hold Teagan back.

"If I get him a drink, is it okay to hand it to him?" Carol asked, as she slid off the stool.

"Yip, just don't linger."

By now the guy had given up trying to keep from laughing. "You're all crazy," he added.

"Yes… and I'm the craziest and you're with me… got it?" Teagan asked.

All he could do was nod 'yes' until he finally quit laughing. "Since I may never see any of you again, I'm Chase Brooks."

Teagan then introduced her sisters, one by one, as they waited for Carol to come back with a beer for him and a refill for her.

14

Drinks in hand, Carol ushered them toward a table off in the corner.

As they stepped away, he heard Keira say, "So Fae, you broke your plane?"

"The S2F broke itself. It's like all five of you, old and crotchety."

***

"Are they all your sisters?" Chase asked as Carol set their drinks on the table and he stopped her. "I'm only going to have water, thank you. Last thing I need is to hurt someone else or get another DUI."

"I can drive you home and have one of my sisters follow us and bring me home," Teagan suggested.

"Better not. Your sister A… O… E…fee is already giving me the evil eye."

"Her name is pronounced Effa." Then she answered his question about her sisters. "Yes we're all sisters but, we have different mothers."

His face scrunched up with a 'huh' look. "And your fathers?"

"Different too."

"So, none of you are really related in anyway?"

"We're related through the ranch and the horses."

He was absolutely sure she was having a hell of a lot of fun with this, but there was no way he was giving up till he knew how they were all connected. "I'll come back to the ranch, and the horses, but that kind of explains why none of you look alike. Well, maybe Aoife and Erin but I think that's because of the red hair and their smiles." He paused. "Actually, Bridget and Keira could pass for sisters too. They both have the same facial structure. Fae appears to be kind of a blend of everybody."

"So, I'm the odd girl out?" Teagan asked.

"Definitely. You're much prettier than the rest... not that they're not pretty... just that your beauty shines above everything else. Plus, you're the only one with dark hair and eyes and that tells me you have a beautiful soul too."

She turned beet red, smiled at him and whispered, "Nice recovery." Then changed subjects. "Looks like they put your nose back on pretty good. Kinda leans to the left a tad though so you might want to go back in for a redo tweak."

"Got it. You don't take compliments well. But changing subjects won't stop me from telling you how beautiful you are."

When she turned even redder, he decided to move on. "So what's this ranch and horses thing all about."

"This is going to take a while so, you first." When he winced, she added, "I promise I'll explain all about us. It's just that it's a long and complicated story."

"Okay. Mine's pretty simple actually. My name's Chase Brooks. I was born and raised in San Diego. I graduated from UCSD with a degree in engineering and I work for a company that manufactures airline seats. I live in Bonita and the day you guys saved me I was coming back from celebrating a promotion and..." He watched her eyebrows go up.

"And?" she asked.

"The accident wasn't my fault."

Her eyes clearly said, 'They all say that, but go on.'

"Yes, I had been drinking. Yes, I shouldn't have been driving. But only the two girls that I hit saw the car that cut me off and ran me into them. Both of them gave a report to the police that another car tried to pass me on the shoulder, slammed into the right side of my car and forced me into their lane. The other car never even slowed down. It just kept going. Once the police had their report, they inspected my car and found paint from the other car all down the right side of my car, and trim from both cars alongside of the road."

His hand was shaking and she reached over and put her hand over his, then gently squeezed. "I'm really sorry we came down on you so hard, but you need to understand what we see on a daily basis. We…"

He put his other hand over hers and squeezed back. "I understand and believe me, I know why all of you reacted the way you did. I just… I just wanted you to understand that if it hadn't been for the other car, the accident wouldn't have happened. If I'd had even a little bit of warning, I would have chosen to slam into it and not the girls… I would have pushed the other car off the side of the road, rather than slam into someone head on. But… they came out of no…"

"It's okay, Chase. I'll let Aoife and Erin know. Have the police found the other car or the driver?"

"Yeah. It was stolen and abandoned. They had just robbed a store and were running, even though no one was chasing them. So forcing me into the other lane, and those two girls, was completely unnecessary. I only got a look at the driver. He actually smiled at me as he pushed me into the other lane… like it was funny… some kind of game."

Teagan slid off her stool and locked him in a big hug. "I'm so sorry about what happened." She leaned back and looked deep into his eyes.

He watched a smile form and knew she was going to kiss him. A moment later their lips met.

She broke the kiss off and smiled. "Okay, my turn. Strap in and pay attention because this will get complicated fast. The best way to explain who we are is to go through the sisterhoods.

"The first sisterhood was three of our mothers. CJ, Aoife's mother by adoption, Shannon, Erin's mother and Christine, Bridget's mom.

"Aoife's mom CJ was rescued from the sex trade here in San Diego. After going through rehab and therapy, the owner of a horse rescue ranch, Horses of Tir Na Nog, hired her to be the manager of the ranch. CJ says she couldn't even spell horse, no less know how to run a ranch. But Christine, Bridget's mom, and Shannon, Erin's mom, both volunteered at the ranch and took CJ under their wings. They formed a sisterhood with her and taught her everything they knew. The three of them were, and still are, sisters in every sense of the word and support each other in every way you can think of.

"Soon, CJ met and fell in love with Shawn, a Bonita fireman. Then Shannon met Bert, another Bonita fireman, and Christine met Matt, a Special Agent assigned directly to the President of the United States." She paused and smiled. "I'll leave out how they each met or we'll be here all week.

"The second sisterhood is Jessie, Aoife's birth mom, Paige, Jessie's mate, and Amber, Fae's mom. Jessie and Paige were also rescued from the sex trade and pretty much taken under the wings of CJ, Shannon and Christine: AKA the first sisterhood. Amber was still in high school and volunteering at the ranch and she, Jessie and Paige quickly became best buds." Teagan paused again and watched him. "Have I lost you yet?"

18

"I don't think so. But remind me, which one is Fae?"

Teagan pointed toward the end of the table everyone else was at. "The young blond at the end. The one who wants to be an Air Tanker jock but can't reach the peddles." Letting out a giggle she added, "I'm sorry. We all tease her but she's absolutely wonderful and anyone who ever messes with her has the five of us to deal with. The poor kid will likely never find a boyfriend though because he'll have to run the gauntlet of three sisterhoods, five dads and God knows how many uncles and aunts at the firehouse and ranch."

Chase let out a snort mixed in with a chuckle.

"What's so funny?" Teagan asked him.

"Please don't take this the wrong way… I'm just glad I was attracted to you, instead of her."

"Hmm, not sure if I should be okay with that, feel complimented or be pissed since she's kind of young for you. Plus, I've not gotten to me yet."

He smiled at her, then leaned over and gave her another kiss. "Trust me, whatever your background is, it'll just make me more impressed with you."

"Nice recovery… again," she said, returning his kiss. "Okay, where was I?"

"The second sisterhood and you and Keira, I think," he reminded her.

"Very good!" That got him another kiss. "My mom and Keira's weren't really part of the sisterhoods. They were kind of tack-ons to the first sisterhood." She let out another chuckle. "I just thought of that but it's an ideal way to describe them.

"The first sisterhood had a habit of picking up 'new members' wherever they went. While CJ and Shannon were on their honeymoons in England, Alice, Keira's mom, was their travel guide… and soon became a BFF and sisterhood add-on when she moved to the US.

"My mom, Leigh, was in the military in Afghanistan and best friends with Shane, Keira's dad. My mom lost her leg there and Shane became her protector. That is until James, my dad, came along. You'll love this. He was the cable guy sent to install cable in her room and it was love at first sight; with me not far behind… Still with me?"

"Uh, yeah, I think so. I'm sorry about your mom losing her leg. Is she okay?"

"Ha. She runs, literally, rings around all of us. The only reason my dad stays in shape is so he can keep up with her… well… and me too."

Teagan looked up and found him staring at her. "What?"

"Your family… uh more like your 'tribe'… is amazing. The unity, support and, I'm sure love, for each other is unbelievable." He looked over at the other table and smiled. "Even without you telling me all that, all I need to do is look at your sisters, and Fae the add-on, to see the glow of love and support from all of you."

He paused again, reached over and took her hands. "Do you all know how lucky you are? I'm pretty sure you do, but some people would kill to have the support and love and caring that surrounds each of you. Someday…" another pause "… I'd love to meet all of your families."

"That's easy. You're officially invited to the ranch next Saturday when we have a get-together planned. A warning though… you'll be running the gauntlet while they all make sure you're good enough to court me."

"Is that what I'm doing? Courting you?'

"I don't know. Is it?"

"I certainly hope so."

"Are you ready you join the group again?" she asked him.

"Sure. But, before we do, can you tell me what each one of you do? I mean job wise."

"Well, we all grew up hanging around the ranch and firehouse. I think it's fair to say the firefighters and EMTs impressed us the most since we're all first responders, in one form or another. I think the fact that fire trucks don't poop or try to kick you when you're bathing them helped too.

"As you know, I'm a Nurse and Helicopter Pilot with Mercy Air.

And Aoife is a Flight Nurse, also with Mercy Air.

Erin is a Firefighter and Arson Investigator with the Bonita-Sunnyside Fire District.

Kiera is a Deputy with the San Diego Sherriff's department, assigned to the Urban Search and Rescue Team for Cal EMA and FMEA.

Bridget is a Law Enforcement and Animal Control Officer with the San Diego Sheriff's Department.

And Fae, the tack-on, is training to be an Air Tanker Pilot with CAL Fire.

Oh… and all of us are also certified EMTs."

"Wow, I'm beyond impressed." He pulled her into a hug and added, "I can't wait to meet the rest of your families and see the ranch."

"Ha, you say that now but wait till you meet everyone. Your first hint at what your day will be like will be when I handcuff you to me so you can't run."

"No handcuffs please. Been there done that with a stretcher. I promise I won't run if you just hold my hand all the time."

"Gladly."

# Chapter 3 – A Day at The Ranch

Saturday arrived and Teagan drove over to Chase's apartment to pick him up. It turned out he lived in the same complex that CJ and Shawn and Jessie and Paige lived in, except he lived where the rental apartments were on the north side of the complex.

She pulled in front of his building and found him waiting out on the sidewalk. "You're not anxious or anything are you?" she asked when he opened the passenger door and slid into her truck.

"Actually, I am. I can't wait to meet your family."

"Well, I'm sorry but the get together has been postponed. Bonita has two fire trucks, 38 and 238, their backup truck. 38's been called up to Camp Pendleton to help fight a fire on base. That means 238's been put on-line and pretty much the whole department is either up north or at the fire station." She let out a small laugh. "As the saying goes, when it rains, it pours. Keira also got issued her search dog and so she and 'Digger', are bonding with each other all weekend, before he comes to live with her… actually us."

"Damn, I was looking forward to meeting everyone and getting a tour of the ranch." Chase's smile grew. "Since you're here though, I hope that means I still get to spend the day with you?"

She stared at him and shook her head, returning his smile. "Nice. Actually, you'll get to see the ranch anyway, since I plan on giving you a private tour… oh and dessert too."

"Lead on McDuff!" he said.

She watched his smile grow into an evil grin. Yup, definitely evil. "You are SO! BAD! And… who's McDuff?"

"Don't know. Just remember that from growing up," he said.

"Who told you you grew up?"

"True, true. Listen we're wasting time. I could be munching on you… ah, dessert, that is."

She pointed at the passenger door. "OUT. NOW."

His smile turned into a very confused look. Then he shrugged, opened the door, slid out and started to close it.

"Don't close the door," she added, staring at him. Then said, "Get back in!"

He got back in, looked at her… she nodded, and he closed the door.

"I got it… we start over again. You're in charge," he whispered.

"Wow, there's hope for you yet." She reached over, pulled him close and kissed him. "You do know I'm only messin' with you, right?"

"Yeah, I got that. You're sick, but I love your sense of humor. Which I guess makes me sicker. With your job though, I suspect that's the only way you can stay sane at times." He paused, pulled her back in and gave her a gentle but longer kiss. "So, where are we going?" he asked, as she started the truck, pulled out and headed up Bonita Road toward the 805 freeway.

"East on 8 to the Julian exit," she told him. "The ranch is just after the Julian turn off, but before you get to Guatay."

"Goo who?" he asked.

She knew he was kidding and let out a chuckle. "Goo You, if you don't watch where you're walking when we get to the ranch. While were on that subject, it's rattle snake breeding time so, in addition to horse, and a variety of other poos, watch out for rattle snakes... snake poo too, I guess."

The two of them started laughing as both had the same thought: *It's been a long time since I've laughed this much and the days just started.*

\*\*\*

Teagan pulled up in front of the ranch gate, put her truck in park, then reached to open her door.

"I got it," Chase said, putting his hand on her arm before she could get the door open.

"Thanks," she told him as he stepped out and headed for the gate.

He waved her through, closed the gate and started walking toward the second gate a short way up the dirt road. *Holy shit. I'm impressed,* she thought, as a giant smile lit up her face. Once again, he waved her through, closed the gate, then came over and opened her door after she'd parked.

She slid out of her seat, reached over and pulled him in for the longest kiss they'd had yet.

"Wow!" he said. "I'm impressed. Not sure what I did to earn that but tell me so I can do it again."

"Stop stealing my lines." She planted another long kiss on him, stepped back and burst out laughing at the most confused look she'd seen on him yet. "What you did was pay attention to things in a place you've never been before, then figure out that the gate needed to be opened, then closed after I got through. While you were doing that, you saw the second gate, walked up and opened it for me too... You're the first person EVER to figure that out without me having to explain it or watch them get in and out of the truck four times."

"If that's all I did to earn those two super kisses, I can't wait till I do something really cool like... buy you flowers or take you out to dinner."

"Come here," she demanded as she grabbed his shirt and pulled him in for what started out as a great kiss and ended up being a tongue duel. A long duel that ended in applause as soon as they broke apart.

"Uh, hi Mom. Hi, Dad," Teagan said as she turned Chase to face her parents and stepped alongside of him.

"Are you okay, son?" James, her dad, asked Chase.

"What the…" Teagan started to say.

Her mom came over, took Chase's hand and said, "Come with us. We'll get you a beer and issue you the appropriate 'dating our daughter' warnings. Be patient with us though, she's never brought anyone home before so we're kinda new at this."

"MOM. You… you… Dad… how fast can you carve her another leg from a tree?... because I'm about to beat her with the good one, after I remove it."

"Ha. Go ahead and try!" her mom said. "You forget I have a pink belt in Super Mario and an orange stripe for Nintendo."

Teagan couldn't help but snort and shake her head when she looked over at Chase who was laughing so hard he could barely stand. Her mom, who you would never know had an artificial leg, was the only thing holding him upright.

"Come on," Leigh told him, then started to tug him up the hill "Let's get you that beer while they decide how many legs I'll end up with."

Her dad pulled Teagan up alongside of her mom and Chase as the four of them headed up the hill toward the volunteer trailer. "Don't believe a thing they tell you," Teagan whispered to Chase when she caught up with him. "I'm really adopted. My birth parents were the normal ones. They…"

"Stop!" he said, bending over and gripping his left side with one hand. "I can't take any more. My side is killing me. You're… you're all crazy."

"Here, let me look. I'm an EMT… remember?" Teagan said, pulling his shirt up. She bent down, kissed his side… all over… then looked up at him. "How's that? Better?"

All poor Chase could do was squeeze his side tighter and shake his head as they eased him onto one of the picnic table benches in front of the trailer. Next thing he knew, someone was handing him a beer.

***

"So, what are you two doing at the ranch?" Teagan asked her parents.

"Well, several of you were supposed to come help at the ranch today when the party got cancelled. Then, everyone suddenly became 'unavailable'," her mom told her. "So your dad and I came out to help."

"Oh crap! I totally forgot." She smiled at Chase. "You okay with getting a little dirty?"

"We got it covered," her dad told them. "It would be nice to know his name though."

28

*Oh God. I've completely lost my brain!* Teagan thought. "Mom and Dad, this is Chase. Chase, this is my mom and dad."

Her dad shook hands with him, then her mom gave him a hug. "We actually have names too, although our daughter's obviously forgotten them…" her mom winked at Chase. "… happens with adopted kids. It's good that she remembered yours. Anyway, I'm Leigh and this cute guy here is James."

"Would someone just go bury me in the manure pile," Teagan pleaded.

Once again, Chase was laughing so hard that Leigh had to grab him around the waist to keep him from falling off the bench. "I love your family," he finally managed to squeak out.

Leigh looked over at James. "Is he asking for permission to marry our daughter?"

"No… I …" Chase stopped when he saw the death stare coming from Teagan. *How the hell do I get out of this?* he thought.

"One tenth of a date and you're rejecting me already?" Teagan asked.

But Chase caught the wink she'd given her parents. "Uh, yeah. You sleeping in the manure pile pretty much ended it for me."

"He's absolute perfect for you," her mom told Teagan. "Now go, you two. We've got the ranch chores covered."

"I actually came out to give him a tour of the ranch."

"Figures," her dad said looking at her mom. Then, turning to Teagan, added, "Okay, go show him the ranch but don't leave any footprints where I raked."

Teagan rolled her eyes and pulled Chase downhill toward Deveny's stall.

"I absolutely love your family's sense of humor," he told her.

"You want them? We can have them disown me and adopt you," she added, slipping her arm around his waist.

"We heard that!" followed them, as she laid her head against him and they both started chuckling.

***

Teagan introduced Chase to Deveny and explained how she had been abandoned out in a field and had the brand cut out of her hide so she couldn't be traced back to her owner. "She wanted nothing to do with people when we first got her, but now she's learned to trust again and everyone loves her."

"How could anyone do that to a horse? Or any animal?" Chase asked.

"Desperation. Almost every horse here was left somewhere or turned into the SPCA because their owners couldn't afford to keep them. It got so bad in 2009, that when the SPCA wouldn't take them, the owners would just take them out of the horse trailer, tie them to a tree, leave them in the parking lot and drive off," she explained, watching his eyes tear up. "Okay. Change of subject. If you do decide to date me, get used to the smell of horse shit, cow shit and every kind of animal pee you can think of because you'll be volunteering out here with me as often as we can." She watched for the 'I'm out of here' look she'd gotten from several guys she'd brought to the ranch but instead got a big smile.

"If… when we come out, what is it we'll be doing?"

She just stood there staring at him. Finally, she broke out of her trance and asked, "Have you ever been around horses before?"

"Nope. Rode a pig once… but no horses."

"A… a pig?"

"Yup. At the county fair. Actually, it was a pig race, and my pig lost. He… or she… made a hard right hand turn halfway around the course and chased some poor kid until he threw his cotton candy at us… which I guess is why the pig chased him in the first place."

Now it was Teagan's turn to bend over and grab her side, laughing hysterically. No one would ever know the picture that popped into her mind: *Chase hanging upside down, arms around the pig's neck, legs around its waist, then crashing through the railing with the pig headed for the cotton candy cart.* The more she tried to get the picture out of her head, the clearer it became, and the harder she laughed.

"I'm…" he started to say.

"SHUT UP. Not another word," she managed to squeak out as he eased her to the ground.

Aoife had almost forgotten about her regularly scheduled visit to her doctor. Fortunately, the second reminder message pinged on her phone the morning before. *Crap. Erin and I were supposed to go out and volunteer at the ranch tomorrow.* Pulling out her phone, she hit 'Mom C'.

"Mom, help. We're supposed to help out at the ranch tomorrow and I've got a doctor's appointment in the morning. Any chance of you spending the day at the ranch?"

"Well, hi daughter... that we never hear from unless she needs help," CJ answered.

"Mom! That's not true."

"Sorry. You're right. We hear from you when you're hungry and want to drop by for dinner, too."

"Ugh. Blame mom J. She should have raised me better... and if she could cook, I'd share meals with her too."

"She would have raised you better and taken cooking lessons, but she was too busy filling in for you at the ranch."

"Ha ha. Very funny, Mom."

"You can relax," CJ told her. "Seems all five of you have some kind of national emergency come up when you need to volunteer at the ranch... Oh, wait. Make that six because Fae got the training wheels on her plane fixed so she'll be back in the air.

Anyway, Leigh, James, Christine and I are going out and Christine corralled a group from the high school so everything's covered."

"Oh, thank you, Mom. I owe you."

"Are you okay? Is this just a regular appointment?"

"Yeah. Just my semi-annual checkup to keep me flight certified. Listen, Mom, I need to run. Catch up with you tomorrow night… for dinner?"

CJ let out a chuckle. "Sure, beef in wine sauce with rice and honey glazed carrots. That work for you?"

"Yum! Love you, Mom… Oh… is Dad up north with Engine 38?"

"Yeah, he and Bert. Hopefully, they'll get a handle on the fire and be back home tomorrow." CJ paused, then added, "Fly safe and be careful out there."

"You too, Mom. Love you… lots!"

They both hung up.

***

Before Aoife could set her phone down, it rang. "Hey, Erin, what's up?"

"Can I hitch a ride with you to the doctor's?"

"Uh… sure. Everything okay?"

"Yeah, sorry. You mentioned you had your flight cert exam tomorrow and mine was scheduled for next Monday so I called, and they can take me tomorrow, right after you… if that's okay?" Erin asked.

"Sure. Love the company. Wanna come over to mom C's for dinner afterward? Beef in wine sauce with rice and honey glazed carrots."

"Yum. I'm in. Dad's up north with your dad so I'm sure Mom will be there… want me to call mom C and warn her?"

"Good idea. I just hung up with her but if I call her twice in one day, she's likely to have a heart attack."

Erin let out a chuckle. "And think your credit card got rejected… again."

"If you start walking now, you can probably make your doctor's appointment by tomorrow," Aoife told her. After a brief chuckle from both of them, Aoife added, "What are you doing for dinner tonight?"

"Not sure. I haven't checked to see if there's anything in the fridge that doesn't have green stuff growing on it and is within a year of its pull date. Why?"

"Feel like running over to Taste of Thai with me?"

"Sure," Erin said. A minute later, there was a knock on the door and Erin stepped in. "It's so nice we all live in the same apartment building," then added, "Change of plans? I'm not in the mood for Thai but Mexican sounds really good. How about Coasterra? I'll even drive."

"Uh, wait…" Aoife told Erin, who was still standing in the doorway. Then she stuck her arm out, turned her hand and wrist. "… Okay. Okay. I'll go with you. Just don't hurt me anymore!"

"Come on, goofball. My stomach's growling and a pitcher of Frida Rita Margaritas is calling my name."

***

Erin pulled up to the two valets standing in the middle of the parking lot entrance. They opened both doors and Erin and Aoife stepped out. Erin handed her keys to the one holding her door open, then glanced over to the spaces reserved for the really high-priced cars. "Oh good!" she said, pointing. "My space is open. It's the one between the Ferrari and the Maserati."

The valet looked at her well-worn VW Bug and said, "Right," as he tossed the keys to another valet who was running up to park her car. "Over in the corner… by the runway," he told him.

"Oh, forgot. That's my space. The 747 soot corner!" she said, smiling at the head valet, then looping her arm through Aoife's and leading her into the restaurant.

One step inside and they both realized the place was packed. They looked at each other and the hostess. *Doesn't everyone know this is Tuesday?* went unsaid as the hostess asked, "Reservation?"

They both shook their heads, while the hostess rolled her eyes. "I can squeeze you in at one of the high-tops by the bar, but you'll be sharing it with other people. Is that okay?"

They both shrugged and she led them toward the high-top tables in the bar area; just as a couple seated at the first table was led out to the patio. That left one person, a cute looking guy, who slid into the middle of the three stools at the table.

"Can I ask you to slide back over so these ladies can share your table, please?" the hostess asked him.

He looked at them, smiled, said, "Sure," and moved back onto the stool he'd been on.

Aoife took the stool next to him and Erin slid onto the one on the other side of her.

The hostess set a menu in front of each of them and looked at the empty space in front of the guy. "Do you need a menu?" she asked him.

He looked over at the front door, then told her, "I'm supposed to meet someone." His eyes moved to Aoife and he asked, "Okay if I share yours if I need too?"

For no reason she could think of, Aoife decided to have a little fun with him. She raised her eyebrows and gave him her best death stare. "Uh, menus are pretty hard to come by." She watched as he fought to keeps his lips from curling into the beginning of a smile.

"Oh, I hadn't realized that," he said, as Erin jabbed her in the ribs with an elbow.

"Tell you what. Buy us each a Frida Rita Margarita and I'll give you five minutes with my menu."

"Five minutes? How about I buy a pitcher for ten minutes? By the way, what's a Frida Rita Margarita?" he asked. The bar server passing by overheard them and set off for a pitcher of margaritas and a Corona refill for him.

"You wouldn't be interested. It's a girly drink." She smiled at him and stuck her hand out. "I'm Aoife... spelled A.O.I.F.E. but pronounced Effa."

"Pretty name. I'm Maverick," he said, taking her hand and holding it way too long.

"Maverick... like the fighter pilot in 'Top Gun?'"

He nodded just as Erin's elbow landed in Aoife's ribs again. "Ouch. Shit, that hurt!"

"What am I? Chopped sausage over here?" Erin asked.

"Liver... it's liver," Aoife told her, rubbing her side as she turned back to Maverick. "This is my good friend Erin.... and good thing she has her own menu."

Maverick let out laugh. "You two always this funny?" Before either of them could answer, he added, "Let me guess. You two work together as a comedy act in bars in the Gas Lamp?"

"Not even close," Aoife said. "I'm a flight nurse and Erin is a firefighter."

"Wow! I'm impressed. Seriously," he said, just as the bar server set a pitcher, two margarita glasses and a Corona on the table.

"Thank you," Aoife told him. "Let me guess, your dad was an F14 jock in the Navy, named you Maverick, and you fly F18s to keep up the family tradition."

Maverick's face broke into a big smile and he shook his head. "Not even close."

Aoife filled the two margarita glasses and passed one to Erin. "Okay, spill. What do you fly?" She took a big sip of her margarita.

"I don't fly... I ..." he reached over and eased her hand with the glass back to the table. "...you probably want to swallow that before I go on." Aoife swallowed and he said, "I'm a pea inspector."

A second later, Erin spit her margarita all over the table. In between coughs and gasps for air, she managed to get out, "Did he say what I think he said?"

Aoife, also gasping for breath, nodded. Then finally added, "I'll bet working in a medical lab examining urine samples doesn't win you a lot of dates... might want to keep your occupation to yourself when meeting women."

"Uh, not that kind of pee," Maverick said, "the other kind. The little round green ones."

A moment later they both sprayed the table and gagged on their second attempt at a drink from their glasses.

Erin shook her head, closed her eyes and managed to get out, "What the hell could possibly go wrong with a pea?"

Suddenly Aoife, who also had her eyes closed, had an image pop into her mind and she burst out laughing. The image of a conveyor belt had formed. It was loaded with peas, rocking down the belt to "I Got a Feeling" by the Black Eyed Peas. As she watched, Maverick, dressed as a little pea person, jumped out and rescued a dented pea from the conveyor belt. He started trying to resuscitate the pea by performing CPR (Cardio Pea Revival). Another pea passing by yelled, "Someone call 911". A second later a miniature ambulance raced up on the little roadway alongside of the belt. Two tiny pea people jumped out and ran up carrying, a stretcher.

"Stop!" one little pea person yelled at little pea Maverick. "You're making a mess of him. He'll only be good for pea soup or mushy peas, if his can gets shipped to England."

*** 

Abruptly, a voice brought her out of her vision. "Would you like to go out with me?" Maverick was asking.

Trying to clear the image from her head and not spray the table again, Aoife stared at him… finally answering. "I don't think that would be a good idea. I'm not sure I could take helping you come down from your high stress job every day. I mean how many peas are lost per day? How many get crushed in the conveyor belt or get into a pea pissing contest?"

He let out a chuckle. "It's... it's not like that. Mostly it's just keeping them happy. I read *The Princess and the Pea* to the baby peas, we go to Black Eyed Pea concerts as often as we can, and we try to give them names that make them proud to be peas. Names like: Peaches, Peace, Peaky, Peanut and Mr. Peabody."

They both turned at the sound of 'thump, thump', watching as Erin smacked her head on the table. "No more!" she said. "If you date him I'll... I'll... turn you into a ...peahen! And... and ... him into a peacock." At which point she slid off the stool onto the floor, laughing hysterically.

Totally ignoring Erin, Maverick went on. "Listen, not to dangle a carrot, but there's talk about my being promoted to the carrot line."

"That would be a lot less stress?" Aoife asked.

"Not really, separating the baby carrots from their moms is heart wrenching... but, it could be worse," he told her.

"What could possibly be worse?"

"Working succotash."

A second later they were sitting on the floor next to Erin, the three of them laughing uncontrollably.

After a warning from the manager, they climbed back onto their stools.

"Not sure I want to know, but what's the best line to work?" Aoife asked.

"Asparagus. They're stalky, but very upright and well behaved."

She wiped the tears from her eyes and attempted to stare at him without breaking into another bout of laughter. "Okay, I suspect just knowing you will make my drinking bill go way up while I bar nurse you through the daily traumas of your job. I'm also not sure how much of what you've told me is true but somehow, I think dating you would be fun. So, we'll do a trial date and see how it goes from there."

He reached over, took her hand and she watched as he turned serious. "I really am a pea inspector. Unfortunately, most of the rest, including a promotion to the carrot line, is BS. Especially the part about going to Black Eyed Pea concerts. Oh, and I don't sing to the baby peas. With my voice they'd all run for their pea pickin' lives."

"I already agreed to go on a trial date with you so I'd suggest you quit while you're ahead."

"Got it." He added a big smile. "Okay to talk about you?" He paused, glanced over at Erin and added, "Sorry… both of you."

Whether he realized it or not, that won him dozens of brownie points with Aoife. Apparently with Erin too, as she leaned forward and mouthed 'thank you'.

Returning his smile, Aoife explained what she did. "I'm a Flight Nurse with Mercy Air. Mostly, we retrieve accident victims who are in critical condition and need to be air lifted to Sharp Memorial Hospital in Kearney Mesa or Scripps Mercy Hospital in Hillcrest. In addition to caring for them on scene, along with Erin who is also an EMT, I monitor them on the flight to the hospital and relay their condition when we arrive at the hospital. We also transport donor organs and critically vital or rare blood, when it's needed." Turning to Erin, she said, "You're up."

"Hi, Maverick... thanks for including me by the way. That earned you a lot of points with both of us." After taking a sip of her margarita, she went on. "I'm a firefighter with the Bonita-Sunnyside Fire District and I specialize in arson investigation. As Aoife mentioned, I'm also an EMT so I often get called to the same accident scenes she gets called to, if they're in our district." Pausing, she looked at Aoife. "Guess we should warn him that there's six of us?"

"Good idea," Aoife agreed.

"Six? You two are related and there's four more of you?" a stunned Maverick managed to get out.

"Yes and no," Erin answered. "We're not related by blood but by a sisterhood. All of our parents are exceptionally close, and

43

we were all born within a year of each other; except for baby Fae who is fifteen years behind us. We're also all first responders in one form or another."

Letting out a chuckle, Aoife added, "And all of them will likely show up on our first date… just to make sure you pass the gauntlet of approval for dating me."

They both watched, expecting him to excuse himself, having just remembered an appointment somewhere that he was late for. Instead, he asked, "Do any of them carry a gun?"

They both broke into a big smile. "As a matter of fact, two do. They both work for the Sheriff's Department. One as an Animal Control Officer so she carries two guns. A regular gun, plus a tranquilizer gun that shoots darts that'll put a gorilla in a deep sleep for several days. The other is a Sherriff Deputy, assigned to the search and rescue office. She carries a gun and has a search and rescue dog."

His smile got bigger as he turned and stared at Aoife. "Got it. I'll be dating six of you on the first date and running a gauntlet. Anything else I should know before we pick a date for our date?"

Aoife couldn't help but like Maverick, even if he was insane. Truly, any sane individual would have headed for the hills at 'there will be six of us on the date' or when the words 'gauntlet' or 'tranquilizer darts' came up. Most of all, she loved his sense of humor and was certain that the date would be fun and full of laughs, if nothing else.

Suddenly his smile disappeared. She followed his eyes and turned just as a guy came up on the other side of Erin and asked, "Okay if I join you? Seems seats are in short supply."

Erin looked over at him, smiled and said, "Sure, I guess." Politely serving notice she had no interest in him, then confirming it by smiling again before turning back to rejoin the conversation with Aoife and Maverick.

Ignoring the hint, the guy pulled a stool over from another table and went on. "Any idea what's good here?" Then, staring at her margarita glass, added, "What's that you're drinking?"

Not wanting to be totally rude, she partially turned back to face him and pasted on another smile. He was about her age, hadn't shaved in a day or two, which might look good on someone like Maverick but only made this guy look like he lost his razor and was too cheap to buy another one. His wrinkled shirt, stained jeans and the smell of cheap laundry soap, mixed with body odor, completed the picture of someone who didn't worry too much about personal hygiene.

"Like what you see?" he asked.

Erin chose to totally ignore his question. "Everything here is good and we're drinking Frida Rita Margaritas." She paused before starting to turn back, then added, "Enjoy your meal."

Finally getting the hint, he said, "Sorry, didn't mean to interrupt... just trying to make conversation."

This time Erin just ignored him. But Maverick could see she'd pissed him off. While Aoife and Erin continued joking about first dates with a member of the sisterhood, Aoife noticed Maverick continuously glancing at the guy.

When the bar server came by, the guy ordered a Frida Rida Margarita and told her he needed more time to decide on what he wanted to eat. A few minutes later she came back, set his drink down and told him, "Just flag me down when you decide on food."

Erin's back was still to him and Maverick could see the steam rising the longer she ignored him. He also noticed how each time the guy took a sip of his margarita, he'd set the glass back down close to hers, as if comparing them. It didn't take him long to figure out what the guy was going to do. He leaned slightly past Aoife and made eye contact with Erin. "I need to…" was all he got out before she smiled.

"Yes, I know," Erin told him, then put her finger to her lips as if she were rubbing them, but clearly giving him a 'shhh' signal.

His eyes lighted on Aoife's smile. *She knew too!* "Thank you for being such a gentleman. I'm really looking forward to our date," she said, adding a wink.

*They're both on to him.* Maverick had no doubt. *This should be good.*

A minute later, Erin slid off the stood and slipped her arm through Aoife's. "Be right back," she said to Maverick, as they headed for the restrooms.

The guy stared at Maverick, who gave him a pasted-on grin, then turned his back on him. *That should really piss him off... and give him a chance to do what they were all sure he would.*

The girls returned from the rest room and as Erin slid onto her stool, she pointed at a couple coming through the front door. "Oh my God! Isn't that Katie G... the porn star?"

The guy had to turn all the way around to look. Erin reversed their margarita glasses, then picked up the one that had been his. When he turned back around, she tipped the glass toward him, smiled and finished what was in it. He smiled back, picked up the other glass, stared at her and emptied it.

Erin turned her back on him again, winked at Maverick and Aoife, then broke into a big smile.

Five minutes went by, Aoife reached over, grabbed their margarita pitcher and refilled each of their glasses. After setting the pitcher down, she pulled her phone out of her purse, set it on the table and took a sip of her drink. Smiling at Maverick she asked, "Is he still upright?"

"Not for long," he said, certain the guy thought he was now on a small boat during a storm.

Aoife waved the server over, picked the phone back up and dialed 911, just as the guy tumbled off his stool. "Yes, this is Aoife with Mercy Air. I'm in Coasterra, just past the bar and we need an ambulance and the Harbor Police... Yes.... We're pretty sure a patron somehow spiked his own drink… Sure, we'll be here… Have a nice day!" Then she hung up.

The server locked eyes with Erin and chuckled. "Nice job with the switcheroo. We were watching from the bar and couldn't see what he was doing but knew something wasn't right. Anyway, I was just about to come over when you pointed at the door, then switched glasses."

A moment later, two Harbor Policemen came through the door, followed by two EMTs pushing a gurney. "Hey, Aoife. Hi, Erin." One of the EMTs said, then looked around. "Where'd you park your helicopter?"

"Ha ha. Very funny, Vinny," Erin said. "Rule one: No drinking and flying. Especially after margaritas."

"So, what did you do to this poor guy?" Vinny asked as they stood him up and helped him onto the gurney.

"Seems he forgot which drink he spiked, then drugged himself," Aoife told him.

Vinny chuckled. "Oh sure. Happens all the time. Especially when they're messing with first responders with eyes in the back of their heads." He paused, looked over at the guy, then said, "He's a frequent flyer by the way. This is like the third time someone played switchie switchie with him. Think he'd learn? See ya later," he added as they pushed the gurney toward the front door.

Maverick sat there shaking his head and chuckling. "Uh, back to our date?" he asked Aoife. "How's next Saturday look?"

"I'm on call as back up. But if you're okay with me driving and meeting you somewhere, in case I get called out, I'm good with Saturday."

"Wow, I'm on call too, just in case there's a carrot-tastrophy on the line. It's seldom that we get called back in, but two weeks ago we had a Brussels sprout break out and we had to launch a search and rescue operation. Thirty of the little buggers rolled their way back up the belt and escaped by dropping into in a box of plums. By the time we got to them, they had already... grafted... shall we say?

Laughing and shaking her head, Erin looked over at them. "He can bring you back," she told Aoife. "I'm going home to start coming up with a list of names for the Brussel-plum babies." Her gaze shifted to Maverick who was just barely holding it together. "How many?" she asked.

He stared at her, let out a snort then asked, "How many what?"

"What the hell kind of foster father are you? Brussel-plums, you dummy."

"Oh... Eight. But actually you only need names for six since two got shipped off with the cherry tomatoes."

By now the three of them were back to laughing hysterically, again. Finally, Erin calmed down enough to slip off the stool and stand up. "I am so glad I'm not double dating with you." Then she turned and left, giggling all the way to the door.

The following morning, Aoife collected Erin and the two of them headed for the doctor's office.

"What time did you get back yesterday?" Erin asked.

"Not late actually. Turns out he got called in right after you left. As soon as he answered the phone he started laughing, but when I asked him what was up, he wouldn't tell me."

"You sure you want to know? He's crazy, but I think he'll be great to date," Erin told her. "If he can't make you laugh after a day of scraping bodies off the roadway, you'll need to start dating a psychologist."

"You do know you're sick?"

"Yip, comes with the territory," Erin answered.

An hour and a half later, their exams finished, they were almost at Aoife's truck when Erin's phone went off with a call-in; followed seconds later by a call-in on Aoife's phone. "I'll drop you off at the station then head for Gillespie Field," Aoife told her. "I suspect we're being called in for the same incident and we'll be seeing each other shortly." Just then her phone rang again. "Hey, Teag, what's going on?"

"Is Erin still with you?" Teagan asked, then went on after Aoife said 'yes'. "Okay, drop her off at the Bonita station, then go over to the softball diamond at Rohr Park. We'll be there in about ten minutes to pick you up."

"Sure. What's going on?" she asked.

"Four injured hikers at Otay Lakes. Keira and Digger just spotted them down near the bottom of the dam. One lost his balance. Another tried to grab him and they both tumbled down the hill. The other two tried to slide down to help them and ended up stuck down there with the first two. At least two of them are pretty banged up, the first one slammed into a rock and is unconscious. No way we can get an ambulance close, so Kiera's team is pulling them out one by one. They'll bring them over to the mesa on the west side, the one overlooking the dam. First one out will be the guy that's unconscious, so Aoife, you and I need to get there as soon as we can."

Erin had already been dropped off at the fire station and, as she zipped up her flight suit and grabbed her helmet, Aoife could hear sirens leaving the fire station and the helicopter approaching from behind her.

Teagan set the chopper down and Aoife slid the door open. Once she was in, she slid the door closed, then strapped in as they lifted off. Teag cleared the trees, dipped the nose and sharply turned the chopper toward the lakes. Less than two minutes later they flew over Erin's ambulance and Engine 238, making their way down Otay Lakes Road.

As Teagan set Air Two down in the meadow on the mesa, they watched Keira and another S&R team member crest the hill in a doon buggy. Strapped to the back was someone on a back board with Digger lying next to him.

The doon buggy pulled next to the chopper, Aoife slid the door open and helped guide the backboard onto a stretcher on the shelf, then strap the guy down. "Hey, sis!" she called out to Keira, then asked, "You want us to wait?"

Keira shook her head 'No' then yelled, "They're bringing the other three up now. They're banged up, but not critical. Better get this one over to Mercy or Memorial, we'll follow with the others." Keira looked over at Teagan, gave her a big smile and blew her a kiss, then slid the door closed.

While Aoife called to see which hospital had an opening, Teagan made sure Keira and the doon buggy were clear, then brought the rotor up to speed and eased Air Two into the air. Just as she turned the nose north, she saw Engine 238 and the ambulance roll onto the mesa. "The rest are all yours Erin," she heard Aoife tell her over the radio. "See you at Memorial."

***

Erin and Jake hopped out of the ambulance and watched Air Two head north toward Sharp Memorial Hospital. As they walked to the back to pull the gurney out, the doon buggy came back over the ridge. Kiera was driving with someone next to her and two guys sitting in the back, Digger between them. Kiera and the passenger next to her climbed out, then helped the guys in the back out.

As Erin and Jake wheeled the gurney toward the doon buggy, Kiera and the guy with her, steadied one guy from the backseat between them, then guided him toward the gurney. Kiera smiled at Erin. "Hi, sis! I think he's more shook up then anything but he's probably the one that should be on the gurney. The other two just got scratched up a bit," she added as they lowered him onto the gurney. Once the guy was safely strapped in, the guy with Kiera looked up at Erin and smiled. "Your sister?" he asked Kiera.

"Yeah... and you'd better be nice to her or she'll leave you on the side of the road and you'll have to hitchhike to the hospital." Kiera added a wink, then introduced him to Erin. "This is Bailey and aside from wanting to take control of everything, he was a lot of help in getting the other three up here... Bailey, this is Erin, one of my sisters."

Erin watched as Digger leaned against Bailey's leg, eyes glued to him like a lovesick puppy.

"What'd he do to 'Sir Digs a Lot'?" she asked Kiera.

Kiera shrugged. "Got me. Digger took to him like he owns a dog treat factory."

"Trader," Erin told him, as she patted Digger on the head, then she and Jake pushed the gurney toward the ambulance. Halfway there, she turned to see Bailey hugging Kiera. "You coming?" she yelled. He turned, followed them, and once they had loaded the gurney, he made sure to get the seat next to Erin.

Kiera watched and a big smile formed as she blew Erin a kiss while Jake closed the back doors then headed for the driver's door.

***

Erin wrapped the blood pressure cuff around the arm of the guy on the stretcher, then turned to Bailey. "So, Mr. Bailey, what do you do?... aside from rolling down hills?"

"You mean for a living?"

"Uh huh."

"I own a Starbucks," he told her.

Her eyes lit up. "Which one?"

"The one in Bonita, on the corner of Bonita and Central... just down the road from your fire house, I think. You are based out of Bonita, right?"

"Oh wow!" she said as she checked the blood pressure reading on his friend, then asked, "Any chance on getting a latte discount when we do the boot drive?" She watched as a cute twinkle moved into his eyes.

"Are you trying to bribe me?" he asked.

"I..." she stopped and stared at him. "How... would my getting a discount be bribing you?"

"You suggesting that you'll come in would be the bribe."

"Cute," she added as she looked over at the third guy, pointed to his arms and said, "Let me look at those scratches."

"Nope, I'm good, and you're one smile away from a free lifetime supply of lattes from Bailey here, so I can wait till we get to the hospital."

She looked back and forth between them twice then asked, "Did you guys come up with this routine while Kiera and Digger dragged you up the hill?"

"Yup. Didn't have anything else to do during the trip," the guy on the stretcher said. "We even had time to do that rock, paper, scissors, finger thing to figure out who was going to get you... and Bailey won."

"Oh?... Bailey won me... did he?"

"It wasn't..."

The back door opened and Jake and Erin unloaded the gurney as Bailey added, "... like that," to an empty ambulance.

*** 

After they transferred the guy from the gurney to a bed in the Sharp Chula Vista ER, Erin backed out of the cubical then turned and slammed into Bailey. Reaching out, he caught her around the waist to keep her from falling and they found themselves nose to nose. "I'm really sorry," he started to explain.

"I didn't win you with the rock, paper thing. We didn't even know you were up there until we got up onto the clearing."

"So, who did you win?" she asked, flashing him an evil grin, but still in his arms.

"Kiera, we uh…" suddenly he remembered they were sisters, but her death stare told him he was too late.

"Oh, so I was second place?"

"No, no. We were going to tell Kiera that I won the stretcher ride. Honest…" Erin watched as he went onto full panic mode. "Please, you have to believe me. My friend was only joking. I would never demean someone lik…"

She reached up, pinched his lips together and said, "Lifetime supply of lattes…"

His face lit up in a big smile. "You got it!"

"… for me and my sisters."

"Not a problem."

"Muffins too."

"Croissants, if anyone wants those instead," he offered.

"Can I get in on this?" Jake asked from the other side of the gurney.

"No!" they both said.

Erin leaned into Bailey, smiled, then kissed him on the cheek. "See you soon," she whispered as she and Jake headed back to the ambulance.

Teagan heard a knock on her door. "Door's open. Come on in!"

"What are you knocking for?" she asked Aoife and Erin as they stepped into the apartment.

"Uh, last thing we need is catching you and Chase in some kind of compromising position," Erin told her.

Teagan stared at her. "The last time I was in a compromising position was when my mom changed my diaper in public. As for Chase, we haven't even been on a date yet, so we've a long way to go before you need to worry about not knocking."

Erin turned and smiled at Aoife. "Me thinks she hasn't paid any attention to the way he looks at her… or her at him."

Shaking her head, Teagan responded. "Ha, you're a great one to talk. Actually, both of you. I've already put two of those little fire extinguishers in my purse so I can put your panties out when Maverick and Bailey are around."

"Better add a third for yourself," Aoife said, as the three of them laughed.

"God. I hope no one is recording this! I don't think we were this horny, even in high school, we're we?" Erin asked.

"Nope… that's because we got more action in high school. Now it's us picking the men up… usually off the highway… and any playing with their private parts involves antiseptic, gauze, bandages and surgical tape," Aoife added, following with another chuckle.

"Okay, let's go, or we'll be late," Teagan said, reaching for the TV remote.

"Wait! Wait!" Erin shouted. "I love this commercial. I have no idea what it's for, other than some type of drug for something or other, but one of the side effects is 'death'." She read the caution on the screen in a deep voice: "*And! If you suffer any of these side effects… you should call your doctor immediately!*" She let out a giggle. "So, your first phone call after dying should be to report to your doctor that you died from the drug?"

After another giggle she added, "Who the hell writes this shit?" as they headed for the door.

***

Ten minutes later Teagan pulled her truck into the driveway of Generate Hope and parked. Janet, the director, was waiting for them and gave each of them a hug as they stepped out of the truck, all three in uniform. "You have no idea how excited the girls are about you doing this. Even though we have classes on various occupations they can go into, there's nothing like having someone that can tell them what their job is really like and answer their questions."

She led them toward the building on the left and added, "I can't tell you how much I appreciate all of you doing this." They stepped into the entryway above a small sunken den and stood at the top of the stairs.

As they watched, one girl had her arms out and was circling the couches. "Tower, this is heli 101, seeking permission to land."

One of the other girls said, "This is tower. Rodger dodger heli 101 you're clear to come in… oh, just watch out for the girl sitting on the runway," she added pointing at one of the girls on the floor in front of a couch.

The girl circling made one more pass, then did a crash landing onto a couch.

Everyone turned as Aoife, Erin and Teagan applauded. "Your landing on the couch was what we call an autorotation," Teagan told the girl. "And, you did a really good job with little to no damage to the couch… not to mention missing the girl sitting on the runway."

Covering her beet red face with her hands, helicopter girl said, "Oh my God. I can't believe you saw that!"

Still trying to stifle a laugh, Janet stepped down into the den. "Okay, girls, everyone onto the runway so these ladies can have this couch." She looked at helicopter girl and added, "Leah, make sure you clean up any debris from your crash site. We don't want anyone sitting on a rotor blade or tail fin."

"Yes, ma'am," Leah answered, saluting, then running her hands over the couch.

Each of sisters lined up in front of the couch and introduced themselves.

"I'm Teagan and I'm a helicopter pilot with Mercy Air."

"I'm Aoife and I'm a flight nurse with Mercy Air."

"I'm Erin, I'm a firefighter and arson investigator with the Bonita-Sunnyside Fire District."

Aoife jumped back in. "Since I'm the oldest, I got tagged to tell you the rest. All of us are also nurses and certified EMTs. On a personal level, we're all BFFs and grew up together, along with three other sisters, who are also first responders. Two of our dads are firefighters, three of our moms were rescued from the sex trade, and two of them were helped by Generate Hope." She paused, staring at all the open mouths. "So, for us, spending time with you, and hopefully, helping you decide what you want to do in life, is our way of paying it forward."

Two girls had their hands up, but another girl just jumped in. "Why should we listen to you tell us what to do?"

"Lisa, I don't-" Janet started.

"I got this," Teagan interrupted, then looked at the girl. "Lisa? I know you've all had a pretty tough life, and we're sorry for that. But none of us here can change what happened to you. We're also not here to tell you what to do. We're here to tell you what we do, why we love doing it, then answer any questions you might have."

Ignoring three hands now raised, Lisa jumped in again. "Are firemen as hot as everyone says? I mean on TV they're all smokin'!" She paused, then added, "I'll bet playing with their hoses would be fun too." That set all the girls to snickering.

"Lisa!" Janet yelled.

Teagan put her hand up in another 'I got this' gesture. "Lisa, I would seriously suggest you look into standup comedy. By the way, Erin and Aoife's dads are firemen, and both of their mothers think they're smokin' hot. Erin here is also a firefighter and she's pretty hot so, yeah, being hot might be a requirement." She turned to Erin. "Erin, you know of any ugly firefighters?"

"Ha ha. Do bears fart in the woods? Ratio of hot to ugly is about five to one leaning to the hot and good-looking side… But, they do fart in the station… and in the truck cab on the way to a call; beans and hotdogs being a main staple at the station."

By now everyone was rolling around on the floor laughing. "Oh, and Lisa? Playing with their hose… just makes them fart more so… definitely NOT a good idea."

The next hour was spent answering as many questions as they could with the girls' questions ranging from, where did you go to college and what did you study, to what's it like to fly a helicopter? Lisa had also quit shouting out and was now raising her hand and waiting to be called on.

Finally, Janet asked each of them to say what they loved most about their job, what they liked least, and who their hero was.

The last part was the easiest as each of them proclaimed all of their sisterhood sisters were their heroes. That resulted in Lisa declaring to the other girls that they needed to establish a sisterhood and support one another.

Afterward, as they reached Teagan's truck, Janet stopped them. "You three are absolutely amazing. Lisa has always been our sceptic, the voice of uncertainty. Yet halfway through it became obvious that you'd won her over. Now she's in there cheering the rest of them on." After giving each of them a big hug, Janet asked if they would be willing to come back. Teagan's suggestion, however, was that they would talk to their other three sisters about doing the next session since that would add a whole different variety of jobs to the mix.

*** 

"Okay, everyone up for some free cappuccinos and muffins or croissants?" Erin asked. "I happen to know this wonderful guy who owns a Starbucks. Plus, I promised him we'd stop by when we finished at Generate Hope so he can try and win me over with free stuff."

Once again, the three of them piled out of Teagan's truck, laughing at something Aoife had said. As they reached the small patio in front of Starbucks, four guys sitting at the closest table blatantly stared at them. "Wow," one of them said. "Are they fucking hot or what?"

Just then, Bailey stepped out and came over to them. He reached out and took one of Erin's hands. Glaring at the four guys he told her, "I'll have a table out here on the patio for you in a little bit," then he led them inside.

Halfway through them placing their order, two Chula Vista police cars pulled up. Four policemen got out, walked over to the table the guys were at and, after a short discussion, handcuffed them and led them to the police cars.

"Ah, your table is ready, ladies," Bailey told them, as an employee rushed past, cleared the table and wiped it down. "Follow me," he added and led them outside to the now clean table.

"This isn't over... turd breath," one of the guys spit out before the policeman shoved him into the back seat and closed the door.

"Turd breath. That's original," Aoife said.

"I take it there weren't enough blueberries in their muffins?" Erin added.

"I've got a restraining order against them," Bailey explained. "They showed up ten minutes ago and sat at the table I'd reserved for you. I told Gigi, their server, to just go ahead and serve them while I called the police. They show up every few days, harassing customers to prove a restraining order doesn't mean anything to them. I doubt any of them can read and their cumulative IQ is probably a negative number, so it's likely they don't even know what a restraining order is."

Minutes after the police left, intuition told Erin to turn and look behind her. As she did, she saw a woman come out from between two cars and start running toward them. She had something in her hand and raised it as she got closer. Erin stood, threw her arm out, stiffened it, and clotheslined the woman in the throat. Gagging, the woman went down like a sack of potatoes. A car leaving the parking lot ran over the small baseball bat she'd dropped and launched it out onto Bonita Road.

Teagan was already on the phone with 911 explaining that they needed the police and an ambulance. Aoife attempted to help the woman gasping for air while trying to spew curse words at Erin and Bailey. With Starbucks less than a block from the fire station, two minutes later an ambulance rolled up and Jake, and Rita, another EMT, hopped out.

Jake looked at the three sisters and Bailey, then the woman on the ground. "Let me guess. Her team lost the softball game and she came after you with the bat we ran over coming in here," he joked.

"Close, but you still don't get a free muffin," Erin said.

Just then two of the same policemen from earlier pulled back in. As they came up, one of them looked over at Bailey. "Wow, you play to a tough crowd of customers." Glancing at the woman on the ground, who was now sitting up coughing and hacking, he asked, "Bad blueberry?"

An hour and three different reports later, the parking lot finally cleared of emergency vehicles. "Wow, that was fun!" Teagan said. Glancing at Erin she added, "And I was sure Maverick the pea inspector was going to be the most interesting guy we've met."

Bailey's face scrunched up in confusion. "Pea inspector?"

"It's a long story. I'll explain later," Erin told him. "In the meantime, who's the batgirl I stiff armed?"

"Uh, that would be the girlfriend of one of the wahoos they hauled away earlier. She's on the restraining order too. My guess is she hid in their car till the police left then decided to attack."

"Do you have any normal customers?" Teagan asked.

"Aside from you three… probably not."

"If you're using us to define normal, you're really in trouble," Aoife threw in.

A second later, all three of their phones went off.

"Does anyone understand what a 'day off' means?" Teagan said as 'Call In' flashed on her phone. "This is Teagan," she answered. "Yes, Aoife is with me. What's up?" After a long pause while staring at Aoife she said, "Oh my God! Okay, we'll be there as fast as we can. Oh, can you notify Bonita Fire that Erin is with us and she'll be responding too. Thanks."

"What's up?" Erin asked, as the three of them headed for Teagan's truck.

"Two idiots racing on the South Bay off the Chula Vista Marina just ran into a float party. We're meeting a Harbor Police boat at the marina in fifteen minutes as part of the search and rescue team."

They reached Teagan's truck, each grabbed a life vest out of the storage compartment in the bed of the truck, then climbed into the crew cab. Teagan flipped on the special blue and red emergency lights and siren as she pulled onto Bonita Road and raced toward Otay Lakes Road.

Twelve minutes later they parked at the Chula Vista Marina, life vests in hand, ran down the dock ramp and boarded the police boat. "I hope none of you just ate because it's really ugly out there," a harbor police sergeant said as their boat raced out of the marina and into the South Bay. In less than three minutes their boat throttled back and coasted into what looked like the red sea. The blood and debris floating everywhere were bad enough, but the screams were right out of a horror movie.

Their life vests barely pulled snug, Aoife and Erin were over the side, each swimming toward a head bobbing in the water. Teagan and the harbor police officer helped the injured onto the boat as each of them guided another banged up partyer to them. One was missing a hand. Another had a foot dangling, skin and muscle the only thing holding it on. Still another with a deep gash across his entire back.

"That's enough," Teagan yelled. "We need to get these three on the way to the hospital or they'll never make it." Aoife and Erin made sure no one else was near them that they could grab quickly, then climbed back on board. The boat raced to the dock just as Air Two set down in the marina parking lot.

The three rescues safely on board, Teagan gave a thumbs up to the pilot. Air Two lifted off and turned for Scripps Mercy Hospital while the three of them ran back to the dock and the police boat.

Four hours and seventeen more rescues, an exhausted trio of Erin, Teagan and Aoife threw their life vests into the bed of the truck, grabbed their backpacks and headed toward the marina's locker room to change into something dry and warm. On the way in, the owner of The Galley stopped them. "After you've changed, I've set a table for you on the patio. Anything you want is on the house."

"Thank you," the three of them said.

A short time later, they stepped out to a loud round of applause, cheers, whistling and whooping. Once they were seated the waitress brought them each a glass of wine, then took their orders.

"WOW!" Aoife said. "I lost count of the rescues, three trips each by Air One and Two and I don't know how many ambulances we filled." She paused as tears soaked her eyes and streamed down her cheeks. "Most of them were just kids... teenagers. It broke my heart every time I reached one of them, looked into their terrified eyes and tried to tell them it would be okay. Then try to make sure I didn't lose a part of them on the way back to the police boat."

Teagan, tears also streaming, was shaking her head. "I... I ... hope they fucking hang those two that were racing. The sergeant said they were deliberately racing to the party group with the intent to turn and wake spray them at the last minute. But, they collided, both of them lost control and slammed into the party group at full speed."

"So many lives ruined... for what?" Erin added, her tears joining the others.

The three of them got up and locked themselves in a hug. "I hope we never have another call like this... ever." Teagan whispered.

"Amen," both Aoife and Erin added.

70

*** 

When they got back to the apartment complex, the three of them headed for their apartments with a shower the first thing on the agenda. Before she climbed into the shower though, Teagan called Chase. "Hi. Feel like some company, then maybe the two of us go to dinner somewhere?"

Even though they'd spent very little time together, he could sense something was off. Plus he had fully expected their first real date to include at least one of the sisters, just to be safe and until she was sure he was okay to date. "Are you okay?" he decided to ask anyway.

"Am I that obvious?"

"No, not really. Just a sixth sense telling me something's off."

"Very perceptive. We went out on a really bad call today and I need help getting it out of my head."

"Wow. I'm honored you called me. I'll be happy to try and help cheer you up and I'd love to have dinner with you." He paused. "Teagan? You said 'we'. Were any of your sisters with you?"

*What is he, a mind reader?* she thought. "Yeah, Erin and Aoife were on the call with me."

"Do you think they'd like to come along with us? Maybe some company, a few drinks and laughs would cheer them up too."

She sat stunned. *What the hell kind of a guy invites his first date's sisters to come along?* "Chase?"

"Yeah?"

"Do you have any idea how wonderful what you just suggested is?"

"You mean being concerned about your sisters too?"

"Yeah, and knowing as hard as I'd try, I'd sit there all night, worrying about them?"

"Well, sounds to me like you need to call them and see if they want to join us. It also sounds like whatever you were called out on was pretty nasty. So how about if I drive and that way the three of you can get as drunk as you want."

"Chase, are you absolutely sure you're okay with my sisters joining us?"

"I'm absolutely certain. This will also give me a chance to explain and apologize about my accident in person… and maybe even get Aoife to like me, just a little."

"You don't need to explain or apologize. I already told them what happened. As for Aoife, she lost a good friend to a drunk driver when she was sixteen and your accident brought all those memories back. She'll get over it; it'll just take some time."

"Will she be okay with joining us? My whole intent was to help all of you get over the call. Last thing I want is put more stress on anyone."

"You really are amazing, you know that? Why don't I invite them and if either one doesn't want to come, they don't have to." She gave him her address and while he was on his way, she called Aoife and Erin.

It wasn't long before there was a knock on the door. Teagan answered it, pulled Chase in and gave him a kiss. Behind her on the couch were Erin and Aoife, both wearing big smiles. A second later, Teagan stepped back and he found himself the filling of an Erin and Aoife sandwich.

"Thank you for inviting us," Erin whispered.

"And worrying about my forgiving you," Aoife added.

"Okay, I'm starved," Teagan said. "Where are we going, Chase?"

"Well, since I may have to carry each of you back to the car, then to your apartments, I thought I'd keep it close. How about Romescos? They have a great selection of both Mexican and Italian. Plus the last time I was there, the food was excellent."

Teagan looped her arm through his and asked, "Why are we taking a car? It's only a short walk. That way you can drink too and don't need to carry any of us. Also, the walk will sober us up. Worse comes to worse, we can roll anyone back that can't walk."

The four of them walked the six blocks to the restaurant. Once they were inside, drinks delivered and their orders placed, the interrogation of Chase started.

"So which airlines do you build seats for?" Aoife asked.

"Pretty much all of them," he answered. "Most of our customers, at the moment, are domestic airlines but that's because they're the ones replacing their fleets with the new 737- 400 and 500s and 767-ERs. We just finished quoting seats for British Airways 777s though, which I'm pretty sure we'll win."

"Does that mean you'll be going to England?" Teagan asked, batting her eyelashes, leaving no doubt she was teasing him and waiting for an invitation.

His smile brightened. "Very likely.. Why, you want to come?"

"I think I could be convinced."

"Uh, I think we all could," Erin threw in, just as their meals came.

Teagan leaned into him and loudly whispered, "I knew inviting them was a mistake!"

That got a chuckle out of everyone, before Chase went on. "Actually, I would love showing you all around London. It's one of my favorite cities and I know it quite well since I was stationed there in the Air Force." He reached over and turned Teagan's head toward him and gave her another kiss. Before his lips left hers he whispered, "Oh, did I mention I get a friends and family discount with British Airways... and the hotel?"

"Okay, everyone, eat quick. We need to go pack!" Aoife mumbled through a mouth full of food.

Chase chuckled. "Relax, my company needs to get awarded the contract first, then they need to pick me to be the representative to BA." He paused, his face taking on a very serious expression. He looked at each of them, stopping at Teagan. "I take it the call you went on was the accident out on the bay? It's been all over the news and looked pretty bad." He watched as each of them stared at the table. "Okay, I got it. Time for a subject change."

"Thank you," Erin whispered.

"What's some of the funny calls you've been on?" he asked.

Aoife let out a chuckle. "The call out to the senior retirement residence?" she asked Teagan and Erin. After they both nodded, she went on. "This was before Teagan and Aoife were flight certified and all three of us were on call as EMTs out of Bonita Fire. Anyway… we get a call from the restaurant in a senior residence. When we arrive, the girl at the reception desk has no clue about a 911 call, so we all head for the restaurant. As we go in, a woman way in the back starts waving wildly at us. When we get to her, she looks fine and Teagan asks her what her emergency is. The woman glares at us then turns to the receptionist. 'I've been down here for over ten minutes waiting for someone to help me!'"

Now it's Teagan's turn to chuckle. "Just then a server shows up. 'I'm sorry, ma'am, I forgot to ask how you wanted your burger done.' 'Medium, of course,' the woman responded." Shaking her head, Teagan added, "The woman had not only been helped but ordered and completely forgotten."

"Oh! Oh!" Erin shouted. "We can't possibly forget the guy that got trapped in his suit of armor on Halloween. His wife helped him get into a full suit of armor and then the two of them headed for a party. On the way there, they got into an argument, so she left him in the car and went inside to the party." She let out a big snort. "Problem was, he could barely move, couldn't get out of the car without help and his wife had his phone. Finally, he managed to attract the attention of another couple coming out of the party. Even then, they weren't sure he was real and reported a robot stuck in a car on the 911 call."

Suddenly, Teagan burst out laughing. "Uh... we ... we can't leave out the guy handcuffed to the bed and his girlfriend with the lightbulb."

"Lightbulb?" Chase asked, as Erin and Aoife burst out laughing.

"She had handcuffed him to the headboard and was... shall we say... entertaining herself with a lightbulb while he watched. Problem was, the lightbulb went in and... got stuck? She was afraid to stand up or walk because the light bulb might break, and he couldn't help because he was handcuffed to the bed. Luckily, he somehow reached the phone and called 911."

"I remember when the 911 dispatcher relayed the call," Aoife added. "She kept trying to say the call was for a 'lightbulb extraction' but was laughing so hard she finally gave up and said, 'you'll find out as soon as you get there.'"

"This was not their first 'adventure' with 911 and EMTs having to rescue them from their strange sexual exploits," Erin said, then added, "Most of which none of us really want to go into detail about."

By now Chase just kept shaking his head, trying not to picture what they must have walked in on each time.

***

After dinner and two rounds of drinks, the four of them walked back toward the apartment complex. Erin and Aoife politely excused themselves and left Teagan and Chase standing in front of her apartment door.

"Would you like to come in?" she asked him.

"Are you sure you're okay with being alone with me?"

"I'm pretty sure you're safe. Besides, all I need to do is knock on the wall and they'll be here in an instant… with a medical bag full of sharp instruments to rescue me." She smiled and added, "Want a beer?"

"I'd better not. I've already had two and I need to drive back to my place." Ignoring his own words, he lowered himself onto the couch.

"I think we both agree, you shouldn't be driving," she told him as she smiled and passed him an open beer.

"You're evil, you know that?"

She set her beer on the end table, climbed onto the couch and straddled him. "Uh yeah. I'm pretty sure my parents warned you about that at the ranch." She took his beer, set it next to hers then locked him into a searing kiss as her tongue searched for his.

"So much for…" he mumbled before she clamped onto his tongue.

"Anyone ever tell you you talk too much?" she said after releasing his tongue. Then she put her arms up and he gently removed her blouse.

Aoife had just filled her blender with a banana, strawberries, wheat germ, milk, and honey when her phone rang. The number looked a little familiar but she couldn't place it. "Hello."

"Hi, Aoife. This is the pea rescue squad calling. We have a position open for an EMT who knows veggie CPR and can train our line workers in mouth-to-mouth. Any interest?"

Trying to come up with a smart reply, without thinking, she punched the 'blend' button. "UGH!" he heard, followed by, "I'm sorry. I'm having a pea-tastrophe at the moment. The top of my blender just flew off and soaked me with my pea smoothie so… I need to get out of my clothes right away."

A second later there was a knock on the door… with no doubt in her mind who was out there, she pulled the door open. "How the hell did you know where I live?"

"Too many Frida Rita Margaritas," he said. "Don't you remember giving me your phone number in Coasterra?" Smiling, he stared at a giant blob of dark green sludge slowly sliding down the front of her blouse. "Well, you put your address on it too," he added, then reached out, scooped a handful of the sludge off of her and slurped it out of his palm. "Umm, that's really good."

She grabbed him by the front of his shirt, pulled him into the apartment and kissed him as he reached back and closed the door.

"Much better than the smoothie!" he said as he bent back in and licked her lips.

"Shut up and help me get out of these clothes," she told him, dragging him down the hallway and into the bathroom.

"Shouldn't we kiss some more before we... uh start peeling each other's clothes off?

She glared at him. "You want me to go get one of my sisters next door to help me take my clothes off?"

"No. No. I got this." He led her into the bathroom, then eased her top over her head. He set it in the sink, then bent over and slurped another blob of smoothie from between her breasts.

"You missed some," she said as she unhooked her bra and threw it in the sink.

The next thing she knew, she was naked, in his arms and being lowered onto her bed.

"Don't move," he whispered as he licked another blob of green stuff from just above the hairline between her legs.

"Oh God! Maverick!" she moaned, while he stripped out of his shirt, pants and underwear. "If you so much as look at me down there again I'm going to cream in my... " She looked down between her legs. "Uh, my jeans seemed to have disappeared? Panties too?"

"You want me to go get one of your sisters to help find them?"

"You want to die young?" she asked as she pushed his head down between her legs. "They can't have gone far. So I suggest you do a thorough search... leaving no crease or fold un... folded?"

***

Erin decided a cappuccino was just what she needed to top the night off... one served by someone that seemed to send shivers to places she'd long forgotten about. Before she made it through the door to Starbucks, Bailey stepped from behind the counter with a giant smile and two mugs in his hands.

A wink and a nod toward a table in the back corner and she intercepted him halfway there. After they settled in at the table and shared a gentle kiss she told him, "Someone said the cappuccino here was much better than at Romescos... oh, and that you needed help closing."

"I don't know who said that because I helped train the staff at Romescos on how to use the cappuccino machine. Guess I'll need to do a reminder class." He smiled and gave her another light kiss on the lips. "As for closing, actually it's Ruby's night to close. I was just getting ready to leave when I saw you across the street, waiting for the light to change. Somehow I knew you were desperate for a cappuccino, so I decided to wait for you."

"I'm really glad. because halfway here, I realized how dark it is out and now I'm afraid to walk home alone."

Bailey's face lit up in a big smile. "You do know your nose is going to grow."

"Yes, I'm aware of that. I thought you might want to walk me home and we can watch it grow together."

Leaving their cappuccinos unfinished on the table, Bailey stood, helped Erin up and the two of them headed for the door. His hand on the small of her back sent chills through her body as he held the door and eased her through it. Once they were outside, he put his arm around her waist and she pulled herself tight against him. "Um, you're nice and warm," she said, then bent over and kissed him.

A few minutes later they were right in front of the fire station when a car passing on Bonita Road backfired. Suddenly, Bailey's warmth was gone. "Bailey?" she called out. Looking around, he was nowhere in sight. "Bailey?"

"Over here," came from behind the half wall with 'Bonita Fire Station' spelled out on it.

Erin carefully made her way through the shrubbery and peeked behind the wall. "Are you okay?" she asked when she saw Bailey sitting behind the wall. He was shaking like a leaf in the wind. Kneeling in front of him, she wrapped her arms around him and whispered, "It's okay. It was just a car backfiring."

"I'm sorry," he said.

She eased herself next to him and pulled him against her chest. "What's going on?" she asked softly. "You're shaking like crazy." As a nurse, she knew something traumatic must have happened to him to cause the reaction he was having.

"My... my brother was killed in a drive-by when I was twelve. We were just walking down the street, then he was lying on the sidewalk, dead. I remember hearing a loud bang, his hands grabbing for my leg as he slid down beside me. They'd shot him in the neck and hit a main artery. Blood was spewing everywhere... I ... I couldn't stop it... it just wouldn't stop."

Erin pulled him in tighter. "Oh my God. I'm so sorry." She gently kissed his cheek just as the front door of the fire station opened.

Someone came down the steps, turned, then stopped. "Erin?" the person said, then rushed over. "Bailey? Are you two okay?"

"Hi, Jason," Erin said. "A car backfired next to us and scared poor Bailey half to death."

"I'm headed home. You want me to run him and you to the hospital?"

"No, but would you mind taking us to my apartment? It's just another two blocks down. I'd rather he not have to deal with cars passing the rest of the way. I think he'll be okay once I feed him a scotch or two."

"Sure," Jason replied, as they helped Bailey to his feet. "Scotch, the cure-all for everything," he kidded.

Ten minutes later Jason dropped them off in front of Erin's apartment. "You sure you're both okay?" he asked her again.

"Yeah, I got this, he'll be fine."

"Who wouldn't be with you nursing them," Jason said, adding a big smile. He turned to Bailey. "You owe me a cappuccino, or two."

"Get in line," Bailey said, pointing behind Erin.

Jason left and Erin put her arm around Bailey's waist and walked him to her door. Once inside, she parked him on the couch, said, "Stay," and went into the kitchen. A few minutes later she was back with two half full tumblers of scotch.

"I think a back rub, along with the scotch, will go a long way to relaxing you and easing the trauma you suffered. But…" her smile grew "…I'll need your clothes off. All of them."

Six am - Three apartment doors opened, three males and three females marched out, all wearing giant smiles. They turned and looked at one another and their smiles grew. "As the elder here, I guess it's my job to lead the 'Walk of Shame' parade?" Aoife asked.

"As long as it leads to Starbucks and coffee, I don't care who's directing the parade," Bailey told them.

Aoife looked at her sisters and let out a chuckle. "Hey, quit staring. I was teaching Maverick mouth-to-mouth… you know, so he knows how to do veggie resuscitation."

"Oh. Is that what we're calling it now?" Erin said.

"Why do I feel like I've missed something?" Chase added, searching all the faces.

"You missed a lot but get used to it. Buy me coffee and I'll fill you in," Teagan replied.

Ten minutes later they all assembled at the door to Starbucks.

"It's a pretty morning. Why don't you all grab two tables out here on the patio and I'll have Grace come out and take everyone's order," Bailey said, disappearing inside.

"Wow. Bossy," Maverick said. "You'd think he owned the place."

Aoife gave him a kiss. "That's because he does."

"Oh wow! You know if he's dating anyone?" Maverick asked. That earned him two elbows in the ribs, one from Aoife and one from Erin, who he happened to be standing in between.

After pulling two tables together they all sat. Erin introduced everyone… adding Bailey at the end, when he returned outside. As soon as their coffee and muffins were delivered, the three women stood up. "Sorry, guys," Teagan said. "Some of us have to earn a living and we're all due on duty this morning."

Each gave their respective dates a kiss then headed for their cars. Teagan and Aoife drove to their helicopter at Gillespie Field, Erin, a short block away to the Bonita Fire Station.

\*\*\*

As soon as she walked into the fire station, the dispatcher called Erin over. "The chief said to send you in as soon as you got here. He's in his office."

"Thanks, Alice. Any idea what it's about?" she asked Keira's mom.

"Nope. He just said it was important."

Tapping lightly on the chief's door, she eased it open when she heard, "Come in."

86

Chief Weston looked up and smiled. "Close the door, Erin, and have a seat."

"What's up, chief?"

He stared at the Starbucks cup in her hand. "Don't you know you're supposed to bring the chief coffee when there's a meeting first thing in the morning?"

"Sorry. Didn't know there was a meeting… you want me to run back to Starbucks and grab you a cup?"

"No, I'm just giving you a hard time. Your dad never brings me coffee so I guess not bribing the chief is a family trait."

She smiled, set the cup on the desk, then eased it over to him. "Here. I only took a small sip… So, what's up?"

"You know that new Mexican restaurant on Sweetwater?" he asked.

"Yeah. The one everyone's wondering… like why do we need another Mexican restaurant when there's already twenty of them in our little village? Especially one out in the middle of nowhere?"

"That's the one. I need to introduce you to FBI Agent Lisa Willis. She'll be here any minute and I'll let her do most of the explaining." Just then there was a knock on the door.

Erin walked over and opened the door. Standing on the other side was a very cute and very young blond. Slim, maybe an inch or two over five feet and 100 pounds, soaking wet. "Hi. I'm Lisa," she said, throwing her hand out.

Erin shook her hand. "Hi, I'm Erin." *This is an FBI Agent? She's not old enough to be in high school yet,* she thought as she studied Lisa.

Lisa's face lit up in a smile as she stepped past Erin. "I know. I look like I'm still in eighth grade. Part of my disguise."

Erin's head snapped back to the Chief. "Disguise? Why does she need a disguise? What's going on?"

"Why don't you both go into the conference room and close the door. I'm sure Lisa can explain everything to you better than I can. I'll have Alice bring in some coffee and water," the chief replied.

The two of them followed his instructions and once Alice had dropped off the coffee and water, Lisa closed the door and they sat opposite each other. "Since we'll be working together, you need to know that, even though I look fifteen, I'm actually twenty-seven. I graduated from the FBI's training center at Quantico six years ago and I've been a field agent for five years. So they're not sticking you with some inexperienced rookie."

"Okay?" Erin said, hesitating from still not knowing what this was all about.

"The restaurant your chief mentioned? We're pretty sure it's a front for bringing young girls into this country illegally and forcing them into the sex trade. Lately, we think they've also

88

expanded into kidnapping locals and girls from other states. If you haven't eaten there... don't! The food sucks. They also do everything else they can to discourage anyone from eating there. That's why there's never any customers inside. There are, however, always at least four or five young girls, dressed as servers, inside."

"Okay, and what does this have to do with me?" Erin asked.

"They want you, and me, to go in under the premise of inspecting the business for fire safety. You're the inspector and I'm to be a college student you're mentoring on an exchange program with the fire department."

Staring at her, Erin said, "You do know I'm a firefighter and EMT not a detective."

"Actually, you are a detective, since you investigate arson cases. We'll just be looking for a slightly different set of clues, but I trust you'll be able to quickly spot the signs of illegal living quarters. Being an EMT will also let you evaluate any of the girls we might come across. Believe me, it's not hard to scope out anyone that's being sexually abused... their eyes will just scream 'help' at you."

"That part I'm more than familiar with," Erin said. "We pick up our fair share of girls that have been abused during sex or beaten after the person they were sold to was not happy with them." She paused and stared at Lisa. "Okay, so what's the plan?"

"Before I go into what I'm thinking, I need to tell you that I know all about Aoife's mom, as well at Paige and Jessie… Also, your most recent visit to Generate Hope. And yes, that was another reason for picking you."

"You've been spying on me!"

"I promise, it was more my own curiosity then spying."

Erin broke into a smile as a light bulb lit. "Okay, here's the deal. I'll go with you, but in exchange, you need to come with us the next time we speak to the girls."

Lisa's smile matched Erin's. "How did I know you were going to come up with that? I've got my notes all ready and I'd love to be a part of your pay it forward talks with them." Lisa's smile grew as she stared at Erin. "What? You're surprised? Don't be. Once I realized what Generate Hope does and how important a role they play in getting and keeping girls off the street, I wanted to help. Then when I found out your 'sisterhood' worked with them also, it made me realize I could help too."

"Thank you. We and the girls need all the help they can get," Erin said, adding, "So what's the plan for getting into the restaurant?"

"Well, it'll be a surprise inspection, just like for any business. But I'll need a day or two to get the paperwork in place, so we look official. Are you okay with doing it on one of your days off?"

"Sure," Erin said. "Can I tell my sisters what's going on?"

"Normally I'd say no, but in this case, I think it'll be okay. Plus, we may need their help a little further down the road. Just please, make sure no one overhears when you tell them."

Lisa stood and Erin joined her. "I'm sorry to get you involved in this but I really need your help to put these guys out of business."

"I'm happy to help in any way I can. Especially if it shuts them down and saves several girls from being forced into the sex trade. Just let me know where we go from here."

"I'll set up the paperwork for the inspection and let you know as soon as it's ready," Lisa told her. Then added, "I can't thank you enough for helping us take these guys down."

***

No sooner did they start for the door when the call horn went off and Alice came over the PA. "Engine 38, EMT 7... Shooting at Costco. Assist CV Engine 51 and EMT 21. CV police and highway patrol on scene."

Erin met Jake in the engine bay, ran around the front of the vehicle and climbed into the driver's seat. She started the ambulance while Jake flipped on the lights and siren, then she pulled out and staged them behind Engine 38 as it rolled out of the bay. Lights and sirens going, both vehicles turned out onto Bonita Road and made their way to Otay Lakes Road. Turning south on Otay Lakes Road they followed 38 up the hill to H Street, turned west and proceeded the few miles to Costco.

Costco's parking lot was a picture of sheer havoc. People running everywhere in panic while the police tried to corral them away from the danger. Engine 51 and EMT 21 had pulled up right in front of the main entrance and the engineer driving 38 pulled it in front of 51 to leave room for EMT 7 alongside of 21.

A policewoman met Erin and Jake as they came around to the back of the ambulance. "What happened?" Erin asked her as they opened the back doors and started to pull the gurney out.

"Three women got into it over a new game controller. The store only had three left and they each wanted two of them. After the sales clerk interrupted a tug of war that destroyed one of the controllers, he explained that he would get more in, either tomorrow or the next day at the latest. But none of them wanted to wait. One woman pulled out pepper spray, sprayed the other two, grabbed the last two controllers and took off. She tripped and went down. One of the other women pulled a display rack over on top of her, grabbed the controllers and ran. In the meantime, the other one pulled a gun out of her purse, supposedly to defend herself, but shot herself in the foot instead. We arrived and caught the other two fighting over the controllers in the parking lot."

Trying to stifle a chuckle, Erin asked, "So who's hurt?"

Pointing at two women handcuffed to a shopping cart by the front door, the policewoman said, "Those two are scratched up from wrestling with the display racks and the cat fight in the parking lot afterward. The one inside has a hole in her foot and some tug of war bruises."

Louise, one of the EMTs from 21, had been listening and turned to Erin. "You want to do rock-paper-scissors to see who gets Annie Oakley inside?"

"Nope, you can have her. We'll get the shopping cart twins over there," Erin replied.

Just as they finished patching up numerous cuts and scrapes on the shopping cart twins, Louise and her partner wheeled Annie Oakley, handcuffed to the gurney, out and put her in the ambulance. The policewoman wheeled the shopping cart, the twins walking alongside it, over to her police car, uncuffed them from the cart and put them into the back seat. She gave a quick wave as Jake and Erin collected all their medical supplies and headed back to the ambulance.

"Another successful Costco rescue," Erin said.

"Yup. We do get called here a lot, don't we?" Jake added, as they locked the gurney down and shut the doors.

"Yeah, can't wait for Halloween, Thanksgiving and Black Friday when the shopping feuds really begin," Erin said as they headed back to the station.

# Chapter 10 – Four Days Where?

Monday morning. Teagan's phone rang. *Chase. Hum, wonder what he wants this early?* "Hi, Chase. What's up?"

"I'm sorry. Did I wake you?"

"Yeah, but that's okay. Actually, my alarm went off an hour ago and I managed to get one leg out before I dozed back off," she added as she sat up and tossed back the bed covers.

"Can I come over? I've got a proposition for you."

"A proposition? Maybe I shouldn't get dressed after I shower?" she teased, letting out a little giggle.

"I'm good with that, but it's not that kind of proposition... uh, well, maybe it is."

"Enough! It's too early to think." She paused. "That could be cured with a latte though."

"Got it. Go shower while I get you a gallon size, triple shot, latte from Bailey's Starbucks... oh... and I'm good with clothes being optional after you've dried off."

\*\*\*

Twenty minutes later, Teagan answered the door in her bra and panties, a towel wrapped around her hair. Before Chase could clear the doorway, she snatched the giant latte out of his hand and took a large sip. "Oh God did I need that!" She added after she came up for air, then kissed him. She took a step back and smiled. "Go ahead, say it, I can be bought for a latte." She took another giant sip and smiled. "Just name it and I'm yours to do what you want with."

"Well, that was easy. How fast can you pack for London?"

Desperately trying not to spray him with her third sip, she gagged as it foamed out of her mouth, ran down her chin and into her bra. "Wha…" cough cough "…Did you just say London?"

He eased her over to the couch, gently set her down and carefully pried the latte out of her hand. "Don't move." A minute later he was back with a damp wash cloth and dish towel. He wiped her chin and neck, smiled into her eyes, seeking permission, then unclipped her bra. Once her breasts were wiped, he dried her with the dish towel and headed for her bedroom. A minute or two later he was back with a clean, dry bra. "Sorry, you're all out of pink but the roses will go with the pink panties."

Her smile grew even bigger. "That does it! You're to report here every morning to pick out my clothes before I get dressed."

"Maybe I should just…" he stopped in mid-sentence. *Too soon, dummy. Don't push it.* "Why don't we save that for another time. About London. My company won the contract to equip British Airways new fleet of 777s with seats and I've been picked to be their representative. That means I need to go do a courtesy call, introduce myself and start laying out a plan for equipping their aircraft. This trip will only be three days and I remembered you saying today was the first day of your four days off. So I was wondering if you'd like to come with me?"

Her face lit up. Then she pushed her excitement aside for a moment, remembering how hard he'd worked to win the contract and had wanted to be picked as the BA representative. "Oh, Chase, that's fantastic. Congratulations on winning the contract and being selected as their representative. I'm so very proud of you!"

He couldn't help but stare at her. Anyone else would have been peeing their pants over going to London… but what did she do first? She stopped and recognized all the effort he'd put into winning the contract. There was now no doubt in his mind about how special she was. His smile grew as he realized that this was just the first step in his showing her how special he thought she was.

Little did he know she was having the very same thoughts about him inviting her to share in his winning the BA contract with her. *Next he'll be inviting Aoife and Erin so they don't feel left out.* She looked up as she reached over, retrieved her latte and took another big sip.

"Just so you know, I would have invited Aoife and Erin but this first trip is special and I only wanted to share it with you." Half laughing and half choking, Teagan sprayed the front of him with latte.

As he cleaned up the latte with the dish towel, it dawned on him, did she have a passport? "Uh, I should have asked this before, but do you have a passport?"

"Yup. We were talking about going to the Caribbean last year, so I got one. Work got in the way so we never went. I even have a stamp in it from Mexico. We walked over to Tijuana for dinner one night and we insisted they stamp our passports at the border so they wouldn't be empty."

Chase was shaking his head and smiling. "I... okay... guess we both need to get dressed now, and you need to pack. Then we'll go earn you some more stamps in your passport. I've booked us on today's non-stop BA flight to Heathrow. It leaves at 8:30 pm and we'll arrive in London tomorrow, Tuesday, around three in the afternoon their time. We'll be there for two and a half days, then return on Friday, leaving London around 1:30 in the afternoon their time and arriving here at 6 pm. I hope that will work."

He watched Teagan nodding. "I'll make it work," she said, grabbing her phone. "Mike? Hi, this is Teagan. Listen, I need an extra day off... no, I'm going out of country and can't get back until late Friday... Sure. Tell him I'll make it up and work one of his days next week or whenever he wants... Great. Thanks, and I'll see you Saturday morning."

She turned to Chase, gave him a big kiss and said, "All set. Let's get packing."

While Chase ran out to grab his suitcase, Teagan pulled hers out of the closet and began throwing underwear in it. As soon as Chase returned, she asked, "Weather in London?"

"Let's see, September. Damp, chilly and good chance of rain. Dress warm but in layers so you can peel stuff off if it turns nice."

"Got it." She grabbed several pairs of slacks and blouses out of the closet, then stopped and smiled at him. "Chase, are we sharing a room?"

Returning her smile as he pulled a new shirt out of his suitcase he said, "I was about to get to that. They only had one room left... are you okay with that?"

Her smile grew. "Very okay. I know you'll need to be at BA for meetings and such but I hope you'll be able to see a little of London with me."

Stripping out of his latte-stained shirt he watched her stare at his chest, then pulled her in for a kiss. "Thank you for coming with me. This account means so much to me and I'm really nervous about making a good impression."

Teagan wrapped him in her arms "Why in the world would you be nervous? You're the most confident person I've ever met. But putting that aside, I'm glad you asked me to come with you and I'll be there to support you in any way I can."

Her phone rang and she picked it up. "Was that Chase I saw going into your apartment?" Aoife asked, her phone obviously on speaker mode. Then she added, "Twice… and the second time with a suitcase?"

After a long pause, Erin in the background asked, "Is there something we should know?"

Chase, watched as an evil grin took over her face. "Uh yes. I'm glad you called because I need to tell you I'll be gone for a while."

She could just picture the two of them staring at each other. "What do you mean 'gone for a while?' How long's a while? Where… where are you going? Is Chase going with you? Teag, what's going on?"

"Actually, he's not going with me, I'm going with him. His company, thanks in large part to him, won a contract with British Airways and he's invited me to go with him to London for three days."

Instinctively she moved the phone away from her ear as "London!" blurted out of it. That was followed by, "Oh my God. Put Chase on, please!"

She let out a chuckle. "They want to talk to you," she said, handing him the phone.

"Hi, who's this? Aoife or Erin?"

"Both", came back. Then Aoife spoke up. "Chase, thank you for doing this. Teag hasn't had time off or gone anywhere in forever. We know it's only a few days but please make sure she has a good time."

A second later Erin chimed in. "Just so you know, we're both jealous but we're so glad you asked her to go with you. She so deserves this. When do you leave?"

"I'm glad the timing worked out with her days off," he told them. "We're off on tonight's nonstop flight and I promise I'll take good care of her and make sure she has a good time. I only wish it could be longer but if things go well, I'll be going back often and believe me, she'll be going with me as much as she can."

"Chase? You're pretty special and we're so glad you two found each other," Aoife said. "Oh, and Chase, I'm so sorry I lit into you when we picked you up from the accident."

"Believe me, I understand." He paused. "You two get ready, because if I have my way, she'll come back with a giant smile and tons of stories about what she did and saw."

***

Teagan insisted they eat at the airport so they wouldn't miss their flight. So, five hours early, they checked their luggage in for the flight, then headed for Planet Hollywood for something to eat.

Two hours before boarding they were the first passengers at the gate. While Chase checked in at the desk Teagan sat squirming like a little kid, unable to believe she was going to London… for three days!

"Welcome aboard British Airways, Mr. Brooks," the gate agent said after he gave her their passports and boarding passes. "I'm afraid I'll need Ms. Moore to come to the desk so I can verify her against her passport."

"Teagan," Chase called, then turned and waved her to come join him. "She needs to check you against your passport picture." He put his arm around her waist and pulled her close.

The gate agent looked up and studied Teagan against her passport picture, then smiled at both of them. "Thanks. I also need to tell you that we've been instructed to bump you up to first class, so you'll be boarding at first call." Her smile broadened, her hand came up and she handed an envelope to Chase. "Also, this is for you."

"Thank you," Chase replied as he and Teagan headed back to their seats.

As soon as they were reseated, Teagan went off like a bottle rocket. Shaking his shoulder, she loudly whispered "First Class! Oh my God, my first flight and I'm going first class. Wait till I tell Erin and Aoife."

Things were working out beyond anything he could have planned. He couldn't believe how happy she was as he opened the envelope. Teagan watched his smile grow and light up his face. "What?" she asked.

"They want us to check into the hotel, then go to the BA Engineering Office right afterward."

"Us? I'm sure they mean you," Teagan said.

"Nope, they specifically said to bring you with me."

# Chapter 11 – London Calling

"What the hell is this idiot doing?" Jake asked Erin as they watched a bright yellow sports car quickly approach from behind, then speed past them in the carpool lane. "He's got to be doing over a hundred," he added as he reached for the radio. "Bonita dispatch, this is EMT 7."

"Go ahead 7," Alice answered.

"We're on southbound 805 just coming up on the Palm Ave exit. Can you notify the CHP that a…." Just then a CHP cruiser, lights and siren going, passed them, giving chase to the sports car. "Cancel the call. CHP is on scene giving chase to a yellow… oh shit," While he'd been talking, they watched as two exits up, the sports car lost control, slammed into the center divider, bounced back into the freeway lanes and was broadsided by two cars.

Reaching up, Erin flipped on the lights and siren and slowed the ambulance.

"Bonita dispatch. Be advised we're on the scene of an accident. Southbound 805 just north of the 54 interchange. CHP on scene. Three cars involved. We'll definitely need 38 and at least one more ambulance."

"Roger 7. Engine 38 was returning from a call near you. ETA five minutes. CV Engine 51 and EMT 12 being dispatched."

To protect the accident scene, Erin eased the ambulance to a stop parallel with the CHP Cruiser so that as many flashing lights as possible would be seen by approaching cars. Just as she and Jake opened their doors, there was a loud squeal of brakes.

***

Chase and Teagan grabbed their carry-on bags from the overhead, thanked the first-class flight attendant and headed into the terminal. As they exited customs and emigration, a BA representative approached them. "Mr. Brooks, Ms. Moore?"

They both nodded and the representative shook hands with both of them. "I'm Ian. I've a black cab waiting to take you to the hotel and then on to BA." Chase glanced at Teagan who had the biggest smile he'd ever seen. She looked back and forth between Chase and Ian, then said, "I had no idea I was traveling with a dignitary."

"This is a little more than we usually do for our vendors but they'll explain more about that when you get to the Engineering offices," Ian told them.

"Is this one of the famous London 'black cabs' everyone said I have to take a ride in?" Teagan asked when they stepped outside to the cab rank.

"I suspect so ma'am," Ian answered.

A short ten-minute cab ride and they pulled into the driveway of the Sheraton Skyline Hotel on Bath Road. Across the street, behind two other hotels, was the south end of Heathrow's runway. A block further to the left they could see the British Airway's office complex and hangers. A British Airways Concord on display next to the closest building.

While the cabbie waited, the concierge and bellman collected their bags, checked them in, then escorted them to their room. After tipping the bellman, he gave them each a room key and they headed back down to the black cab. Five minutes later it dropped them off in front of BA's engineering complex across the way.

***

They checked in at the reception desk in the lobby. "Welcome to British Airways, Mr. Brooks and Ms. Moore," the receptionist greeted them. "Mr. William Weston, the 777 Program Manager, will be down in just a minute. Might I bring you some tea or water once you're settled in the conference room?"

"Water will be just fine," Teagan said. Chase nodded at her and she added, "For both of us please."

Mr. Weston came out of the elevator, introduced himself and shook hands with both of them. "Please, call me William," he said, then escorted them to a glassed-in conference room just off the lobby. They all took seats and the receptionist brought in a tray with a pitcher of water and glasses.

"I'm afraid I've good news and bad news," William said. "The bad news is, we're not ready for you. Seems the chaps that were assigned to layout the seats for our new 777s are stuck in

New Zealand on a project with Air New Zealand. As best we can predict, it'll be a week, more likely two, before they can finish up and get back. Then it'll be at least another week before they can finish up their draft specifications for the 777 seating. But on to the good news. That means you're free to enjoy your time here in London playing tourist. It also means we'll need you to come back in about three weeks." He paused and looked at Teagan. "I hope that's not too inconvenient, Ms. Moore, since I assume you'll be joining Mr. Brooks on his future trips?"

Teagan stared at Chase and broke into a big smile. "Uh, I hope so but that's up to Mr. Brooks." She also couldn't help but notice the look on Chase's face. The one that said, 'Why is he playing up to her. I'm the one he's supposed to be meeting with.'

"Forgive me for being nosy, but what is it you do, Ms. Moore?"

"I'm a helicopter pilot. Actually, an air ambulance pilot, for Mercy Air in San Diego."

Mr. Weston's mouth dropped open as he stared at Teagan. "Fascinating! What an interesting job," he finally said. He turned to Chase and lit up in a big smile. "You must bring her back. My team will have a thousand questions for her at the next meeting. We'll be lucky if we get anything accomplished on the seats, but I suspect that will just lead to more trips to London for both of you. Now I'm glad I brought this," he said as he pulled a card out of his pocket and handed it to Teagan.

She looked at the card, looked at Chase then back to Mr. Weston. "This... this is a friends and family pass for British Airways. I ... I don't understand?"

"Simple. We inconvenienced you by not being ready for you and now you'll need to return, so the least we can do is pay for your next trip... and any additional trips after that." His smile grew and he winked at Chase. "I'm sorry if I'm intruding in your relationship, but I just assumed she would be joining you on future trips."

Teagan locked eyes with Chase. *He's mad,* she thought. *Of course he's mad. You've unintentionally distracted Mr. Weston and taken over his meeting.* As she was thinking of how to turn things around, Chase raised his eyebrows as if to say, 'go with it'. Obviously, he had an idea. "Mr. Weston, Teagan actually has two sisters who will likely be joining us on future trips. They too are first responders. Aoife, is a flight nurse and flies with Teagen, and Erin is a firefighter and EMT who goes on callouts with them."

William smiled at Teagan. "Well, isn't that funny. I just happen to have two more passes in my pocket." He pulled them out and handed them to Teagan. "We certainly can't have you leaving your sisters behind while you enjoy our lovely city."

Teagan watched William's smile grow again. *What's he up to?* she thought as she smiled back. She would need to apologize to Chase when they got back to the hotel. William was acting like *she* was here to meet with BA, rather than Chase.

William must have read her mind. "Of course, you'll need to warn them that we'll want to know all about what the three of you do… and hear some of your more interesting stories."

"So noted. I… I can't begin to thank you enough." She stood up and pulled him into a big hug. *I need to talk with Chase. I can't let my sisters and I unintentionally take over his meeting… make that meetings.*

"My pleasure. I somehow think these meetings with be a lot more enjoyable with the three of you in them. I do have one request though. On your flights here and back, please take note of our cabins, the seating and the amenities. Our team would love your input, as unbiased passengers of course." He paused and smiled again. "Simply ignore the friends and family passes. They're certainly not meant to be a bribe in any way. Just a thank you for helping."

They watched a light bulb light above his head and his smile grew again. "As a matter of fact, I just had an idea." He turned to Chase. "I'll be changing your class of service on each flight into Heathrow. That way you'll get to sample each class of service. On your return flights, of course, we'll book you back in first class."

***

After they left, Teagan couldn't believe what had happened. "Erin and Aoife are going to pee their pants when I give them these passes." She stopped, kissed him and gave him a big hug, adding, "Thank you for bringing me." Pulling him to a stop, she looked into his eyes. "I'm so sorry I became such a distraction. I feel like talking about what Aoife, Erin and I do, took the meeting way off course. Maybe us attending the next meetings is not such a good idea?"

Chase had the biggest grin. "At first I would have agreed with you. But then I realized, I could never generate that much interest in a meeting on seats. Believe me, I can handle keeping the meetings on track, but their interest in what the three of you do will make everyone want to attend. Once they're there, it'll be easy for me to pick the right moments to steer the meetings toward selecting seats. Of course, I'll need a little help from the three of you." He paused. "I think that's why William has us changing where we sit on each flight. He's as much as said he values and looks forward to your opinions."

"How did you get so smart?" His smile earned him another kiss. "Are you okay with walking back to the hotel? It's only a few blocks and it'll give me a chance to absorb the differences... like driving on the left and the traffic circles at every intersection."

"You mean roundabouts." He pulled her in tight and returned her kiss. "Just so you know, I think bringing you with me was the best thing I could have done. If you didn't figure it out yet, William is fascinated by you. I suspect Erin and Aoife joining us will only add to his, and everyone else's, fascination with what the three of you do."

"Well, if it helps you in the meetings, I'm sure the three of us will find a way to suffer through multiple trips to London. I'll be hard but we'll manage, somehow! Now let's go eat, I'm starved, and I have to call Aoife and Erin."

Intuition told Erin to pull her arm back in and not to step out of the ambulance. Just as she leaned back in, there was a loud crash. The driver's side door disappeared and the side of a pickup truck sealed the opening where the door had been.

"Are you okay?" Jake asked.

"Yeah. That was close though. Something just told me not to step out."

"Your guardian angel, I suspect."

"Do you believe in that stuff?"

"Yup, too many unexplained close calls for me not to."

The two of them slid out of the passenger side and made their way around to the pickup truck. The driver had managed to wedge his truck between the ambulance and the CHP cruiser. Shaking her head, Erin surveyed the situation. "Are you okay?" she yelled to the driver.

"Yeah, I think so," came back.

"Okay. Try not to move around. It's going to be a while till we can get to you." She looked at Jake and smiled. "Hope he likes convertibles. Even if we pull his truck out, the roof's going to have to come off so we can get to him."

Just then Engine 38 pulled up, the driver angling it to protect the two emergency vehicles and accident scene. "You alright?" Bert asked his daughter as he climbed out of Engine 38.

"Yeah, we're good, Dad," she replied as she locked him in a hug. "Think you can pull his truck out while we check on the people up front? I'm pretty sure the top needs to come off once you get it out."

Her dad returned her hug and told her to be careful as she and Jake headed for the main accident scene. Bert turned around to find at least three cars had pulled up behind Engine 38 making it impossible for them to back the truck up. He flagged down a CHP officer and asked him to clear the cars from behind their truck so they could pull the pickup out.

"Why are people so fascinated by accidents?" he asked Shawn.

"They wouldn't be if they had to deal with the blood and guts we do on a daily basis," Shawn answered. He waved the closest car toward the far side of the freeway, around their engine and the accident scene.

Finally, they cleared enough cars out of the way and Bert aligned Engine 38 behind the pickup. Ten minutes later, they pulled the truck out, with the most God-awful metal to metal screeches. Once the truck was loose, they told the driver to cover his head with his arms and lean away from the window so they could smash it and put a blanket over him. Next came the windshield, then four cuts with a saw and they lifted the roof off, before easing the driver out.

Jake came back to check on the pickup driver. "How is he?"

"He's good. A bit shaken up with a few minor cuts and bruises, but nothing major," Shawn replied.

"Good. Can you walk him over to 12 and let the EMTs check him out. Then we could really use your help up front. It's a mess up there," Jake said.

Shawn and Bert approached the main accident just as Erin and one of the EMTs from ambulance 12 covered the driver of the sports car with a yellow tarp. His body was ten feet away from what was left of his totally unidentifiable sports car.

Erin looked up at them and shook her head. "He never stood a chance. We watched it unfold. His car hit the center divider at full speed, bounced off, then got broadsided by these two." She pointed at the two cars imbedded in the driver's side of the sports car. "That launched him clear out of the other side of his car." She paused. "Not sure if he didn't have his seat belt on or took it off just as he got broadsided." Looking at the mangled steering wheel and dashboard controls, now almost on the passenger side, she added, "Either way, I'm not sure it would have made a difference."

Fortunately, the occupants of the other two cars came out with only minor cuts and scrapes. Everyone had been wearing their seat belts and both drivers had just enough time to react and were riding the brakes when they slammed into the sports car.

"Hey, Dad? Any chance on getting a ride back to the station with you?" Erin asked Bert.

"Sure," Shawn answered for him.

"Okay. give us a second to grab the drug case and lock the back of the ambulance," she said as she and Jake headed for ambulance 7.

***

An hour later Jake and Erin were sitting in the station conference room filling out reports when Aoife walked in. "What's this I hear you're taking lessons from Fae in tearing parts off your vehicle?" she asked.

"Ha ha. No lessons involved. Other than be sure to look before you jump out. Especially at an accident scene," Erin replied.

"Are both of you okay?" Aoife asked.

"Yeah, thanks to intuition and my guardian angel."

Jake pointed at his watch and whispered, "I need to go meet my girlfriend," then headed for the door.

Just as the door closed Aoife's phone played "Danger Zone" from Top Gun. "That's Teagan." She put the call on speaker. "Hey, Teag. How's London?"

"Where are you? Is Erin with you?"

"We're at the station and yeah, Erin's right here."

"Good. Are you both sitting down?" Teagan asked, adding a chuckle.

"Uh yeah, we're sitting. Is… is everything okay, Teag?" Erin asked.

"Way more than okay. Turns out BA wasn't ready to have a meeting on seats because their crew got sent to New Zealand. So, we're free to run and jump and play for a few days, then head home. It also means we need to come back in about three weeks and… and you two are invited."

"What!" Erin and Aoife yelled at the same time.

"Why would we be invited? The only thing we know about seats is cleaning blood off them after we do a pick up," Aoife added.

"Seems the head of the project at BA is fascinated by what the three of us do and wants everyone in his crew to meet us so we can tell them interesting stories."

"Do they know there's blood, guts and mangled body parts in most of our stories?" Erin asked.

Teagan let out a chuckle. "Yeah, I think that's why they're so interested. Anyway, I'll explain more when we get back. I just wanted to give you both a heads up. So, don't use any of your time off… you'll need it for multiple trips to London."

"Have you been drinking?" Erin asked.

"Not yet, but we're walking back to the hotel and the pub will be our first stop for food and drinks. Then it'll be off for some much-needed sleep."

Aoife was shaking her head. "Okay, we'll let you go but plan on spending most of your next call explaining what's going on."

"Have a good night you two! Love you and promise I'll explain everything in the morning. Hugs." Teagan hung up, leaving Erin and Aoife staring at each other.

# Chapter 13 – CC and J ?

Teagan peeled one eye open, looked around then down at the arm propping her bare breasts up. Following the arm, she found a pair of eyes watching her. "My boobs haven't looked this perky in a long time. You need to follow me around and hold them up." She watched Chase's smile grow.

"Gladly." He looked down at her breasts. "Although I think several love making sessions from last night had more to do with their being perky this morning than my arm."

"I don't think my nipples will ever return to normal."

His eyes moved back to her breasts and his smile grew. "I love the new normal."

She reached over and gently lifted his chin and looked into his beautiful sea blue-grey eyes. "Chase, this is getting complicated." She leaned in, kissed him, then stared at him. "This… 'us' … has happened faster then I think either of us ever expected. So if you feel overwhelmed and want out before things go too far, please say so. Everything you've done, like being concerned about my sisters and inviting me to come to London with you, just makes me fall more in love with you… Actually, I think it's already too late."

"Good, because I'm in love with you and have been since I locked eyes with you in 57 Degrees. So, the last thing I need is an 'out'." He returned her kiss. "I suggest you just go along with my plan."

"Uh, do I want to know what your plan is?"

"It's simple. I plan on spoiling you so that no one else will want you." He paused and added, "That's part one. Part two is to spoil everyone in your sisterhood so they think the two of us, together, are the best thing since cream cheese and jelly."

Teagan gaped at him, a look of total confusion on her face. Finally, she let out a snort. "Cream cheese and jelly? Don't you mean peanut butter and jelly?"

"Nope, can't stand peanut butter."

Another snort slipped out. "Uh, who's the cream cheese and who's the jelly?"

"Take your pick. You're sweet and creamy so you can be either or both."

"That would make you … the bread?" she asked.

"How about a cracker?" he replied.

"Okay! Enough. Now I'm hungry, so how about a quicky in the shower, then take me to breakfast."

"You're evil! And I love it, my CC and J." He slipped out of bed, pulled her up and led her to the shower.

\*\*\*

Six thousand miles to the west, Maverick kissed the top of Aoife's head as he pulled her tighter into his arms. "Hey, easy. I'm not one of your peas... but a little mouth-to-mouth would be appreciated," she said, batting her eyelids.

After an extra-long kiss with a lot of tongue dancing, she broke it off and turned in his arms to gain a little space. "I hope you're as comfortable with this as I am..." she said, staring into his sparkling hazel eyes "... because this is not just a couple of one-night stands and it's getting serious for me."

"Me too. And, just so you know, I knew you would never be a one-night stand. I knew it was all in or nothing from the very beginning, and I'm way more than fine with that."

Her look turned serious and she cocked her head. "Did you just ask me to marry you?" She watched as his eyes went wide and he began to studder.

"I... I... uh..."

*I can't do this*, she said to herself and broke out laughing. "I'm just teasing you. I do think I'll wait till next week though to tell you I'm with child."

"Crap! I knew I shouldn't have bought those condoms from that pea on the corner."

"Ewww," she yelled and pushed him. As he rolled off the edge of the bed and hit the floor, the two of them broke into hysterical laughter. "I'm sorry... I didn't mean to push you off the bed," she tried to squeak out.

They both looked up as someone knocked lightly on the wall. "Can you kind of hold it down in there?"

"Oh shit, that's Bailey," Aoife whispered.

"Sorry. We're trying to come up with names for our kid and got carried away," Maverick said.

A second later, the door opened, and Erin charged in, Bailey a step or two behind her. "Kid? What kid! Are you pregnant? Didn't you listen in the birth control class at school?"

Aoife desperately tried to keep from laughing as she pointed to Maverick. "He borrowed condoms from one of the pea people and they were… uh… a wee bit too small."

Erin glared at him. "Was the carrot or asparagus line too far away?"

"I… I didn't know anyone over there."

Aoife broke in. "Trust me. He's definitely bigger than an asparagus spear, or a carrot, so it wouldn't have helped."

By now Erin and Bailey had joined Maverick on the floor and they were all laughing and holding their sides. "God, I hope no one is recording this," Bailey managed to squeak out. Before he finished his sentence, Erin's phone rang.

"Hi, Teagan." She decided to have a little fun with Teagan as she put the call on speaker. "Your timing is perfect. We're all over at Aoife's trying to come up with a name for the baby."

"The what?" came back.

"Uh, seems Maverick went cheap and bought his condoms off a pea peddler who used a defective rubber by-product. That resulted in the condom being attracted to Aoife's IAD which ripped a hole in the…"

"Stop," Teagan yelled. After a long pause came, "I'm pretty sure it's her IUD, and I hope you know you're all crazier than a herd of loons."

"I think that would be a flight of loons?" Bailey said.

"Nope, definitely a flock of loons," Maverick threw in.

"Okay. Shut up! All of you. I've important news. So ditch the kid and the condoms and listen up," Teagan said, desperately trying keep from bursting out laughing. She spent the next ten minutes explaining about their short meeting with William at BA. How his way to apologize was to give each of them a BA friends and family pass and invite them to the next several meetings. "Of course, along with that, we need to rate their seating by class and tell them all of our crazy stories."

Maverick and Bailey were both polite enough not to assume they were invited to London on these trips and stayed quiet. If either Aoife or Erin wanted them to come along, that was a subject for later.

"Oh my God, I can't believe this," Aoife said.

"Yeah, I can't wait to see London," Erin added. "Speaking of which, what have you done so far and what are you going to do with your next two days there?"

"Well, last night we had dinner here at the pub in the hotel. I had bangers and mash... with mushy peas. Teagan told them. "Then this morning we had the hotel breakfast buffet with eggs cooked to order, more bangers, bacon, baked tomatoes, baked beans and portage. Oh my God. I think I gained ten pounds."

"What are bangers?" Erin asked.

"English sausage and the mash is mashed potatoes. It's soooo good," she replied.

"So have you gotten to see anything yet?" Aoife asked.

"Yeah. After breakfast, we caught the hopper bus to the airport, took the tube - subway for you non-Brits - to Westminster, then took the double decker tour bus all around London. It's such a cool city. I can't wait for all of you to get here and see it. Oh, and then tonight, we've got tickets on the London Eye."

"You sound like a little kid who just found a new fantasy world. I'm not sure we've ever heard you this excited about anything," Erin said.

Teagan looked over at Chase with the biggest smile he'd seen yet. "You have no idea how happy I am that Chase asked me to come with him. When you get here, you'll understand. There really is no way to describe London. It's everything you've read or heard about or seen pictures of, but none of that does it justice." After a pause and a wink to Chase she added, "Being here with Chase is as fantastic as the city too. He's so knowledgeable and an absolute pleasure to tour with. He points out stuff I missed and insists I try the local food. Oh, and you know all those stories you heard about English food being so bland and boring? Well, don't believe a word of it. If you know where to go and what to order, it's fantastic."

"I can't wait to get there," Aoife replied. "Where are you off to tomorrow?"

"Oh wow. Wait till you hear this. We're on a tour to Salisbury Cathedral. Then from there we go to Bath with a walk through the village, its old Roman baths, the aqueduct, the village and Stonehenge. The hotel concierge made me promise to bring back a dozen Bath Buns for him and the staff. Of course, there'll be a dozen for us, not counting what we eat there. Hee hee."

"You do know we hate you. We're sitting here picturing all this and drooling and now we need to wait three weeks before we go. Ugh!" Erin complained.

This time it was Aoife's phone that rang, while 'Call-In' flashed on Erin's. "Gotta go. We're being called in," Erin said, adding, "See you in two days."

Aoife answered her phone. "This is Aoife."

Erin answered hers.

"This is an emergency call-in for all first responders in the south bay area. You're requested to report to nearest fire station as soon as possible. Full turn-out gear will be required." After a long pause, the message repeated. "This is an emergency call-in for all first responders in the south bay area … "

"Sorry guys. We need to go," Aoife said, while she grabbed her call-in backpack and Erin ran next door for hers. Two quick kisses were exchanged then they headed for the Bonita Fire Station.

# Chapter 14 – A Pea Free Vacation

As soon as they pulled into the fire station parking lot, they knew something serious was up. The normally almost empty lot was not only full, but every type of emergency vehicle from the south bay was either there or pulling in behind them: Local police, sheriffs, CHP, lifeguards, search and rescue… even a US Navy NCIS vehicle.

But it was the two people coming out of the fire station and heading for them that made them realize this was very serious: Bridget and her father, Matt, the Secret Service Agent attached to the President's office.

Bridget and her dad met them in front of Aoife's truck. "What's going on?" Erin asked.

"Were not sure yet," Bridget answered as she hugged each of them. "The Chula Vista Police, National City Police and San Diego Sherriff's Departments, all received a phone call, warning of *payback* early this morning. The calls were from one of the gangs here in the south bay. They claimed that the police are arresting *their girls* and then releasing them to whatever gang bids the highest for them. That was followed by disarming bombs at two local police stations and explosions at the hangouts of three of the gangs, with a promise of more to come."

"That… that's the most ridiculous thing I've ever heard," Aoife replied.

Matt looked at each of them. "Intelligence is not a requirement or strong suit of gang members. We believe one the gangs is spreading the rumor and hoping some of them will attack the police, and the gangs supposedly on the *preferred list* of the police. Probably to eliminate some of their competition." He paused, then added, "This is not just happening here. The same rumor is spreading to gangs in all the big cities. That's why the President asked me to get involved. We think, however, that it started here."

"What can we do to help?" Erin asked.

"Obviously law enforcement will take the lead on this, but if this gets out of hand, there's likely to be a lot of clean-up. So, we're trying to assemble quick response teams and station them around the south bay. Hopefully, we can stop this soon. So far only one person has been injured but if this goes much further it'll be a very ugly mess," Matt answered. "Come on inside. We're about to explain what our plan is, and issue assignments."

They headed inside and joined the large crowd of first responders and police. Bridget's dad seemed to be in charge and asked for everyone's attention. He repeated what he'd told Aoife and Erin out in the parking lot. Next, they assigned teams of EMTs and first responders and told them where they would be assigned. The locations covered much of the south bay area and made sure at least one team was no more than five to seven minutes away from responding to an area.

Erin and Aoife were assigned as a team to the old Bonita fire station on Bonita Road. "They've already staged ambulance 3 there and it's been fitted with everything you'll need, including bullet proof vests and weapons," Matt told them. "Only select EMT teams will be armed, those who are qualified with the weapons we've given you." He looked around at the rest of the room. "Whether your armed or not, a police team will be assigned to join you on any call out. I want to be clear that you're to wait for your police team to join you before you respond to the call out. Is that clear?" Everyone nodded. "Okay, God's speed and be safe out there!"

Keira and Bridget joined them as they walked outside. "We're in ambulance 6 and we'll be staging out of the Sharp medical facility over on Third Street in Chula Vista."

"Wow, is it my imagination or does it seem like we're surrounding Chula Vista?" Erin asked.

"Definitely not your imagination. That's because of the number of gangs there," Bridget told them. "Listen, we'll only be ten minutes away so, call if you need help. We're all sisters you know."

Aoife gave them a big smile. "Uh yeah, don't forget, that works both ways and we're there for you too. But we only admit being related to you on good days."

"Yeah, ditto the other way. Oh, and how's Teagan's London trip going?" Keira asked.

"She's super excited and we're pretty sure she and Chase are definitely a couple now," Erin told them. "They'll be back on Friday, so we'll see about all of us getting together over the weekend."

The girls all swapped hugs, then headed to their assigned stations.

\*\*\*

Aoife and Erin arrived at the old fire station. After parking their pickup truck out back they grabbed their gear and unlocked the station. First thing was an inspection of the station and ambulance 3. A quick inventory and weapons check followed. "Been a while since I've used an AR," Erin said, while they both inspected their ARs and 380s, made sure they were loaded, then secured them.

"It's like riding a bicycle. It'll automatically come back to you," Aoife told her, as they holstered their 380s.

"Hopefully, it won't need to come back. I signed up to be a nurse and EMT, not an Annie Oakley wanna be."

Aoife let out a series of snorts.

"What's so funny?" Erin asked.

"You! I remember you out back on the ranch when we did target practice. We had to load you up with a banana clip and hope at least one round made it to the target." Aoife broke out laughing.

"Any idiot that messes with you is going to look like a sieve before you stop them,"

Aoife's phone rang. "Hey, Maverick."

"Are you two okay? We just drove by the old fire station and saw you pull in." He paused. "We're out front. Okay to come in?"

Aoife stared at Erin, "They're out front. Okay if they come in?"

"Got me? I don't see why not."

"Sure... but we may have to torture and kill you afterward," Aoife said to Maverick.

"Oh, torture! I'm in," came back.

A moment later there was a knock on the front door of the station. Aoife walked over and opened the door. "We were worried abou..." Maverick stopped in midsentence as he and Bailey stared at both girls in their turn-out gear, a 380 decorating each of their hips. "This... this is serious, isn't it?" he finally managed to get out.

"Very," Erin said. "Especially considering Aoife can't shoot worth a shit. If she unholsters her gun, I'd suggest you turn sideways and make yourself as skinny as possible."

"Is she serious?" Maverick asked Aoife.

"She's just kidding. I shot a rattlesnake out on the ranch at forty paces."

In between snorts, Erin added, "Yeah, we found sixty rounds in the ground around him but none in him. She went through four banana clips before he finally gave up. We're pretty sure he died from fright, not from being shot."

***

The four of them settled into the station lounge and the girls explained about the gang threats and what was going on. Bailey and Maverick volunteered to go get cappuccinos and muffins and, of course, before anyone could get a bite of their muffin, all hell to broke loose.

"Ambulance 3. Shots fired. Car wash on Bonita Road at 805. Use extreme caution. Apparent gun fight in exit area. Multiple injuries. SD Sheriff will escort you. Ambulance 6 with CHP also responding." The girls slipped into their bulletproof vests, checked their 380s and headed for the ambulance bay.

A sheriff's car pulled up out front as Erin opened the bay door and Aoife started the ambulance. Lights, siren and whoop horn came on as they followed the sheriff's car up Bonita Road toward the freeway.

Bailey turned to Maverick. "Those two women are amazing. I don't know about you but I've never met anyone like Erin, and Aoife and Teagan are both just as wonderful. I certainly plan on trying to take our relationship to the next level."

"Well, I think it's fair to say that Chase taking Teagan to London won him more than a few points. And you with your lifetime supply of cappuccinos and muffins for Erin has put me in a tough position. Anything pea or veggie related is not going to do much but I think I've come up with an idea for something she'll appreciate. I've already got most of it, but I need to run to my apartment and wrap it. If they get back before I do, can you ask her to wait for me?" Maverick turned and started for the door. "Oh, and please tell her not to eat anything because I've got lunch covered."

***

By the time the police and EMTs arrived, the shootout at the carwash was over. The deputy sheriffs and CHP officers went in first, while ambulances 3 and 6 waited a short way down Bonita Road. Once the police gave the all-clear, both ambulances arrived to find only dead bodies.

"Nothing much we can do except call the coroner," Aoife told the officers. Turning to Bridget, she said, "You may as well go back to your station. No sense in all of us standing around waiting on them to clean up the bodies."

As ambulance 6 left, Matt and another federal agent pulled in. After conferring with the deputies and CHP officers, he walked over to Erin and Aoife. "Well, looks like the gangs solved everything for us. The six of them lying dead over there, include the head and next in line of the gang that started all this. Plus the leaders of three of the largest gangs in Chula Vista. I think it's fair to say that any immediate threat died with them. It'll be a while before any of them can regroup. Especially since we've done a sweep and the top echelon of every gang in the south bay is sitting in jail. Not sure how many of the arrests will stick but we've certainly put a big dent in their plans. Once the coroner gets here, you're free to return to your station. We'll likely be disbanding the teams and cutting you lose within an hour or two."

By the time they got back to the fire station, Maverick had returned. His timing couldn't have been better. They received the all-clear and relieved from duty call before Erin had the door to the ambulance bay closed.

"We came up with a plan for lunch while you were gone," Maverick said.

"We did?" Bailey asked.

He winked at Bailey. "Well, I did and you two are invited," he told Erin and Bailey. He took Aoife's hand and added, "May I have the pleasure of my fair lady's company for lunch?"

Aoife did a half curtsey. "Of course, my knight of the round pea conveyer belt."

"Where are we going, sir fine knight of the cappuccino machine?" Erin asked Bailey.

"Uh, no idea," Bailey answered. "But we need to take veggie man's steed since mines in for his 2,000 gallop oats change."

Erin locked up the station and laughing, the four of them headed for Maverick's truck.

Twenty minutes later, they pulled into the parking lot of Shakespeare's restaurant.

As they got out, Maverick reached behind the back seat and pulled out a four-inch square, foot-long package, wrapped in wrapping paper with red, white and blue British flags all over it. Once they were settled at a table inside, he handed the package to Aoife. "This is for you. I've also arranged for the owner to come over and explain British food to you. That, and the contents of the package, should make sure you have a fantastic time in London."

Flabbergasted, Aoife just stared at him. Finally, the feelings rushing around inside her began to ebb as tears formed and ran down her cheeks. Holding up the package she smiled. "Maverick, I've no idea what's in here, but bringing me here for a translation of English food is the kindest, most considerate thing anyone could ever have done."

"I... I was so afraid you'd take it the wrong way... like I was trying to say you had no idea what English food is."

Her smile grew even bigger. "I never would have taken it that way... even though I really have no idea what English food is. So, this is perfect. And... let's see what's in here," she added as she tore into the wrapped package.

The first thing out was a red, white and blue, collapsible, travel size umbrella. Next, a power adapter kit fell into her lap... along with a packet of cards in a plastic baggie. Inside the baggie was an Oyster Card, good for a month's transportation on the

London tube and water taxi system. Next, a gift certificate for afternoon tea at the Ritz Hotel in London. Then, a no-wait ticket for a sunset ride on the London Eye. And finally, a ticket, good for a week, for the hop on hop off London tour bus.

"Uh, there's something else. Actually, two something elses," he said, handing her two more plastic baggies. Each contained a duplicate set of tickets and passes. "One's for Teagan and the other's for Erin, since I know all three of you will be doing everything together." Turning to Erin he added, "Sorry, you and Teagan will need to get your own umbrellas and borrow a power adapter from Aoife's kit."

Her mouth hanging open, Aoife locked eyes with Maverick. "You have to be the most wonderful person in the world. I will never be able to tell you how meaningful what you've done is. You've put so much thought into this but…" she reached over and took both of his hands in hers "… all of this is not going to work." Reaching over she picked up the umbrella. "Well, maybe this will, but the rest we're not going to be able to use." Her smile grew as she watched confusion take over his face.

"I… I don't understand," he said.

"Simple. Pay attention. There's only one ticket for each of us and… I've no plans on doing any of this without you coming with us. So other than sharing the umbrella, your one ticket short on everything."

"Does that mean you… you want me to come with you?"

134

She bent over and kissed him. "Of course it does. My friends and family pass is good for two people. I just hadn't had a chance to tell you, you're the second person." Her smile grew into an evil grin. "Think you can leave your pea people long enough for us to run around London together?"

"Can I bring a can of mushy peas? Just one? Kind of as a peace offering?"

"No! This will be a pea free vacation. No asparagus or carrots either. You get me to play with - all you want – that's it."

"Oh, and you better check with Erin, because I suspect Bailey will be joining us too."

# Chapter 15 – What are Bath Buns and Who's Igor?

Teagan and Chase arrived in San Diego at 6:30 on the BA flight from Heathrow. Waiting for them were Aoife and Maverick and Erin and Bailey. No sooner had they collected their luggage when they were whisked off to a reserved table at Coasterra on Harbor Island.

"Oh my God. It is so good to be home," Teagan said as she locked Aoife and Erin in a giant hug. That was followed by hugs for Maverick and Bailey. "You better have taken good care of my sisters."

"They both took excellent care of us," Erin replied. "But we want to hear all about London. Where did you go? What did you do? When are we all going back? What should we do for the meetings? Where are we staying? If it's where you stayed, what's it like? Oh! Food! What's the food like? Maverick took us for English food. Is it like what we had? What do we need to bring? We're all packed but we left room, just in case. What's ..."

By now everyone was watching Bailey who was running his hands all over Erin's back and sides. "There's an off switch here somewhere. I need to find it again."

Erin stopped talking and stared at everyone. "Was I that bad?"

"Nope, worse," Aoife said. "I thought we were going to have to do mouth-to-mouth if you didn't stop and take a breath."

"Sorry, guess I'm just excited."

Chase's eyebrows went up. "Gee, you think? When we get to BA in a few weeks, we should just push her into the room. Lock the door and come back a few days later. Maybe by then they'll have answered all her questions."

"I'm so sorry," Erin started to apologize, but Chase locked her in a big hug. "No need to be sorry. Your just super excited and frankly, I'm glad this is working out the way it is." He turned to Teagan. "I can't wait till they get to see some of the places we went to."

"Ha, you say that now but wait till you've had a week of them. We'll be putting them on the train through the Chunnel over to Paris just to get some peace and quiet," Teagan replied.

"Paris! Did you say Paris? Oh. My. God," Aoife yelled, and half the restaurant turned around.

"Nice going... big mouth!" Chase said. "Going to Paris was supposed to be a secret... and only if they were good."

"We'll be good. I promise," Aoife yelled and locked her arms around Chase's neck and hugged him for all she was worth.

"Uh, Eff? You might want to let up? He's turning blue?" Teagan said.

"Sorry." She let go, stepped back and kissed him on the cheek as she rubbed his chest trying to get him to breathe again. Everyone else was holding their side and laughing.

Maverick leaned over and loudly whispered to Bailey, "This is definitely going to be an interesting trip." Turning to each of them he added, "Please don't take this wrong. I'm just asking out of curiosity. Have any of you ever been out of the country before?"

They each nodded and Teagan spoke for the girls. "We've been out of the country, but mostly local, Canada and Mexico." Her focus turned to Chase. "I promise we'll be good. If any of them so much as thinks of doing something that would screw up your contract with BA, I'll personally kill them and dump their body in the Thames River."

To make sure he didn't embarrass any of the girls, Maverick turned to Bailey and Chase, his expression asking the same question.

"Uh, yeah, a few times," Chase said.

"Actually, only across the border into Mexico for me," Bailey said. "I was booked on a Mediterranean cruise, but I got sick the week before and had to cancel."

Watching Bailey, Maverick smiled. "Well, we're pretty even. I've been across the border but the one up north. I also kinda cancelled a trip through the Panama Canal. Actually, the girl I was dating met someone else and gave him my ticket." Everyone let out a chuckle, until Erin noticed the hurt feeling wash over his face and wrapped him in a big hug.

Turning serious, Bailey looked around the table. "I need to say something. This has to be the most mismatched group I can think of. The exception being you three girls, who pretty much grew up together. Even there though, the background of each of your families is drastically different. Were it not for the ranch and your moms' sisterhoods, I'm not sure you would ever have met or become friends. And that would have been a shame…" he turned and smiled at Maverick and Chase "…almost as bad as the three of us not meeting them."

He scanned the table again and stopped at Erin. "Please understand. I'm just trying to tell you how happy I am to have met you." he turned to the others. "All of you." He paused again. "I'm complimenting all of us for being so accepting of how different we each are and I love the way everyone has accepted everyone else." His smile grew and he reached over and took Erin's hands in his. "And you for inviting me to go to London with you."

A snort escaped Teagan. "I warned you he was weird! Oh, and I thought you invited Igor, the hunky fireman from Boston. The one who promised to buy you Bath Buns?" she asked Erin.

Panic took over Bailey's face. "Boston? They don't even speak English there. I… I'll buy you Bath Buns… whatever those are. I'll order them as soon as I get back to the store. I'll even give you a bath while you eat your buns." In a poor attempt at a whisper, he asked Chase, "What the hell are Bath Buns?"

139

"I suggest you ask Igor after we get back," he answered.

Still holding hands with him, Erin almost fell out of her chair she was laughing so hard. "You're adorable!" She finally managed to get out. "There is no Igor and I too have no idea what a Bath Bun is. Oh, and yes, you're coming with me."

*\*\*\**

Once the laughter settled down, Teagan described where she and Chase had gone during their three days in London. "We took the hop on, hop off bus all round London. I was amazed at how vibrant a city it is. On the other hand, so many of the things you see have such a fascinating history. Things like the Tower of London, Big Ben, Parliament, Tower Bridge, Westminster Abbey, a ride on the London Eye and on and on. Actually, I can't wait for everyone to get there because I know I missed stuff."

"Where else did you go?" Aoife asked. "I know you mentioned Bath and Stonehenge."

"Yeah. We took two separate tours. One went to Bath, Stonehenge and Salisbury Cathedral and the other went to Canterbury. I'm not going to tell you much about them because I made Chase promise we'd take all of you to each, while you're there. Trust me, going back to any of them would not be an issue. I could visit all of them over and over and over. I will tell you that Salisbury Cathedral is the most beautiful thing I have ever seen. Bath will make you wish you'd paid a lot more attention to Roman history in school and Canterbury is like right out of a fairytale."

"Oh my God. I can't wait to see everything," Erin said.

After Bailey mentioned finding both of them armed and dangerous at the Old Bonita Fire Station, the rest of the evening was spent with Aoife and Erin explaining about the gang shootings.

Finally, Chase looked over and found Teagan's head about ready to hit the table. "We need to get you home so you can get some sleep," he said.

"You too," she added. "Care to join me?"

"Only if we promise each other we'll get some sleep. You're on duty tomorrow and I've got my trip report to turn in. Not that that will take long."

"I promise," she replied as they all filed out into Maverick's truck and headed for their apartment complex.

The following morning it was back to work for everyone. Chase and Maverick reported to their companies and Erin drove Bailey to Starbucks. Teagan and Aoife headed for their helicopter at Gillespie Field. Cappuccinos in hand, thanks to Bailey, Erin's next stop was the Bonita Fire Station.

She just barely made it through the station door where she was met by the fire chief and Lisa, the FBI agent. Stopping to stare at Lisa's coveralls, Erin smiled as she read the embroidered name on the coveralls. "County Building Inspection, cute. I take it this means we're headed to the restaurant for our 'inspection'?"

"You okay with that?" the chief asked. After Erin nodded, he added, "There's a pair of coveralls hanging on your locker. Like Lisa's, they only identify you as an inspector with Bonita Sunnyside Fire. There's also a building inspection check sheet and a backpack with some tools that you might need in it."

Following Erin into the locker room, Lisa waited until she stripped out of her uniform, then stopped her before she could put the special coveralls on. Reaching down to the large pocket on her right leg, Lisa pulled the pocket flap up and revealed the grip of a pistol. "There's a low-profile leg holster strapped to my leg. I know you're weapons qualified, so I have another one for you… if you want it. Your coveralls also have the same fake pocket flaps as mine."

Staring at her, Erin asked, "Do you think we're going to need them... the guns that is?"

"I hope not, but these people are crazy. They'll often do anything to keep from getting caught, and keep their girls from getting away. That means that at least some of them will be armed."

"Ugh, now you tell me," Erin said as she reached for the holster, then strapped it to her left leg. Slipping on the coveralls, she stepped back into her boots and adjusted everything. Lisa handed her a Colt 38 Super Pistol with a two-inch barrel. Once it was holstered, and the pocket flap closed, there was no trace of the gun; even when Erin did a test walk around while watching her leg in the mirror. Satisfied, she opened the flap, removed the pistol and did a final check to make sure it was fully loaded and the safety was on.

The chief met them outside of the locker room and watched Erin for a moment. "You okay with all this?"

"Yip. With luck I won't blow my leg off, we'll put a bunch of bad guys away and give the girls they're holding captive their lives back."

"Okay. Let go," Lisa said. "I've got a borrowed county car outside... Oh, and before I forget. I'm wired for sound so the deputy who will be watching us will be able to hear everything."

***

It only took ten minutes for them to drive down Sweetwater Road and pull into the restaurant parking lot. Lisa knocked on the back door, but no one answered. She knocked harder and finally someone yelled, "We're not open. No deliveries are scheduled for today."

"We're not customers or purveyors. We're here for an inspection," she yelled back.

The door opened and the guy standing in it looked both of them up and down. "I told you, we're not open."

Lisa pasted on a phony smile and said, "You don't need to be open. As a matter of fact, we prefer that you not be since we'll be climbing over everything and moving stuff during our inspection."

The guy stared at her like she had just spoken in some foreign language. Finally, he came back with, "You have a warrant?"

Shaking her head, Lisa told him, "We don't need a warrant. You're required to submit to a health inspection and a fire safety inspection once every six months. Our records show that you haven't been inspected for either since you opened so we need to do both." She tried to step inside, but the guy blocked her way. An 'I'm not fucking around' smile appeared on her face as she glared at him. "Look... we can do this the easy way, or the hard way. Either you let us in or we have the sheriff's deputy over there..."

she pointed to the sheriff's cruiser parked on the far side of the parking lot "…escort us in."

Glancing across the parking lot, the guy shook his head. "Okay. But make it quick. I don't want you here when we open and customers start arriving."

"We'll be at least an hour, depending on how much we find, and your sign out front says you don't open for another two hours. So, plenty of time," she added as they both stepped past him. Lisa's 'fuck you' grin that followed had Erin desperately stifling a snort that she buried behind a cough.

The kitchen, that the back door opened into, was empty not only of people but food. Nothing was cooking on the stove or grill and nothing on any of the prep counters. The only sign that this was a kitchen was a pile of dirty dishes by the dishwasher.

Erin looked around and smiled at Lisa. "Well, this is your area so I'm off to inspect the rest of the building for fire hazards while you do your thing here."

They both watched panic set into the guy's eyes. "Uh, excuse me but you need to wait till she's finished. I can't be with both of you so you need to wait!"

"I really don't need you with me. If I have any questions, I'll address them when I'm finished. So you can stay here while she does her health inspection."

Just then, two young girls in their early teens, came in through the doors to the restaurant. Both were dressed in extremely tight short shorts, low cut, revealing tank tops and high heels. "We need some coffee before we hit the street," one of them said, before looking up. Her eyes locked onto Lisa, then moved slowly to Erin. "Oh, sorry. We'll just get our coffee and leave," she added as fear flooded both of their faces.

"Oh, perfect!" Erin said as she quickly made her way next to the two girls. "Both of you can show me around while I do my fire inspection." She started leading them out the door but the guy got to her first, grabbing her by the arm.

"I said you don't go anywhere without me! You got that?" he said, squeezing her arm till it hurt.

Erin glared at his hand on her arm. "You've got two seconds to let go of me before I rip your arm off."

"Fuck you…" was all he got out before he found himself slammed against the wall, his arm twisted halfway up his back.

"Well, look what I found here," Erin said, as she removed a pistol from the waistband of his jeans.

"Deputy, I think it's time for you to make an appearance," Lisa said. Less than a minute later, two San Diego Sherriff's deputies came through the back door. "Please read this gentleman his rights and arrest him for interfering with government inspectors and carrying a concealed firearm without a permit."

The two girls tried to back out of the doorway without being noticed but Erin stopped them. "I'm sorry girls, but you need to come with us."

146

"Do you have any idea what will happen to us if we go with you?" one of them said.

"I know what will happen if you don't," Erin told them. "They'll put you back on the street and sooner or later you'll both be sold and whoever buys you will do whatever they want with you. So please, let us help you." She reached out and took one of each of their hands. "Please come with us. We'll - no, I'll make sure your protected. I know a wonderful place that will take you in and help you get your lives back."

As the deputies led the guy outside, Lisa joined Erin and the girls. "Are there any other girls here?" she asked.

"There's only two more," one of the girls answered. "They're out on the streets somewhere. Three others escaped last night. That's why the guy you arrested is the only one here. The others, four of them, are out looking for the girls that escaped."

"Okay," Lisa said. She ran to the door and stopped the deputies from leaving, then dialed a number off her contact list. "Yes, this is agent Willis, badge number 337. I need backup at my location right away." She paused and listened. "Yes. I've two deputies that I'm holding until you can get me backup. There are four more suspects out looking for three girls that escaped last night. They could return any minute so I need you to expedite my request." Another pause. "Sure, Chula Vista Police will do just fine." She hung up and not five minutes later two Chula Vista policemen came through the door.

"We had just passed and wondered what all the activity here was when our dispatcher told us you needed backup."

The second policemen added, "It's about time someone shut this place down. What can we do to help?"

"Four of the suspects are out hunting three girls that escaped last night," Lisa told them. "They might return at any minute. So can you move your car out of sight and then back us up if they do return?"

"Sure," one of them said as he went to move their car and the other stepped just outside the door to stand guard.

Lisa began questioning the two girls when suddenly they heard voices coming from inside the restaurant. Erin was standing by herself off to the side of the door to the restaurant. Instinct told her to make herself invisible so she stepped next to a large refrigerator, putting her out of sight from anyone coming through the door from the restaurant.

The door opened and three guys, each holding a girl by their arm, forced them into the kitchen.

Lisa and Erin looked at each other, both having the same thought, *Where's the fourth guy?*

"Who the fuck are you?" one of the guys asked, finally noticing Lisa and drawing his gun.

With the girl between them, Lisa had no clear shot and hoped that Erin did. Just then, the fourth guy, with his pistol already drawn, stepped in and locked eyes with Lisa.

Erin watched as his finger started to move inside the trigger guard toward the trigger. "I wouldn't do that if I were you," she said, stepping out into the open. She'd startled both guys and they turned their guns toward her.

*Decision time.* She knew Lisa didn't have a clear shot at the guy with the girl, so she aimed at him. Before his finger found the trigger, she shot off a round. His gun disintegrated into pieces, he let out a loud scream and blood rushed from where two fingers on his hand had disappeared. No longer a threat, Erin refocused her attention on the fourth guy just as two shots rang out. She watched as a red spot appeared on his forehead, but out of the corner of her eye she saw Lisa crumple to the floor. For some reason, he'd turned and fired at Lisa instead of her.

Waving the barrel of her gun between the last two, she said, "Who's next?"

Without being told, two set of hands went up, the three girls ran to where the other two girls stood. The two policemen, who had been caught halfway through the door, came in and handcuffed the two men. Erin sidestepped over to Lisa, her gun still trained on the guys as they were led outside. "Call an ambulance," Erin said, as she holstered her weapon and bent over a smiling Lisa.

"You okay?" Erin asked.

"Yeah, I think so," Lisa answered. "Not sure why he turned to me, but I'm glad he did. He had a clear shot at you. He fired before he brought his gun around, so he just grazed me in the leg."

Just then there was a loud moan from behind them. Two of the girls grabbed the one between them as she slid to the floor. "Oh shit," Lisa yelled. "One of you grab the first aid kit from your car," she yelled at the two policemen.

Thanks to Lisa being wired for sound, two ambulances pulled up a moment later.

One ambulance crew attended to Lisa while the other to the girl behind them. She had also only been grazed but had gone into shock. Both ambulance crews ignored the guy missing two fingers until they finished caring for Lisa and the girl. Once they were both bandaged up, Lisa insisted Erin take her to the hospital while the ambulances transported the wounded girl and guy. The one with the hole in his head would have to wait for the coroner for his ride.

While one of the policemen retrieved their police car, the other turned to Erin and Lisa. "Where the hell did you two learn to shoot like that?" Turning to Erin, he added, "By the way, you're Bailey's girlfriend, aren't you?"

"Yes, I'm seeing Bailey," she answered, adding a big smile. "As for learning to shoot, my dad, Bert the fireman, taught me."

"Quantico," Lisa threw in.

"Well, I think you're in the wrong profession, Erin. Anytime you want a job with the police department just let me know."

"Sorry. Too late. The FBI already has dibs on her," Lisa said, winking at Erin.

# Chapter 17 – How Stupid Can You Be?

Erin ran Lisa to the Chula Vista Hospital Emergency Room, where she was in and out in an hour. The doctor and nurses commended the EMTs that had tended to her. From there it was back to the fire station where Aoife and Teagan and all the firefighters on duty engulfed the two of them in a giant hug.

"You're supposed to plug holes in people, not make them," Teagan told Erin, adding a chuckle.

Lisa was shaking her head. "Yeah, I told her that was my job, but she said she needed the practice. Tell you what though, the guy that messed with her will not be giving anyone the finger, or pulling a trigger, anytime soon."

"Are you okay Lisa?" Aoife asked.

"Yeah. It's all in the line of duty."

"Line of duty my ass," Erin said. "The bullet she took should have been mine. He had me dead on with nothing between us. I don't know what made him turn and shoot at Lisa but thank heaven he did." She realized what she had just said and with a smile added, "Only because he just grazed you."

"We'll probably never know what made him turn," Lisa said. "It's the business we're in When it's your time to go, you're gone. When it's not, something steps in and you get to live another day."

Bailey came rushing through the door and headed straight for Erin. "Are you okay? Please tell me you're not hurt." He ran his hands all over her. Finding no holes, he wrapped her in his arms and kept kissing her - all over.

Finally, she eased him back and kissed him on the lips. "I'm fine. It was Lisa that took the hit." She studied his face. "What's with the constipated cat look?"

"I was talking with two policemen out on the patio when the call came over their radio saying one of you got shot. I'm pretty sure I lost ten years off my life on the way here. I'm... I'm so glad you're safe."

Teagan and Aoife looked at each other. "Constipated cat?" they both mumbled, looked at Bailey, and burst out laughing.

Erin pulled him back in and hugged him even tighter. "You're adorable. I'm fine and I'm sorry I worried you," she whispered in his ear.

"Hey, I'm the one that got shot. Don't I get any more hugs?" Lisa asked. A moment later she found herself in the middle of a second giant group hug, yelling, "Ouch. Ouch."

As the group broke the hug, Erin's eyes found her dad in the doorway. "Something I should know about?" Bert asked his daughter.

Erin held her arms out and did a three-hundred-and-sixty-degree turn. "Nope. No holes and I'm not with child, Dad... yet."

153

"Uh, about the second part, your mom and I would like a little advanced notice," he said.

"Sure. How's nine months work?"

"Uh, ten would be better."

"Now who looks like a constipated cat?" Bailey asked, letting out a chuckle and watching confusion flood Erin's face.

*** 

Lisa and Erin's 'adventure' had made the news and by the time they all retreated to Teagan's apartment, Lisa and Bailey in tow, they found Chase and Maverick sitting in the hall waiting for them. After introducing Lisa, the seven of them broke out what beer and wine Teagan had; fortunately, just enough for one round.

"Bailey and I will go get more in just a minute," Erin said, after winking at him. "But first I want to say something." She scanned the group, stopping at Bailey again. "What happened today made me realize that we all need to say thanks for things in our lives. I know the three of us meeting Maverick, Chase and Bailey was by chance. But somehow, I can't help but think, someone out there, planned it. All three of you instantly recognized how important the sisterhood was to us. Something most of our dads realized when they met our moms.

"Then, all of you, instead of being jealous of our closeness, have gone out of your way to make sure you include all three of us as much as you can. To make sure none of us feel left out. Not with personal things, like hanging out while we make out on the

154

couch…" she bent over and kissed Bailey and whispered, "thank heaven," then went on, "… but including all of us because we're family. I don't think any of us could have picked better men to bring into our lives." Another scan of the room and she reached over and grabbed Bailey's hand. "Okay, beer and wine run. Let's go."

***

Everyone had applied for two weeks' vacation to coincide with Chase's meetings in London. The next several weeks went by quickly. The calls for Erin fell into the typical; car accidents and two calls to patch kids up after performing stupid stunts. Meanwhile, Aoife and Teagan did several organ delivery runs, answered two auto accident calls and transported a cyclist to Mercy Hospital after being hit by a driver who was busy trying to text while driving. Pretty much normal days for each of them. That is, until two days before they were scheduled to leave for London.

The call started out pretty normal with Erin and Jake arriving first. What they found was yet another cyclist who had been hit by a driver not paying attention. Hovering over the injured cyclist were five other cyclists trying to render aid to him. A few yards away, another twenty cyclists surrounded the car that had hit him. It was wrapped around a tree, with the driver and passenger trapped inside; the cyclists screaming and pounding on the car.

The first thing Erin and Jake did was confirm that the police were on their way as they headed for the injured cyclist. Even though he'd been wearing a helmet, he'd suffered head and

155

neck injuries and his whole left side was covered with road rash from when he'd gone down. "His neck hurts and he's pretty dazed," one of the bikers standing over him told Erin as she eased a neck brace onto him.

"I'll call for the chopper, then go check on the driver," Jake said. Squeezing the mike on his shoulder, he called in. "Mercy Base this is EMT 7. We've a cyclist down with neck and head injuries and need helo transport. We're one mile south of the softball field on Sweetwater Road in the preserve. The south end of the field we're in is clear for the helicopter to land."

"Roger EMT 7. Sweetwater Road, one mile south of the softball field in the preserve. Air 1 is just lifting off. ETA ten minutes."

Jake worked his way over to the car. That's when things started to go south.

"Forget that son of a bitch," one of the bikers yelled and blocked Jake's path. "He and the dumb broad with him were busy fucking around with each other and slammed right into Jimmy." The biker reached out and pushed Jake back toward Erin and the injured biker. "You tend to him first. Those two can wait," he added pointing to the biker on the ground.

"Bonita Fire. We need Engine 38 at our location. Please confirm police are being dispatched too," Jake said into the mike.

Instantly things went from bad to worse. Three bikers surrounded him. "What are you… fucking deaf? Get over there and help your partner. Those two in the car can die for all we care. Jimmy comes first... you hear?" One of the bikers screamed as the three of them pushed Jake back over to where the biker was laying.

Just as Jake knelt down next to Erin, Engine 38 pulled up, a Chula Vista police car right behind it. "Thank God," Erin whispered to Jake. "Where's Air One? We need to get this guy to the hospital soon."

No sooner had the words left her lips and they could hear Air One approaching.

Teagan brought Air One to a hover over the field just south of the accident scene and started to ease the collective down.

"Abort! Abort! Abort!" Aoife yelled just as Teagan watched a van drive right under them.

"What the fuck!" Teagan yelled as she pulled up on the collective and her heart rate went through the roof. Once the chopper was clear and leveled, she maneuvered it further south in the field and set it down. "I almost set our left skid on top of that idiot! That would have tipped us over for sure. When we get out, whoever's in that van is mine."

Erin and Jake guided the gurney through the field with the biker on it as Teagan threw her helmet into the chopper and stormed past them. "Oh shit!" Erin and Aoife said at the same time.

Back at the van, a young woman was standing next to it with a microphone in her hand. She turned as Teagan stomped toward her, then jammed the microphone into Teagan's face. "I'm Grace with the Bikers U-Tube Channel News and I'd like your opinion on…"

Teagan ripped the microphone out of her hand and, with the strength of a discus thrower, launched it into the middle of Sweetwater Road, where it was run over by two cars.

The woman reporter put her hands on her hips and glared at Teagan. *Perfect,* Teagan thought. Her fist came up and she decked the reporter with one punch. Another woman came around the van, looked at the reporter out cold and stared at Teagan. "You'll pay for that. Our station will sue you for everything you've got!"

Before Teagan could say anything, Erin's dad Bert, Aoife's dad, Shawn, and the fire chief came up alongside her. "I think it's your station that will be paying. You damn near killed the crew of that helicopter," the chief told the woman, then turned to the policeman that had followed them. "Please arrest these two women. Interfering with first responders on an emergency call. Endangering the crew of a rescue helicopter. Ignoring a direct order to clear the area of an accident scene… that's it for now. I'm sure we'll think of more once we get everyone here off to the hospital."

By the time they were done with the reporter and the police had hauled her and the van driver off in handcuffs, the cyclist had been loaded into the helicopter. Teagan watched as they passed her again, this time with the driver of the car. "You think putting them both in my helicopter is a good idea?" she asked no one in particular.

"No choice," Erin answered. "Air two is off somewhere else and he and his girlfriend won't both fit in the ambulance. Besides, they're both still arguing so better to split them up," she answered, throwing Teagan a phony grin.

"Oh, thanks. And like he and the biker are going to swap hugs in my bird?"

As Teagan had predicted, the biker and driver got into it before the door to the chopper was even closed. A few minutes after they lifted off and headed for Sharp Memorial, Aoife had had enough. "Both of you! Shut the fuck up or we'll detour over to the ocean and dump you in." Turning to Teagan she smiled. "You still need one more save for your merit badge, right?"

Teagan nodded. "Yeah, but rescuing dummies doesn't count. So, no points for these two."

\*\*\*

The helicopters skids set down on the helipad of Sharp Memorial's parking structure across from the Emergency Room entrance. With the copter settled, Teagan did one last check of the instruments, then shut everything down. As the rotor blades slowed to a stop, she climbed out, came around to the side door and helped unlatch the stretchers. A moment later two nurses came up, each pushing a gurney. Teagan turned and greeted them, "Hey, Beverly, Jose."

"Hi, Teag, Hi, Aoife," Jose answered. "Haven't seen you two in a while."

"Been busy on organ runs and dropping accident victims off at Mercy while they redecorated your ER," Aoife said.

"Redecorated?" Beverly said. "More like rebuilt, after Covid had the place overflowing for over a year."

Aoife stepped out and they started sliding the stretcher with the car driver onto one of the gurneys. "Better stash these two in different ends of the ER. This one is the reason the other one is here, and they definitely do not get along."

"Surprised they both made it here. You usually 'lose' one of them over the ocean," Jose said, both he and Beverly in on the joke about dumping obnoxious passengers in the ocean and earning merit badges. They moved the first gurney out of the way and slid the biker's stretcher onto the second.

"Couldn't help it. My dad and the police watched us load both of them. Would have been hard to explain if one got 'lost' on the way," Aoife said as the four of them pushed the two gurneys toward the elevators.

When they came through the doors of the ER, Beverly announced, "Look who we found illegally parking up on the helipad." Instantly, Teagan and Aoife were surrounded. Both, along with their other sisters, had helped whenever they could at both Sharp Memorial and Scripps Mercy during the peak of the Covid epidemic. Not only did the entire staff at both ERs know

160

them, but they considered the six sisters the only reason they ever got a moment to rest during the pandemic. In the eyes of both hospitals, they were true heroines, in every sense of the word.

"Hey! I heard you were going to London," one of the nurses yelled out.

"So much for sneaking quietly out of the country," Erin said as she came up behind them, having just wheeled the driver's girlfriend in.

"Can you hide me in your suitcase?" another nurse asked.

"Sure. You're number 26 in line," Teagan replied, then turned to Erin. "How the hell did you get here so fast?"

"Traffic. There was an accident on the 805 north, just south of Bonita Road, They closed the freeway so it was just us all the way up. Didn't even need the siren or lights."

Aoife looked at her watch. "Hey, we're on vacation as soon as we turn our bird in. Let's go, Teag." Giving Erin a hug she added, "Meet you back at the apartments."

The two of them headed for the parking structure and Erin back to her ambulance.

# Chapter 18 – London Here We Come!

That evening, everyone gathered at Teagan's apartment. Chase broke out a bottle of champagne to celebrate their leaving for London the next day. As he poured everyone a glass and Teagan passed them out, he told them about his latest conversation with BA. "I talked with the folks at BA and they can't wait to interrogate the three of you," he told Teagan, Aoife and Erin. "Actually, all of us, but you three especially."

"Don't they have firefighters in England?" Aoife asked.

"Yeah, but I think it's the fact that the six of you are related, even though not by blood, and all chose kind of the same path, that makes them very curious about you. They also admitted that because of what you do, what the rest of us do and our varying experience with flying, we are an excellent sample group," he went on, adding a big smile.

"So, we're guinea pigs, are we?" Erin asked.

"Uh, very well rewarded guinea pigs. And we haven't even done anything yet," Teagan reminded them.

Looking at Chase, Erin apologized. "I'm sorry. Teag is right. This is the chance of a lifetime and they can pick my brain all they want... what little of it there is. As long as they leave enough grey matter for me to master Brit Speak and absorb as much of London and England as I can."

"Hey, I love your brain," Bailey said, pulling her into a hug. Then adding, "Your other parts too."

"Can we send them to Ireland? Please!" Teagan begged no one in particular.

***

The remainder of the evening was spent looking at a tube map and tour bus routes in London and planning all the places they wanted to stop and see. After breakfast the next morning, they all reassembled, each going through their suitcase and making a list of last-minute things they might need. That was followed by them dividing into three teams with each heading off to a different store. By early afternoon they reassembled and finished packing the last-minute items.

A quick poll and they all agreed that eating at the airport would be the easiest. Three Uber rides later, they checked in at the BA counter, then headed for the food court. Without realizing it, by the time they finished eating they only had a little less than an hour before the boarding area opened for their flight.

"Let's go stroll through the duty-free shops," Chase suggested.

That lasted a fast ten minutes. No one really needed anything, nor did they want to be lugging something all the way to England, then back again. "Okay, why don't we save the shopping for after we get to England? I'm sure there will be all kinds of neat shops in London, Bath and Salisbury," Maverick said.

Aofie stopped them. "Wait. We need to get something for the team at BA. Nothing big, just something from the US, actually San Diego, that says thank you. It's the thought I'm going for here, not how fancy or expensive it is."

"Wow, what a great idea," Chase said. "Whatever it is, I'm paying for it. It'll come out of my marketing account." He paused and added, "Just remember, no food or plants. They'll never get through the security check or customs."

"Crap! There goes my taco, burrito and tortilla chip basket idea," Erin said.

"Hey, Chase. Are there more than the six we met with?" Teagan yelled from next to a rack filled with souvenir mugs.

"Nope, just the six. Four guys and two women," he yelled back.

"Great. How about panda tea mugs from the San Diego Zoo? There's about eight different ones and three have female pandas on them," she said, as everyone wandered over next to her.

"Those would be great but we-" Chase started to say.

"How much can we spend?" Aoife asked, reading his mind.

"Don't worry about price," Chase said.

"Okay, what if we put one of these in each of the tea mugs? But... they're a hundred dollars each." Aoife handed him a $100 gift certificate for San Diego Restaurant Week.

"I don't know if they'll be here for restaurant week," he answered.

"They don't have to be. They can be redeemed at any restaurant that participates in Restaurant Week at any time and they'll get Restaurant Week prices."

"That's perfect," he said. "Grab six of them," then added, "Teag, we'll need six tea mugs; four male and two female."

When they got to the checkout counter, Chase was smiling. He asked the clerk to put a Restaurant Week gift certificate in each mug, then put the mug back in its own small box.

Teagan couldn't believe how excited he was. "This is perfect," he said. "Everyone gets a mug to put in their carry-on luggage and give to a BA team member when we have our first meeting. These are business gifts so, no wrapping paper or ribbon. Just keep it simple."

Turning back to Teagan he pulled her in for a long kiss. "You are fantastic." He kissed her again, looked at everyone, then kissed her four more times. "That's from each of us because the BA team is going to love their mugs... and us!"

Hand in hand, the three couples strolled back to their gate. Since all of the seats in the waiting area were taken, they ended up standing along the wall near the boarding door entrance. A moment later, Teagan watched as another couple joined them along the wall and started a conversation with Erin and Bailey.

Less than five minutes later, the boarding gate attendant came up to them. "Mr. Brooks?" she asked, staring at Chase. Chase nodded. "Good I see your entire party is here, so if you'll follow me, I'll get you all seated on board." She checked each of their passports and scanned their boarding passes, then led them down the ramp to the aircraft; the other couple following them.

"We've placed two of you in First Class, the other four in Business Class. You choose."

"Chase and Teag, you're in First… this time," Aoife said, adding a big smile.

"Fine, you two follow me. The rest of you wait here and I'll be right back to seat you," the attendant said, then stopped before guiding Chase and Teagan into First Class. Once again, Teagan noticed that the other couple started following them. "You'll all get pre-boarding service once you're seated. That's normal for our VIP customers. Also, I've been asked to remind you to please take notes as you'll be asked to fill out a questionnaire at your first meeting at BA."

She turned to guide Chase and Teagan into First Class and stopped again. "On behalf of the flight crew, I've been asked to warn you that we'll be checking your notes throughout the flight." She gave them a big smile. "Anyone who gives us less than a perfect score will not get their bag of peanuts and will be swimming the rest of the way to London."

She watched as Teagan, Erin and Aoife looked at each other and started laughing. Finally, Erin asked her, "Are you working on a merit badge?" as they observed the confused look that flooded her face.

Aoife let out a chuckle. "I'll explain when you come back and seat us."

***

The attendant seated them in the first row of first class. As she started back to tend to the others, she almost ran over the other couple. Realizing they weren't with Chase's group and had simply followed her instructions, she smiled and asked, "May I see your boarding passes please?" She checked their passes, smiled again, and seated them across from Teagan and Chase.

Chase took the window seat, while Teagan settled into the aisle seat. A moment later, another attendant, champagne in hand, welcomed them aboard. "My name is Alicia and I'll be attending to your needs during the flight." She handed a menu to each of them, and the couple across from them.

Voices from across the aisle filtered over to them. "Make sure your seat belt is buckled and snug," the guy told the woman.

*Oh joy! First time flyer*, Teagan thought.

"Breathe, you'll be okay. It'll be a while before we take off. Just close your eyes and breathe in and out," he added.

"I... I can't. I need to see. What if we're going to crash? I won't know it and I'll die." The woman turned and locked eyes with Teagan, just as Teagan let out a snort and Chase elbowed her, gently, in the ribs.

"Be nice," he grunted, disguising it with a big smile.

Teagan didn't hear him because she was too busy staring into the terrified eyes of the woman across from her. They smiled at each other, but the woman's smile was pasted on and her eyes were pleading with Teagan for help. So too was the guy with her when Teagan looked over at him.

A moment later she flagged down the attendant. "Is it okay to swap seats?"

"Sure, but make it fast, we're just about to close the doors."

Teagan undid her seatbelt and stood up. "Chase, would you be okay with swapping seats?" Chase had already figured out what she was doing and nodded, then stepped across the aisle. Teagan guided the woman into her aisle seat, then stepped over her and sat in Chase's window seat. She glanced at the guy across the aisle who whispered, "Thanks," as everyone settled into their new seats.

"First time?" Teagan asked the woman. She nodded like a bobble head doll, then her face relaxed as Teagan took the woman's hand and gave it a light squeeze. "Okay, they just closed the doors, so we'll be backing out of the gate in just a minute.

From there, we'll taxi over to the runway, and as soon as it's clear, we'll take off." She gave her hand another squeeze. "Here's what I want you to do… as soon as we turn onto the runway, I'll let you know. Then, I want you to close your eyes."

"I… can't. I need to know if we're going to crash so I can get to the d… door."

"Don't worry. We're not going to crash but… if we are, I'll let you know and lead you to the door. How's that?"

"Okay. Ta… Thank you."

The poor woman was shaking like a leaf and Teagan squeezed her hand a wee bit harder to let her know things were okay. "My name is Teagan. What's yours?"

"Britney… where… where are you going?"

"London, I hope… since this is a nonstop flight," Teagan answered before she could stop herself. "I'm sorry. That was a dumb ass answer."

"No," Britney said, letting out a small chuckle and giving her a smile. "It was a dumb ass question." Her smile got bigger. "I seem to have left my brains on the ground."

"Well, we're still on the ground. You want me to run out and get them?"

Britney let out a snort. "You're funny. And thank you for babysitting me."

Teagan looked out the window just as the plane turned onto the active runway. She gave Britney's hand another squeeze. "Okay, I want you to close your eyes. Now pretend you're a fairy and you've just come into the stable and taken your unicorn out of his stall."

"He's a she," Britney said, her eyes still closed.

"Okay, you've taken *her* out of *her* stall and now, I want you to swing your leg over her and pull yourself up onto her back." She paused, then added, "You up there?"

"Yip. Should I say giddy-up yet?"

Teagan looked over at her. "Are you messin' with me?"

"Nope. Just never took unicorn commands in school". Teagan watched as her smile grew. "Uh, so, what should I say?"

*Oh crap.* Teagan thought for a minute then managed to get out, "Up, up and away. Off to the land called Honah Lee, my beautiful unicorn," before she broke into a fit of laughter.

"Uh, are we meeting Puff the Magic Dragon?" Britney asked.

Distracted, they barely realized the 777 was racing down the runway and starting to lift off.

Britney snickered. "I think my unicorn heard you and is taking off... either that or she has to go to the bathroom."

Teagan glanced across the aisle at Chase. He and Britney's mate had obviously been listening and were laughing hysterically.

"Okay, we're airborne. Keep your eyes closed. Now, put your arms... uh wings out... now gently flap them. That's it. We're climbing up into the beautiful puffy white clouds. Now we're going to make a slow turn to the right, so gently lean to the right. Your unicorn will sense your weight shifting and glide to the right."

The 777 continued to climb, then went into a slow right bank, turning toward Canada.

"I'm sorry. You can't have your wing out in the aisle like that," the passing flight attendant said. She turned to Chase and smiled. "Gotta watch these fairies all the time."

"Oh, sorry," Britney said, as she folded her arm and leaned further to her right until her left elbow was out of the aisle.

Teagan watched as Britney's head tilted to the left, her left eye squinted and her right eye tried to find the window. "Are you looking?" Teagan asked her.

"Uh huh. Are we really in the air?" she asked, then closed her eyes again.

"Yip. Are you okay?"

"I can't believe it. I forgot all about being scared." She squinted again, but this time at Teagan. "I'm a fairy... I'm not afraid of flying any more and I'm on my unicorn, so we need to go someplace magic?"

"I'm sure there's a castle in London you can land at." Teagan thought for a minute. "How about the tower of London?"

"Istanbul," Britney said.

"Why would we go to Istanbul? What's there?"

"The Grand Bazaar… so I can get a necklace like yours."

Teagan sat stunned. How did she know about the Grand Bazaar? Or the necklace, that she was certain was hidden inside her blouse? "How… how did you know about my necklace or that it came from the Grand Bazaar?"

Britney's eyes were now wide open, and she was staring at Teagan, a big smile on her face. "I was standing next to one of your sisters in the boarding area and asked about her beautiful necklace. She explained that you each had one and where they came from." She paused and her smile got bigger. "Sorry, I'm kind of nosey like that."

Without realizing it, they were now over an hour into their flight to London. Britney had totally forgotten that she was supposed to be afraid as she watched out the window, and Teagan couldn't help but chuckle whenever she glanced at her. When the flight attendant came by with a second round of drinks, Britney snapped out of her trance. "I'm sorry! I got so engrossed with watching the world go by that I forgot I'm keeping you and your boyfriend apart." She stood up, offered another apology, then swapped seats with Chase. "You think I'm too old to become a helicopter pilot?" she asked her mate before she was even settled in her seat.

Chase leaned over and kissed Teagan. "You're amazing, you know that?"

Several hours into the flight, Erin and Aoife visited, more to see what first class was like than anything else. Other than that, the flight went fast and they landed in London fifteen minutes early.

*** 

"Follow us," Teagan said as if she and Chase were expert Heathrow Airport Tour Guides. They led the parade over to the elevators to the lower tunnels. However, they soon discovered they needed a special key to call the elevator.

Luckily, an airport employee pulled up on a cart just as they were about to hoof it to baggage claim the long way. "Oi, going to baggage claim, are we?" he asked. Chase nodded.

"Hop on, I'm headed right past there, so I'll be happy to drop you off."

The six of them climbed into the cart as he unlocked the elevator, and they were on their way. Five minutes later he dropped them off in front of the baggage carousel for their flight.

Once they had collected their bags, Teagan steered them to a ticket vending machine near the exit door. "Thanks to Maverick, we've all got Oyster cards for the tube, but I suggest we each get a 'Ten Fer' roundtrip Hopper Bus Pass since we'll likely be going back and forth to catch the tube."

Bus passes in hand, they headed out to the hopper bus stops, just as their bus arrived.

Aoife, Erin, Maverick and Bailey oh'ed and ah'ed every time they passed something unique: The BA Concord on display at the entrance to the airport. The big red double decker buses that seemed to be everywhere. The roundabouts at every intersection. "Oh my God. We're in London. This is so cool!" Erin said as they pulled into the driveway of the Sheridan Skyline.

"I remember my mom talking about how much she and my dad loved London when they came here on their honeymoon," Aoife said. "Now I understand why, and we haven't even seen anything yet. I can't wait to see all the places they raved about."

"Yeah, my mom and dad too," Erin added.

BA had all their reservations in place, so check-in took but a few minutes. "Throw your bags in the room and we'll meet you all down in the pub," Chase told them, pointing to the pub entrance at the end of the lobby.

A half hour later, Aoife and Maverick were the last two to stroll into the pub. "We took a stroll around the hotel to check things out," Maverick said. "The dining area out by the pool looks really nice. I can't believe the size of the sago palms out there!"

"The pool bar looks like a great place to kick back and relax too," Aoife said. Looking around, she added, "The pub is pretty cool too. And I love having Starbucks in the lobby… a cappuccino and scone, what a way to start the day. Thanks for finding this place, Chase."

"Thank BA," he said. "Speaking of which, I need to confess something. I kind of unloaded on Teagan for taking over the meeting the last time. In fact, it wasn't her fault. William from BA jumped on the fact that she was a helicopter pilot, and it took off from there. Pun intended. I suspect that will happen again now that they know you're all first responders. So I'm going to ask you to let me coordinate things and take the lead in conducting the meeting."

Aoife covered her mouth and let out a snort. "Surely he jests… We're about as coordinated as a bunch of hotdogs trying to escape from a pot of boiling water… make that, escape through a pile of sauerkraut, relish and mustard."

"Hey, don't forget catsup… I like catsup on my dogs," Teagan threw in.

"Oh God," Chase mumbled. "Maybe I should just turn you all loose on them and forget about seat selections."

"See. He's learning," Erin said.

"Everyone good with Black and Tan's to drink?" Teagan asked when the barmaid came over. Everyone nodded and a few minutes later they all clinked glasses as Teagan toasted to Chase having a successful meeting with BA.

With almost everyone yawning, Chase suggested eating out by the pool. Erin grabbed the menu from the center of the table and after a fast perusal said, "Why don't we just move to a bigger table and eat here? There's quite a good selection."

Hungry and tired, they all quickly agreed as the barmaid carried their drinks to a six top table in the dining area. "Okay. No burgers, hotdogs or American stuff," Teagan said. "English food for our first meal here."

A minute later the barmaid had their orders: Two fish and chips with tartare sauce and, of course, mushy peas. Two orders of beef and wild mushroom pie with red wine sauce, creamy mashed potatoes and mixed vegetables. Two shepherd's pies with Maris Piper mash, whatever that was. For dessert, they all had the sports bar cup: Chocolate ice cream, brownies, fresh strawberries, crushed Smarties and topped with fresh whipped cream.

"What are Smarties?" Teagan asked the barmaid after their dessert order was in.

"They're our version of your M&Ms," she explained. "But there's a much bigger selection of colors and coating flavors."

"Thank you," Teagan said. "By the way, I love your accent. Where are you from?"

"Wales," the barmaid answered with a big smile.

"Is that close by?" Aoife asked her.

"I'm afraid not love. It's all the way up the west coast, several hours by train." She paused and added, "A few more hours if you're going up to Holyhead to catch the ferry over to Dublin."

"Oh my God. Dublin. I've always wanted to go to Ireland." Aoife turned to Maverick, then Chase. "Maybe we could go there?"

The barmaid's smile brightened. "It's an all-day trip if you'll be taking the train and ferry... but you'll love Dublin. Plus, once you're there, you can book passage on day tours all over Ireland."

Chase looked around the table and his smile matched the barmaid's. "Perhaps on one of our future trips. How about if we see London and England first?"

"I'm sorry. You're right," Aoife said. Suddenly an evil smile crept across her face. "Maybe we should just stay here and see if we can become first responders with London Fire?"

The barmaid giggled. "Uh... sorry love... but no one's going to understand you with that funny accent you have," she said, adding another giggle.

"Okay, time to get some sleep. We're all getting silly," Teagan said. Then turned to Aoife. "We're not counting out Ireland though. Being this close, it only makes sense to plan a trip there on one of the next trips to London. Chase is right though, let's explore England first."

***

The following morning, they met down in the restaurant for the breakfast buffet. They all settled on a typical English breakfast; eggs cooked to order, baked beans, baked tomatoes, portage, toast, a wide variety of fresh fruit, coffee and tea.

"We're due at BA at 9 am," Chase said. "It's just a short walk across the street and it's only 8:30 so it'll be a casual walk if we leave now."

Ten minutes later they were standing in front of another BA Concord on display next to the engineering building. "Wow. That must have been a great ride to the states," Maverick said. "Just under three hours. London to NY if I remember right."

"Yeah. I never got to ride in one," Chase replied. "They retired them just before I started working with BA."

Just then William walked up to them. "You're early I see." He introduced himself to everyone and guided them into the building, then to a conference room on the second floor. A conference room with seven people waiting for them, three of them in uniform.

Once they were seated, he looked at Teagan, Aoife and Erin. "I've taken the liberty of inviting three of our firefighters from our Heathrow Airport Fire Station. I hope you don't mind but I thought having some of your own kind might help you feel more at home."

After going around the table so everyone could introduce themselves, William took command of the meeting. "I'm going to

178

break this into two meetings, that is, if no one minds. I know my team, and our firefighters, are anxious to talk to the women about what they do so I thought we'd cover that first. Then the rest of you can go run around London while we talk about seats with Chase."

Everyone from the US turned and stared at Maverick as Aoife let out a very unladylike snort. "I think we should start with Maverick," she said, adding a big smile. "He's got the most interesting job of all of us."

"You'll pay for this," he half whispered to Aoife.

Teagan wrapped her arm through Chase's and smiled at him, then William. "I'm staying for the seat meeting, if that's okay. You asked us to take notes and I did so I'd like to sit in on the meeting." A second later, everyone else said they'd like to stay too, since they had all taken notes, as requested.

William turned to Chase, then his team. "Everyone okay with that?" he asked. Everyone nodded. "Okay, now I'm extremely curious, Maverick. What exactly is it you do?"

"I guess you could say I'm a pea whisperer. I'm in charge of a pea production line... occasionally I work carrots and asparagus too," he tried to add over the gasps, giggles and snickering.

"I see," William responded, desperately trying to be serious. "Uh, Bailey?"

"My job is very boring compared to Maverick's. I own a Starbucks coffee shop."

Pulling Bailey in close, Erin looked around the table. "At least I get all the free cappuccino I want. All Aoife gets is smashed peas and an occasional bent asparagus spear."

Diane, a female British firefighter, looked around the table. Desperately trying to control her laughter, she said, "You're all bonkers. While we're doing Heimlich's to dislodge a peanut from a passenger's throat, you lot are back at the fire station sucking up cappuccinos and playing billiards with peas."

"Oh! So not true!" Teagan finally joined in. "Erin, Aoife and I re-rescued a DUI after he accidently fell into the ocean on the way to the hospital." She paused. "It was perfect timing too, since Erin was with us and needed her 'DUI Water Rescue Merit Badge'. Since he'd barfed, she uh, skipped the mouth-to-mouth part. So, she only got the pink badge. Next DUI run we'll get her the 'Dangling Red Tongue Ribbon' that goes with it."

By now, everyone was in stitches and holding their side. "Bloody hell. And we thought rescuing luggage from cheese runs to Amsterdam and Surströmming fish runs to Sweden was bad," Peter, one of the male firefighters, said.

"Surströmming fish?" Aoife asked.

"Yip, the foulest smelling fish in the world. Think days' old soiled nappies," Richard, the third firefighter, explained.

"What's a nappy?' Erin asked.

"A diaper to you lot," Diane threw in.

"Ewwww! Definitely TMI," Aoife mumbled.

"Okay, I can see this convo has gone down the crapper… quite literally," William said, trying to steer the conversation elsewhere. "How about if all you firefighters swap some of your funnier stories?"

"We don't deal with the airport or incoming flights, but I'll bet you get some real wierdos," Teagan said, looking at the three British firefighters.

"Oh, you've no idea," Diane answered. "The body odor alone sometimes is enough to make you want to just tell the crew to return them from whence they came… then burn the seats they were in. Oh, and the stuff they drag onboard. You wouldn't believe how many call outs we get for fights over someone trying to store everything they own in the overhead. Often, just to avoid paying an overweight fee."

Erin jumped in. "Yeah, I couldn't believe the stuff I saw being pushed around on luggage carts at the airport. Not just here but in San Diego too."

"Try dealing with that stuff when it gets jammed up coming down the luggage shoot," Richard said. "Or… when someone's skis or golf clubs turn sideways, rip open the cardboard boxes someone is using for luggage then jam up everything behind them."

"And launch the contents of said carboard luggage all over the baggage area, once enough weight builds up behind them," Peter threw in, then burst out laughing. "Remember the bloke with the golf cleats stuck in his forehead. Turned out it was his own shoe. Launched from his golf bag, it was, when it flipped up just as he reached for it."

"I guess we're lucky," Aoife said. "DUIs are usually our biggest source of entertainment."

"Ha, you forgot holiday Bar-B-Qers who use a gallon of gasoline to light their BBQ and try to burn everything around them down," Teagan added. "Oh, and lest we forget the ones who try to blow fingers, toes, arms, legs and other body parts off with illegal fireworks."

Erin couldn't help but chuckle, then add, "I can't believe you're leaving out deep fat turkey fryers. Responsible for most of our Thanksgiving and Christmas ambulance runs and house fires. Truly a device invented by turkeys to speed up the annihilation of mankind."

William looked around and shook his head. "I'm so glad I went into engineering. All we have to worry about is getting the right seats in the right place and making sure they're comfortable and barf proof."

The two sets of firefighters went on for the next hour trying to outdo each other with crazy stories. Finally, the remaining two team members from William's seat design team entered the room.

"While I love the stories you've all told, and I know you could go on forever, we need to get on with the seat design meeting. I want to especially thank our London Fire Brigade members for joining us and making their counterparts from across the pond feel welcomed." He paused and looked at each of the women, then added, "At the suggestion of our firefighters, I've taken the liberty of arranging for a tour of one of our firehouses here at the airport. I've scheduled that for tomorrow morning if that's okay."

Everyone nodded and the LFB members waved, then filed out of the room.

Chase stood and set a shopping bag on the table. "Before we get started, and now that all of your team members are here, my team would like to give you each a little gift of appreciation for your wonderful hospitality and the Friends and Family Air Passes."

Teagan and Aoife passed out the San Diego Zoo mugs with the gift certificates in each, while Erin explained about the restaurant week certificates and which pandas were male and which were female. Noticing the smiles on the BA team members, Chase gave Teagan, Erin and Aoife credit for selecting the gifts.

"On behalf of the BA team, thank you for the unique gifts. We'll all have to chain the mugs to our desks I'm afraid, since everyone else within engineering will certainly be jealous," William said. "Okay, who wants to go first on what you thought about our seats?"

Teagan's hand shot up. "I have to be honest, when we first entered the first class area, it looked more like a hedge maze. Once the flight attendant helped us wind our way through and pointed out our seats, I found the seating, and area, to be comfortable and private. In fact, almost a little too private.

"With the partition between us up, I felt like I was in my own little cell. I also found it very difficult to hold a conversation with Chase. Then, when he swapped seats with the woman across from us so I could console her - she was afraid of flying - it was like they had to jump the hedges to swap seats."

William's smile broadened. "What I'm hearing is more consideration needs to be given to couples, or people flying together. Is that a good assumption?"

Aoife raised her hand. "We found the same thing in Business, or what you call your 'Club World'. There did seem to be more consideration to providing seating for couples or people flying together. In both cases though, I couldn't help but think about how difficult it would have been if all six of us were seated in the same class and wanted to chat during the flight. Even for the four of us it was hard to chat without leaning out into the aisle."

Chase looked around the conference room at everyone scribbling notes. "What I'm hearing is we need to come up with a design for first and club world classes that allows more flexibility. We'll still need to provide the privacy for those traveling alone but be able to adjust the seating for pairs of two and small groups...

perhaps up to six people?" He scanned William's team for confirmation.

Once they all nodded, he added, "I think we can do that. I'm thinking of an area within each class where the seating could be adjusted. That way the current privacy of the present seating for singles wouldn't be disturbed, yet groups of two to six could be accommodated, when requested."

"My genius!" Teagan declared, then rewarded him with a kiss. "Maybe you should redesign the gurney shelves of our helos. Just remember, we'll need an eject button for difficult patients… oh, and deployable water wings, to keep them afloat till one of us can stage a merit badge rescue."

One of females on the BA team raised her hand. "Can we add hidden restraints that we can automatically deploy to lock unruly passengers in their seats? Our flight attendants will love you to death for that one. Not to mention letting you fly free forever."

Maverick, who was noisily flipping through his notes, raised his hand. "I was thinking more along the lines of entertainment." He held up a sketch that made everyone's forehead wrinkle.

"What is that?" Aoife asked."

"It's a tray-sized, snap on, pea pool table with built-in pool cues. It would tie into the audio system so the peas could dance to the music the passenger selected. Each dancing pea the passenger drops into a pocket wins him a beer or glass of wine." He paused. "Uh, that would be for coach though, since beer and wine are free in first and world class. Maybe in those classes they could get an extra bag of peanuts?"

In between snorts, Aoife pointed at him and said, "I have no idea who he is. He just followed me onto the plane... Maybe Chase should work on seat security?"

"Yeah, just add a gag to the seat restraint system," the woman who suggested the restraints said.

William finished shaking his head, then looked around the table. "Look, I know you're kidding about some of this, but I'm reading between the lines and I frankly love the suggestions." He turned to Teagan. "Not the ones for your helo, as you call it. Those, you'll need to deal with.

"But, I love the idea of an adjustable area for small groups... and, Maverick, I don't think a tiny pea pool table will work, but perhaps adding some games to our in-flight-entertainment package might be a good thing to look at." Turning to Teagan he added, "Teagan, I understand you helped a woman who was afraid of flying. Thank you for that and do you have any suggestions for the flight crew in that area? Things they might be able to do to help passengers overcome their fears?"

"Not really," Teagan answered. "But let me sleep on it. Maybe I can come up with some suggestions. Unfortunately, something like that needs to be tailored to the person and their particular fears."

In mid-sentence, Teagan's face scrunched up. "Actually, I do have some ideas. Maybe have a question about 'fear of flying' somewhere in the reservations. Then, try to seat people who say their afraid to fly next to an experienced flyer. Don't just dump them on the experienced person though. Somehow make sure they're okay with helping others... maybe have a special category of BA World Travelers who are willing to help... you'd have to screen them though. Last thing you'd need is them going off and calling the person that's scared, a wimp or telling them they shouldn't be flying."

Before she finished her answer, Teagan reminded herself that this was Chase's meeting. She needed to hand it back to him, or at least let him steer it back to seating design. Before she could pass it back though, William beat her to it. "I think you've given my team enough to think about for the moment. So, why don't we let you go explore London and we'll have a look at some of the things you've brought up." With that, everyone stood up. "Oh, and don't forget the firehouse tour tomorrow morning. They'll be picking you up in front of the hotel at eight am."

Once they were back outside, they started to walk toward the hotel when Bailey spotted one of the big red buses. "We definitely need to ride one of those... and take a ride in a black cab."

"Both are on our must do list," Aoife answered.

Chase put his arm around Teagan and gave her a big kiss. "Okay, here's what Teag and I suggest. Back to the hotel, dump off whatever you don't need then, and we'll catch the Hopper Bus to the airport. From there we can take the tube to Westminster. That's kind of a central point for a lot of the things in London, especially transportation."

Kissing him back, Teagan jumped in. "I suggest we take the hop on hop off tour bus first. That will give everybody a good idea of all the things to see. From there, we can head to whatever

188

appeals to everyone." She hesitated and smiled at Chase. "I need to warn you though. We could spend a month running around London and not see everything. Plus Chase and I have some trips outside of London that we think we all should do so, we're going to need to leave some of the London stuff for the next trip or two."

Everybody nodded as Maverick raised his hand. "Yes, you in the back," Teagan said, pointing to him while everyone else chuckled.

"Uh, can we ride the London Eye? I heard it's one of the must do things in London."

"Actually," Chase answered, "We'll stop at the concierge's desk at the hotel and see if he can get us 'fast track' tickets for tonight or tomorrow night. That's what he recommended when Teag and I took it, and London at night is spectacular from the top of the eye."

"Make sure to bring your pass packs." Teagan reminded everyone as they headed for the elevator and their rooms to leave whatever they didn't need. Less than ten minutes later, they were all assembled back at the concierge's desk.

"Okay, we've got reservations at Gillray's Steakhouse, just a short walk from The Eye, for dinner and reserved fast track tickets for the nighttime eye," Chase told them as they boarded the hopper bus to the airport. "If we time it right, we can catch the eye ride at sunset. That's what Teag and I did and it's unbelievable, watching London light up at sunset."

A tube change at Acton Station to the District Line and thirty minutes later they exited at Westminster Station. By the time they reached the station, the sun had come out and so had everyone in London. Coming up the steps from the station, everyone's eyes locked onto Westminster Cathedral, Big Ben and the Westminster Bridge. As they watched the line of pedestrians cross the bridge, The London Eye on the other side of the Thames River rotated in slow motion with Tower Bridge off in the background.

"Oh. My. God! This is so cool," Aoife said, pulling her phone out and snapping picture after picture.

Herding them all to the side of the walkway so they weren't blocking the station exit, Chase once again suggested they do the bus tour first. "I know you're all going to want to go tour Westminster Cathedral, but let's catch the bus and do the tour of London first. That will give everyone a good overview of things to see. Plus it'll drop us off back here and we can do the cathedral when we get off."

Everybody nodded, more out of having too many choices, than agreeing with Chase. The cathedral, Parliament, Big Ben, The London Eye, Westminster Bridge, St. Paul's, Tower Bridge and Waterloo Station all a short walk.

Erin, with a giant smile on her face, summed it up nicely as she snuggled into Bailey. "I feel like I just stepped into a picture from a tourist brochure for London."

A few minutes later they boarded the big red hop - on hop - off tour bus, then made their way to the open top deck.

"I can't believe our timing," Aoife said, as they all found seats next to each other. That would quickly change at the next stop though.

The bus crossed the Thames River on the Westminster Bridge and they couldn't help but notice the crowds lined up along the river walkway, waiting to get on the London Eye. "I'm sure glad we got fast track tickets," Chase told everyone.

"Yeah, we learned the last time, when the concierge told us about the wait time, especially at sunset and nighttime," Teagan added.

The bus turned left on York Road, passed Waterloo Station and proceeded along the south bank of the river. "Holy crap. Look at the size of Waterloo Station!" Erin said.

"Yeah, it's the largest in London," Teagan said. "By the way, the last time we took the bus tour, the driver said there are 334 train stations and 270 tube stations in London. Waterloo is the biggest and busiest of all of them. Wait till we get on the Eye. Then you'll see how big it really is."

The bus continued along the river, past Waterloo Bridge, Blackfriars Bridge, Shakespeare's Globe Theater, The Millennium Pedestrian Bridge, Southwark Bridge, the new London Bridge, then finally turned onto Tower Bridge to re-cross the river.

"Holy crap! How many bridges are there?" Aoife asked no one in particular.

As if the driver heard her, he announced, "For those of you who are curious, the Thames River is crossed by over 200 bridges."

Everyone stared up at the towers and overhead walkway as the bus passed under the bridge's superstructure. Coming off the bridge, the Tower of London appeared on the left. The bus then worked its way toward Fleet Street, passing St. Paul's Cathedral, Old Bailey, then the Temple Bar. Along the way, there seemed to be a pub on every corner, each with flower boxes in full bloom, under every window.

"It's certainly not hard to see why people love London," Maverick said. He turned to Aoife with a big smile. "We could spend our lives just crossing bridges and visiting train and tube stations."

"Don't forget pubs," Aoife added.

The bus continued past Piccadilly Circus, then Oxford Circus to Bayswater Road. From there they passed Marble Arch, then circled Hyde Park and Kensington Gardens. Finally, turning back toward Westminster, they rode past Buckingham Palace, St. James Palace and St. James Park before arriving back at the little square across from Westminster Cathedral.

As they came down the stairs and stepped off the bus, Bailey finally spoke. "Wow! I'm in total tourist overload." He looked at the crowds lined up in front of the cathedral and shook his head. "No way I'm dealing with that right now. Anyone want to join me on a pub hunt?"

"I'm in," Erin answered.

"Me too," Aoife added. Turning, she pointed down Bridge Street. "There's St. Stephens Tavern right there."

"Looks good to me," Maverick said, as he grabbed Aoife's hand and started towing her down the street, everyone else falling in behind them.

"Wow. I love it," Chase said as his arm slipped around Teagan's waist, and they brought up the rear. "Just mention 'pub' and everyone heads for it. No arguments, no discussions."

"Yip, our kind of people... Pub crawlers," Teagan threw in, pulling Chase in closer and adding a chuckle.

Two hours and several Black and Tans and glasses of wine later, they decided to give the cathedral another try. As they started down the street, Teagan told them, "We're actually going to Westminster Abbey Cathedral, not Westminster Cathedral."

"Huh?" Aoife said. "There's two of them?"

Chase let out a chuckle and turned to Teagan. "Okay, history buff. Let's see how much you remember from our tour of the abbey."

"The abbey is the older of the two. It's over 900 years old and belongs to the Church of England. The Cathedral is a Catholic church and was consecrated in 1910. It's down the road a bit, past St. James Park, near Buckingham Palace."

Luckily, they found the line to get into the abbey was now only a few people long. After getting in line, they stood gaping at the two giant towers defining the entrance. "I have no idea what the inside is like," Maverick said, "But the outside is impressive as hell."

"Ha. I should warn you; be prepared for a major shock when we get inside," Teagan replied. "Trust me, it's nothing like what you could imagine, or the pictures you may have seen during royal events."

Stepping through the entrance, they stopped and gaped at the nave. "Holy shit," Erin said, then covered her mouth, adding, "Sorry."

Staring at the wooden pews lining each side, their eyes weren't sure what to take in: The elaborate golden gothic cathedral trim behind the pews. The beautiful alter that seemed miles away at the end of the Nave. The arched ceiling that towered above them. The giant array of windows letting daylight inside so that everything sparkled and lit up. Or the diamond patterned floor that formed a pathway and led your eye to the altar far off in the distance.

"Oh. My. God. This is the most beautiful and stunning church I've ever seen," Aofie whispered.

"Yes, it is, isn't it," a voice from behind them said. They all turned to find a young gentleman smiling at them. "I'm Johnathon and I'll gladly be your guide if you wish." A second later his eyes lit on Teagan and his smile lit up. "You're Teagan, the helicopter pilot... if I remember correctly."

Teagan smiled back. "I'm amazed that you remembered."

"Ah, but you asked the most intelligent questions when you were here... like you were studying for an English history exam." He turned to Chase, as if asking permission, then added, "And, if I may be so bold, your lovely smile is impossible to forget."

Teagan's red face faded as she recovered by introducing everyone else.

"I'm very pleased to meet all of you," Johnathon said, as he turned and led them into the nave, while explaining the overall history and pointing out the various architectural details of the abbey. "Perhaps the most fascinating part of the abbey is the North and South Ambulatories, where some of England's most renowned kings, queens and other famous people lay," he explained as he led them into the South Ambulatory, then behind the altar.

As they entered, he pointed out the tombs of: Anne of Cleves. Richard II and Anne of Bohemia, Edward III, Saint Edward the Confessor, Lyonel and Anne Cranfield, Henry V, Eleanor of Castile, Edward I, various bishops and archbishops from the Church of England, and on and on it went. A veritable who's who of England's famous figures.

From there he directed them to Poet's Corner, pointing out the tombs of William Shakespeare, Jane Austen, the Bronte Sisters and Charles Dickens. Finally, they entered the Cloisters as he led them back outside.

"It was a pleasure being your guide, again," he said, looking at Teagan and Chase, then adding, "I hope everyone enjoyed your tour. I'm sure you're all quite overwhelmed and I suggest that, like Teagan and Chase, you'll visit us again. It really is quite a lot to take in on one visit." He shook hands with everyone, then turned and headed back inside.

Once he was out of hearing range, Bailey was the first to speak up. "Holy crap. Overwhelmed doesn't even come close to covering it. I had no idea so many kings and queens and poets and famous people were entombed in there."

"I suggest we all head back to the hotel and grab something to eat, then maybe relax out by the pool bar before we rest up for tomorrow's BA and Fire Brigade meetings," Chase suggested. "After the meetings, we'll be headed for Salisbury Cathedral, then Bath and Stonehenge."

As they headed back to the tube station, Maverick and Aoife jumped out in front of them, turned and stopped everyone. "Chase and Teagan, Aoife and I need to tell you that we can't thank you enough for doing this. For getting all of us the friends and family passes, suggesting the tours and acting like advanced scouts." He paused and kissed Aoife. "I… we… can't tell you how fantastic this trip has already been and it's only the first day. But between the bus tour and the tour of Westminster Abbey, London has already become my favorite city."

"Ditto!" Aoife added.

# Chapter 20 – Surprise Surprise

A few minutes later, they were back in the tube station waiting on the platform. A District Line train pulled up and one of the cars stopped right in front of them. The usual "Mind the Gap" announcement came over the speakers as the doors opened.

"Mind the fucking gap yourself," a high-pitched voice mimicked the announcement, then added, "Out of my way you bloody bitch," as someone shoved Teagan into Chase and started past her into the car.

Chase caught Teagan just before she lost her balance and her legs gave way. At the same time, Maverick reached out and grabbed the back of the guy's collar and jerked him back out of the car. Off balance, the guy tried to turn and land a roundhouse punch on Maverick. Maverick stepped aside and the guy slammed himself into the edge of the subway car door.

"Oh shit… that hurt," Bailey said, as the guy rocked back, threw up and his legs caved in as he slid down the door.

An alarm sounded somewhere as Teagan yelled, "Someone call 911," then joined Aoife and Erin as they tried to tend to the guy, now sitting against the door.

"You mean call 999," someone in the crowd that had now formed said, then added, "already done."

"Whoah! What the hell's this guy been drinking?" Teagan asked, as she reached out for some tissue Erin had pulled out of her purse. Teagan started to blot the blood running from the guy's forehead as Chase watched his leg come back. Realizing he was going to kick out at Teagan, Chase aimed for the guy's other ankle and stomped. A snap, pop and excruciating moan was followed by a loud scream as his foot flopped to the side at a very unnatural angle. Then he passed out.

"Sorry about his foot, but there was no way I was letting him kick you," Chase told Teagan.

Looking up at Chase, she said, "Thanks. He was aiming for my face."

Just as the three American EMTs stopped the bleeding, two bobbies came up. While one called for medical assistance, someone in the crowd explained to the other what had happened, as three ambulance workers with the London Ambulance Service arrived pushing a gurney.

"Good thing he passed out," one of them said, as she pulled his foot and snapped the guy's ankle back in place. They braced and taped his leg and foot in place, then bandaged his forehead. "Nice job stopping the bleeding," one of them said to the three women. "You should think about becoming ambulance nurses."

Erin let out a chuckle. "I'm Erin, this is Teagan and Aoife," pointing each of them out. "We're all EMTs back in San Diego, where we come from."

The woman's smile lit up. "Pleased to meet you. I'm Betty, and this is Alice and Jane. We're NHS, National Health Service, ambulance nurses, based just across the bridge in Waterloo." She paused, then frowned. "One of the Bobbies told us what this shit did. We're really sorry." She turned to Alice and Jane and added, "What's say we dump his arse in the river and get some water rescue credit?"

The three of them turned as Erin, Teagan and Aoife broke into hysterical laughter.

Once they quit laughing, Erin looked at Teagan and Aiofe then shook her head. "I can't let this go. We have to tell them." Turning to the three NHS Nurses, with very confused looks on their faces, she explained that Teagan was also an air ambulance pilot and Aoife a flight nurse. Then went on to tell them how DUI drivers were an excellent source for ocean rescue merit badges, on the trip to the hospital.

That left the six women in fits of hooting, howling and snorting while the men just stared at each other. Finally, Bailey looked at the guy on the gurney and asked, "Think we can get him and the gurney up the stairs and over to the pub?"

Teagan turned and shot him a look that could kill. "Trust me. The last thing he needs is another drink."

The nurses wheeled the gurney and the guy toward the service elevator while the crew from the US caught the next

District Line train heading west. Forty-five minutes later, they stepped off the hopper bus and headed straight for the pool bar.

Settled in and drinks ordered, Teagan was the first to speak up. "Well, that was fun! I'm thinking we should have brought along our medical bags." She paused and then added, "I've got a bunch of questions for when we tour the BFG Station tomorrow morning. Assuming they have an ambulance with NHS Nurses at the airport fire station."

"Yeah, I'm curious as to just how different being a nurse here is compared to our jobs back in the states," Aoife added.

"Well, first thing you'd need to learn is to yell 'call 999' instead of 911," Erin threw in, adding, "That might take a while."

Maverick chuckled. "I wonder if they have a pea rescue brigade?"

"Of course they do… where else would mushy peas have come from?" Aoife couldn't help but add after a chuckle and sip from her beer.

Finally, Bailey switched the discussion to Westminster Abbey. "I don't know about anyone else, but I was absolutely amazed and fascinated by the abbey. I had no idea that people's tombs were there, no less all those famous people."

"I agree," Erin said. "That and the architecture were amazing. I mean, I'd seen some of the royal weddings on TV but they didn't come close to showing how enormous and stunningly beautiful the place is. The view of the nave when we first walked in will always be what I remember about the abbey."

"That and the first glimpse of the tombs behind the altar," Aoife added. "I had always wondered where they buried their kings, queens and famous people. Now I know."

"I can't wait till tomorrow when you all get to see Salisbury Cathedral," Teagan added. "It's as beautiful, actually... I think more beautiful... than the abbey." She paused, then smiled. "I think that may be because, unlike the abbey, it stands by itself. When you first see it, it's beauty stuns you and makes your mouth drop open."

"Wow, I can't wait," Erin said.

"You know, I think the most surprising things about seeing all this is not only the beauty but the history," Aoife told them. "When we were touring the abbey I couldn't help but wonder what it was like back when the kings, queens and people entombed there were alive. What it must have been like to go to the Globe Theater and watch a Shakespeare play or watch a schooner sail up the Thames River into London."

Shaking her head, Teagan stared at Chase. "Oh my God, talk about history. Wait till they see the aqueduct and baths at Bath... and the pillars and stone altar at Stonehenge." Turning to Aoife, she added, "You have no idea of the Roman influence, or how vast the Roman Empire was until you see the aqueduct and baths."

"The hell with touring the Heathrow Fire House, let's just head for Salisbury first thing," Bailey suggested.

"That would be way beyond rude!" Erin, obviously not happy with his suggestion, told him. "The firefighters are going out of their way to give us a tour. If you want, you can wait here at the hotel. Then you can join us afterward, when the tour bus comes to pick us up here at the hotel."

Realizing he'd fucked up, big time, Bailey tried to smooth things over. "Sorry, I didn't mean to…" Hearing Maverick snort, he turned to him. "What's so funny?"

"You," Maverick answered. "It's usually me that puts both feet in his mouth, then tries to walk. So it's nice not to be on the hot seat for a change."

"None of this is funny," Erin said, giving Bailey a death stare. "If you're not happy, Bailey, I suggest you stay home next trip. That goes for you too, Maverick," she added, turning her death stare to him.

"Obviously no one warned you two that Erin's temper matches her red hair," Teagan told them, giving Chase a look that clearly said, 'time for you to jump in'.

Picking up on the hint, Chase took Maverick and Bailey to the other side of the pool. "You both need to understand that these three women love what they do. It's not a job to them, it's a chance to save a life, help someone and, when an opportunity presents itself, learn from someone else. When BA presented them with passes, the first two people they thought of was you two. You both need to return that tenfold. You need to make this trip about them."

He started to turn to Bailey but stopped. "The other thing we all need to keep in mind is that, while they're not related by blood, they're sisters in every respect... and there's not three of them, but six. They grew up together. They played together. They went to school together. They often work together and they pretty much live together. So, if you date one, you're really dating them all. You need to keep that in mind because, believe me, if you don't it'll be a very short relationship."

Turning to Bailey he added, "Look, I don't know what your feelings are for Erin, but you need to think about what I just said before you spit shit out. I'll also add that if you hurt her, I'll be the first one to make sure you pay dearly for it."

"Wow!" Bailey said, shaking his head. "Bad enough I've got six of them to deal with. Now I need to worry about you too?"

Maverick held his hands up before Chase could turn to him. "I got it." But he was staring at Bailey. "You can add me to that list," he told Bailey. "As a matter of fact, I'm not sure how long you and Erin are going to last. None of them are your average date and, no insult intended, but it's obvious you're having a hell of a time sharing things you have no interest in with her."

"Thanks guys. I got the message... loud and clear." Bailey said, shaking his head.

The three of them retuned to the table by the bar but it quickly became apparent the mood had changed, drastically. The first hint was when Chase and Maverick sat down, but Bailey remained standing.

Finally, Teagan couldn't take it anymore. "Okay, enough everyone. Chase is here on business and while the rest of us are here to help him with our suggestions on seating, we're also here to have fun and enjoy exploring England. So let's all go back to being good friends, sharing a wonderful adventure." Her focus turned to Bailey who was still standing. "You okay?" she asked.

"No, actually, I need to talk to Erin… in private."

The two of them walked far enough away from the table to not be overheard. After several minutes, Erin returned while Bailey headed for the elevators.

"You told him to leave?" Aoife asked.

"No, he figured that out on his own," Erin answered. "I told him he was welcome to go do something else while we visited the fire station but he said the point was, I was supposed to be with him not with a crowd or each of us running off on our own."

"Uh, you're kidding… right?" Teagan asked.

"I… I… should have known we weren't going to work. He's been dropping hints all along about how we needed to do things on our own… like without all of you. He said, this was the last straw." She looked around the table. "I knew it was coming,

I'd just thought maybe this trip would help or at least a blow-up wouldn't have happened till we got back."

"Yeah, I overheard both of you on the way here," Maverick said. Then he turned to Chase. "That's why I said what I did over there."

"Uh, where was I during all this 'overheard conversation'?" Aoife asked.

Maverick bent over and kissed her. "Napping."

"I really can't blame him," Erin said. "He was raised an only child and honestly, dealing with us has to be difficult, even for someone from a big, close family."

"Ha! Probably a good thing you broke up now," Teagan added. "Just think what it's going to be like when Bridget, Keira and Fae join our happy group, along with whoever they drag along with them."

"There's three more?" Maverick asked Chase.

"Yip. Didn't you read the date disclosure agreement?" Pausing, with a big smile, he added, "You did get a copy of the disclosure agreement, right? The one that said there are six of them and they each come with five sisters, tons of parents, aunts and uncles and a bunch… oops sorry… a herd of horses."

"Keep it up you two and we'll volunteer you for the first class luggage evacuation drill tomorrow," Aoife barely got out before breaking into a snort fit.

"First class luggage evacuation drill?" Chase asked.

"Yip," Teagan answered. "That's where you two get to play like a suitcase from first class and we get to rescue you from the cargo bay and toss you into the baggage cart." Turning to Erin she asked, "We only missed the cart eight out of ten times when we did it at home, right?"

"Yeah, unless they don't let you count 'hangers', in which case we missed ten out of ten," Erin answered.

None of them could take any more as they all broke up laughing.

An hour later, with dinner done and most everyone yawning, they all headed for their rooms. On the way up in the elevator, Teagan asked Erin if she'd be alright. "Yeah, Bailey will probably be in the room. He said he wasn't going to leave until tomorrow and wanted to talk before he left. We'll be fine. We both knew this was coming and I'm sure we'll part friends."

The following morning, as they finished breakfast and made their way to the lobby, they found Diane, Peter and Richard waiting for them. Outside in the driveway, sat a Giant Scania, Crew Cab, Domestic Pumper with a Land Rover Fire Tender behind it. The three Fire Rescue Service (FSR) firefighters ushered them into the two vehicles, then headed for the airport's Northern Perimeter Road Firehouse.

As they arrived at the fire station and stepped out of the trucks, Erin stood staring at the fire station. "Oh my God. This place is huge!"

"Eight engine bays at this station and six bays at the south side station," Peter replied, as they were escorted into a small briefing room just off the engine bays.

"Diane is a crew manager and our official Heathrow FRS Public Relations Representative. So we're going to let her explain about our appliances - vehicles to you Yanks - and the type of calls we answer," Richard explained.

"Hi, everyone," Diane said with a bubbly smile. "I am so glad to be able to do this and, if you have any questions as we go along, just shout them out. The number and type of firefighting appliances based at an airport in the UK is determined by the airport's category. We categorize airports from 1 to 10, depending on the type and size of aircraft they handle. Heathrow is a category

10 since it caters to the biggest aircraft and therefore requires extensive rescue and firefighting coverage.

"Erin, as Peter mentioned, we have two stations, one at each end of the airport. That's because we are required to maintain a three-minute response time to any location within the airport or just outside its perimeter.

"The fire appliances used by airport fire and rescue services normally consist of a fleet of large, high-volume, pumping vehicles, capable of carrying an enormous amount of foam, other fire extinguishing media and equipment on bulk. They are able to apply it under massive pressure and volume at the fire scene.

"Most airport fire appliances are equipped with a roof-mounted high volume 'monitor' or 'nozzle', which can shoot fire extinguishing media huge distances. This means that an approaching fire appliance can begin tackling flames before it has arrived close to the scene of the fire.

"A new type of roof-mounted monitor has been introduced here in the UK; commonly known as a 'snozzle'. It consists of an extensible boom capable of reaching the upper decks of the A380 to extinguish fires. It is equipped with an infrared camera, a variable output 'nozzle' and a device resembling a spike that can pierce the fuselage of an aircraft and deliver large amounts of water and foam inside the aircraft. This makes airport firefighting safer as firefighters do not need to set foot inside the aircraft to extinguish fires as they can do it from the safety of their fire appliance using the snozzle.

"Each station here operates a Scania domestic pump, two six-wheel-drive major foam tenders and a similar but smaller four-wheel-drive light foam tender. We also have a Scania hose-layer, several auxiliary vehicles, such as a personnel carrier, along with a couple of reserve foam tenders and, the Scania 42 m aerial ladder platform I mentioned to reach the upper deck of the A380.

"The Heathrow FRS also operates two Mitsubishi Shogun command vehicles out of this main, north, fire station."

Turning to Teagan and Aoife she added, "Heathrow Air Ambulance also operates out of our airport. It's a private company that has both small and large fixed wing aircraft, not helicopters. It's meant to provide emergency transportation throughout Europe and even the Middle East, rather than just the UK.

"We also have Southern Ambulance Service, which typically has one or two ambulances housed here. It's also private and provides ground transportation from Heathrow Airport to London hospitals or homes, or indeed to any hospital, care home or residential address across the UK."

She stopped and her smile brightened. "I know you've got questions, so fire away."

"Wow. Doesn't sound like you have much in the way of emergency services based here at the airport. What do you do if there's a traffic accident here or someone gets hurt in a terminal or there's a plane crash?" Aoife asked.

"Well, there are two main scenarios. If one or two, or more people are injured, our FRS firefighters are trained as medical technicians, like you as EMTs. We choose not to have separate EMTs, instead, we train all of our firefighters as medical technicians. In the case of only a few injured, the firefighters would treat them and call Southern Ambulance Service to transport them to the nearest available hospital.

"In the case of a major plane incident, such as a crash, our firefighters would triage those injured, out away from the crash site. They would treat whoever they could and call Southern Ambulance Service, as well as several other local ambulance services, to transport everyone. There are over ten hospitals within five miles of the airport, so doing round-robins to deliver the injured is very feasible."

"Wow. You've certainly got a handle on pretty much anything that could happen," Teagan said, then added, "Your equipment is quite specialized. What do you do when you respond to something outside of the airport?"

Ready with an answer, Diane's face lit up again. "Well, first off, we only respond within a very small area close to our perimeter. That's because we must still maintain our three-minute response time. Also, we would only respond with our light, non-specialized, appliances. Then once the local fire brigade arrives, we would pull our equipment and people out and return them to their station."

"I'm totally impressed with your knowledge," Teagan said.

"Thank you. I truly hope so, but that's my job," Diane responded, then asked, "My turn?"

"Sure, fire way… no pun intended," Teagan said, adding a chuckle.

"I'm quite familiar with your fire departments in the states but not with your air ambulance service," Diane said. "What type of calls would you respond to? I mean, from what I remember, each fire station we toured had its own EMTs and ambulance. So when would you be called out?"

"Like you, there would be two scenarios. First, if someone was severely injured and needed to be transported immediately. A life-or-death situation, if you will, where a ground vehicle couldn't get them to a hospital quick enough.

"The second would be if their injuries need special treatment. For example, injuries involving nerve damage or a damaged organ that likely could require an organ transplant. In San Diego, each hospital group has a hospital that specializes in cases like that and those hospitals all have a heliport on grounds.

"For example, Scripps Mercy Hospital specializes in traumatic injuries, while Sharp's Neurology Department is at its Memorial Hospital. Both have a heliport and Emergency

212

Departments at their facility. It would be the call of the EMTs arriving on scene, like Erin, to determine if helicopter transport is required, and to where.

"Once we land at the incident site, one of the EMTs would join us in transporting the patient or turn their care over to Aoife if they need to stay on scene." Teagan paused. "We also do organ delivery for transplants and occasionally patient transfers from one hospital to another if needed."

"Thank you. It sounds like our abundance of hospitals, especially in the London area, would eliminate the need for helicopter transport. I know we have helicopter ambulance service outside of London but it's all private, so I'm not familiar with it," Diane replied.

Before turning them loose, Peter rejoined them, then escorted them out into the engine bays for a quick tour of the vehicles. As they finished up, Richard pulled up in one of the Mitsubishi Shogun command vehicles, then delivered them back at the hotel.

# Chapter 22 – Walking in Their Parent's Footprints

They had an hour to kill before being picked up for their tour of Salisbury, Stonehenge and Bath, so they headed for the Starbucks counter. Once everyone had something to drink, they claimed one of the couch groupings across the lobby.

"That was really interesting," Aoife said. "It's surprising how different our approaches to firefighting and emergency medical services are. I realize their typical response is unique to being at an airport or dealing with hundreds of people on a plane, but even outside of the airport they separate fire and medical. Maybe it's just because it's *different* and I'm not used to it, but it's hard to imagine response times being much longer than ours."

"Well, you heard them, they're tied to a three-minute response time. That's a hell of a lot better than ours, typically. Actually, always," Teagan said, adding a chuckle.

"Yeah, but that's because their response area is limited. They also have two firehouses covering what, a 12,000-foot runway? That's a 6,000-foot worse case response distance from either station? With no traffic to fight their way through." Erin paused. "We've got to cover all of Bonita and half our calls are into Chula Vista or National City."

Chase looked at the three of them. "Apples and oranges."

Everyone nodded in agreement.

A moment later the concierge came up to them. "Your bus is here for your tour."

***

A little over an hour later, their small tour bus crossed the River Avon and the cathedral's spire filled the sky off in the distance. Some four hundred four feet tall, it was the tallest spire in England.

The bus pulled into the parking area, and they exited the bus. As they stood looking at the massive cathedral, its spire disappearing into the clouds, Aoife stared and said, "I remember my mom telling me this had to be the most beautiful building in the world."

Agreeing, Erin added, "My mom said the same thing."

Seeing it for the second time, Teagan just nodded. She couldn't agree more. Nothing she would ever see could possibly compare to what stood in front of her. Its parapets, its flying buttresses, stained glass windows of every size and shape imaginable, many of them hundreds of feet up. The hundreds and hundreds of statues, each standing in its own niche, designed specifically for it. The ornate spire overwhelming the massive ten-story structure it was part of.

Their guide led them through the front doors, explaining that the cathedral was built over 800 years ago and finished around 1220, but their minds were already totally into overload. They stepped through the doorway, barely walked into the nave, and stopped. Each leaned back, looked up and tried to take everything in.

"Oh my God," Erin whispered. Even with her head tilted back until her neck hurt, she still couldn't see the top of the cathedral's ceiling.

Unaware, they ended up sitting in the same pew their parents had. "Stunning, isn't it?" Teagan said, as they all looked up toward the stained glass windows high above them, each casting a rainbow of colors throughout the chapel.

"My mom said she felt like she was in heaven, sitting at the bottom of a rainbow with God shining his light down on her," Aoife said. "Now I see why."

"I suspect it was designed to make you feel like that," Maverick whispered, not wanting to break the spell.

Together they took dozens of pictures, covering both outside and inside, while Aoife, mimicking her mom CJ, was glued to their tour guide's every word, asking hundreds of questions.

Before they knew it, it was time to head to Stonehenge and Bath. As the bus pulled out, they all watched as the cathedral faded into the landscape behind them.

***

Their next stop was Stonehenge. As they stepped off the bus a young woman approached them. "My name is Shala and it's my pleasure to personally guide you through one of the oldest and richest prehistoric landscapes in the world. We'll be waiting here for a bit to let the previous group get through the tunnel. Once they've moved off and onto the perimeter of the circle, I'll be taking you up to the opposite side. That way it doesn't get too crowded, and I can answer any questions you might have. Our tour usually takes about an hour and afterward the bus will take us on to Bath. There is no time limit though since we have our own bus, so please feel free to ask as many questions as you want.

"We can't go inside the circle?" Aofie asked.

"I'm sorry," Shala apologized. "Guests are no longer permitted near the stones because so much vandalism has been done in the past. So it's only by special tour that guests can go inside the circle." She paused. "I'll also be going on to Bath with you. If you think of something afterward, please don't be afraid to ask."

Shala looked up the hill toward the circle. "Okay. They're up at the circle so let's wander up." As they walked up the path, she explained that the temple is over 5,000 years old and was last in use over 3,500 years ago. "There is a place where I will let you touch one the stones that fell away from the temple. That way you can brag about having touched it and tell all your friends."

She went on to explain, "Stonehenge was produced by a culture that left no written records. Thus many aspects of

Stonehenge, such as how it was built and for what purposes it was used, remain subject to debate. A number of myths surround the stones. The site, specifically the great trilithon, the encompassing horseshoe arrangement of the five central trilithons, the heel stone, and the embanked avenue, are aligned to the sunset of the winter solstice and the opposing sunrise of the summer solstice. A natural landform at the monument's location followed this line and may have inspired its construction."

Dozens of pictures, and questions; an hour and twenty minutes later, they came back through the tunnel and climbed into the bus waiting for them.

In Bath, she told them all about the history of the Romans occupying England as she walked them past the aqueduct and through the Roman baths. Then she explained about the Georgian village of Bath as they strolled along the main street.

At the end of their tour of the village, the baths and the aqueduct, Teagan, Chase, and Shala waited outside while the others wandered into a gift shop. "Your group has been a pleasure to escort through the ruins and Bath. Most of the tourists I get are only partially interested and ask only a few questions. You lot, though, have been a pleasure and I loved all of your questions."

On the way back to the bus, Shala steered them into in a small bakery where she purchased two dozen Bath Buns, then handed them to Maverick who was next to her.

"All for me?" Maverick asked.

Shala let out a chuckle and shook her head. "No! One dozen is for all of you. Then it's tradition to take the rest back for your hotel staff. They will love you forever, and believe me, you'll have no problem being bumped to the head of the queue any time you need something. Just make sure everyone at the concierge's desk gets one."

***

After collecting a hug, she put each of them back on the bus. Then, sporting a giant smile, Shala stood waving at them as the bus pulled away.

"I hope you gave her a good tip," Teagan said to Chase.

"Way more than good. She was an excellent guide. The one we had a month ago was good, but Shala put her to shame."

The rest of the trip back to the hotel was filled with chatter about everything they had seen.

"I can't believe we're leaving tomorrow," Maverick said as they pulled into the hotel driveway.

"What's everyone want to do about dinner?" Erin asked as they strolled back into the hotel.

"I'm exhausted and vote for a nice meal here in the pub, then getting a good night's sleep. Plus we've got an early morning meeting at BA before we catch our flight home," Aoife said.

It only took a minute for everyone to agree and the group to turn and head for the pub. They claimed a table in the pub's dining area.

"Black and Tans all around?" The barmaid called over and already had three of them poured.

A few minutes later, they each ordered something different so they could share, while the server set their drinks down.

Chase held up his glass. "To a fantastic couple of days," he toasted as everyone clinked their glasses. "We'll know better after tomorrow morning's meeting at BA, but I suspect we'll be back in a few weeks. I'll try and give you all as much advanced notice as I can. That way you can see about getting time off again.

"They've already messaged my office that they're okay with the six of us returning and that they thought the comments from us were very helpful. William also added that he'd love it if we came up with any other ideas and to be sure to bring them to the next meeting. He said that everyone loved the suggestion for the small group seating. So put your thinking caps on."

***

The meeting the following morning lasted a quick fifteen minutes. "You've created a monster," William said. "My team loved your idea so much that they're off working on several options for seating small groups in both first and business class. No small task given the lounge type seats in both, but trust me,

220

they'll come up with something our passengers will love." He paused. "They're unbelievably creative."

He scanned them with a big smile. "Your job is to come up with more ideas and keep them busy. So put your heads together and we'll see you in a few more weeks. Oh, and on your way back I'd like you all to look at and comment on our in-flight entertainment package, especially the gambling we offer. We've had a lot of comments - both good and bad - so I'd really like your opinions; also, on the selection of movies we offer."

Returning to the hotel, they collected their bags from the concierge and caught the hopper bus over to Heathrow. On the flight back they were all seated in first class and kept passing notes with ideas on them back and forth. Finally, Chase suggested they plan a get together over dinner in the next few days since passing ideas on notes was just not working. He also suggested that Erin might want to offer her second friends and family pass to one of their other sisters. If need be, he'd find a way to get two more passes for their other sisters.

"We'd only need one more," Teagan explained. "Fae is off working on her S2 tanker certification with Cal Fire and there's no way she'd give that up... for anything."

Chase promised to work on another pass, along with some kind of trip for Fae as a reward for getting her S2 certification. That earned him a big kiss and a, "No wonder I'm in love with you," from Teagan.

The flight home had been smooth, with clear skies. So clear in fact that the pilot obtained permission to bring the aircraft down to 20,000 feet as they flew along the sun lit face of the glaciers in Iceland. Everyone on the right side of the aircraft gladly shared their windows with those on the left. As they skimmed across the sun lit face of the glaciers, they were provided with a view none of them would ever forget; a view of the changing vivid blue swirls and streaks imbedded in the ice as the angle of the sun changed. "Oh my God! That is unbelievable. That view will stay with me forever," Aoife said as they all gathered around her window.

Their flight landed on time and everyone decided to crash and catch up on sleep. Erin was due to start her go-around the following morning, while Teagan and Aoife had another day before they were due back. Maverick and Chase were both due at work the following morning too, so it would be an early evening for all of them.

Arriving at the station in the morning, Erin found Bailey, cappuccinos in hand, waiting on the steps for her. "What do you want, Bailey?" she asked, trying very hard not to make it sound sarcastic.

"I want to apologize," he answered.

"Apology accepted, but if you're going to propose we get back together... I don't think that's going to happen."

"I wasn't going to suggest we get back together. I think it's fair to say we're different enough that being together is just not going to work. I do want to stay friends though, if that's alright with you."

"Why?" she asked.

"Because we work right down the street from each other and are bound to keep running into one another. Not only don't I want that to be uncomfortable, for either one of us, but I really like and respect you. So staying friends, I hope, will work for both of us?"

"I can do that," she said. "I really do like you too, but liking you and being with you are two different things."

Just then, the alert horn went off inside the station. "I have to go, Bailey. I'll stop by Starbucks when I get a chance," she said, adding a big smile. She ran in, threw her backpack in her locker and headed for the engine bay.

As she climbed into the passenger seat of the ambulance, Jake said, "805 Freeway, northbound, just north of the 125. Multi-car accident. Apparent road rage incident. Highway Patrol is on scene."

Reaching over she flipped on the lights and siren, then heard 38 start up in the bay next to them.

Bert's voice came over the radio, "Engine 38, EMT 7 responding."

"Roger 38 and 7, be advised, shots fired… I repeat… shots fired. Approach only after CHP declares scene to be safe," Alice advised them.

"Copy dispatch," Bert said as they followed 38 out of the bay and onto Bonita Road.

CHP cleared the scene before they reached the freeway and Chula Vista EMT 12 pulled in behind them as they passed the 125 interchange. Up ahead they could see two cars, partially on the shoulder, smoke pouring from the hood of one of them. Engine 38 angled in behind them to protect the scene, while EMT 7 and 12 stopped on the shoulder just behind the big pumper.

"The driver of the car on fire is on the shoulder in front of the car. He's dead. The father and daughter in the silver car are both wounded and trapped inside the car," the Highway Patrolman told them.

They all watched as Bert and his crew pried the doors open, then bent them back to break them off and gain access to the two gunshot victims. "God, she's just a teenager," Erin said, as they approached with the gurney and watched them lift the girl out of the front passenger seat and onto a backboard. From there, they slid the backboard onto the gurney and strapped her down. In the meantime, the EMTs from 12 tended to her father.

The patrolman came up just before they slid her gurney into the ambulance. "Can you tell me what happened?" he asked, as Erin tightly taped a large gauze pad to her shoulder to stem the bleeding.

"I'm not sure. My dad and I were driving along, singing to our favorite U2 song, when this nut pulls up alongside of us and starts yelling out his window."

"Had you cut him off?" the patrolman asked.

"No. He just came out of nowhere. I would have seen it if we'd cut him off. Next thing I know a gun comes up in his hand… my dad starts to shove my head under the dashboard and I feel this sharp pain in my shoulder. I looked over and there was blood all running down the back of my dad's neck." She paused, then went on. "My dad didn't even look… he just jerked the steering wheel to the left and we hit the guy's car. I'm… I'm not sure what happened next because my dad was yelling 'stay down' so I kept my head under the dashboard as much as I could."

"Anything else?" the patrolman asked her.

"Yeah. My dad pulled over and just after we stopped, I heard another shot. I thought it was him shooting at us again, but then I realized it must have been you because, before the shot, I heard you yell 'drop the gun.'"

"We need to get her to the hospital," Erin told him. "You can finish your questioning there."

"Which hospital?" the patrolman asked.

"We just got clearance for Sharp Memorial for both her and her dad," Jake replied, as they locked her gurney in place in the ambulance. Jake climbed in the back, Erin closed the door and headed for the drivers door.

"Is my dad okay?" she asked Jake.

"Yeah, I think he'll be okay. It looks like the same bullet that hit you grazed the back of his head before it hit you in the shoulder. Like most head wounds, there's a lot of blood but the EMT said there doesn't appear to be much damage so I think he'll be alright."

*** 

After pulling in next to EMT 12, they unloaded the young girl and wheeled her into the Emergency Room bed next to her dad. They changed the bedding on the gurney and just as they slid it back into the ambulance, another call came in.

"EMT 7, Engine 38, house fire. Valley Road, corner of Sweetwater and Valley… EMT 7 advise of ETA."

Erin reached up and keyed her radio. "Bonita Fire, ETA on Valley Road call, fifteen minutes."

"Roger 7. 38 is already on scene."

Their ambulance pulled up in front of a farmhouse that sat back from the corner. Just as they stopped, Shawn came up to Erin's door with someone, or something, wrapped in a blanket, in his arms. Erin opened her door and Shawn slid whatever it was

226

into her lap. "Their cat was in the shed that caught fire. He got out, but his feet were burned when he dug his way out under the door. Can you run him over to the VCA vets on Bonita Road? I'll call and let them know you're coming."

Erin was nodding her head as she opened the blanket the cat was wrapped in. Out popped the head of the cutest marmalade kitten she had ever seen. The brightest golden eyes stared at her, begging her to help him. "Oh. My. God. He's adorable," she said as she pulled him against her chest. "Go Jake!" she added as she flipped the lights and siren on and started to carefully examine his paws. "It's okay, baby, Auntie Erin's got you and she's not going to let anything happen to you. We'll get you all better in just a little bit."

Jake glanced over as the cat, just barely out of kittenhood, who was feverishly licking Erin's chin, while she giggled up a storm and spoke to him in her best 'kitten voice'.

"Uh, I need to pull over and throw up," he said.

"You pull over and I'll make you a gelding."

He stared at her, then asked, "What's a gelding?"

"I'll let the vet explain it to you. Just get our baby there so we can get him fixed up."

"Our baby?"

"Shut up and go," she added as they pulled into the VCA parking lot.

Erin pulled the blanket tight against her chest and eased herself out of the ambulance. One of the vet assistants came up and tried to take the blanket and cat from her. Turning her shoulder to block her, Erin said, "I've got him," and headed for the front door.

"Of course you do," the assistant said, adding a big smile. Then she led Erin, with the cat, into one of the exam rooms.

A moment later, the vet came through the back door. "Hi. Who have we got here?" She looked first at Erin, then Jake.

"Uh, a cat?" Jake said.

The vet looked at Erin and rolled her eyes. "Yeah, I figured that much out. Does he have a name?" She lifted him to double check that he was a he.

"He was rescued from a shed on a farm over on Sweetwater Road," Erin said.

"Well, judging from his coat, I'd say he's a stray," the vet told her as she reached for her chip scanner. After waving the chip scanner over him and checking his teeth, she added, "Yep. He's not chipped and his teeth look like he's been eating anything he could find." Next, she checked his feet. "They're a little singed but nothing a bit of salve can't cure. Cats are amazing. They always seem to find a way to save themselves from a fire." She picked him up and stared into his eyes. "Isn't that right?" Turning to Erin she added, "He's adorable and marmalades are notorious for making great pets."

Erin keyed her radio. "Engine 38, this is EMT 7."

"Go 7," Shawn answered.

"Shawn, do you want to report on the condition of the cat to the owners?"

"Uh, the owners said they don't have a cat. They think he's just been making his home in the shed but he's not theirs and they were adamant that they're not paying a vet bill for him."

"Copy that," Erin said, as she noticed the smile fade from the vet's face. She reached over and scratched the cat's neck. She was sure he smiled back as he leaned into her hand. "Can you please chip him and give him all the shots he should have?" He meowed at her and rolled in the vet's arms so Erin could scratch his tummy.

"I'm pretty sure he knows you're his new owner and is more than okay with that," the vet added.

"Can I pick him up after I get off shift... a little after eight tonight?" she asked.

"Sure. I'll let the night staff know. Just come to the back door and knock," the vet said. Looking at the name on her uniform, she added. "Oh, I noticed we share a name. I'm Erin too." The two of them shook hands and Erin, the vet, added, "We'll give him a bath too, and set you up with a cat bed, carry case, treats, food dishes and food, if you'd like."

"That would be fantastic," Erin replied.

"Please stop at the desk and give the receptionist your name and address and she'll get you and... uh, sir cat... all registered."

"Uh, I got the hint. He needs a name... How about Marshmallow... since he almost got toasted."

"I love it!" the vet said. "We'll have him all soft and fluffy, like a jet puffed marshmallow, when you pick him up."

The two Erins hugged each other, then firefighter Erin, with Jake trailing, headed for the front desk. "I somehow think you're the marshmallow, not him," Jake said. "Meet you out at the truck."

*** 

Erin finished her shift, picked up Marshmallow and all his supplies and headed for her apartment. Halfway down the hall to her apartment Marshmallow announced his arrival with a series of very loud meows. Just as she got to her door, Teagan and Aoife came out to see what all the racket was about. "Oh. My. God. He's adorable.!" The two of them announced at the same time.

"You spoil him and you get to buy food and treats for the next year." Erin told them, as Teagan eased Marshmallow out of his crate, then scratched his ears, while Aoife scratched his belly.

"God, listen to him purr. When's the last time this poor guy got any attention?" Aoife asked.

"Would one of you, actually both, go down to my truck and lug the rest of his stuff up? I kinda ran out of hands."

Teagan set the cat back in his carry crate and closed the door. Then she and Aoife headed for the front door and Erin's truck. "Don't forget the whirly toy on the passenger seat," she yelled after them."

"We fly helicopters, how could we possibly forget a whirly toy," Teagan yelled back.

Smiling down at Marshmallow, Erin let out a chuckle. "You have no idea what you're in for." Then she carried him into the apartment.

*** 

Teagan and Aoife reported to the air base and headed to the lounge for coffee after signing in. "How was London?" a voice from the doorway asked.

Turning around, Aoife smiled at Mitch, the pilot for Air Two. "London was fantastic!" she said. "We got to tour a whole bunch of places and BA loved our suggestions. As a matter of fact, they liked them so much they invited us to come back in a few weeks."

"Wow. I'm super jealous. Any chance on you ditching your boyfriend and taking me next time?"

"Sorry, I'll put you on the list. You're number 27." She added a big smile so he'd know she was just kidding. While she had no intention of giving Maverick up, Mitch was cute, actually, very cute. Plus, they got along really well.

Just then the call alarm went off. "Air One, Air Two. Apartment fire, multiple injuries. Bonita and Chula Vista fire responding." Both crews headed for their aircraft. Just as they were ready to crank both aircraft up, the dispatcher came back on. "Air One, Air Two, Stand Down. Repeat, Stand Down."

Mitch came on asking the question they all had. "What's up? False alarm?"

"No," the dispatcher said. "The closest place to land is the high school sports field, but transport to you from the apartment complex would have to be by ambulance. We checked with Chula Vista Hospital ER and they can handle initial treatment. So it was decided to just transport them directly there."

"Roger dispatch. Makes sense," Mitch came back.

Both crews headed back to the crew lounge. Twenty minutes later, the call alarm went off again. "Air One, Traffic Accident. 805 South, East Palomar Road exit. Wrong way driver. CHP has southbound lanes closed for landing."

"Roger," Teagan said as she brought the helo up to speed and they lifted off. Ten minutes later she eased the aircraft onto the freeway as Erin and Jake wheeled their gurney up and Aoife helped them slide and lock the stretcher into place.

"Broken arm, multiple broken ribs, possible collapsed lung and internal bleeding," Erin said as she followed the stretcher in

232

and smiled at Teagan. "Hi, Sis! I'm going with you. Jake has the second victim and will catch up with us at Memorial."

"Thought you were at the apartment fire?" Aoife asked, as she made sure the stretcher was locked down and Teagan relayed the patient information to Sharp Memorial.

"We were. We just finished dropping one of the burn victims off when we got called out for this," she answered, pointing at the two mangled cars against the center divider. "The hospital's only three blocks up so we were less than five minutes away," she added as she slid the door closed.

"Roger Memorial, ETA ten minutes," Teagan said into her headset as she eased the collective up and their bird lifted off.

Nine minutes later they set down on the roof of Sharp Memorial's parking structure. As the rotors came to a stop, two ER nurses rolled a gurney over and they all helped transfer the stretcher onto it.

"Just can't stay away?" a male ER nurse said as they entered the ER, obviously addressing all three of them.

"Hey, I thought you guys were in England," another nurse said as she hurried by.

"I hope you didn't double park on the heliport again," Janet, the nurse at the sign in desk said, as they approached.

"You're all just jealous because we got to go to London and you all didn't!" Aoife said as she signed them in. That earned them raspberries from the whole ER staff.

After they deposited their patient to the designated ER bed, they came back to the desk to sign out. "So, how was London and what did you get to see?" Janet asked them.

"Wow," Erin said, then went on to explain where they had gone and what they saw. "Teagan had seen most of it on her previous trip but honestly, I could go back and see most of it over and over again. The history there is just fascinating and the beauty of the cathedrals takes your breath away."

Aoife jumped in. "Oh, and Bath Buns are soooo delicious! We had to tape the box for the hotel staff shut or they never would have made it back to the hotel. Speaking of food, I know everyone talks about how bad British food is but everything we had was really good."

"Thanks," Janet said. "Now I feel like calling the airlines and booking myself on the next flight."

"Trust me, if you get a chance, go to London. Like Eff said, this was my second trip and I'm looking forward to going back again and again. It's everything you've heard and more," Teagan told her.

Once they finished signing out, Erin joined Jake while Teagan and Aoife headed back up to the heliport. Cranking the helicopter up, Teagan got on the radio. "Mercy Air Base, this is Air One."

"Go ahead Air One."

"Roger, we're cleared from Memorial and headed back to base."

"Air One, be advised we need you on another run. Unknown injury, Chula Vista Golf Course in Bonita. They've cleared a place to land right behind the clubhouse. Bonita fire is tending to the individual and will meet you there."

"Roger base, on our way. ETA ten minutes," Teagan responded as their helicopter lifted off.

As Teagan brought the helicopter to a hover, Erin waved at them, removed the flag from the green and waved her over to land. As she set down, she and Aoife noticed someone laying off to the side with a group of firefighters tending to him and a crowd of golfers at the back of the clubhouse.

Once the rotors stopped, Aoife opened the door and slid a stretcher out to Erin and Jake. A few minutes later they were loading the golfer, who sported a giant lump on his forehead, onto the lower stretcher shelf. "Wow!" Aoife said. "What did he run into?"

"A duck and a golf ball," Jake answered, adding a chuckle. "He and his buddy were putting on the green when a duck landed off to the side. His friend decided to take a shot at the duck.

Unfortunately, he had a really bad slice, the ball made a sharp left and nailed his friend in the forehead."

By then his golf buddy had come over to see how he was. "I never should have taken the shot with a putter," he said, then added, "is he going to be okay?"

Aoife had just finished hooking him up to the blood pressure and heart monitors. "Not sure yet. Everything looks okay. Blood pressure's a little high but that's to be expected with a head injury. We need to get him to the hospital so they can do a CT Scan to see if there's any damage." While she was explaining she was putting him through a series of tests: checking his eyes for their reaction to light, follow my finger, squeeze my fingers, push on my hand, and so on.

"Everything looks pretty normal. His responses are a bit weak and slow but again that's not unusual after suffering a trauma. Still, we need to get him to the hospital where they can do more extensive testing." She looked at Teagan. "Memorial?"

"Yeah, they have a bed open in the neurology ward," Teagan answered.

"We'll be taking him to Sharp Memorial," Aoife told his friend.

"Can I fly with you?" he asked.

"Nope, sorry. We're not allowed to transport passengers. He should be assigned to a bed by the time you get there, so check with the ER desk. They'll know where he's being assigned, because there's a good chance he'll be in the CT chamber when you arrive."

He thanked Erin, Jake and Aoife, waved at Teagan, collected his golf gear, his friends gear, then headed for the parking lot.

***

For the second time in a little over an hour, Teagan set their helicopter down on the roof of Memorial's parking structure. Two nurses, the same two that had met them on the last run, came up to the door as the rotors came to a halt. "Just can't stay away, can you," one of them said as Aoife slid the door open again.

"Wow. What the hell did he run into?" one of them asked, looking at the guy on the stretcher.

"Uh, a duck and a golf ball," Aoife told them.

"Let me guess," the nurse replied. "The duck was playing golf and this guy tried to play through, so the duck beaned him."

"Close. This guy's partner got tired of waiting for the duck to get off the green and tried to bean him. Unfortunately, he learned putters don't make good drivers. But they are good for slicing a shot. So, his ball made a sharp left and beaned his partner, while the duck and his partner stood there laughing… or quacking as it were."

"Where the hell do you find these pickups?" the nurse asked, desperately trying to stifle a laugh.

"Hey, weird call? Dispatch the sisterhood," Teagan said. "You name it, we've seen it."

"Yeah, I can't wait till Fae gets her tanker certification. Next thing you know, she'll be having arresting wires installed up here so she can bring patients in and land her S-2 or C-130 tanker up here," Aoife added.

The four of them wheeled the patient over to the elevator, then took him down to street level and across to the ER entrance. As soon as they stepped inside, Janet, the administrative nurse looked up. "Back so soon?" she said, adding a big smile, then logged the patient in and assigned him to Bed 4. As Teagan and Aiofe headed for Bed 4, she called the nurse assigned to that bed over. "Don't go far. I'm sure he'll be going down for a scan once the doctor has a look at him."

As Teagan and Aiofe headed back out, Janet said, "That's it for today. No more patients please. The inn is full."

The two of them just smiled and waved.

# Chapter 24 – DUCK!

All three of them finished the day with no more call outs. A bit unusual since people seemed to lose their brains and do the dumbest things in the afternoon and evening especially after a few drinks.

After showering and changing into PJs, they assembled in Teagan's apartment and curled up on the couch. "What a friggin' day!" Aoife said, as she set three beers on the coffee table. "Every time you think you've seen it all, along comes someone who tries to bean a duck." She paused, then started laughing hysterically. Finally, she managed to spit out, "I wonder if he yelled 'Duck' before he teed off?" That had them all bursting into a round of laughter.

Turning serious, Teagan looked at Erin. "Should we start working on finding you a Bailey replacement?"

"Oh God no! I'm just fine, thank you. I may just declare myself gay. You guys are so much easier to deal with then men. I mean Bailey, on the surface seemed fine, but several times I felt like he was forcing himself to do something he didn't want to do. I'd even mention that we could do something else, but he'd go, 'Oh no, I'm fine,' then he'd become Mr. Grumps. Even though he never said it, the looks he'd shoot at me were like, 'this is the worst time I've ever had… oh, and it's your fault'. That's why I blew up so easily in London."

"We're so sorry," Teagan and Aoife said and wrapped Erin in their arms.

"Don't be sorry," Erin added a big grin. "Which one of you wants to have sex with me? Or… maybe a threesome?"

"Uh, I've got a blow up Ken doll you can borrow," Teagan replied.

"You can use my vibrator… it fits in Ken's hand," Aiofe added.

"And you know that how?" Erin asked Aoife, then shook her head. "Never mind. Definitely TMI."

By now they were all laughing again and rolling on the floor.

\*\*\*

The next morning found them all curled up on the floor in front of the couch, a king-size quilt over them and a dozen empty beer bottles on the coffee table.

A minute after Teagan opened one eye, her alarm went off in the bedroom. Both Erin and Aoife bolted upright.

"What in the hell is that?" Erin asked, looking all around.

"Uh, my alarm," Teagan said.

"Even the call horn at the fire station isn't that annoying," Erin replied. A second later all three of their phones went off.

*Countywide alert! All available first responders report for duty.*
The message on each of their phones said.

"Oh crap, now what?" Teagan asked.

The three of them quickly dressed and headed for their cars. Out in the parking lot, they ran into Keira and Bridget. "Either of you know what's up?" Aoife asked.

"Something about major injuries from a concert at Petco Park?" Keira replied.

"A concert at five am?" Teagan asked.

Keira shrugged. "Hey, I just told you more than I know. We'll find out more when we get to the station. Oh, it's great seeing you three. You'd think we lived on the other side of the earth. Oh wait, that's right, you're all busy buzzing back and forth to London." That earned her three raspberries.

"I promise, we'll catch up with you soon," Teagan yelled as she and Aoife closed the doors to her car.

Sure enough, when they reached the airfield, they were told to gear up and head for Petco Park. Erin met with the same instructions when she arrived at the firehouse. "Uh, Petco Park's a little out of our jurisdiction, isn't it?" she asked Jake as she buckled into the passenger seat of ambulance.

"I'll explain on the way," he answered. He pulled out of the engine bay and she flipped on the lights and siren. "So, there was some kind of rock concert at the park last night. It went into

241

the wee hours. The crowd went nuts. Drugs were everywhere. Multiple people went over the railing from the upper decks. Security called for help around midnight, but the arrival of the police just made things worse. By 3am it had turned into a major riot. So every ambulance in San Diego County is responding... that includes Navy, Marine Corps and Coast Guard medical personnel."

As they approached the stadium, Mercy Air One and Two set down in the back parking lot. Two Navy Medivac CH-53s were already on the ground with navy medical personnel pushing gurneys toward the entrance of the stadium.

"Holy crap - this is bad," Erin said, as they joined a dozen ambulances already backed up to the stadium's gates. Inside, it was pure pandemonium. People yelling, screaming and staggering everywhere. Teagan and Aoife joined them as they stepped out of the ambulance.

"Be sure it's locked up." Jake watched people trying to open the doors of the ambulances down the line from them.

"Please! You've got to help my friend!" a young woman screamed as she ran up to them. "They... they pushed her over the railing and she's hurt... really bad." She grabbed Teagan's arm and started dragging her through the gates. "She landed head first on the seat below."

Somehow, she and several of her friends had managed to drag their injured friend to just inside the gate. Aoife bent over and examined her. A second later she had a collar on the girl's neck. "We need to get her to Mercy... quick." She looked up at Erin and Jake. "Grab someone else that's hurt and bring them over. No sense having an empty stretcher with this many people injured," she added, as she and Teagan pushed the gurney toward the helicopter.

Jake looked over at another of their friends, the one holding a blood-soaked sweatshirt against her side. "Hold on," he said. He picked her up and set her on the gurney. Then they followed Teagan and Aoife with her on their gurney.

Both patients secured in the stretcher racks, Erin closed the door and rapped on the side to let Teagan know she could take off. Then she and Jake headed back to the stadium for another injured concert goer.

\*\*\*

Before the day was over, Teagan and Aoife made five runs, three to Mercy and two to Memorial. Jake and Erin had made four runs to four different hospitals as the nearest ER wards quickly filled up.

At a little after six pm, they found themselves back in Teagan's apartment this time joined by Bridget and Keira.

"I have a much better appreciation of the Heathrow firefighters because I'm pretty sure I now know what it's like to deal with an airplane crash," Aoife said to no one in particular.

243

"At least things eventually got organized. It was pure chaos at first," Keira replied.

"How in the hell do you prepare for something like that?" Bridget asked.

As she passed around the first round of beer, Teagan said, "It's a good thing some of them... hell, a lot of them... were stoned. If they weren't high or sober, I think there would have been a lot more injuries. How else do you explain some of them falling from the second tier and just laughing it off?"

"Yeah, that poor security guy wasn't so lucky. He got pushed over backward. The navy doctor who looked at him said he never stood a chance. He landed on a seat back and it snapped his spine in two. The doctor said he was pretty sure he died instantly," Aoife said.

"What the hell is wrong with people?" Teagan shook her head. "Last count I heard was over sixty were injured enough to be hauled to hospitals, with three dead."

"Uh, change of subject, please," Kiera announced, turning to Erin. "What was going on with you and that other security guard?"

"Oh, I know him from school. His name is Ray and he only moonlights as a security guard. He's actually a Chula Vista Policeman. The other security guard, the one that died, was his partner on the police force. They grew up together and he's the godfather to the children of the one that died."

"That's such a shame," Teagan said. "Did I hear you say you two were getting together?"

"Yep. I promised him I'd go with him to visit the wife and kids tomorrow and go with him to the funeral."

"Did you two date in high school?" Teagan asked.

"Yeah, for a little bit, but he was all full of himself back then, so we didn't last long. He asked me to the senior prom, then started flirting with anyone wearing a skirt that walked by, so I left and went home alone."

"You think this might go somewhere?" Aoife asked.

"Who knows. If he's still got a stick up his butt, probably not. The fact that he thinks having me there will help the wife and kids feel more comfortable already tells me he's changed. But… who knows. I'm keeping it at 'a friend helping a friend', nothing more."

Kiera looked at her watch and her eyebrows went up. "Holy crap. No wonder my eyes are closing. I need to go and get some sleep."

Four "Me Toos" joined her as everyone stood and good night hugs went around.

*** 

The next morning and Teagan and Aoife were restocking their helicopter when the call alarm went off. "Air One. couch accident, 805 Freeway South at Palm Ave." The dispatcher let out a snort, then added, "Duck involved."

Teagan stared at Aoife. "Uh, she did say couch accident… did she not?"

"Yip, and 'Duck involved'. So I think our duck may be at it again," Aoife answered, then shrugged. "And I thought this job was going to be all blood and guts… not golf balls, couches and duck poop."

Teagan eased the collective up, both of them laughing and unable to look at each other.

Fifteen minutes later they arrived over the accident scene. Two cars, each with a couch across the hood. A pickup truck on its side, buried under four more couches. Another pickup with six couches hanging from the bed and a dead duck, spread eagle, across the windshield.

"Only in San Diego!" Aoife managed to spit out.

"Poor duckie. He should have stayed on the green. Maybe he thought 'drivers have bad aim' applied to pickups too," Teagan added as she set Air One down on the closed off freeway.

Both pickups had been headed for the border, part of the weekly parade of used furniture on its way to be sold in Tijuana. As best the Highway Patrolman could speculate, the duck had been coming in for a landing on the other side of the freeway. He, or she, had misjudged the added height of the couches stacked on the pickup, panicked, tried to avoid them at the last minute, and

246

slammed into the windshield. The pickup driver slammed on the breaks, the second pickup did the same and couches went flying.

Teagan and Aoife checked and no one from the pickups or cars seemed to be injured, so they loaded the duck on the gurney, then into the helicopter. On the way back to the airfield, Aoife called the dispatcher and told her to contact the SPCA office just down the street from their base and tell them they needed a 'dead duck transport'. She tried explaining over the radio, but both she and Teagan were laughing so much the dispatcher couldn't understand anything beyond 'SPCA and dead duck transport'.

# Chapter 25 – A Duckless Day

The next afternoon everyone had gathered at Teagan's apartment to get ready for their next trip to London. This time joined by Chase, Maverick and Erin's latest date, Ray. Keira and Bridget were both on duty and had taken a rain check. As Teagan and Aoife tried to explain about the couch-duck call, Erin decided there definitely wasn't enough beer and placed an emergency delivery order with Vons.

"That was you guys?" Ray said in between snorts. "Every station, police and fire, in San Diego has heard about your call." He turned to Erin. "Uh, can we keep our dating quiet until this kind of dies down?"

"Hey, I wasn't there! We were busy rescuing a cat held captive in a tree by a rattle snake," she said, sticking her tongue out.

"We need to write a book," Aoife added.

"Why? No one would believe it," Teagan replied.

"The fire brigade at Heathrow will," Aoife said. "I'll even bet they could add a bunch of weird and funny stories from stuff they've seen."

"Speaking of which," Chase chimed in. "We need to come up with some more suggestions for our next meeting at BA. Has anyone thought of anything?"

"What kind of suggestions?" Ray asked.

Erin told him about the friends and family passes and BA's request that they rate their flights. Also, try and come up with suggestions for things that might make their flights more enjoyable. As soon as she finished, he smiled at her and said, "I have an idea."

"You haven't even been on one of their flights, have you?" Erin came back with.

"No, but I've been on long flights." He paused. "This may not work because it could take up a lot of space. But if it were designed into the seating right, it might work and be a big attraction. I remember my dad bragging about how he loved flying Continental Airlines back in the eighties. Why? Because they had what they called 'Pub Flights'. On all their wide-bodied planes, the ones used for long distance flights, they had converted the center section, what would now be business class on most planes, into a pub. Up against the front bulkhead they had a bar and there were tables with four seats at each down the center. Along the sides there were couches. The layout was very much like what you would find in a private jet. The pub was only open during flight and you had to reserve a table or place on the couch. Once the flight reached altitude, you could make your way up there and spend the entire flight, until just before landing, in the pub if you wished."

"What a fantastic idea," Aoife said.

"Hey, that could solve the issue we brought up last time… that there was no place for small groups. They could reserve a space in the pub," Teagan added, obviously excited.

"My hero," Erin said, laying a big kiss on Ray.

"Does that mean I get to go to London with you?" he asked, adding a big smile.

"Oh, you get to go to a lot more places than London with me, but only if you're good." she told him, batting her eyes.

"Uh, perhaps you'd like to take the rest of this conversation to your apartment, Erin? It's about to go TMI," Teagan said.

"Okay, back to the important stuff: aircraft seating and entertainment," Chase interrupted and was bombarded with a bunch of boos. He looked around. "How quickly you all forget who set this up." Suddenly he was in the middle of a giant hug.

"Yay! Back to seats and entertainment," Aoife added.

Shaking his head, Chase replied, "Seriously, what has anyone noticed about the entertainment?"

"I thought the movie selections were pretty current and there was a nice variety," Aoife said. "Music, not so much. Maybe it's just me but there wasn't much that appealed to me… oh, and way too much hip hop."

"Yeah, I noticed that too," Erin threw in. "Oh, and not enough country western or classic."

"How about games?" Chase asked.

"Didn't even look at them," Teagan answered, and everyone else nodded.

"Okay, no gamers in the group," Chase parroted back. "Anything anyone else thinks might be added? Remember, they don't need to do it. It's just food for thought."

"Some of the latest popular TV shows? *Dancing With the Stars, America*... or *Britain's Got Talent, the Chicago Series*?" Teagan said.

"Hey, you mentioned food! How about regional food served onboard?" Maverick added. "Shepherd's pie and Bath Buns on the way to London. Mexican food and churros on the way to San Diego. You know, a sample of food from the destination."

"All good ideas," Chase said. "I think that gives us some good things to bring up at the next meeting. I just want to make sure we let them know we're earning our passes and thinking about the things they asked us to."

Ray looked puzzled so Chase went over what BA had asked them to do in return for the friends and family passes. "Thanks," Ray said. "I thought it was just things pertaining to seats or seating."

"Nope," Chase answered. "We can comment on anything pertaining to the flight. Actually, we could probably comment on anything else, like the boarding procedure, but they just asked us to look at the flight."

Everyone couldn't help but notice Erin staring at Ray. He was definitely not the overconfident, full of himself, jerk who had gone to the prom with her. He smiled at her. "Do I have something stuck in my teeth? You're all staring."

"No, I just can't believe how much you've changed," Erin answered, returning his smile.

"You mean I stopped being an asshole." It was a statement, not a question. He paused and looked around. "Being a cop will do that to you. But I guess being first responders, you know what I mean. Reality quickly sinks in your first week on the street… when being an asshole gets thrown at you on half the calls."

After winking at him, she added, "Yep, you've definitely changed. For the better."

"Uh, so have you. You've become even prettier."

Her smile brightened. "Aw, keep it up. You're winning lots of points."

"Excuse me while I go throw up," Teagan said. Looking at Aoife she added, "Want to join me so we can save on toilet flushes."

"I'd tell you to ignore them and they'll go away but that's not going to happen," Erin said.

"You know, I remember all of you hanging out together from school… and a ranch? Don't all of your parents own a ranch somewhere?" Ray asked.

Erin shook her head. "No. Three of our moms worked there and we all volunteered at the ranch whenever we could." She couldn't help but notice the genuine interest he seemed to have. Another change from the old Ray. She reached over and took his hand. "Tell you what. Buy me lunch before we visit your friend's family and go to his funeral. I'll tell you all about us while we eat. But… you need to tell me all about you too. If I remember right, you went into the Air Force right out of high school?"

"Yeah. That's definitely where I grew up," he said as he stood and helped her up. "Thanks for inviting me," he told everyone else, as they headed for the door hand in hand.

As soon as the door closed, Aoife, who had been the closest to Erin growing up, said, "He's really changed. I remember what a total asshole he was in school. I'm amazed Erin didn't kill him, or at least make him a gelding, after the shit he put her through at the prom."

Maverick let out a loud, painful groan.

"Well, she certainly seems to be well on her way to forgiving him," Chase said, adding a chuckle. "By the way, I love his pub flight idea. I hope it'll go over well at BA since it really fits perfectly with England and their flights."

\*\*\*

Erin suggested CPK, California Pizza Kitchen, since it was close to his friend's house and the funeral home. Ray parked and they came through the back pick-up entrance and headed for the hostess stand at the front door. They both glanced at the empty stand, then Erin spotted the hostess off in the small dining room by the bar, seating a couple. "She's seating someone over there," she told Ray, as she nodded toward the dining area.

While they waited for her to return, something at the pick-up register caught Ray's attention. He watched as the guy in front of the counter kept glancing around and the cashier seemed to be emptying the cash register. It only took a second for him to realize what was happening. Gently, he took Erin's arm and turned her away from the pick-up entrance. "Take your phone out please," he whispered.

She realized something was going on but didn't question him as she took her phone out of her back pocket.

"Keep your back to the pick-up door and call 911. Tell them there's a robbery in progress and that there's a policeman on scene in plain clothes." He kissed her on the cheek and added "Stay here. I'll be right back." Then he headed out the front door.

As she dialed 911, she watched him go out and turn to go alongside the building toward the back. "Yes, my name is Erin. My boyfriend is a policeman and he said to tell you there's a robbery in progress at the CPK at Otay Ranch Town Center. He said to be sure and let the police know that there's a policeman on scene in plain clothes." She stopped and listened, then casually glanced toward the back entrance. "Yes, there's one person at the back pick-up counter. I can't tell if he's armed or not. He's got blond hair, about six foot, jeans, a gray hoodie and a plastic bag over his arm." Pausing again, she added, "There's a beige pickup truck outside in the pick-up area that appears to be waiting for him. One person inside... a male, is all I can tell."

Suddenly she heard two shots ring out and watched as the back window of the pickup truck disintegrated. The truck started to pull away, another shot rang out, the pickup veered sharply to the left, went up over the curb and slammed into the front of a car parked in the parking lot. The door of the pickup flew open, the driver came out, gun in hand and two more shots rang out.

The guy at the register had watched the whole thing and went into panic mode when his friend in the truck slid down the side of it. Scared, he ran around the counter and grabbed the girl on the other side.

While the guy was being distracted, Erin grabbed two menus from the hostess stand and carefully worked her way toward the pickup station. She was almost at the register when the guy noticed her, raised a gun and pointed it at her.

"Whoah!" She stopped in her tracks and eased the menus up in front of her. "Easy. I just came back to see what's going on."

"One more step and you'll definitely find out what's going on." He paused and glanced outside then back at her. He must have realized she would be a lot easier to get out the door since she was right in front of it. A second later, he shoved the cashier toward the kitchen so hard she lost her balance, stumbled and fell to the floor. Before Erin realized it, he was behind her and she had replaced the cashier as his hostage. He jabbed the gun into her side and started pushing her toward the door.

As they came outside, her eyes locked with Ray's. He was standing off to the side, looking for all the world like a confused restaurant patron who was on his way in to pick up his order. Ray winked at her and she winked back.

The robber looked around. When he saw no one but Ray, he eased the gun out of Erin's side and pointed it forward, along her hip. She looked down and it was sticking out in front of her enough that she was sure she could get a grip on the barrel. She could also feel his hand shaking badly against her hip. She winked at Ray again, grabbed the barrel with one hand, his hand with the other and pushed down on both with everything she had.

The gun went off, the robber let out a loud scream and a second later Ray was wrenching the gun out of his hand. Erin spun around, her knee came up between his legs, the robber let out another God-awful scream. As he hunched over, the gun flew into the garden, Ray came up with both hands locked together and scored a direct hit under his chin.

Somewhere during all that, the police must have arrived because the next thing she knew, he was handcuffed and being put in a police car parked by the curb.

"Wow!" Ray said as he wrapped her in his arms and kissed her forehead. "Remind me never to mess with you. I'm pretty sure

he blew at least three toes off when you pushed the gun barrel down."

She smiled at him. "It was your wink that did it. I could just hear you in my head saying… go for it!" Staring at him, she added, "I'm just glad he swapped me for that young girl inside. She was petrified and I wasn't sure what was going to happen if he'd dragged her out here."

They both gave statements to the police and the manager of CPK came out to thank them for saving the cashier. Included with his thanks was lunch on the restaurant.

An hour later they pulled up in front of his partner's house. The wife, with tears in her eyes, met them at the door and he introduced Erin. The wife apologized, telling them she'd had her husband cremated, so there would be no funeral, just a small get together. Ray said they understood and after they spent a proper amount of time socializing with everyone, they offered their condolences again and left.

"Wow, she's really torn up," Erin said as they made their way back to Ray's car.

"Yeah," he said. "They were only married for two years and hung all over each other every time you saw them. I suspect she'll move back to Ohio, where they were both from."

"What a shame," she added. She slipped her arm through his and pulled herself in tight. Neither of them said anything on the way back to her apartment, until he started to pull into a parking space. "Feel like a Coasterra Frita Rita Margarita fix?" she asked before he was all the way into the space.

Without answering he put the car in reverse and backed out. "I guess that's a 'yes'," she said, adding a chuckle.

"Not sure I want to know what a Frita Rita Margarita is. Sounds awfully 'girly' but I know they have Corona so, I'm okay." He turned, pulled her into a kiss, then headed for Bonita Road and the freeway.

No sooner had Ray and Erin left for the funeral when Teagan and Aoife were called in. "Sorry," the dispatcher told them. "Air Two's crew is stuck in Mexico. They ran down to Tijuana yesterday evening and there's some kind of ruckus at the border this morning and no one is allowed to cross till it gets cleared up. So, 'tag' you two are 'it' till they get back."

The two of them apologized to Chase and Maverick, changed into their uniforms, then headed for the airfield. No sooner had they settled in the crew lounge when the alarm call went off and the speaker announced, "Air One, traffic accident, San Ysidro DMV parking lot."

"Uh… someone didn't pass their driving test?" Aoife joked, as Teagan eased their helicopter into the air.

Twelve minutes later, they set Air One down in the blocked off street in front of the DMV office. Just inside the parking lot, two cars sat smoldering as San Diego Fire and Rescue loaded two people into ambulances and someone else lay on a gurney nearby. As soon as Aoife slid the back door open, two firemen pushed the gurney over and started loading the patient onto the shelf.

"Broken ribs, possible pierced lung and neck injury. The airbag smashed her purse into her chest and snapped her head back," one of the paramedics told Aoife. While Teagan relayed the information to Sharp Memorial, they locked the patient's stretcher into the shelf. "The other car belongs to a teenager who celebrated his passing his driving test by doing a wheelie. He lost control and slammed into her as she was going out."

Aoife shook her head, thanked the paramedics and slid the door shut. "Well, guess he passed his test, but I doubt he'll get his license anytime soon." She tended to the patient as Teagan eased up on the collective. Fifteen minutes later they set down on the heliport at Memorial and two waiting nurses eased their passenger's stretcher out.

***

On their return to the airfield, they both noticed Air Two sitting out on the tarmac in front of the hanger. "Well, looks like Air Two's crew made it out of Mexico," Aoife said. They logged in when they reached the office, where the dispatcher told them they were released from duty for the rest of the day.

"How about an early lunch?" Teagan suggested as they stowed their helmets in their lockers and headed for her truck.

"Sure," Aoife said, then suggested Romesco's.

Teagan cruised past the front of the restaurant, but all the parking spaces were taken. Finally, she found a space further down in the L-shaped shopping center. As they walked back toward the restaurant, they both noticed a parking enforcement officer ticketing cars parked in handicap spaces without either handicap plates or a placard. They both nodded to her, and Aoife said, "Glad to see they finally sent someone out here. It's getting so people think they can just park anywhere."

The officer smiled back at them. "You've no idea. I just started and I've already written out six tickets in this row alone. Three for handicap infractions, two for taking up two spaces and one for blocking a walkway. People think they can just park anywhere and anyway they want. Heaven forbid they should have to walk an extra few feet." The officer added, "Have a good day," then headed in the opposite direction from the restaurant. Three cars later, she shook her head and started writing out another ticket.

Teagan and Aoife smiled at each other. When they got to the end of the row, they turned right toward the restaurant. As they passed along the row in front of the restaurant they noticed the car in the handicap space right in front of the entrance, had a ticket on it. "Wow, she wasn't kidding, was she," Teagan said.

Before they could turn into the restaurant, the door opened and a woman came rushing out. "I don't believe you," the woman screamed at Teagan. "I just ran in to get my order and you give me a ticket?"

Teagan was quite sure the woman was yelling at someone else. Perhaps the officer had circled the lot and come back this way. But when she turned and looked behind her, there was no one even close. A second later, the woman was poking her in the back. "You... yeah, you. I can't believe you gave me a ticket."

Hearing a grunt, Teagan looked over toward Aoife, who had all she could do to stifle a laugh.

"What's so funny?" the woman said, turning her scorn on Aoife. "You two meter maids couldn't hold down a decent job if you had to. I'll bet neither one of you can even spell ticket." She glared at Aoife's name tag. "A O If-ee. What kind of a name is that? What the hell country are you from?"

"Ma'am, we're not parking officers... we're-" Aoife started to explain.

"Listen, I know a meter maid's uniform when I see one." She stared at Teagan's name tag. "Do I look stupid? Your name's Treagan and you work for Mercury Air Parking." She pulled the ticket out from under her windshield wiper and waved it in Teagan face. "Write 'Void' on it then sign under it," she demanded.

Teagan did as directed and handed the ticket back to the woman. She and Aoife watched as the woman got in her car, backed out and drove away. As her car turned onto Bonita Road, both of them burst out laughing. "Oh. My. God. I'd give a week's salary to be there when she turns that ticket in," Teagan said.

"Before I forget, remind me to ask Mercury Air Parking for one of those little three-wheel carts that seats two," Aoife said. "All the other meter maids have them. Why should Treagan and A O If-ee have to hoof it?

Arm in arm, still laughing, they marched into Romesco's.

Another week went by with surprisingly, only a few call outs. For Teagan and Aoife it was the usual traffic accidents, with a lost hiker and a gunshot victim from a party argument, in between. For Erin, she too had mostly auto accidents. Interspersed was a dog bite, a child with a frisbee dent in their forehead and a homeowner who tried to amputate his toes while cutting the hedges with sandals on.

Friday evening, they assembled at the airport early, bags packed and checked then settled in the boarding lounge. Erin turned to the group. "Ugh, another week of traffic accidents. I know air bags save lives, but I can't believe the number of broken noses and imbedded sunglasses they leave behind."

"Oh wait," Teagan said. "You have got to hear our meter maid story." Just as she started her story, the flight attendants walked up behind her. When she finished, everyone was laughing hysterically.

"I want to be an EMT when I grow up," one of the flight attendants said. "You guys always have such interesting stories."

"Ha. Be careful what you wish for. We deliberately leave the blood and guts stuff out," Aoife said.

"And the DUIs and druggies that are so sloshed or stoned they have no idea what planet they're on," Teagan tossed in.

"Oh, we get those on the flights too," one of the flight attendants said. "We've actually had to duct tape a few passengers to their seats." She paused, then one of the others added, "When I became a flight attendant, disobeying or putting your hands on one of us was a definite 'No No'. Now, it's like anything goes."

The boarding agent came over. "We're ready for all of you," she said.

It was pretty obvious that it hadn't taken long for the flight crews to get to know and adopt them. The flight attendants, Erin, Aoife and Teagan all locked arms and headed for the boarding ramp. Chase, Maverick and Ray following, while everyone in the boarding area watched, wondering why they got special treatment.

As agreed, they were spread out in the aircraft so they could report on their experience in each class. That put Teagan and Chase in Executive Club class, Aoife and Maverick in first class and Erin and Ray in coach. Once Erin and Ray were seated in the last row and the flight attendant had served each of them drinks, Ray turned to Erin. "I can't thank you enough for inviting me to join you." He looked around, then added, "I never thought being in the very last row would still feel like we're being treated with first class service, but it does."

"The flight attendants do treat us pretty special, but a good part of the service is simply what every other passenger experiences," Erin said. "The whole purpose is for us to evaluate the service everyone gets, in all three sections, and offer suggestions to add new things, and improvements… and let them know what they're doing right. I think you'll find BA's service is impeccable and most of our suggestions have been to add things to make it even better."

Ray smiled at her but then his smile faded as he stared at her. "Can I tell you something?"

"Sure," she answered.

"You have changed so much since school." After a long pause, he added, "You need to know that I love the relationship between you and the other women in your sisterhood. It's so much like what we develop in the Air Force... and the police force. The way we all have each other's back, watch out for each other, help each other with little to no questions asked. I see the same kind of camaraderie with all of you. You help each other, share the good times and are there for each other when things go south." He paused again. "I can also see the sense of fulfillment, worth and accomplishment when you save someone. That, and the dedication and leadership you've taught each other."

Erin was caught totally off guard. Ray was the first person ever to recognize what the sisterhood meant to her, to each of them. A tear rolled down her cheek and he pulled her in and kissed it away.

"You're all pretty special. You need to know that. When we first reconnected, I was afraid I'd have to compete with the other five of you, but I don't. I just need to remember how special they are and why... something I could never compete with. Well, not and win." He paused, just before kissing another tear away. "So, the one thing I hope for, is that all of your sisters adopt me too."

Staring at him, her smile grew, and her eyes brightened. "When the fuck did you become so smart? Especially when it comes to women?"

"When I saw you again and realized what I lost back then, what I don't ever want to take a chance on losing again."

"You keep that shit up and they'll be hauling us off this plane for indecent exposure. I'm already thinking of suggesting BA reserve a row of seats in each class for a 'Mile High Club' experience." She looked around and pointed up to the luggage compartment. "Let's see. Extra space between the rows, a heavy curtain up there, all around, for privacy and a little sound proofing. Retracting arms and fully reclining seats to form a bed."

"Uh, don't forget an in-flight-entertainment porn flick or two," Ray added. "You know… to get us in the mood."

Suddenly, Ray went quiet as Erin followed his eyes, and found herself looking into the eyes of a smiling flight attendant. "Has anyone told you you're both sick?" Abby, the flight attendant told them. "If you think being a flight attendant is hard now, just imagine trying to tell couples their time in 'The Play Room' is up and they need to vacate for the next couple or for the guy who wants to masturbate to the porn flicks? Hell, getting them out of the bathroom now is hard enough."

"Guess we scratch that suggestion?" Ray said.

"You think?" Abby added before strolling off giggling.

"Five minutes from now the whole plane is going to know about our suggestion," Erin whispered.

"They already do," came from the guy in the seat behind them.

***

Up front, Aoife and Maverick too were chatting with Belinda, one of the first-class flight attendants. "So, what do you do Maverick?" she asked him.

"Um… I'm responsible for a veggie production line – specializing in peas."

"You need to give yourself more credit," Aoife told him, adding a snicker. Turning to the attendant she added, "He does carrots and asparagus too."

"I see," said Belinda, glaring at both of them since she was sure they were putting her on. "Let me guess. You're really a spy with Her Majesty's Secret Veggie Service. Your name is Maverick Pea Bond. And…" pointing at Aoife she added, "She's Hollandaise Sauce Galore and you're headed to London to spear the Asparagus Gang that's terrorizing all of Europe."

They were all chuckling so much it was hard for any of them to say anything. Finally, Maverick composed himself enough to speak. "Oh, I love that. Maverick Pea Bond, much better than 'Pea Herder.' The name's Bond... Maverick Pea Bond." He pointed his finger like a gun barrel, then blowing smoke off of it, like it'd just been fired.

"Is he serious?" Belinda asked Aoife.

"Thanks to you... very," she said.

***

In the Executive Club Class, Teagan and Chase had settled in as Sarah, the flight attendant, came over with a beer for him and a glass of wine for her. Right behind her, a guy in jeans and a T-shirt started to push past her, almost causing her to spill Teagan's wine. Teagan grabbed the wine and held it away as Sarah almost landed in her lap.

Turning to glare at the guy, Teagan said, "That was pretty rude of you."

"Who the fuck are you?" the guy asked. "She's blocking the aisle and I need to get through... not that it's any of your business."

Chase stood up behind him and Teagan shook her head – *No.*

"Well, are you going to move your ass... or what?" the guy yelled at Sarah.

Abby, who had moved forward to help direct passengers, overheard him, picked up the flight attendant station phone and called forward. "Uh, I think we're going to need security back here. Sarah is dealing with a very unruly passenger."

Just as the guy reached out to shove Sarah, Chase grabbed his arm and pulled it back. The guy turned, intending to take a swing at Chase, as Teagan launched herself out of her seat. She grabbed his shoulder and shoved the guy into the empty seat on the other side of the aisle. Trying to hang onto his carry-on suitcase with one hand and block his fall with the other, he went over the seat arm and slid onto the floor. A second later an airport security guard arrived.

The security guard pulled the guy to his feet, spun him around and put handcuffs on him. No sooner had he snapped the second cuff shut when another passenger went off. "We're trying to get to our seat... you think maybe you could get out of the way?" the woman rudely said.

Turning to her, the guard shook his head. "Patience... or I'll be hauling you out of here next."

Trying to ease the situation, Sarah smiled, then told the woman, "It might be faster to go around us." She pointed toward the other aisle. Then mumbled, "It's going to be one of those flights," to no one in particular.

\*\*\*

Fortunately, there were no other incidents during boarding, or the flight, which landed right on time at Heathrow. Catching the hopper bus and check-in at the Skyline was a breeze. While the concierge had their luggage taken up to their rooms, Erin gave Ray a quick tour of the lobby, pub and restaurants on the first floor of the hotel, while Maverick and Aoife asked the concierge to call over to the Pheasant to see if they could get dinner reservations. Since they were early again, they had no problem getting a table at the Pheasant.

As they left the hotel to walk to the Pheasant, Ray held Erin back. "You're absolutely amazing. All of you. I thought you'd only been here once before, but it seems more like you live here. You know where everything is, where to go, and the hotel staff seems to know all of you."

Aoife, who was close enough to overhear him, slowed Maverick down to let Erin and Ray catch up. "You'll find its very easy to learn your way around in London. As for the hotel staff, British Airways is one of their biggest customers and since BA books our rooms, that's made us kind of royalty."

"I think being 'Yanks' helps make us stand out too… so we tend to get catered to," Erin added.

"Well, all I know is it feels like all of you are totally at home here."

By now they had caught up with Teagan and Chase. "Ha, wait till tomorrow morning's meeting at BA. Somehow, they think we walk on water," Teagan said.

Chase let out a chuckle. "Actually, they just know how to treat their customers. They appreciate the chance to get honest feedback on what they're doing right and some unbiased suggestions on what they can do to make their flights better."

"Well, all I know is, so far, this trip is nothing like what I expected, and you all have impressed the hell out of me." Then Ray added, "And we just got here."

Their table was waiting for them at the Pheasant and, once again, they were greeted like they owned the place. Ray just kept shaking his head. "I'm never going anywhere unless you guys are with me," he said.

"Well, I guess that counts out spending any *alone time* with him," Erin replied, adding a big grin.

"Oh crap. That backfired," Ray said.

The waitress, standing behind Erin asked, "Would you like me to shuffle him off to a separate table in the pub?" She paused. "Oh, wait, he'll not have any idea what chips or shepherd's pie or puddin' is. Perhaps one of you can order for him and I'll just deliver it… I suppose I'll have to teach him the proper fork to use too."

Ray was laughing so hard he couldn't think of a comeback. Finally, he got control of himself and laid his head on Erin's shoulder. "I know I'm the newbie and everyone is picking on me, but I'm loving every minute of it. And I've never felt so accepted."

"Good, then you won't mind us hiding in the corner while I teach you to read the menu and the proper use of a fork." Erin stood up, took his hand, and led him to a table back in the corner.

"Well, I suspect that'll be the last you'll be seeing of them tonight," the waitress told the rest of the table.

Over in the corner, Erin was instructing Ray in the proper English use of utensils. Fork in left hand, tines down, knife in right hand. Use the knife to help pile things onto the upside down fork.

At the main table, everyone was shaking their head, watching Ray, who was infatuated with Erin and obviously not hearing a word she was saying.

Dinner was fantastic as usual, with lots of tasty dishes. Ray let Erin order for him, then couldn't stop moaning over his steak and ale pie with 'proper' chips. His black and tan, a mixture of Guinness Stout and ale, was a perfect complement to it. When Erin topped it off with a sticky toffee pudding for them to share, she was sure Ray had creamed in his jeans. Wearing a giant smile she kissed him just before they got up from the table. "I'm not sure what was better, the meal or watching you love everything I ordered for you," she said.

After studying her for a moment, he pulled her in and kissed her. "I have never enjoyed a night like this in my entire life. While the meal was fantastic, it's your company that I'll always remember."

Returning his smile, Erin whispered in his ear, "If you're trying to get in my pants, you've succeeded. Now shut up and walk fast, before I have my way with you in the bushes out front."

"You're adorable," he replied as he steered her toward the stairs to the front door.

By now, the others had given up waiting for them and were likely in the hotel pub snickering and wondering if Ray and Erin would stop and get a room at the Marriott next door because they couldn't wait to get to the Skyline. "Ray is so different from Bailey," Teagan said.

"Yeah. I've never seen Erin laugh and carry on so much. Not to mention wearing bedroom eyes ever since we got off the plane," Aoife added.

Maverick looked over at Chase and let out a chuckle. "If he doesn't get any tonight, there's no hope for him."

"Fat chance. All he's got to do is lay there and Erin will do the rest," Teagan said, in the midst of a chuckle.

\*\*\*

As Erin and Ray exited the Pheasant, three obviously drunk guys staggered out of the back door of the pub. "Wasn't that the piss," one of them yelled as he shoved one of the others… right into Erin.

Wrapping his arms around her as she tried to keep from falling, Ray managed to keep her upright. "You okay?" he asked her.

She nodded just as the guy who crashed into her said, "Watch out where you're going …bitch!"

"Don't. He's not worth it," Erin told Ray as he released her and started toward the guy.

"Oh shit. Bloody Yanks!" one of the other guys said, then tried, unsuccessfully, to spit on Erin, who was closest to them.

She knew that did it and didn't even try to hold Ray back. Before the spit could drip off the guy's chin, he found himself on the ground. A second guy stepped forward and quickly joined his friend on the ground. "Next?" Ray asked the third.

Suddenly, a scream came out of the first guy. Ray looked down to find Erin's foot on his hand, blood oozing around the knife he had pulled out.

"You cut me... you fucking bitch," the guy yelled.

"Oh, I'm sorry. I meant to break your fingers." She stomped on his hand and he let out a blood curdling scream.

Just then, two policemen came through the parking lot. "You lot... again." One of them said to the trio.

"Guess they'll never learn," the other one added.

They both looked at Ray, who pointed at Erin. "I tried to tell them not to mess with her but... would they listen? Nope."

"You are so bad," Erin told Ray. Adding a kiss, she slid her arm through his and guided him toward the lane back to Bath Road and the hotel. "Come on. There's a spanking waiting for you!"

Ray turned with a big smile, raised his eyebrows, and waved at the policemen.

The next morning, they all met at the breakfast buffet, the giant smiles on Erin and Ray's faces impossible to miss.

After returning from the buffet with at least one of everything, Ray looked around the table. "What?" he asked,

"Nothing," Maverick answered, then turned to Aoife. "I think we should give each other matching hickeys like theirs. That way everyone will know you're mine and I'm yours."

"You been smoking asparagus again?" she asked.

The server who was just setting Chase's second glass of orange juice in front of him, started laughing so hard she dumped the whole thing in his lap. "I'm so sorry. I'll request another station… I can't deal with you lot without cracking up." Off she went, giggling like a fool.

Chase ran back to the room to change while everyone else finished their breakfast. He returned with an arm full of clothing, which he dropped off at the concierge's desk as they all headed for the BA van waiting outside.

As the van paused to turn onto Bath Road, Maverick glanced across the street at the two girls loitering near the bus stop. "They must catch the bus to work each morning. I remember seeing them on our last trip." He nodded toward the other side of the road.

Letting out a chuckle, Chase shook his head. "I'm pretty sure they're not waiting for the bus."

"Oh my God. I can't believe we didn't notice them before," Teagan said, just as the van turned onto Bath Road, then into the airport, headed for BA's Engineering offices. As they exited the van, Teagan pulled Aoife and Erin aside. "We need to get hold of Generate Hope and find out what we can do… who we can contact here to get those two girls off the street. They can't be much older than fourteen or fifteen."

Partially overhearing them, Chase asked, "What's going on?" Turning to him, she found Maverick and Ray next to him, all staring at her. "This is about the girls out there, isn't it?"

"Yeah," Teagan said. "We work with an organization called Generate Hope back in San Diego. They take in girls rescued from the sex trade and help them get their lives back. I… I can't believe we didn't notice those two girls out there. We need to do something to help them."

Maverick put his arm around Aoife. "Before you three run up and try to rescue them, you need to pay attention to the two sleazeballs in the parking lot just down the street from them. They look totally out of place and I'm pretty sure they're watching the girls to make sure they do what they're told and don't run off."

"Why didn't one of you say something the last time?" Teagan spit out, a lot more bitter than she had meant it to sound.

"You mean like… 'Hey honey, did you notice the two hookers over there?'" Chase said.

"I'm sorry, you're right. Neither of you knew about Generate Hope or our working with them. But now that you do, you need to know that we've got to do something to get those girls off the street."

Turning to Chase and Ray, Maverick told them, "I'm in. You two okay with a little side rescue mission?" Both of them nodded as the three women locked them in hugs.

"Thank you," Teagan said. "We need to know what to do with them once we rescue them, so wait till we call back and find out who here takes in girls that are rescued from the sex trade."

"I think asking our fire brigade friends might help?" Chase suggested, as they walked into the building and made their way to the conference room. They entered the room and took their seats around the table, while Chase headed directly for William. After a short conversation, William smiled and nodded, then took out his phone.

Everyone settled in and William asked Ray his name, then welcomed him after introducing his crew. While Chase's group went over their comments and suggestions from the flight, three members from the Heathrow Fire Brigade quietly slipped into the room and took seats at the end of the table.

As the meeting ended, William and Chase worked their way over to the fire brigade members. A minute later, the girls, along with Ray and Maverick, joined them as Chase explained about the young girls on Bath Road.

"Bloody hell. We've been here before and have got this," The brigade chief said, turning to the other two firefighters, one a man, the other a woman. "Same plan as last time?" he asked them. They both nodded in return and all three of them stood. "Brenda, you'll go pick up the girls, while Sean and I distract whoever's watching them?" Both Sean and Brenda nodded, then headed for the door.

Turning to Chase's group, the chief asked, "Care to ride along and have a bit of fun?" They all nodded. "Ladies, I suspect going to help Brenda with the girls would be best." Turning to the guys he added, "You three can come have some fun with the rest of us while we deal with the rubbish watching them."

Everyone made their way outside and a few minutes later the Giant Scania, Crew Cab, Domestic Pumper and the Land Rover Fire Tender pulled up in front of them. "Okay, gentlemen, you're in the Pumper and ladies, you're in the Rover," the chief told them.

"Can I swap with one of you?" Teagan asked, looking at Chase, Maverick and Ray. "I want a piece of them if the opportunity comes up."

"Sure." Ray climbed out of the Pumper's Crew Cab and into the Rover, then collected a kiss from Erin.

Both vehicles pulled out onto Bath Road, the Rover hanging back until the pumper turned into the car park where the two guys were smoking up a storm in their car. The giant pumper pulled right in front of their car, almost taking the car's front bumper with it; completely blocking their view of the two girls down the street.

Teagan, Sean and Chase jumped out. Teagan walked up to the driver's side window, while Sean and Chase headed for the passenger door. She waved the smoke pouring out of the window away and bent over slightly so she could see both passengers.

"What the fuck do ya think you be doin'?" The driver took another drag on the cigarette and blew the smoke directly at her.

She was sure they were both Eastern European: Dark hair, dark eyes, olive skin, tobacco-stained teeth, and the driver at least, a heavy Eastern European accent. Both were wearing put-on 'I dare you' grins, and she had to stifle a chuckle as she realized, the two of them together couldn't make half a set of teeth.

"You're in violation of fire code 6.19.003, smoking in a public car park…" she glanced into the car and noticed the driver's pants were open "… and civil code 44.69.7, masturbating in public." She opened the door and stepped back. "Out of the car… NOW."

"What'd they do… send you across the pond to watch me playing with meself?" the driver said. He flicked his cigarette butt at her, but missed, as he started out of the car. When he stood up, he reached for her, a brown toothy smile on his face.

No sooner was he clear of the door when her foot came up and scored a direct hit on his genitals. The smile disappeared, he grabbed his crotch and went down on his knees.

She looked down at the cigarette butt that had landed next to her. "Oh, mussn't litter." Her palm came up and smashed into the bridge of his nose. His head bounced back and hit the car door. He slumped forward, and her knee came up and slammed into his chin. "Sorry about that... I had a leg itch and was just trying to scratch it."

In the meantime, Chase and Sean were staring at the passenger, now on the ground on the other side of the car. Seems he'd accidently slipped and fallen while trying to get out of the car. Poor guy. His pants too were unzipped and apparently he'd been 'jerkin' his gherkin' (as Maverick would later explain) when they'd approached the car. Unfortunately, his gherkin had bent back and lost several layers of skin when he'd launched himself across the asphalt.

Teagan looked up, and Maverick, who was in the truck and watching Ray while the girls loaded the two sex-trafficked young women into the Rover, passed Ray's thumbs up on to her.

Certain that the two young women were safe, they all loaded back into the pumper, leaving the two guys lying in the car park moaning and clutching their privates. "The police and the folks from Refuge, an organization that helps sex-trafficked women, are waiting at the North Station for us," Sean told them. "Refuge will put the girls up and help them reclaim their lives. The police will take care of these two," he added, pointing as a police car, its blue lights flashing, passed them as they started back into the airport.

*\*\*\**

Two women from Refuge thanked them, then escorted the young girls out of the fire station's conference room, while a third stayed behind. The next hour was spent with her and the fire chief explaining that the hotels along Bath Road were a common place for sex trafficking. "We try and keep a watch out but as fast as we rescue them, there's more behind them."

"By the way, thank you for helping rescue these two," the woman from Rescue said. "Most visitors just walk right past, and even if they do notice, they want nothing to do with it." She smiled and added, "Thank you also for working with our organizations to help these young women. I met several members from your Generate Hope organization while I was at a conference on trafficking in New York last year. One of the things that surprised all of us was how coordinated trafficking is between countries. It seems that trading young women from one country to another is becoming quite common."

"Are you serious?" Maverick asked.

"Quite. It's becoming an 'on-line order a sex slave from whatever country you like.' Accents, along with physical traits, are on the order check list… right along with age, eye and hair color, skin tone, height, weight and build.

"While we've not worked with Generate Hope directly, we do work with several agencies in New York City and up and down your East Coast," she added. "It seems English girls are very popular on your side of the pond, while Hispanic woman are considered exotic and desirable here and in Western Europe.

"I should let you go. Thank you again and I hope you enjoy the rest of your stay." She shook hands with each of them, nodded at the chief, then turned and left.

The chief, Brenda and Sean added their thanks and the chief asked if they wanted him to call for the van.

It'd been a crazy morning. Nothing like they'd expected.

"Well, everyone still up for some sightseeing?" Maverick asked. They all nodded. "Good, I was looking at the tube map and what would everyone say to catching the water taxi over to Greenwich. There's lots to do over there and it'll help get our mind off of this morning's events. Plus, we can walk over to the terminal and catch the tube from here." They thanked the chief and walked the short distance over to Terminal 5 to catch the tube.

***

As they came up the stairs at the Westminster Station, Ray said, "I'm getting hungry. Anyone else?"

Remembering their last trip, Aoife pointed to the other side of the small park next to the tube station. "There's a pub right over there. The one we ate at the last time."

"Is everyone okay with waiting till we get to Greenwich? I'd like to see if we can find something with a patio on or near the river," Erin asked.

Everyone nodded and they walked over to the quay and down the ramp to the water taxi. Twenty-five minutes later, the boat tied off at the dock in Greenwich.

Before they even stepped onto the dock, Ray pointed and yelled, "Holly shit… that's the *Cutty Sark*. The real one!"

"Uh, you were expecting a fake one?" Erin asked, adding a chuckle.

"Cheeky wench!" he came back with. Then added a kiss so she was sure he was only kidding with her.

"Ah, how quickly he's turned into a Brit!" Aoife said.

As they stepped up onto the quay, Teagan pointed over toward the *Cutty Sark*. "There's the Cutty Sark Tavern, according to the review on the map they serve British food and have a great view of the river."

"Works for me, but only if it's the *real* Cutty Sark Tavern," Ray said, as everyone shook their head, collected their mate and headed for the ship and tavern. Once they were settled at a table overlooking the river, it was black and tans all around. Sticking with British fare, they shared three orders of fish and chips and three orders of shepherd's pie. That was followed by sticky toffee and bread pudding with whiskey sauce for dessert.

Lunch finished, they wandered over to the ticket booth, purchased tickets, then went onto the *Cutty Sark*. As they strolled through the ship, they learned she had been built in Scotland in 1869. Her prime duty was to transport supplies to England and she was one of the fastest and last 'tea clippers' to be built: Tea because her cargo was often tea from the far east and Clipper because of her speed.

Another hour and a half of admiring the ship's fantastic woodwork, sleek design, and history, then they disembarked, turned and headed for Greenwich Park, The National Maritime Museum, The Royal Observatory and Queen's House.

After taking in each of the sites, they walked around to the side of the Royal Observatory where the Greenwich Mean Line was embedded in the side of the building. They each took turns spanning it with their partner while the others took pictures. Finally, they commandeered a passing couple and begged them to take their picture as one couple kneeled, the second crouched behind them and the third stood against the wall, all three couples spanning the line.

"We just stood on opposite sides of the Greenwich Mean Line, on opposite sides of the globe, each of us in a different hemisphere. That is so cool. How many people get to do that?" Aoife said afterward, a giant smile on her face.

From there, they wandered back to the dock and caught the next water taxi back into London proper. Exiting at Westminster, they walked over to the tube station, then made their way back to the Skyline. As had become habit, they congregated in the pub after quick stops in their rooms to freshen up.

"I've booked us on tomorrow morning's tour to Leeds Castle, Canterbury and the Cliffs of Dover," Teagan said. "Hope that's okay with everyone."

"Oh my God. I remember our mom's telling us about going to Canterbury on their honeymoon and how much they loved it. They said it's like a fairytale village, especially at Christmas time." Aoife paused, trying to remember something. "Oh, they raved about the cathedral, and its history. So, we have to be sure and take that in while we're there."

Erin kept nodding. "Yeah, my mom said it was one of her favorite places." After adding a chuckle, she said, "Of course, by the time they got back, every place was her favorite."

"To Canterbury," Maverick toasted.

"To Canterbury," everyone added raising their glasses.

"I gather you'll be going to Canterbury," the barmaid said. "Tis one of my favorite places and you'll all be loving it. It has such a fascinating history, especially the cathedral you've just mentioned."

"Care to join us... Belinda?" Teagan asked, after taking note of her name tag.

"I'd love to but I'm afraid I'm scheduled to work tomorrow. Perhaps another time." Then she headed off to wait on another patron.

Just as Teagan started to go over the brochures on tomorrow's tour that she'd grabbed from the rack, a ruckus broke out at the other end of the bar. They all turned just in time to see a guy reach over the bar, trying to grab Belinda. "That's the sleazeball I kicked in the nuts this morning," Teagan said. Leaning back to see the guy behind him, she added, "And his partner, sleazeball number two." Before she finished, all six of them were headed to rescue Belinda.

Teagan arrived first, just as sleazeball number one turned and saw her. "You!" he said, as she got right up in his face.

"Hey. You recognized me. I'm flattered!" she said, as her knee came up and nailed him right in the crotch… again. "Never learn… do you?" She stepped back.

Moaning, he bent over, then dropped to his knees, holding his privates. That was Teagan's signal to let him have it again. The side of her hand slammed into the bridge of his nose. His head bounced off a bar stool leg and he face planted into the floor. "You're absolutely no fun. I'd love to try some new moves on you, but you keep setting yourself up for the same stuff."

By now, sleazeball number two had turned to head for the door but ran smack into Maverick's chest. "Oh…  I'm sorry. Am I blocking your pathway?" Maverick asked. That earned him a smile with every other rotting tooth stump leaking drool down the guy's chin. "Yep, definitely need a dentist." His fist collided with the guy's mouth. Maverick stepped aside and watched sleazeball two face plant next to his buddy.

Someone had obviously called the police as two Bobbies came into the pub. They immediately scraped the two sleazeballs up off the floor. "Never can take a bloody hint, can we?" one of the Bobbies told the two guys. Turning to Maverick, who was closest, he added, "We've jailed these two enough times they should own a cell in our lockup."

The excitement over, everyone turned and started back for their table on the other side of the bar. Suddenly, one of the policemen yelled "Watch out," as the man he'd been leading to the door, slashed him with a knife, broke free and headed for Teagan. Maverick was the first to realize what was happening and intercepted him just before he reached Teagan. The man slashed Maverick's arm, then stabbed him in the chest. Teagan turned to see what the noise was all about, just as the guy pulled the knife out of Maverick and imbedded it in her shoulder.

Teagan's moan reached Chase's ears as he and Ray doubled back. "Teag! Are you okay?" he yelled as he wrapped her in his arms.

At the same time, Ray grabbed the guy's wrist, before he had a chance to stab Teagan again. That was followed by a bone crushing punch to the guy's face, then a loud snap as Ray slid the guy's arm up his back and over the back of his head.

Chase wrapped his arms around Teagan, eased both of them to the floor and pulled her into his lap just as Erin and Aoife reached them.

Aoife felt panic setting in, but her training took over. "We need towels over here," she yelled as she helped Maverick down next to Teagan and held her hand against his chest wound, while Erin did the same with Teagan's shoulder. Belinda appeared with a hand full of bar towels and handed half the pile to each of them.

"You better not die on me," Aoife whispered to Maverick.

He looked up and smiled at her, then let out a wheezy groan. "Oh, that hurts... I've no plans on dying... but my plan to ravish you will have to wait," he managed to squeak out. That was followed by another sickening wheeze, as he tried to breathe in.

"I don't want to die," Teagan told Chase.

"We're not going to let either of you die," he answered, and bent towards her.

"Good," she said and tried to reach up with her injured arm to pull him in for a kiss. "Ow! Ow! Ow! Shit, that hurts."

"Uh, can we... hold the noise down over there..." Maverick managed to wheeze out, and even add a chuckle.

While the girls tried to stop the bleeding, Belinda called 999 and told them several people were injured and they needed at least two ambulances to the pub at the Skyline.

When the second guy had broken lose, the first policeman had handcuffed the first guy to the door pull at the pub's entrance and called for ambulances. So, moments later, true to their three-minute response time, the airport fire brigade rushed through the door. As soon as the chief realized who was involved, he directed the EMTs to tend to Maverick and Teagan while his firefighters looked after the guy out cold on the floor.

The EMT tending to Maverick looked up at Aoife. "He's wheezing and I think his lung's been nicked. We need to get him to hospital right away."

As they loaded both Maverick and Teagan onto gurneys, the brigade chief came over. "I've just called them into West Middlesex University Hospital," he told the EMTs. "My team will escort you there. The two under arrest can wait."

Out front, they loaded Teagan, into one ambulance, with Erin riding with her, and Maverick into the second, with Aoife riding with him. Chase and Ray both climbed into the fire brigade Range Rover that would escort the two ambulances.

# Chapter 30 – What do You Mean, no Ugly Babies?

The hospital ER staff met the ambulances at the Emergency Department entrance. While the ER nurses settled Maverick and Teagan into beds so they could assess them, Aoife and Erin called back to the states. Erin called Teagan's parents, Leigh and James, while Aoife called Maverick's parents. Both got the same response: "They've been hurt? Are they okay?" Based on their experience as EMTs, Erin and Aoife assured the parents that they were sure Maverick and Teagan would be fine and promised to keep everyone updated as they knew more.

Joining Ray and Chase in the waiting room, both found themselves wrapped in their arms as the tears finally let loose. "Oh my God. I can't believe this is happening," Aoife whispered.

"They'll both be fine... I'm sure of it," Chase replied, pulling Aoife in as close as he could.

"I'm really worried about Maverick," she said. "Teag too, but I'm pretty sure he just stabbed her in the shoulder muscle. That means she'll need stiches and be really sore but will heal quickly. With Maverick, the way he was wheezing, I'm worried that his lung was punctured, that he'll need surgery."

The next hour was spent downing coffee, chewing fingernails and pacing the floor of the waiting room.

Finally, the doctor stepped into the room wearing a big smile. Two words and they knew he was an American. "Before I say anything else, you need to know, they'll both be fine." They all locked themselves in a big hug as he went on. "Teagan's wound punctured only the muscle and missed any critical stuff like veins or arteries. We've stitched her arm up and, other than a scar to brag about and her arm being very sore, she'll be good as new in a few weeks."

He paused and his smile grew. "Maverick is one very lucky chap. The tip of the knife just nicked his right lung. The body, being the amazing thing that it is, has already sealed the tiny hole. So, they'll be no need for surgery. Like with Teagan, the knife missed anything critical. Unlike Teagan, he'll be out of action for at least a month."

"Thank heaven," Aoife whispered. "The peas will just have to get along without him." The doctor's face scrunched up with a definite 'Huh' look.

Pulling out her phone, she took a deep breath, tried to calm her nerves and walked into the hallway to get some privacy. She dialed Maverick's parents to let them know he was okay but would be a while recovering. After she explained what the doctor had told them, they asked if she would stay with him in London till he could travel. Without giving it a thought, she replied, "Of course." *Oh boy. I can't believe I just told them that*, she thought, as she walked back into the waiting room. Then realized, *promise or no promise, I'd never leave him here alone, even if I can't get time get time off. Now, I need to tell everyone I'm staying.*

Erin took care of any concern as she smiled at Aoife and announced, "We talked it over and we're all staying in London till they're both healed and it's safe for them to travel." Aoife's mouth dropped open and she stared at Erin. "We discussed it while you were calling his parents and we called Leigh back. There is no way we're letting them travel till they're healed," Erin insisted. "Nor are we leaving them here by themselves."

"You okay?" Ray asked Aoife.

"Yeah... I just can't believe you're all doing this."

"Ha." Erin said. "You thought we were going to leave the four of you to mess around and run all over England while Ray and I went back and tried to explain to everybody how we let Maverick and Teagan get stabbed? Fat chance. Oh, and before I forget, as soon as the doctor says they can travel, we're getting tickets on the train through the Chunnel to Paris... Our present to all of us for them only getting themselves maimed and not killed."

The doctor, who they all had forgotten about was still standing there, shaking his head. "You're all crazy... Oh, I forgot to tell you because of the damp weather here in England I need to add another two weeks to their recovery. I strongly suggest you let them rest for the next two weeks, then, after Paris, take them to Ireland, have them kiss the Blarney Stone and stop at the Guinness Factory. That will definitely hasten their recovery."

"Got it," Aoife said. "We were supposed to do Canterbury and Leeds Castle tomorrow. I suppose that's out?"

The doctor shook his head in agreement. "Like I said, two weeks. Then, two wheelchairs, a good English breakfast and a stop in a pub for Black and Tans if they look like they're getting tired." Pausing he added, "Do you need a note?"

"Uh, yes, but please leave the side trips to Paris, Ireland and the Black and Tans out," Ray said. "On second thought, let's skip the note."

*** 

Four hours later, the hospital released both of them and two nurses wheeled them out in wheelchairs. Waiting out front was the Range Rover, the fire brigade chief and William from BA standing next to it. "I've already contacted your employers, told them what happened, that Britain considers you all heroes and that you'll be staying till both of you recover. I've also arranged with the hotel to move you to business suites and explained that BA will be paying for your rooms till it's safe for you to travel back to the states," William explained.

Fifteen minutes later they walked and were pushed into the lobby of the Skyline to a round of applause from the staff and guests alike. Belinda ran up and gently hugged first Maverick, then Teagan. "Thank you for rescuing me," she declared. "We've a late dinner all set up for you in the pub," she added as she took over Teagan's wheelchair and steered her toward the pub, everyone else following.

As soon as they were settled, Erin called Maverick and Teagan's parents again. This time to confirm that they were both fine and out of the hospital. Maverick's parents thanked her again. But when she told Teagan's parents that they would be staying... for uh... six weeks... maybe longer... Leigh let out a big laugh. "I knew it," she said. You guys are going to milk this for all it's worth, aren't you?"

"Uh, we're just following doctor's orders," Erin explained. "He's ordered us to Ireland and Paris too, so that's why the six weeks."

"Is Teag there?" Leigh asked, trying to choke down another bout of laughter.

Erin looked at the other end of the table. "Uh yeah, but she's busy swapping spit with Chase and can't talk right now."

"Okay," was followed by another snicker. "Tell her just to be careful. We don't want to be stuck raising any ugly babies. You all be careful too. We love you and have fun recovering."

Erin hung up to the sound of laughing from the other end, while staring at the phone. *Ugly babies? Chase and Teag? Ha. Those two would have to guard their babies in the maternity ward. Come to think of it, Ray and I wouldn't do too bad in the cute baby department either. Neither would Aoife and Maverick.* She thought back to all five of the sisters playing together at the ranch and teasing poor Fae. *Maybe she meant unruly, not ugly. Yup, that would have been us. Maybe that's why Fae wants to be a tanker pilot; her chance at revenge by doing a water strafing run on us.*

***

"Earth to Erin!"

"Huh?"

"Are you okay over there?" Teagan asked.

"Uh… yeah."

"What did Mom say? Is she okay with us staying?"

"Yeah, she said just don't have any ugly babies."

Teagan just stared at her.

"You had to be there," Erin finally added.

"I am here and… uh, never mind." Teagan shook her head.

Everyone's attention turned to the other end of the table, where Aoife, in Maverick's lap, had her arms around his neck, her head on his shoulder and tears running down her cheeks. "You okay down there?" Chase asked.

"I almost lost him," Aoife said, just above a whisper. She lifted her head and kissed Maverick. "I… I'm not letting you out of my sight. I'm in charge of bathing you and kissing your stiches to make sure you heal right." She paused and smiled at him. "I promised the peas I'd take care of you, so you're mine till I tell you otherwise."

Returning her smile, he said, "I'm kind of a slow healer so I hope you're free for… a lot of years."

"I'm not free but I'm reasonable." She added a kiss and as soon as she leaned back, she realized everyone was smiling at them. Things were getting serious with Maverick, between all of the couples, actually. Two of them had almost lost a partner and today had been a wakeup call. Was she ready for this? Maverick was a lot of fun. He was smart, his feelings for her ran deep and he wasn't afraid to show them. Of everyone, he had the craziest, most useless job, some would say. Yet he took it seriously. He truly believed his lot in life was to protect the peas… asparagus and carrots too, if called on. As silly as that might seem to anyone else, she loved him for his dedication to them. That made her as crazy as he was. Which was likely why they got along so well. Yip, 'Helicopter Pea Princess', that was her. Kind of like a Helicopter Mom, looming over her veggie kids.

She could feel her smile growing as she looked up and locked eyes with Teagan. Oh God, Teag knew exactly what she was thinking. She turned and Erin was also smiling at her. She knew too. *Wow. Talk about three peas in a pod. Oh God. I've gone totally berserk and taken my two sisters with me.* She mouthed, "We need to talk," and both Erin and Teagan nodded.

*** 

As soon as they'd all finished eating, the three women stood. Erin looked around the table and announced, "We girls need to have a conference. We'll be out by the pool bar, so you three please find someplace else if it's too early for bed."

"I'm going to go up and rest," Maverick announced.

"You want me to help you upstairs?" Aoife asked him.

"Would you, please?"

As soon as the elevator doors closed, he wrapped her in his arms. "I really can make it on my own, but I needed to tell you that I love you." He kissed her just as they arrived on their floor. They stepped out and he turned her so he could look right into her eyes. "I'm not sure what this *girls' conference* is about, but I suspect it has something to do with me... actually all three of us. So, I just want you to know. I was pretty sure I was falling in love with you before we ever left Coasterra. Now that we've spent time together, there's no doubt in my mind that I want you in my life... long term."

She realized he was trying to leave her an out, in case she was going to break his heart and dump him. "Relax, big guy. We're good - more than good. Go warm up the sheets and we'll talk more when I get back up." She punched the elevator button, gave him a kiss, then stepped inside when the doors opened. The smile and wink that followed told him he was probably not going to get a lot of sleep after she got back.

Ray and Chase headed for a high-top table in the pub, while the girls hijacked a table near the pool bar. After the server set two Black and Tans down and a glass of water for Teagan,

Teagan held up her glass. "Being on medication and not being able to have a drink sucks! But... here's to all of us being alive and, falling in love, which I'm pretty sure is the topic de jour." The girls tapped glasses to toast them all being on the same page. "You're up, Aoife, since this is your meeting," Teagan added.

"I don't know why I even need to say anything. The three of us - actually the six of us sisters - know each other so well, we may as well be a sixtet."

"I think you mean sextuplets," Teagan said.

"Whatever. All I know is I'm falling more in love with Maverick every day. Then when he got hurt, I promised myself that I would tell him I want him in my life, forever. That will happen when I get back upstairs... well, the first time we come up for air... while I tend to his wounds... and other parts."

"Cute. Believe me, I understand," Teagan said. "When I was laying there and Chase was trying to stop the bleeding, I looked up and his eyes told me I was the most important thing in his life. And he in mine. Then he whispered, 'Don't you dare die. I've a whole life I plan on spending with you, if you'll have me.'" She looked at each of them. "Ha, if I'll have him? How could I not want the most caring and unselfish guy in the world? The guy who knew how close all of us were and made sure my two sisters, and their boyfriends, could come with us every time we come to England. The guy who stands me up in front of British Airways, claiming I'm much smarter than anyone he knows. Me! The one who hauls around two prone passengers on DUI Airlines, while you two get to play Betsy Ross, Patch-um-up, flight attendants. Us, the one's he brags to BA about. Us, who get to clean up the barf with a garden hose so we're ready for the next merit badge run."

By now the three of them were giggling uncontrollably. Finally, Erin caught her breath. "Remind me to tell Mercy Air to never let you do the recruiting videos."

She took another deep breath. "My turn?" Erin asked. "I know Ray seems like the new guy in town but really, he and I go way back. Maybe that's a good thing… along with what happened with Bailey. All I know is Ray ranks right up there with Chase and Maverick now. Who he is today is so different from the Ray that dumped me at the prom. He's kind, considerate and he treats me like I'm the prettiest girl in the world and walk on water. That last part actually had me worried, but I think he's realized he can't put me on a pedestal. I am who I am and he lets me know he loves who I am."

She let out a snort and took another deep breath, since she still wasn't quite done laughing. "Sorry, that's a lot of 'who I am's.'" She stopped and looked at both of them. "You know what? What's most important, other than my feelings for him? Chase and Maverick both like him. The three of them are so alike. I watch Chase and Maverick watch him, watch the way he treats me. Watch how different he treats me compared to Bailey." She stopped and her smile grew. "Oops, I forgot to mention; he's the most caring and tender person I've ever slept with. He feels me out…" Teagan let out a big snort… "out, not up… you sick-minded sister," she told Teagan. That sent all of them into another bout of giggles.

"Okay, so I think it's fair to say we're all in love," Aoife said. "I just wanted to make sure what I was seeing was how you both felt."

"Phew! Here I thought you were going suggest a six way," Erin said.

"Nope, there will be no sextuplet… uh, triplet-twin packs? Whatever. I'm not sharing Maverick with any of you."

The three of them finished their drinks, hugged, locked arms, and still chuckling, headed for the lobby. A final hug and Aoife turned for the elevator while Teagan and Erin wandered into the pub.

Aoife came into the room and found Maverick sprawled on the bed, sound asleep with a blanket wrapped around him. As she eased the door closed, his eyes partly opened and he smiled at her. "I'm sorry. I tried to stay awake," he said as she sat down next to him and kissed his forehead.

"That's okay. You've had a rough day." Lifting the blanket, she peeked under it. Other than his jockey shorts, he was naked. Her eyes and hand went to the stiches in his chest. "I'm so sorry you got stabbed but I need to tell you; I'm so proud of you for saving Belinda. He obviously was about to go off on her when you jumped in."

Maverick looked up at her and a big smile formed. "I'm just glad it was me that got stabbed and not her. I'm really sorry about Teagan too. I should have just broken both of his arms to begin with… before he could hurt anyone."

"I think you did everything you could. It all happened so fast none of us realized what was happening till it was too late." She looked down and he was staring at her. "What?"

"I… I'm worried about my job," he confessed.

"BA called your employer, explained everything and even told them you're a hero in the eyes of everyone here."

"Like that's going to do a lot. They couldn't care less, Eff. They need someone to monitor the production line, that's all they care about. I've already stretched things to the limit with the trip here." His smile faded and she realized he was right. He was replaceable and there was no way they were going to hold his job open.

She stood up, slipped out of her clothes, then slid in next to him. Another kiss to his stitches before she wrapped him up in her arms. "Let's not worry about it right now. Tomorrow we can bring it up with the group and see if we can come up with something." She gently pulled him in tight, as they both fell asleep.

\*\*\*

The following morning, they all headed for the breakfast buffet. Teagan and Chase rode down in the elevator with Aoife and Maverick. Teagan stepped out of the elevator, Chase behind her, turned and headed toward the bathrooms. "Be right back," Aoife said, as she followed Chase, hoping that no one would notice as she followed him into the men's room.

"Uh, I think you're in the wrong room," he said, holding the door open for her.

"I need to talk to you… in private."

He smiled. "Okay if I go to the bathroom first?"

"Sure." She added a smile. "I'm going to use one of the stalls. Be right back."

After she came out and as they both washed their hands at the sinks, she explained. "Mav is worried about losing his job. As a matter of fact, he's pretty sure they've already replaced him. They just haven't told him yet."

"That's why the two of you look like your puppy ran away."

"Chase, is there anything you can do to help? Any suggestions?"

"I've got an idea," he said as they stepped out. He turned toward the pool area and pulled his phone out. "Go get breakfast. I'll be there in just a minute."

Once everyone had gone through the buffet line, filled their plates and returned to the table, Erin looked over at Maverick, then Aoife. "You two okay?"

Before either of them had a chance to say anything, Chase came in. "I just had a chat with my boss. BA called him and we all need to talk, after I get brekky."

"Brekky?" Teagan asked, but she seemed to be the only one that picked up on it.

When Chase settled back at the table, he looked around at each of them, then explained. "BA told my boss they had accepted most of our suggestions. That means we'll need to design several new seats and rearrange the configuration for each class. They also explained what happened, and since we're stuck here..." he smiled at Teagan and Maverick... "they told him we could start working on the new seat designs and layouts with BA while we're here."

Pausing, he turned and stared at Maverick. "I told my boss I'd need a project coordinator. Then I mentioned you, how well you got along and worked with the BA team. So I suggested we ask you to come work for us and he told me to make you an offer."

No one was sure who was happier: Maverick, Aoife, or Teagan. They all were smiling so much it looked painful.

"Well? What do you say?" he asked Maverick. "Would you like to come work for us?"

"Of course he would!" Aoife answered for him, then looked at Maverick. "Right?"

"Uh, that means I need to leave my children," he replied.

"It's the peas or me!"

"When do I start?" Maverick turned and asked Chase.

"You just did." Chase shook his head and snickered.

"I can't believe you did that," Teagan whispered to Chase, then pulled him into a long kiss.

Aoife stared at Chase, then mouthed, "Thank you so much." She pulled Maverick into a big hug. "Congratulations."

His eyes narrowed and he smiled at her. *He knew. He knew she had talked to Chase. Oh God, I hope he's okay with what I did.*

Reading the concern on her face, Maverick's smile grew, he kissed her and said, "Thank you."

"To Maverick's new job." Ray held up his orange juice glass.

Everyone toasted with their OJ, V8 or water glasses.

Toast over, Chase looked around the table. "That's the good news."

"The good news?" Erin asked. "That makes it sound like there's some not so good news?"

"BA wants a coordination meeting next Monday morning… assuming Mav is cleared by the doctor."

"What do you mean Maverick is cleared? What about me?" Teagan asked.

"Well, that's the other part. You three ladies will not be attending the BA meetings. The fire brigade called back to Mercy Air and Bonita Fire and the three of you are now designated as 'San Diego's International Fire and Emergency Coordination Team'. So while we're meeting with BA, you'll be meeting with the Heathrow Fire Brigade."

"To do what?" Aoife asked.

"Search me. You're the fire people, not me… I mean us," Chase replied.

"What about Paris and Ireland?" Erin asked.

"Last I looked they were both still there. I'll check when I get a chance." Chase added a big grin.

"You are so going to die!" Teagan replied, then turned to Aoife and Erin. "We need to borrow a chopper and work on our course for deep-sea rescue merit badges… and I've just the three dummies to throw into the ocean."

"Hey, what did I do?" Ray asked.

Erin smiled. "Guilt by association. There's also three of us so we need three of you to throw in the ocean to practice with."

"Uh, who drives the chopper while you're all rescuing us?" Chase asked.

"It's on autopilot," Teagan answered.

"Oh, that's comforting. Can we do this close to shore… like on the beach maybe?" Chase added.

"No. It's an ocean, deep-sea rescue badge course, not a beach rescue badge course. Besides, the beach would leave sand burns. Plus, if we go out far enough, we'll attract sharks and can do our shark rescue badge course too," Teagan added.

"Oh joy," Ray said, as Erin wrapped an arm around his waist and pulled him into a kiss.

"Okay, I assume the four of you are going to lounge around today while Teagan and Maverick heal. So is it okay if Ray and I go off on our own? I was thinking I'd take him to see Salisbury Cathedral, Stonehenge and Bath. It's only about three hours and you've all seen everything." She stopped and looked at everyone. "We can stay here if you'd like."

"No way!" Aoife said. "We're just going to go lounge around by the pool and, like you said, we've already been there. You two go and enjoy yourselves." She stopped and a big smile formed. "Almost forgot. You need to bring back three dozen Bath buns. A dozen for us and two dozen for the hotel staff."

# Chapter 32 – Funny Ghosts

While Erin and Ray headed for the front lobby to book their tour, the other four went into the pool area. Maverick wasted no time in thanking Aoife and Chase. "I know you talked to Chase, and I really appreciate it," he said to Aoife. Turning to Chase, he thanked him too.

"Actually, the timing worked out well for both of us. I really do need a project coordinator and, honestly, I think you're perfect for the job," Chase replied. "Aoife just beat me by asking if I could do anything to help, but I was already thinking of asking you. So, I hope you're not mad at her, or me. And, just so you know, BA also mentioned that you'd impressed them and hinted that they'd be pleased if I brought you onto the team."

Maverick locked his arms around Aoife and pulled her in tight. "I could never be mad at her. She knew that taking the time off to come on this trip would put my job at risk and so did I. But I'd already made up my mind; if it was my job or her, it was a 'no contest'. There's plenty of jobs out there, but there's only one Aoife."

"Aw, thanks," Aoife, who was now sitting in his lap, said, "You just melted my panties."

"Eww. Back to the room you two," Teagan told them. Then she turned serious. "Change of subject. We need to start thinking about this Fire and Emergency Coordination stuff."

Jumping in, Aoife said, "I'm at a loss for even where to start. How about if we work up a list of questions, then schedule a meeting before the weekend with the Fire Brigade? That will give us the weekend to work up something for the meeting on Monday"

"Can we help?" Chase asked.

Both Teagan and Aiofe nodded.

"I can help. I've done lots of pea rescues," Maverick added.

"I am so glad you've got a new job." Aiofe stopped. "You know what? Seriously, I'll bet there are lots of things about the hazards of working around machinery that you can help us with. I would think the fire brigade here at the airport runs into that a lot."

"Be right back," Chase said, as he jumped up and ran out into the lobby. A few minutes later he was back with a pad and pencil. "Okay. Dealing with hazards of working around machinery. What else?"

"Well, what about clearing the landing space for us? Remember that stupid reporter who drove right under us and almost tipped us over. If I hadn't seen her at the last minute, we would have come down right on her roof," Teagan explained.

"Having someone clear the landing space and keep it clear?" Chase asked, then added it when Teagan and Aoife nodded. He paused, then asked, "Isn't that pretty obvious? I mean if I knew you had to land to pick up someone injured in an accident, I'd make sure we cleared a place for you to land."

"I know you would," Teagan said, then added, "But do you know how much space… clearance we need? Plus, if you, and everyone else, is busy dealing with the accident, traffic and looky loos, chances are no one is concerned with keeping our landing space clear, at least not until we get there. Maybe, not even then. My point is, you need to assign someone to specifically make sure our landing space is clear and keep it clear. If not, they get busy and we're either delayed or can't get in at all."

"Got it. Assign someone to be responsible for the landing site," a very proud Chase added.

Leaning over, Teagan gave him a kiss. "A lot of this may seem stupid, things everyone obviously knows or is just plain common sense. But, you need to remember, accident scenes are typically chaos and panic situations. People running all over shouting and sometimes, even being shot at. So what we need to come up with are things you need to do to make sure things go smoothly. So that everyone knows what they need to do and who's assigned to do what."

Looking back at her, Chase's smile grew even bigger. "Doesn't that go for any scene, not just the ones Mercy Air is called out to?"

"Actually, yes, it does," Aoife added. "For us, it's critical that we have a clear landing spot, but you're right: maintaining calm and preassigning things at any accident scene is important. For example, making sure the first fire trucks arriving block off the scene with their trucks."

312

"Got it," Chase said, his smile growing again. He was totally enjoying this. Suddenly, his eyes grew large. He looked at Teagan and started scribbling. A moment later he added, "I remember Erin saying something about the fire truck always going first on the way to a scene. She said that's because the fire engine is big and bright red and people get out of their way, while the ambulance is smaller and might not be seen."

"Very good," Teagan replied. "But not all fire engines are red. They can be green, dark red, white or even orange; usually a bright color though, so they easily stand out and can be seen."

Maverick wildly waved his hand while Chase captured all that. Finally, Chase pointed at him. "Yes, you on the second stool over there."

"When you run into a situation where someone is stuck in some kind of machinery, it's really important that you know how to disable it. Also, how it's assembled so you can disassemble it to free them and-"

Interrupting him Teagan asked, "How are we supposed to know that for every piece of machinery we might run into?"

Lighting up, Aoife read Maverick's mind and winked at him before jumping in. "We can't, but when we do an inspection for fire safety, we can require that they keep a current set of manuals close and in a place where they're obvious." She paused and waved off Maverick, who was about to jump in again. "Oh… Oh… they should also have someone assigned for each piece of equipment, someone who knows it inside out and backward, just in case something happens. They would be the one to assist us or even start a rescue before we get there."

"I'm so proud of my cute little 'firebird'," Maverick whispered as he high-fived Aoife, then pulled her into a long kiss.

While Chase played catch up, trying to write everything down, Teagan said, "I was so worried about what this International Team was going to do. Now I'm worried a couple of weeks here will not be enough." She turned to Maverick. "I love the name you just came up with. Firebirds. I think that would be a great name for our team!"

Aoife stared at her. "Hey, you just stole my name."

"Oh, sorry. We're just borrowing it. You can be the Firebird Team leader, how's that?" Teagan asked. "Of course, that means you get to conduct all the meetings."

"Oh joy. Thanks." Aoife turned to Chase. "You're our sexretary. Be sure to take copious notes and I'll keep you stocked up with Black and Tans and… bread puddin' with whiskey sauce as a special reward."

"Hey! What do I get?" Maverick asked.

"Me, with whiskey sauce if you're good," she loudly whispered, adding a long kiss.

***

Teagan glanced around and what she saw brought a big smile to her face. Feeling his eyes on her, she turned and locked eyes with Chase, who winked at her. He saw it too. How well they all got along. How he had planned to help Maverick before being asked. How he had made sure Maverick didn't get mad at Aoife for helping him find a job. How they all, good naturedly, kidded with each other, yet supported each other.

For her though, his unselfishly making sure her sisters and their boyfriends came with them to England made him beyond special in her eyes, and that didn't include how he was constantly bragging to BA about how smart and talented she was. Was he a keeper? You bet. They were all keepers.

Suddenly, a loud scream echoed throughout the pool area.

Aoife was the first one to spot a woman near the back door screaming and hugging a baby in her arms. "Help," the woman yelled as she held the baby upright in front of her, staring, like the baby was going to tell her what was wrong. The child looked like a rag doll, its arms and legs flapping all over. Then, it quit moving, its head leaning listlessly to the left, its eyes stuck wide open and staring off into space. Mom screamed again and pulled the baby in and kept incoherently, mumbling something.

Clearing a pool lounge chair with one leap, Aoife rounded the end of the pool and reached out for the baby as she stopped in front of the woman. Spying a plastic sandwich bag in the hand of an older child next to the woman, she asked, "What was the baby eating?"

315

"A grape... I gave her a grape," the older child said.

Aoife held the baby face down and flat across the front of her. Then, firmly, but gently, smacked the palm of her hand on the baby's back. Nothing. Another smack and still nothing. The third time though, a whole grape flew out of the baby's mouth. A second later, her scream filled the air. Aoife turned the baby toward her and hugged her to her chest. "It's okay, we got that nasty grape." She snuggled the baby closer and rocked it in her arms. The baby quit crying, looked up, smiled, then giggled as she reached for Aoife's nose.

By that time everyone else had reached them. "The baby's okay," Teagan told the mom and pulled her in. "She's giggling. She's fine."

"Oh my God, thank you, thank you, thank you," the mom said staring at Aoife with a big smile.

The ambulance team from the airport fire station rushed through the door just as Aoife returned the baby to her mom. One of the EMTs they had met with before took the scene in and figured out what must have happened. "Yanks to the rescue, are we?" she asked.

Mom nodded and laid her head on Aoife's shoulder. "She saved my baby. She was choking on a grape."

Everyone looked down at the boy, the bag of grapes still in his hand. "I... I'm sorry. She kept reaching for them, so I finally gave in and gave her one." More to himself than anyone else, he added, "Won't be doin' that again."

Mom took her son by the hand and as they went out, the bag of grapes went in the trash can next to the door.

"That's rescue number three. You lot should just sign on with us," the EMT added as she and her partner picked up their gear, then headed for the door.

***

Ray and Erin returned from their tour. After giving two dozen Bath buns to the front desk for the staff, they took the last dozen into the pool area. "I can't believe you guys are still in here. I thought for sure you'd all be nursing Black and Tans in the pub," Erin said.

"We've been working on a list of things for the Fire Bird Team," Teagan replied.

"The who?" Erin asked.

"We'll explain over dinner," Chase said. "How was your trip."

With Erin beaming next to him, Ray said, "Wow! I'm still trying to digest Salisbury Cathedral. That has to be the most beautiful cathedral I'll ever see. And Bath and Stonehenge were amazing too. All in all, it was like a trip back through multiple centuries... from ancient, to Roman to the thirteenth and fourteenth centuries."

317

Waiting for Ray to finish, Erin winked at him, then added, "Something very interesting happened during our trip." Her smile grew and she suggested they might want to grab beer refills, since this might take a while. Ray caught the eye of the barmaid at the pool bar and made a circle with his finger, indicating another round for everyone. The barmaid smiled, nodded and a few minutes later, delivered six more Black and Tans.

"Since they moved us into our new room, weird things have been happening," Erin said. "The nightstand bedroom light that flickers. Shadows passing by the door between the front room and bedroom. Strange noises like the floor creaking from someone walking. Bathroom faucets that turn themselves on. The mini bar fridge that moans."

Letting out a chuckle, Ray added, "We've nicknamed the mini bar fridge, Moaning Myrtle. It moans, groans, hums and clicks." He looked at the other two couples. "At first we thought it was one of you messing around next door."

Everyone ignored his joke and Teagan asked, "So, what happened on your trip?"

"We ran upstairs to grab jackets and ran into a couple from BA, both pilots, as we were coming out of our room. Turns out they were on the same tour with us. On the way to Salisbury Cathedral, they asked how we liked the haunted room," Erin explained.

"What?" Maverick said.

"It turns out that room was always reserved for two BA flight attendants," Erin went on. "They were both females, who had graduated from school together, gone through flight attendant training together, often flew together and were madly in love with each other.

"They worked a quick turnaround to Frankfurt, Germany, and had left everything in the room since they were working a London to Hong Kong flight the following day. Unfortunately, on their way back to the boarding area in Frankfurt, a drunken passenger stole an airline courtesy cart and ran them over. They never heard the electric cart coming. One died in the arms of her mate and the second never made it to the hospital."

Ray jumped in to finish the story. "The hotel staff adored them and refused to rent out the room or clear their stuff out for a year, as a tribute to them. Just a little over a month ago, BA cleaned their stuff out and… guess what… we're the first ones to occupy their room."

"Is it scary?" Aoife asked.

"No, it's actually kind of cute, almost like they're teasing us, having fun with us," Ray answered. "They wait till we're in bed, do the weird stuff but then leave us alone so we can go to sleep. After the first night, they've had us laughing as we lay there trying to guess what they're going to do next."

"Now that we know who they are, we'll try and find a way to mess with them back. I think they're just lonely," Erin added.

Deciding to eat in, everyone headed to the pub for dinner. Once they were seated, Aoife explained how Maverick had come up with the Firebird nickname and Teagan had adopted it as the International Team's name. From there, Chase and Teagan went over the notes they had started for things they thought they would cover in meetings with the Brit's Fire Brigade. Finally, Teagan told them about Aoife's doing a grape rescue and saving the baby.

Looking at Ray, Erin asked, "How many days were we gone?"

"Uh, less than one... I thought. Maybe we blacked out and missed a day?"

After another fantastic, shared dinner, they all headed for their rooms. "Do not send the ghosts to our room," Aoife said to Erin and Ray, just before everyone waved goodnight and closed their door.

Once their door was closed, Ray wrapped Erin in his arms and the lights flashed. "Ugh, not tonight, please!" he mumbled as they both yawned.

The lights flashed again. "Thank you." Erin looked at the ceiling fixture and told their invisible roommates.

Turning back to Ray, she added, "Can we talk? I'm worried."

They both undressed, climbed into bed and he rewrapped her in his arms. "What are you worried about?"

"You. I'm worried that the police department is going to let you go because you're taking too much time off."

"Thank you," he said, adding a kiss. "I need to call back and tell them to change my vacation over to a leave of absence."

"Oh, Ray, what if they let you go instead?"

"Then they let me go, and I'll find something else. But I'll still have you, and that's much more important."

Erin was speechless. After staring at him for what seemed like forever, she recovered enough to talk. "Are... are you serious?"

"Yeah, very." He kissed her, then added a big smile. "In case you haven't figured it out yet, I'm in love with you."

The lights flashed and they both broke up laughing.

"Ray, I can't let you get fired over me... us... because we all need to stay and have temporary jobs here."

He pulled her into another kiss. "Uh, the worse that happens is I have to take a job as a security officer at the stadium - with an increase in pay and forced to watch football, women's soccer and rugby games."

Her smile brightened. "I'm fine with the pay increase and football. The women's soccer and rugby we'll need to talk about."

The lights flashed again.

"Thank you," Erin added, looking up and winking at the light fixture.

Turning back to Ray, she gently kissed him again and told him, "I love you too. I've actually been in love with you since high school but didn't know how to get you out of 'dork' mode." She gave him another kiss, then leaned back and looked into his eyes. "Something else I should tell you before you decide to risk your job on the police force. I... I may stay in England. Not forever, but maybe a year or two."

His serious look morphed into a smile. "Would you like some company... if you were to stay that is... or even if you don't?"

"Oh, Ray, I would love your company, but what would you do here? For a living I mean?"

322

"Don't know. No way I'm wearing one of those weird 'Bobbie' hats though. I'm sure there are lots of options. There's airport security, private security companies, and even an FBI office in London."

"Would you really stay if I do?"

"Would you want me to?"

Their questions were answered by the lights flickering again and both of them locking each other in a very serious kiss. Kiss over, she leaned back. "Thank you. You've no idea how much you wanting to stay means to me. You confirmed that my idea about staying wasn't just a whim. Ray, this may sound stupid, but from the minute I stepped off the plane, I felt like London... no, England... was calling to me. Telling me to discover how unique it is. To not leave until I've explored its fascinating history, made friends with people here and let it into my heart, actually, it's already in my heart."

Staring into his eyes she paused. "You feel it too, don't you?"

He nodded. "Yeah, but I'm blaming you, because every time I look at you, you're lit up like a Christmas tree. I've never seen you smile so much." He paused again and wrapped her tighter in his arms. "You need to know how much I'm in love with you. Wanting me to stay in England, wanting to share a place you obviously love-"

Reaching over, she lightly clamped his lips together with her fingers. "I need you to stop talking…" with her other hand, she slid his hand between her legs and wrapped her hand over his "…and make love to me."

"Got it." He smiled, then disappeared under the covers.

The lights flashed wildly and the refrigerator moaned, but neither of them noticed.

The following morning everyone met at the breakfast buffet. They all did their usual, full English breakfast and a variety of other items with enough to share, then found a table off to the side where their antics wouldn't disturb others. "How are you two doing?" Erin asked Maverick and Teagan.

"I'm a little sore still," Teagan answered.

"Me too, but less so each day," Maverick added.

"I was thinking maybe we could do something easy like the Thames River Tour. We'd be sitting for most of it and there's only a few steps, mainly getting on and off the boat."

"Can we take one more day?" Teagan asked. "I think I'll be good to do the river tour tomorrow. Now that we're all here, maybe today we can add to the Firebird list we started yesterday?" Looking at Erin and Ray she added, "Unless you two want to go do something on your own again."

Glancing at Erin, Ray smiled, took Erin's hand, winked at her, then answered for them. "Nope, we're good with hanging around here. We'll have plenty of time to play tourist."

Aoife looked around the table to make sure she wasn't the only one that picked up on whatever was going on between Ray and Erin. "What are you two up too?"

"We… uh, we've decided to stay in England… not sure for how long yet," Erin answered, then gave Ray a kiss.

"Why does that not surprise us?" Aoife replied. "I think we'd all stay longer if we could."

"What are you two going to do, job wise?" Chase asked.

"I sent an email off to Bonita Fire this morning to see if I could extend the Firebird thing into an exchange with the London Fire Brigade. I also asked them to contact San Diego Fire at the airport to see if I could coordinate between them and the Heathrow Fire Brigade." Looking at Teagan and Aoife, her smile grew. "Of course, I'd also have a special 'in' with EMTs, Air Rescue and Forest Fire Fighting too."

Looking over at Aoife, Teagan asked, "Wonder who those 'ins' would be?"

"Search me? You know anyone in any of those organizations?" Aoife came back with.

"If you two ever want to see Bath Buns again, you'd better sign up to be my secret information sources," Erin threatened.

"Bath Bun blackmail. I love it," Maverick said as they all started laughing.

Knowing he would be interrogated next, Ray jumped in. "I just had an idea. I know girls with various English and Irish accents are in high demand in the sex trade. What if I were to see if I could be assigned to the FBI office in London? I could specifically deal with girls being traded between the US, England, and Ireland?"

Staring at him, Erin wrapped her arms around him. "Oh, Ray, that would be wonderful. I'd help wherever I could. We've done some things with Generate Hope. They help girls rescued from the sex trade in San Diego. Maybe they can contact the FBI here and put in a good word for you."

Letting out a chuckle he said, "I've never had anything to do with rescuing girls from the sex trade in San Diego, or Chula Vista, or even working with the FBI. So, they wouldn't know anything about me."

"They will by the time I'm done talking with them."

"Why do I get the feeling they'll be promoting me to head attaché in the London office when you're finished talking with them?"

"Uh, you'll need to develop your 'Proper British Accent' first," she said, adding a chuckle. "For now you'll just have to look adorable in one of those cute Bobbie hats."

"Oh! We can get a rotor for the top of his hat," Aoife managed to get out before a chuckle escaped.

"Uh, a four-bladed main rotor and a little tail rotor for the back. Then he'll be known as Rotor Ray the Helo Bobbie," Teagan threw in, just before the image of him in his hat registered and cracked them all up.

"Might I suggest we adjourn to a table out by the pool bar. We're starting to attract a lot of attention, plus I'm sure they can use the table," Chase suggested.

"Aw, are we embarrassing you?" Teagan asked.

"Not at all. I just thought if Ray is going to become a secret agent, and we're all becoming informants, we shouldn't be blabbing it all in public."

They all headed for the pool area and took up two couches near the door from the lobby. Maverick broke out his Firebird notes and went over what they'd listed the day before. As soon as he finished, Erin jumped in. "I think we need to have two lists. One for firefighters and one for EMTs. Also, we can't forget that this is a two-way street. I'm sure the fire brigade is going to have suggestions of their own and we need to look at those."

"Yeah, the whole purpose of this is to combine ideas and come up with what will work best for each organization," Aoife added. "For example, a three-minute response time is a great goal but that depends greatly on where the fire station is located. For us, the station is where it is and a three-minute response time might be impossible without building a new station."

Ray listened until Aoife finished then added, "Can we add coordination with local police authorities? I don't expect the fire brigade to enforce laws, but often they're first on the scene and they're going to need to be able to recognize when something like trafficking is going on. I guess what I'm suggesting is maybe a training program where the FBI could teach them to look for signs of trafficking or drug smuggling."

Looking around, it was impossible to miss the overwhelmed look on Maverick's face.

"Are you okay?" Eff asked.

"Uh, no. I need a course in minute taking or note taking, or something. I think I'm going to beg for my pea herding job back."

"Aw, my poor baby," Aoife said, adding a kiss to help soothe him. "We did kind of stick you with getting all this down. I'll get hold of a friend of mine. She teaches Minute Taking Madness classes and we'll get her to come do a one-on-one class with you."

"Is she cute?"

"Very, but I trust her. She'll make sure you concentrate on taking minutes and not her cuteness."

Pulling out her phone, Aoife called her friend. When she learned she was in Dublin, Ireland with her boyfriend and writing partner, she bribed her. "She'll be down tomorrow to do a one-on-one class with you," she told Maverick. "She also suggested that it might be a good idea to break things out into separate lists. One for firefighter stuff, one for EMTs and one for police stuff."

"Uh, I was just about to suggest that," Maverick said, then added a big smile.

329

"Sure you were," Aoife teased him, softening her skepticism with a kiss.

The rest of the morning was spent breaking things out into three lists, then adding to each as they thought of more ideas.

***

Right after lunch, Chase called William and they set up a meeting with BA, the Heathrow Fire Brigade commander and the local police commander. Chase and William did introductions, then Chase outlined their proposal for trading ideas and coordinating the various agencies. While no commitments were made, everyone agreed working together was a good idea and they each promised to support the American team.

The police commander explained that dealing with women, and young males, kidnapped into the sex trade had become one of the biggest issues they faced at the airport. "We can use all the help we can get. I'll be happy to contact the FBI office here in London, and back in the states, and suggest they talk to you about your ideas. Having the extra eyes of the fire brigade, BA and an FBI agent assigned here would be a tremendous aid in dealing with the problem."

He paused. "I'll warn you though, drug smuggling and sex trafficking run hand and hand, so you'll need to treat them as one. That means your training must cover both. And... be prepared for dealing with some pretty ugly blokes."

The fire and police commissioners left, and William from BA closed the door to the conference room. "You know, as everyone was talking, it dawned on me that a lot of what came up is also having to be delt with by our flight crews and ground crews. I wonder if you'd be willing to put together an outline for a training course. Training for things like; recognizing someone high on drugs or possibly smuggling drugs, someone kidnapped or being forced to fly. I know there's a lot to cover, but I'm looking for guidelines they can follow for the most likely situations they'll come across."

Everyone nodded; they got it. He could see the excitement as ideas started to pop into their heads. "Obviously, I'll pay you for your time."

He paused and turned to Teagan and Aoife and a big smile lit up his face. They both looked at each other, What was he up to now? "I've a special request for both of you." Another pause and smile. "I need you both to promise not to get mad at me. You also can refuse to do it, or back out at any time." A third pause and smile.

*This could not be good,* they both thought.

"I've gotten permission from Mercy Air to let both of you fly with our Air Ambulance and Trauma teams."

Both of them looked at each other, then lit up in smiles. "We... we'd love to fly with your teams!" Aoife spoke for both of them. "I'm sure we could learn a lot."

331

"Actually, I think it's going to very much be a two-way street with each side learning as much as teaching the other teams new things." William watched as the obvious question dawned on both of them. "Now you're wondering what BA has to do with our Air Ambulance Teams," he added before they could. "Well, it seems we just took on training new Air Ambulance pilots and flight nurses. They'll come to us already trained as pilots and EMTs, but what will be lacking will be practical experience. That's where we - and I hope you - will come in."

The smile on both of their faces told him they were not only onboard but couldn't wait to get started. Then Teagan added a 'but'. "We'll only do it if Erin is a part of the team. She's logged almost as many flight hours as we have. She's also working toward her certification as a flight nurse, so she's probably more current on things then we are."

Immediately, William's smile confirmed, not only was he in agreement, he'd been about to include Erin in his offer. "There's no doubt you three are a team and I wouldn't think of breaking you up." He paused. "One of the biggest things I hope you'll pass on to the students is how critical working together as a team is. How you complement each other, learn from each other."

\*\*\*

Afterward, they headed back to the pub to spend the rest of the afternoon adding to their sex trade recognition list and starting a new list for flight training. Before they got started, Maverick jumped in. "I would like to be a part of the training as much as possible. Even if it's just passing out pens and paper, I'd like to help as much as I can."

Wrapping him in a giant hug, Aoife lit up. "Do you have any idea how special you are?"

"Yeah, but don't quit telling me." He added a long kiss to make sure she knew how much he appreciated her recognition and everything she'd done for him... that they'd all done for him.

Now it was Chase's turn. Nodding toward Maverick, he told Teagan, "I'm not doing this because he did... well, mostly... but I want to be a part of the training too. I need to add that seats come first though. Maverick and I need to make sure our contract with BA takes priority, but after that, we'll devote as much time to helping with the other things as we can."

Teagan led them as everybody stood and formed a giant hug. Even the barmaid in the pub who came over with their round of drinks joined in their hug.

"What are we hugging for?" she asked.

"Uh, it's complicated. We're putting together a list of tells to recognize when girls have been kidnapped into the sex trade," Teagan replied.

"Oh." Her smile disappeared. Then she turned and started for the door.

Noticing the sudden change, Teagan gently put her hand on her arm and stopped her. "Are you okay?"

"Yeah, I'm fine," she said, adding a very fake smile. "I need to go check on another table."

"Okay," Teagan said.

While everyone continued their discussions on who could help with what, Teagan kept glancing over at the barmaid. Something had made her very uncomfortable and Teagan was sure it had been the mention of sex trafficking. Several times they caught each other's eye and finally, when she saw the barmaid was free, she excused herself and approached her.

"You were trafficked, weren't you?"

"I... I don't want to talk about it."

"You don't have to. I just wanted to tell you that we're here if we can help in any way."

The barmaid smiled, added a thank you, picked up her tray from the bar and headed for another table. A second later Erin and Aoife joined Teagan. It only took a second for them to figure out what was going on.

"She was trafficked, wasn't she?" Aoife asked, and Teagan quietly acknowledged with a nod, as they wandered back to the rest of the group.

Fifteen minutes later, the barmaid approached Teagan. "Can we talk?" she asked quietly.

"Sure," Teagan said. "Be right back," she told everyone else as the two of them headed for a table off by itself.

"I'm sorry. I didn't mean to be rude. It's hard for me to talk about it but if it'll help, maybe I can tell you what happened to me... even though no one else would be as stupid as I was."

Giving her a big smile, Teagan replied, "First off, I doubt you're stupid. I'm also willing to bet what happened to you is pretty common."

The barmaid explained how she had met a guy at a friend's party. They had danced for a few songs, then retired to a couch and spent the next hour or so talking and getting to know each other. "He really seemed nice," she said. "Polite, interested in me, where I'd been and what I'd done. When I told him that my ex-boyfriend had just dumped me for his old girlfriend, he said my boyfriend had to be nuts. That I was not only pretty, but smart, and had a fantastic personality.

"Anyway, the party broke up early and he told me he wanted to spend more time with me and that a neighbor was having a party where he lived, so he suggested we go join them. I said sure, why not? By the time we got to where he lived, I wasn't feeling too well. He proposed we go up to his apartment where I could lay down on the couch for a bit just till I felt better. The next thing I knew, I woke up, tied to a bed, with him on top of me. I had the hardest time trying to focus on what was happening. I felt like I was floating above me, looking down.

"I don't remember much after that. I think I woke up several times and someone different was on top of me each time. Sometimes I thought I knew what was happening and others, everything was just a blur. A day, maybe two, someone woke me and offered me some water and fed me a stale sandwich. I was still tied to the bed, completely naked and really sore. I had peed and crapped all over myself and the bed. Finally, this girl came in, untied me and took me into the bathroom and told me to shower and clean myself up.

"I locked the door, grabbed a bath towel and went out the window. I landed in an alleyway, followed it onto a side street and there was a policeman. He ran to me and I collapsed into his arms just as he got to me. I must have passed out again because that's all I remember till I woke up in the hospital. It turns out it was actually a week before I escaped."

"I'm so sorry you went through that. But just so you know, your story is more typical than not. Being picked up in a bar or at a party or having a boyfriend recruit you, are the most common ways women end up in the sex trade. Sometimes they're forced, like you were, but more often than not, their traffickers prey on their vulnerabilities. Vulnerabilities that often lead to being groomed into trafficking. Victims frequently feel indebted to their traffickers by the time sex for money is introduced. They often think they love their traffickers and that their traffickers love them. Victims may be told, 'It's just for a minute, one time,' then those minutes turn into years stolen from teenagers who become trafficked adults before they know it.

"Had you not escaped, I suspect the next step would have been your trafficker confessing his undying love for you and that what he did was only because he was desperate for money. That if he didn't pay what he owed, they would have killed him, and you. That what he did was only to save you and from now on he would protect you, no matter what. It always seems to be a variation on a pretty standard plotline."

"I'm not sure if I can be of much help then," she told Teagan.

"Well, to be honest with you, we're just trying to figure out what we're going to do, but I'd love for you to be able to help if you're willing. That is, once we figure everything out."

"Okay if I work on some things that I think might help?" she asked Teagan.

"That would be great."

"Can... can I ask what you all do? I mean, are you some kind of social workers? I heard little bits and pieces and know you're involved with BA and the fire brigade somehow."

Wrapping her arm over her shoulders, Teagan steered her back toward the group. "Come on over and let me introduce you. Then we can explain who we are and what we do." She paused then added, "I'm Teagan, by the way."

"I'm Veronica," the server said as they reached the group.

"Hey, everybody. This is Veronica and I've asked her to join us for a bit. She went around the table, pointing out each of them, their names and what they did for a living."

337

"Wow. I always wanted to be an EMT," Veronica said, then focused in on Aoife. "I love your name by the way, and I never thought of being a flight nurse till just now."

"Well, we'll just have to spend some time together. Being an EMT is great, but being a flight nurse is extra special, I think," she paused then added, "I should warn you that we get called out on some of the gorier calls. So, if you're not into blood and guts, a plain old EMT is probably more for you."

"Hey! What's with the 'plain old EMT'?! I'm not plain and I'm certainly not old… and …and we get plenty of blood and guts on our calls," Erin said.

"Can I get credit for cleaning up barf from drunks, or blood and boogers from someone picking their nose too enthusiastically?" Veronica asked, then added, "Other than that, wiping up spilled drinks, and occasionally pee from a bar stool, is about as exciting as it gets,"

"Sounds like excellent training for becoming an EMT or flight nurse," Aoife said, then added, "DUI's are our specialty."

Veronica had overrun her break and had to get back to work. She took their order for another round of Black and Tans and headed for the bar as everyone else dove back into their lists. First up would be issues for the Air Ambulance crews.

# Chapter 35 – Training, Training and More Training

"BA said their course material covers the formal training requirements for both the pilots and EMTs, so what we need to do is add the practical experience things we've learned," Aoife said, adding, "Teagan, can you start with flight safety since we're always landing in places most helicopter pilots would only crash in? Not to mention areas crowded with looky loos."

"Okay," Teagan said. "But I'm going to start with 'You're an Air Ambulance crew, not an Air Rescue crew.'" She smiled at everyone. "The first thing everyone thinks of is Air Rescue and I think it's important that they understand their job is transporting injured people to the hospital, not repelling down into canyons or jumping into the ocean to rescue people. That's Kiera's job."

"Uh, how are they supposed to get their rescue merit badges if they can't jump into the ocean?" Aoife asked, as the three women giggled at their private joke.

"We'll cover rescue merit badges in the cross-training session. For now, we'll just cover air ambo drivers and EMTs," Teagan answered, adding a chuckle. "The pilot should also be an EMT. I know that's not a requirement everywhere, but I think it should be since often we get the worst of the worst as far as accident victims go. That overloads the Air Nurse if there's no

339

help from ground ambo crews. So, they need to be well trained, prepared and compassionate."

"They also need to stay current on the latest medical procedures and technology," Aoife added, "Oh, and they'll need to make sure their ambo is stocked with everything they might need for the areas they service. Like snake bite kits for the venomous snakes in the area."

"Don't forget splints and braces for areas with rough terrain, where hiking is popular," Erin threw in. "Oh, and special training for treating snake bites and major fractures."

Maverick pulled Aoife in and kissed her neck. "The three of you are beyond impressive. I think BA is going to love having the three of you teach their Air Ambulance courses."

"They need to work as a team… along with the ground EMTs…" Teagan started to say.

Sitting toward the back corner with Ray, Erin kept waving her hand, finally yelling out, "Could you possibly mean a CRM for HAA operations?"

"Oh crap. How could I forget the CRM?" Teagan said.

"Yeah. It's the key thing we studied in my HAA Operations Certification Course," Erin said.

"Okay… what in the world is a CRM and HAA operations?' Chase asked.

"It's actually an FAA requirement. I'll let Erin explain. She's studying to become a certified flight nurse and can cite the requirements in her sleep."

"Thanks, Teag. In August of 2011, a Eurocopter AS 350 B2 helicopter was dispatched to a hospital for medical transport of a patient to another hospital. During patient pick-up, the pilot informed the company's EMS communication center that he didn't have enough fuel to complete the second leg of the mission. While en route to refuel, the helicopter ran out of fuel and crashed, resulting in the death of the pilot, flight nurse, flight paramedic and patient on board. Up until that time, the pilot was solely responsible for the aircraft and the only one trained in in-flight safety and aeronautical decision making.

"That accident caused the FAA and NTSB to launch a special investigation into helicopter air ambulance (HAA) crashes. The NTSB special investigation found that between January of 2002 and January of 2005 alone, fifty-five helicopter air ambulance accidents occurred in the United States. These accidents resulted in fifty-four fatalities and eighteen serious injuries. The investigation highlighted the causes and the need to establish better communication procedures and practices directly related to Crew Resource Management (CRM) principles specific to HAA operations.

"Specifically, the CRM recommendations of the FAA's Advisory Circular (AC) 135-14B, Helicopter Air Ambulance Operations, recommends combined CRM training between air and ground crews to build 'effective integration and coordination during routine flight operations.' That includes issues such as the use of medical personnel to supplement flight crews, as needed and appropriate, during emergency operations."

Erin continued. "In layman's terms, what is CRM? Crew Resource Management is identified as a means to train teams to work together. Specifically, it is utilized to coordinate flight crews and to allow for cross-checking and back-up. The premise of CRM stresses that strengthening communication skills between team members allows technical skills to be seamlessly integrated into an operation for an efficient use of resources with a greater chance of successful outcomes. Skills associated with CRM components and their associated behavioral markers fall into two fundamental CRM component groups: Cognitive skills (e.g., decision making, situation awareness, and workload management), and social skills (e.g., leadership and teamwork)."

Erin paused and took in the confused looks on Chase, Maverick and Ray's faces. "I've obviously put you into information overload."

"You think?" Aoife said, throwing in a chuckle. "Let me see if I can help. What the studies of the crashes showed, was that the pilots had no back-up, no cross checks if you will. The obvious solution was to have the pilot and medical personnel work as a team. The immediate argument to that was that medical personnel had no technical or aeronautical training. However, studies showed that the cognitive and social skills of each crew member was what was really important. That technical skills would be integrated into the crew as they worked together as a team. In short, what they needed to know to make critical decisions, and back each other up, would automatically be integrated into their knowledge base through training and performing as a team; on the job training to supplement classroom training, if you will."

"Holy crap!" Ray said, looking at the three women. "I knew you three were smart, but I had no idea how smart. Not only can you patch people up, but you can fly a helicopter if you have to."

"Thank you," Erin said. "The key is… if we have to. Teag is the one trained as a pilot, but we've sat next to her enough to know what to do to keep it up in the air or land it if we had to."

"It works the other way too," Teagan said. "Even if I wasn't trained as an EMT, just working with Aoife and Erin, I would pick up enough to be able to keep someone alive, if I had to. So, to go back to the CRM, the whole purpose of it is cross training and back up in both directions."

After going around the table, Aoife agreed to summarize everything and the group moved on to what they could contribute to help identify sex trafficked victims. However, Ray immediately jumped in and suggested they wait until he had a chance to work with the FBI's London office. "I contacted them yesterday and they want to talk to me. They also directed me to Homeland Security's website, which I took a quick look at this morning. It's loaded with information and training videos on recognizing sex trafficking that I'm sure we can use. Give me a day or two to come up with an approach that might work best for us."

"Okay, enough work. What's everyone want to do this afternoon?" Maverick asked.

Veronica came up and asked if anyone needed anything else. Teagan looked at her watch and said, "It's kind of late to do anything today. How about if we do another round while we figure out what to do?"

"Do you think we can get some service over here?" Came from a table across the room.

"I'll be right back," Veronica said and headed for the other table.

"Nothing like being impatient," Aoife whispered. "They hadn't even sat down when he yelled at her… they've also been staring over here since they came in."

Teagan watched Veronica as she approached the table. One of the two guys reached out, grabbed her arm and pulled her toward him. Chase had also been watching and started up out of his seat, but Teagan put her hand on his arm and stopped him. "Easy. He hasn't done anything… yet."

Sensing he was being watched, the guy looked over at them, smiled and let go of Veronica's arm. She took their order and mouthed, "Thanks," as she passed by, headed for the bar.

Everyone settled back down and a few minutes later, Veronica slowed on her way back to the other table. "I'm sorry. I should have taken your order first but I don't trust those two, so I want to get them served and out of my hair," she whispered.

"No problem. We're not going anywhere," Maverick said. Then added, "We'll be keeping an eye on them. Just in case one of them grabs you again."

"Thank you," she said and headed for the other table.

She started to deliver the drinks to the far side of their table so she wouldn't be trapped between them, but one of them motioned her to the other side. "You need to learn how to serve," he told her. "You can't put the drinks in front of us from over there," he instructed, adding a pasted-on grin.

"I can reach just fine from over here," she said.

"Listen... I'm the customer and I said get your bum over here," he grunted, then forced an even more phony grin onto his face. "Just because you're pretty doesn't mean you can get away with being rude to customers."

"I... I'm not being rude. I can reach just fine from over here and my next table is over this way... so it's easier for me to serve you from here."

"You really need some lessons in serving customers and we'd be more than happy to teach you. I'm sure we can teach you how to make people happy... not just with drinks but in other ways."

346

"I've been a server for a fair number of years so I'm pretty sure I don't need lessons," she told him.

"Wow, feisty… I like that," He got out of his chair and reached out to grab her again.

"Please keep your hands to yourself," she told him just as Maverick reached them.

Maverick forced his way between them, as he body checked the guy. "Oh, I'm sorry!" he said, pasting on a grin. "She needs to get our order and it seems you're holding her up. By the way, she's a good friend and we really don't appreciate you grabbing her like that." He paused then added, "We're pretty protective of her and you never know, we might just break your arm so you don't keep grabbing her."

"Who the bloody hell do you think you are?" the guy asked, stepping up into Maverick's face.

"Well, I'm a cop, and he's pretty sure he's Superman," Ray said, from behind the guy. "Either way, I suspect you'd rather not mess with us." He paused, looked at both of them, then turned and looked at the two Bobbies standing in the entrance to the pub. "Oh, and I'm pretty sure it's time you both left. The two gentlemen at the door will be happy to help you out and give you a ride home… eventually."

"We just got our drinks," the guy said.

"That's okay; we'll finish them for you. We'll even pick up your tab," Ray said. "So, have a wonderful day. Oh, and I suggest you find someplace else to harass women because if we see either of you again, we're likely not going to give you another warning."

The two guys got up and the Bobbies shadowed them out into the lobby and out the front door.

***

Veronica, along with Ray and Maverick, joined everyone back at their table. "Thank you so much for coming to my rescue," she said. "Those guys have been in before and my boss had to throw them out. Trust me, they'll be back. They work the hotels along Bath Road, looking for girls."

"I'm getting the feeling that we don't need to leave the airport area in our quest for putting a dent in sex trafficking in London," Ray said. "We could set up a Kool-Aid stand in front of the hotel and just wait for the traffickers to come to us."

A burst of laughter escaped from Veronica. "This is London. Me thinks you'll do much better with a tea stand then Kool-Aid… whatever that is."

"Okay. Iced tea stand then," Ray said, desperately trying to stifle a chuckle.

"The only thing he'll be catching with Kool-Aid or Iced-Tea is a cold," she told the rest of them, then turned back to Ray. "Don't know if you've noticed but this is England. Last thing anyone needs is their tea iced or an aid to help cool them. Although … I suspect…"

Ray knew Veronica was putting him on. She had cranked her English accent up to full and was desperately trying to keep a straight face. Everyone at the table was also, unsuccessfully, trying to stifle giggles.

When she finished, she said, "Thank you. I haven't laughed that much in I don't know how long."

"If I want to attract sex traffickers, what do you suggest I sell at my stand?"

Trying to stifle another giggle, Veronica stared at Erin. "Is he for real?"

"Unfortunately, yes," she answered.

"Uh, I'd suggest Black and Tans with Scotch chasers," Veronica finally managed to get out. Suddenly she turned serious. "Were you lot thinking of staying here?"

"Ray and Erin are. The rest of us will be heading back as soon as Teagan is healed and Chase and Maverick finish their business with BA," Aoife told her.

"Yeah, I think we'll be looking for a place to rent like back by the Pheasant since we'll both be working at the airport," Ray replied.

"Over my dead body are we living by the airport," Erin chimed in.

"Might I suggest you look for a flat in either Hillingdon or Uxbridge. They're just north of here but out of the Heathrow pattern. They're also on the tube line to both London proper and Heathrow. That makes it convenient to get around, avoid the airport noise and have reasonable flat fees," Veronica said.

Ray and Erin thanked her, then he turned serious. "Would I be asking too much if I asked you to help me?"

"Help you how?" she asked, then added, "Don't be asking me to go back into the world I escaped from. I'll be having nothing to do with that."

"I wouldn't ever think of asking that," he replied. "I'm thinking more of you acting as an advisor. You not only know the area, but where the traffickers are most likely to hang out." He paused, then waving the tube map he'd gotten from the tour rack by the concierge's desk, added, "But first I need to figure out how to get to the West End." After a chuckle he said, "I thought we were already at the West End."

"We are," Veronica answered. "But we're in Hillingdon, not London. Plus, the West End is the West End in London proper, not the west side of London." She watched his deer in the headlights look, shook her head and added, "here give me that," and snatched the tube map out of his hand.

Erin couldn't help but laugh. "Oh, this is going to be a fun adventure."

The following morning, everyone met at the breakfast buffet. "These English breakfasts are going to ruin me," Aoife said. "Who ever thought I'd be craving baked beans, broiled tomatoes and portage, to go with my eggs and bangers every morning?" she said, while watching everyone haul their overflowing plates to their table.

Breakfast finished, everyone except Ray headed for BA. Ray with tube map in hand caught the hopper bus to the tube station at Heathrow's Terminal 5. From there, following the map and, Veronica's instructions, he'd take the tube to Acton Station, transfer to the Central Line, then work his way through several more transfers to get to the Faringdon tube station in London's West End. A short walk later, he'd not only be a London Tube expert but hopefully, be at the FBI's office on Kerby Street.

Teagan, Aoife and Erin met with BA's director of training and the head of London's Air Ambulance Service. While two conference rooms down the hall, Chase and Maverick met with BA's design staff.

After a brief discussion of Air Ambulance operations in England, BA's director of training and the Air Ambulance head agreed that the best way to approach integrating US and England operations was to just let them go fly together. Ten minutes later, Erin, Teagan and Aoife were climbing into an Airbus H145 idling on the parking apron in front of the firehouse at the south end of the runway. Already inside were a pilot, a flight nurse and a flight trauma nurse. "Ready to go fly?" the pilot asked them.

"Uh, no. Please shut it down?" Teagan told him from the back of the helicopter. Once he'd shut it down and the rotor noise had dissipated to a woosh, she went on. "First off, who are you all? Names would be good here."

"Sorry," the flight nurse said. "We didn't mean to be rude. We're just overexcited to work with you."

"Apology accepted," Teagan replied. "Aside from your names, please tell us a little about yourselves and your certifications, please."

"I'm Richard. I'm a pilot with five years experience flying H135s and H145s."

"Are you an EMT too Richard?"

"Bloody hell no," he answered. His tone obviously reflecting that he thought himself above being an EMT. Aoife also couldn't help but notice both flight nurses roll their eyes.

"Don't like blood?" Erin guessed.

"Can't stand the stuff. Especially if it's mine," Richard answered, adding a smart ass grin.

Teagan looked over at the flight nurse in the copilot's seat. "I'm Grace, the flight nurse. I'm also a certified EMT. Don't know if you lot in the states separate the training but we do here."

352

"Thank you, Grace." Teagan said, adding a smile and turning to the trauma nurse. "And last but not least, you are?"

"I'm Nellie. I'm a trauma nurse and also EMT trained."

"Thank you. I'm Teagan, a pilot and Certified EMT. I'm certified on EC-130s, EC145s as well as H135s and 145s." She nodded toward Aoife.

"I'm Aoife, spelt A.O.I.F.E and pronounced Effa. I'm also EMT certified, an RN and a flight nurse." Turning to Grace she added, "And yes, we too separate being an RN and EMT as well as special training for flight nurses because…" she stared at Richard "… there's usually lots of blood involved in our calls."

That earned her a wink and big smile from both Grace and Nellie.

Finally, it was Erin's turn. "I'm Erin. I'm a certified EMT, a firefighter and arson investigator and working on my flight nurse certification."

"Hi everybody!" everybody said to everyone else.

"Grace, I need to swap seats with you so I can observe Richard as we prepare to take off. Erin and Aoife will also be watching both of you from back here." Pausing, Teagan added, "I want to stress that we're not being critical with our comments. We have, however, been asked to point out things you do different from us and explain why you might want to consider doing things our way, or tell us why your way is better." Everybody but

Richard, who was busy flicking switches in the cockpit, nodded. "Richard, I need you to stay shut down till I can observe you."

"Uh, I think I know how to fly without your help," he said with a snarky grin.

"I'm sure you do but I want to watch Grace and Nellie do their checks with you."

Nellie burst out laughing. "Surely you jest. Richard would chop off our hand if we touched anything in his chopper... pun intended."

"Anyone touching my controls will find themselves walking back," Richard added.

"Richard, I need you in the back," Teagan told him as she got out, walked around to the pilot's door and opened it."

"Bloody hell, bitch, you'll not be touching my bird."

"May I?" she said, reaching over and indicating the microphone on his shoulder.

"Whatever..." He handed her the microphone.

"Air Ambulance dispatch, this is Teagan with US Mercy Air. Could I please speak with your Air Ambulance service director?"

Richard let out a 'harrumph' as the director came on. "This is Mark. How can I help you, Teagan?"

*Ain't that the piss, they're on a first name basis*, Richard thought.

"Hi, Mark. We're out here with Richard, Grace and Nellie. Richard is having a bad day and I wondered if you'd be alright with me flying your bird while Richard sits this one out and does an attitude adjustment."

"More than happy to let you fly. Please send Richard into the dispatch office. We'll find something to keep him busy."

"Uh, nothing that will lower his status as a pilot, please. He's hard enough to live with now," she said, adding a smile while the others tried to stifle their snickering.

"Got you. I'm sure there's some loo cleaning and barfed on bedding we can find for him to wash."

"Thanks," Teagan said as Richard slid out of the copter and glared at her.

"You'll pay for this." He turned and marched toward the Air Ambulance office in the fire station hanger.

As soon as he was out of hearing range, Grace and Nellie burst out laughing. "Oh my God. He is going to be impossible to live with from now on. Messin' with his bird is the kiss of death!" Nellie said.

"Too bad. From now on you'll both be messin' with his bird so, he'd better get used to it," Teagan told them.

355

"Part of what we're going to implement with you is called a CRM, Crew Resource Management. It's a means to train teams to work together and implement a series of cross checks so that Richard isn't the only one monitoring the status of the aircraft," Aoife added.

"Likewise, Richard's going to have to learn to like blood because we'll be teaching him to help back up both of you too," Erin added.

They all watched as Grace tried desperately to stifle a snort. "Tis going to be hard to help us while he's barfing out the bloody door at a thousand meters. Richard wasn't kidding. He's been known to take off and leave us till we've cleaned up the scene and are ready to transport a patient to hospital."

Turning serious, Teagan told them, "Well, it's because of the Richards in the Air Ambulance community that the CRM was implemented. An accident investigation into an Air Ambulance crash in the states found that when only the pilot was monitoring the aircraft, mistakes were often deadly. So the CRM was introduced to let each of you double check things so Richard's not the only one making sure your bird is ready for flight."

"We know," Aoife headed them off, "you're not qualified as pilots, and we're not asking you to be. We're just going to teach you the basic things you need to look at, over Richard's shoulder, to make sure your aircraft is a 'go'."

Climbing into the pilot's seat, Teagan pointed out the various gauges and controls, explaining what each was for and what was considered 'normal' for each. When she finished, she turned to Grace. "I want you up here in the copilot's seat next to me. I'll explain what I'm doing as I do my ground checks, then prepare to take off, and you're going to watch what I do. Take notes if you want." Turning to Nellie she added, "You can watch from back there. We'll be doing several takeoffs and landings and you'll be swapping seats with Grace. I'll be happy to answer any questions you might have. Actually, Aoife or Erin will answer them because I'll be busy flying the aircraft."

"Uh, where's the petrol gauge?" Nellie asked from the back.

Aoife gave her a giant smile. "Outstanding first question," she said as Teagan pointed out the fuel gauge and explained what the minimum indication should be before taking off.

After going through each step, Teagan called the tower asking for clearance to take off. "Hold Air Ambulance 1451… Air New Zealand flight NZ1 is on final approach." A moment later Air New Zealand's 777-300 passed them as it touched down. "Air Ambulance 1451, you're cleared for takeoff," came over the radio.

"Roger, tower," Teagan said as she brought the main rotor up to speed and eased up on the collective. While she did that, Erin explained each thing as Teagan did it.

"You don't need to memorize each step," Aoife told them, "Although you will, just from watching Richard each time you take flight or land. That's the whole point. Pretty soon you'll instinctively know what's normal and what's not; you'll both become his second pair of eyes."

"Oh, he's bloody well going to love that," Nellie said behind a loud snort.

"Uh, Excuse me Sir Richard... you'll be needing to tweak the rotor thingy or you'll be using too much petrol... sir!" Grace added, as they all burst out laughing.

***

Teagan flew east to Northholt RAF base in South Ruislip, where they had been given a corner away from the active runway. There they would practice their takeoffs and landings.

After several takeoffs and landings, explaining each step, Teagan shut the helicopter down and climbed out. "Everyone take a minute to stretch your legs." They all climbed out, and imitated Erin as she rotated her upper body, did a few leg squats and rotated her arms.

"Okay, back in everyone. Nellie, I want you up front this time." As they all climbed in, she added, "Nell, you'll be taking us off."

"What?" Nellie yelled, looking all around like there was another Nellie somewhere behind her.

358

Teagan was laughing so hard she almost drooled on herself. "Relax, you'll be only taking us a few feet off the ground... just so you get a feel for what it's like to take off and land our bird."

"Ugh, you mean Richard's bird. If he ever gets wind Nellie flew it, he'll have her ground up and made into bangers," Grace said.

When she finished giggling, Teagan said, "You mean he'll have 'both' of you ground into bangers, because you'll be taking her up next."

"Yay," Grace yelled out. "Rich can banger me for breakfast anytime, as long as I get to play with his bird." She stopped and looked around as everyone broke into hysterical laughter. "Uh, guess that didn't quite come out right."

Grace and Nellie each got several go's at lifting the helicopter off the ground, then setting it back down. Shakey at first but improving with each lift off and landing. "Wow. It's a lot harder at first, but once you get the feel for it, it gets easier," Nellie said.

"Perfect. That's exactly what I wanted you to learn. Richard, for all his faults, and arrogance, I'm sure is a good pilot. And... you both need to appreciate that." Teagan paused, then added, "By the way, right now he's back at the hanger getting lessons in basic first aid... using real blood."

That caused another burst of hysterical laughter.

Practice liftoffs and landing over, they all climbed back in, Erin in the copilot's seat this time. As Teagan when through each step of her pre-takeoff procedure, Erin mimicked it and explained things again. "I know… it's getting boring, but this will be the last time we'll explain things. From here on out, it's up to you to watch what's going on and, if you're not sure of something, ask."

Teagan lifted the copter off and brought it up to 1,000 meters, ready to head back to Heathrow. Suddenly Grace yelled out from the back, "What's that? That thing headed for us?"

"Ah, perfect," Teagan answered. "That's some idiot flying a drone where they're not supposed to. If you hadn't seen it and we were to hit it, we'd likely crash." A second later, she was on the radio. "Northholt tower. This is Air Ambo 1451. We've got a drone in our face. Permission to take it out?"

A second later the tower came back. "1451, permission granted. He's been warned twice this morning… uh, do a good job because we'll all be watching."

"Roger that," Teagan said, adding, "no pressure here." Then followed it with a chuckle, as she turned the helo and headed toward the drone.

Erin faced everyone in back and said, "Teagan is somewhat of an expert in drone elimination."

Teagan brought the helo alongside the drone and almost level with it, at about 500 meters. "Ah, he's watching us and wondering what I'm going to do," she told everybody. Suddenly, she hopped the chopper up and over the drone. Before the drone operator could realize what she was doing, the wash from the rotor trapped the drone and drove it downward. It hit the ground like it was shot out of a canon and disintegrated into hundreds of pieces.

"Aw, sorry buddy… NOT!" Teagan said, as she turned the helo and headed back to Heathrow. Everyone applauded and Teagan, Erin and Aoife started singing "Come fly with me, let's fly, let's fly away."

Air Ambulance 1451 set back down at Heathrow in front of the South End Fire Station. As everyone came out, Grace, Nellie and Aoife met Teagan and Erin in front of the chopper. "This is one of the best days I've had since becoming a flight nurse," Grace said to everyone.

"Me too," Nellie seconded. "Not only did I learn a lot, I feel like I'm a lot more valuable than I knew."

"You're both more valuable than you know, or I gave you credit for," Richard said as he came up to them. Taking everyone in, he smiled and added, "The chief and director would like to see all of us in the conference room."

As soon as they all sat down in the conference room, the director of Air Ambulance Services smiled at Teagan. "So how did it go?"

"Excellent," Teagan responded. "Grace and Nellie are naturals. They're both smart, paid attention, asked all the right questions and are going to make excellent CRM team members."

The director looked at Aoife and Erin. "Ladies, you agree with that?"

"You bet," Aoife said. "I'd work beside either or both of them any day."

"Me too," Erin chimed in. Turning and looking at Richard she added, "Richard is lucky to have them flying with him."

"I think Richard discovered that while you were out doing the CRM training with them." Turning toward Richard he added, "Isn't that right, Richard?"

Addressing all five women, Richard smiled. "Yes. And I need to apologize to all of you especially Grace and Nellie. After the chief and director explained CRM and why it was formed, I realized how important all of us working together is. I also understand what a piss arse I've been and how badly I've treated both of you." After a short pause, a smile grew on his face. "I hope all is forgiven because I'm going to need your help in dealing with the blood and guts from your side."

"We've got you covered," Grace replied. "We'll just ease you into it and, before you know it, while you won't love it, you'll be used to it."

"To start we'll take the worse cases while you stand back and watch," Nellie said. "But, no running away. You need to watch so you get used to it."

"Thanks... I think," he answered, adding a smile.

"Pub barf will be a good start. Oh, less we forget, you're buying at the pub after our shifts... until you can handle the blood, guts and barf," Grace threw in.

"I can do that. Having you two to chat with afterward will be a bloody lot nicer than sitting in the pub alone." Noticing them both staring at him, he added, "Yip, up till now, I've had no one to sit in the pub with me because I've been such a *buffoon*."

"Uh, Richard. No one uses *buffoon* anymore," Aoife said.

"I think *arshole* is the word you were searching for," Erin offered.

"Hey! Quit picking on our Air Ambo driver," Grace said.

"Yeah, or we'll be starting his blood and guts training right now," Nellie added, both of them desperately trying to keep from bursting out laughing.

***

The chief looked over at the director. "This is working out a lot better than I thought it would. One session and we've got our first CRM crew." Turning to Teagan and Aoife he asked, "Are you sure you two can't stay? With the three of you, we can have all of our crews trained in no time."

"Sorry," Teagan said. "Mercy Air is screaming for us to get back." Turning to Erin she smiled. "Erin will have your crews trained in no time. Plus we'll be back off and on when Chase and Maverick come back so she can set up extra training during our return trips. Just remember though, we need to leave time to work with Ray on sex trafficking too."

"We totally understand," the chief replied, the director nodding behind him.

***

Everyone assembled back at the Skyline Pub, where Veronica, chatting with Ray, were waiting for them.

"How was your London Tube tour?" Erin asked Ray as she kissed him.

"Hey, I'm a tube expert. I can get lost in just two stations."

"Don't believe him," Veronica said. "He actually made it to the Faringdon tube station with no problems, then got lost twice trying to find Kerby Street." She shook her head and added a chuckle.

"Hey, it's not my fault none of the streets go straight. Everything is twisty, turny and turning left, or right, can mean you end up doing a three-sixty and reversing course." His big smile gave away the fact that he was actually enjoying learning his way around London. "Anyway, I made it to the FBI office and we had a good talk. They had already spoken with the Chula Vista Police Department and I'm now 'on loan' to the London FBI office. So, I don't have to quit, then try to get rehired by the FBI. That's a big relief."

Before he finished, Erin wrapped her arms around his neck and pulled him into another kiss. "I'm so proud of you. Now, we need to find a flat."

"That's tomorrow's problem. How did things go with the Air Ambulance group?" he asked.

"Very well," Erin answered for them. "The flight nurses were both wonderful and very receptive. The smart-ass pilot even

365

did a turnaround and they all think CRM is a great idea. That's really important because with Teagan and Aoife leaving, I'm going to recommend that this flight crew help me train the others."

***

The following morning the group did their usual breakfast buffet, then sat out by the pool. Teagan, Chase, Aoife and Maverick were headed home to San Diego, but their flight wouldn't leave until a little after one in the afternoon so they had a couple of hours to kill before catching the hopper bus to Heathrow.

"I'm going to miss you guys," Erin said.

"We'll be back before you know it," Teagan replied, then turned to Ray. "We're trusting you with one of our sisters. You need to promise to take good care of her."

Squeezing Erin's hand, Ray smiled at her and announced, "You have no idea how important she is to me. How much a part of my life she's become. I'd never let anything happen to her." No one could miss the matching smile on Erin's face as she kissed him again.

At 9:30, they all caught the hopper bus over to Terminal 5 at the airport. Everybody checked their bags, then hugged Erin and Ray before turning for the security check point.

"We're going to really miss you two," Aoife said. "Keep us up to date on how the training is going. You too, Ray. We're all curious, our moms too, about what you come up with. Plus, I'm sure we'll get lots of questions during our next visit to Generate Hope."

Pulling Erin in closer he nodded. "We'll definitely keep you up to date on everything." He kissed Erin and asked, "Right?"

She kissed him back then gave him a sexy grin. "Well, not everything."

"Let's go. I can't take any more of these two," Teagan said. They swapped another round of hugs, then the four of them turned into the hallway marked 'Passengers Only', as Ray and Erin headed back outside to the hopper bus stop.

***

Back at the Skyline, as Ray and Erin settled in by the pool bar, Veronica approached. "You might want to have a look in the pub. The two blokes that harassed me are back again. They're chatting up three girls. I tried to warn them but one of the guys pulled me away and threatened me if I so much as said a word to them."

"We'll definitely see about that," Ray said. Turning to Erin, he told her, "Stay here. I'll be right back."

"Over my dead body. I'm coming with you. You'll need back up and that'll be me."

"Erin, this is serious. If they start something I don't want you getting hurt."

"Sorry, I thought you knew. All of us 'sisters' have a black belt in karate and are certified Military and Police 'Experts' in Krav Maga," she added with a big smile.

"Uh, remind me to never piss you off. Okay, Ms Backup, let's go kick some ass!" They let Veronica go in first and gave her a few minutes so the sex traffickers wouldn't think she'd gone and gotten them. Erin went in first and took the table next to the women and traffickers. She smiled at the three women as she sat down, then looked over at the two traffickers.

"Oh, you two again!" Turning to the women she added, "I'm sure these two are sweet talking you into going to a party. You should know that once you're there, they'll drug you and you'll wake up tied to a bed with someone on top of you."

The trafficker closest to her got up and came up next to her. He reached out for her neck, but his hand never made it there. Her elbow came up and collided with his Adam's apple. His mouth flew open, and he gasped for air. A second later her closed fist came up under his chin. His mouth slammed shut and the front half inch of his tongue landed on the table, followed by blood spurting out of the new front of his shortened tongue.

Erin jumped back, the piece of his tongue and blood, just missing her. "Eww," she said, then added "Sorry." She shrugged, just as Veronica arrived with a baggie and a spoon.

Veronica scraped the piece of his tongue into the baggie with the spoon, sealed it and handed it to him. "I think you'll be needing this, and some speech therapy."

His friend grabbed the baggie and shook it at Erin and Veronica while glaring at them. "You'll bloody well pay for this... both of you," he told them.

"I doubt that," Ray said from behind him. "If either of you show your face around here again, you'll likely be leaving with your balls in a baggie, instead of your tongues."

"Eww," one of the girls at the next table let out. "You guys don't mess around... oh, and thank you. We were starting to get some bad vibes from those two, but we probably would have gone to the party thinking there's three of us... so, nothing would happen."

"They pray on that kind of thinking," Erin told them. "It's just as easy to drug the three of you as it is one."

The girls thanked them again then left the pub, while Veronica went back to work waiting on people in the bar area.

Watching Ray's eyes watching her, Erin smiled. "What?"

"You're pretty amazing."

"I'm not, really. What brought that on?"

"Watching you. Not just now, but ever since we got back together. You're smart, have a good sense of humor, care about people and I adore your smile. Now, I find out you're a black belt, twice over, and could probably beat the snot out of me." After a pause he added, "Maybe we should swap places. You be the FBI agent and I'll be the EMT."

"Uh, sure. Where's your EMT Certification? Your Flight Nurse Endorsement? Your Arson Investigator Accreditation? Your deep-water life-saving merit badge? Your CRM training Certificate? Your…"

"Okay, Okay. I'll just be your sidekick, follow you around and scrape up and finish off anyone you leave standing. How's that? Oh, and don't forget, I can be your tube guide!"

The longer she stared at him, the bigger her smile got. "I… uh… have other plans for you. Like doing things I already know you're really good at." That was followed by a very sexy wink.

The two of them migrated back to one of the couches in the pool area. Ray sat, then reached up and pulled her into his lap. "I'm so glad we re-found each other." He thought for a moment then added, "I was going to say I wish we'd stayed together back in high school, but if we had, I don't think I would have ever appreciated you as much as I do now. I was too young and wasn't smart enough back then to realize how intelligent and talented you are. All I saw was how beautiful you are, and it blinded me to all the other wonderful things about you. So, I'm glad you kicked me to the curb at the prom. It made me realize I needed to see women for more than just a pretty face and wonderful body; that I needed to treat women with respect."

Just as she started to answer, her phone went off. "Hello? Oh, hi chief. Sure. We're just across the street. We can be over there in a few minutes." Turning to the curious look on Ray's face she told him, "The chief wants us over at the South End Fire Station."

The two of them got up and ten minutes later met the chief at the door to the fire station. "I'm sorry to bother you, but I just got notice that another air ambulance crew is being restationed here. They're due in tomorrow morning and I wondered if you'd be available to go through the CRM training with them right after they arrive?"

"Sure," Erin replied. "By the way, Ray's been officially transferred to the FBI office here in London and assigned to work the Heathrow area. So you'll be seeing a lot of him too."

"That's all good. Perhaps you can brief this new crew on the sex trafficking situation here and things to look out for?"

"I'd be happy to," Ray replied.

The two of them headed for the door but stopped when the chief yelled, "Oh wait. I almost forgot." He turned, went into his office, then a moment later, returned with a package. Handing it to Erin he said, "I took the liberty of getting you one of our Air Ambulance uniforms. Inside you'll find a pair of our flight coveralls and a jacket. I've also assigned you the rank of major, thus they'll be no doubt of your authority."

Dumbfounded, Erin stared at him. "I... I'm flattered," she finally managed to get out.

The chief smiled, then added, "See you both in the morning."

"Well, so much for flat hunting tomorrow," Erin said as they crossed Bath Road and headed back to the Skyline.

***

The following morning, after their usual trip to the breakfast buffet, they headed for the airport. As they came out of the hotel and reached Bath Road, a wind swirl hit them and blew Erin's hair all over the place. "Wow, hold on," she said as she stopped, fished an elastic hair tie out of her bag, then tied her hair back in a ponytail. "This should make today's flight interesting," she added as they continued on. As they rounded the hanger and came out onto the parking apron, another, even stronger gust hit them.

Just as Ray reached out to open the door to the hanger, the pitch of the engines on a British Airways A321, about to touch down behind them, changed drastically. They both turned and watched the left wing dip, come back up, then dip again. The wings leveled out, but a second later, the nose came up and the tail scraped the runway with the most God-awful sound. Aborting the landing, the engines roared to full power as the plane clawed its way back into the air, leaving the runway behind.

"Holy shit!" Erin said. "The wind down near the surface of the runway must be swirling all over the place." She paused and pulled in a deep breath. "That is one fantastic pilot! Anyone else would have over fought it and sent them nose first into the runway."

Watching the plane circle and come back for a second approach, Erin pointed to a place further down the runway. "He'll be touching down just beyond there."

"Why?" Ray asked.

She brought her hand over, her finger pointing between the hanger and the next building. "The wind gusts are being funneled between the hanger and the next building. That's what hit him just as he tried to touch down."

"How did you get to be so smart?" Ray asked.

"Teagan is one of the best pilots I've ever seen. She loves to explain everything, and I pay attention to whatever she tells us. That's one of the things I love about her and CRM."

They watched as the A321 came in on a second approach. It touched down exactly where Erin had said it would. Once it was off the active runway and safely taxiing over to the terminal, they headed into the office in the hanger.

The chief met them just inside. "Impressive landing, aye?" They both nodded. "I'm afraid I needed to call off the new air ambulance coming in till tomorrow. I hope that's okay. There's a storm coming in. That's what's causing all these bloody winds and I don't know how experienced this new crew is"

"Sure," Erin answered. "Same time?" The chief nodded and she looked at Ray as they headed back for the door. "Guess we'll be flat hunting after all."

***

After collecting their research on flats for rent from their hotel room, Ray and Erin headed for the Terminal 5 tube station where they caught the tube to Hillingdon Station. Finding the first flat they looked at unacceptable, the second one proved to be perfect for them, fully furnished with all utilities included. On the recommendation of the flat manager, they set out for Argos Department Store in Uxbridge. Loaded with bed linens, pillows, a warm snugly comforter, silverware, dishes and glasses for four, they headed back to the flat. Next up was Farm Foods in Hillingdon to stock up on some food, drinks, and snacks. By midafternoon, their flat was stocked with everything they'd need so, it was back to the Skyline to collect their luggage and checkout.

"I don't know about you but I'm going to need some more clothes," Ray said on the tube back to the flat.

"Yeah, me too." She turned and gave him a big smile. "You know, never in a million years did I think I would be in London, England with a new job and sharing a flat with someone. But you know what? I'm glad it's you I'm sharing it with."

"Me too," Ray added, then locked her in a soul-searching kiss.

"Get a flat you too," a young guy said as he and his girlfriend walked by, both adding big smiles.

"Uh… we just did, thank you," Ray responded as all four of them snickered.

Their flight back to San Diego landed right on time. The flight crew held them back as everyone else exited the plane. "You're to follow us," the head flight attendant said as she handed out British Airways Photo IDs to each of them. "From now on, use these whenever you fly back and forth. Just show your IDs at check-in and they'll direct you to the flight crew lounge. Oh, and welcome to British Airways." The four of them were standing there dumbfounded. Finally, the flight attendant smiled and told them, "Clip your IDs on your jackets and let's go."

They followed the crew through the doors marked 'Flight Crews Only'. At the end of the hallway, they found themselves in a separate queue for customs and Immigration. Someone had even collected their luggage and set it near the customs officer's booth for their queue. After next to no questions, they exited outside, where Kiera and Bridget were waiting for them. Behind them was one of Kiera's Urban Search and Rescue vans with Digger, her search dog's head, hanging out the passenger window.

"Digger! How you doin' guy?" Aoife yelled, as she ran up, kissed him on the forehead and scratched behind his ears.

"Wow, lights and siren ride home. Nice," the head stewardess said.

Teagan introduced Kiera, Bridget and Digger to the flight crew, then hugs went around before the BA crew climbed into their van, parked in front of the Search and Rescue vehicle.

"Shit. I'm totally impressed. Look, they even have BA ID Badges," Kiera told Bridget as they loaded the luggage into the back of the van. Once everyone was in, she looked at them in the rear-view mirror. "Unless you guys are totally pooped out, we're headed to 57 Degrees and you're going to spend the rest of the afternoon telling us all about your trip. By the way, Baby Fae's already there, holding down our tables." She paused then added, "Oh, and don't forget, we need all the dirt on Ray and Erin."

They pulled into the parking lot of 57 Degrees, everyone filed out, then through the back door of the wine bar. Fae was waiting for them and gave hugs to everyone as they gathered around their reserved tables. Digger, with his bright orange 'Search Dog' vest, attracting the most attention. Once they were all settled, Sharon, the server, came over and took everyone's order. Drinks out of the way, Bridget said, "Okay, spill. Is there an engagement in the near future for Erin and Ray?"

"Not sure," Teagan said. "They've definitely gotten a lot closer. Personally, I think they're good for each other. They joke and kid around a lot but there's no doubt Ray would throw himself on a hand grenade to protect her."

"They've both taken on jobs over there," Aoife added. "BA has her doing CRM training for their Air Ambulance crews and he's been transferred to the FBI office in London. He'll be based at Heathrow and teaching BA's crews and ground personnel on how to spot, verify and report sex trafficking." She paused then added, "As for getting engaged, I doubt it. More likely they would just run off to Dublin or Paris and get married."

Maverick jumped in. "Yeah, or ask the Queen if they could borrow Salisbury or Westminster Cathedral for an hour or two. Both cathedrals are friggin' huge! You could spend all day in either one, and still probably miss half of it."

"And, what about you guys?" Kiera asked, smiling at Maverick, then Chase.

"Honestly, I think we all love England," Chase answered. "We've not had a lot of time to run around playing tourist but what we have seen is fascinating. I think we're all a little jealous of Erin and Ray and would move there, at least temporality, if the opportunity came up." The rest of them were nodding their heads.

Fae stared at him, smiled, then added, "Nice job avoiding the question about your love lives! So, moving on, where's our friends and family passes?"

"In the works," Chase assured her, returning her smile. "BA is moving more and more into training. They already train their people on spotting potential sex trade situations, but it's minimal at best. Now their big target is training for the London Fire Brigade. I'm subtly mentioning at every meeting about how great it would be to integrate their training with your training here in the US. Before our next trip I plan on having Erin and Ray start dropping hints about inviting all of you to do a presentation on where you could be of help in developing various training courses for BA to present. So put your thinking caps on and start coming up with ideas."

Suddenly Digger stood up, trotted over to the window and started growling. Bridget looked outside just as someone disappeared behind the van. "Uh, excuse me." Grabbing Digger's lead, she headed for the back door, while everyone else turned their attention back to Chase.

Everyone that is, except Fae. A moment later, her stool went over, she cleared the railing around the back area in one leap, then headed for the back door, the rest of them only a few steps behind her.

Alongside the van, Bridget was in some kind of standoff with a guy with a knife in his hand. At the back of the van, Digger had someone else trapped inside.

Chase and Aoife lined up next to Bridget while Teagan came up behind the guy with the knife. In back, Fae grabbed Digger's lead and eased him away from the open doors as Keira and Maverick joined her. Keira held her sheriff's badge in one hand and her gun in the other.

"You're under arrest..." turning toward the guy threating Bridget alongside of the van, she added, "...both of you." The guy inside duck walked out and the one alongside put the knife down, as both raised their hands. Shaking her head, Keira said, "You've got to be some kind of imbecile to try and rob a sheriff's van."

Once both of them were handcuffed, Keira requested a Harbor Police cruiser to transport them to the Harbor Police Station for booking. Her explaining what had happened, caused the policeman to look up at the windows along the back of 57 Degrees. "Oh, this is peachy. I can't wait to write this one up. Not only did they try to rob a sheriff's van, they did it with all of you sitting right there by the windows?"

"Yup, you got it," Kiera said. "Just goes to show, intelligence is not a requirement to qualify as a thief."

As soon as the two, not too bright robbers, were loaded into the cruiser and off to the police station, everyone retreated back into 57 Degrees. "So, where were we?" Fae asked. "Oh, that's right, you we're about to tell us about your love lives!"

Shaking his head side to side Chase decided he needed to give them some crumbs or they'd never leave the four of them alone. Turning to Maverick, he winked then said, "I'm pretty sure Maverick and I are madly in love with your two sisters."

"They're not really our sisters but... Ouch!" Keira yelled, as Bridget kicked her under the table.

"Shut up!" Bridget said. "They're about to confess their undying love and we're about to get two Brotherhood-in-laws. Actually, three, counting Ray."

"I am soooo sorry!" Teagan told Chase. "The good news is we're not related to any of them, so the kids should come out normal."

"Ha. With this cast of aunts, uncles and whatever we are? Good luck with that," Aoife said, finally joining in.

After everyone quit snickering, the four of them launched into what little sightseeing they has gotten to do and their plans for working with British Airways. Chase explained that his company had hired Maverick and the two of them would be working with BA on the seat layouts and new seat designs. When he finished, Maverick added that, while in London, they, along with Teagan and Aoife, would all be helping Erin and Ray whenever they could. Not only with the CRM training but also shoring up BA's training on spotting sexual predators and their prey.

Turning serious, Kiera put her hand over Maverick's. "Maverick, I know we've all teased you a lot about pea herding, but I'm pretty sure I speak for all of us when I say we recognized your herding and organizing talent and skills... pun kind of intended. Chase obviously did too. The one thing we will all miss is your wonderful sense of humor and ability to make pea herding sound like one of the most prestigious jobs in the world."

"Wow. Thank you, ma' lady," Maverick said, with a bow. He put his arm around Aoife's shoulder and pulled her in close. "Thanks to this wonderful woman, my job never embarrassed me. The fact that it was so opposite hers, and all of yours, has never been thrown at me, by any of you."

"You're really special, you know that." Aoife wrapped her arms around him.

Copying Aoife, Teagan wrapped her arms around Chase and pulled him close. "We all are, and I think we all realize it. That's what makes us such a great team. We complement each other, both as couples and as individuals." She paused and smiled at Maverick. "Maverick, sometimes your jokes were the only thing that let us keep our sanity after a horrific call. You somehow always seem to know when and how to cheer us up."

"Yeah, pea guts and mangled asparagus spears are a lot easier to deal with then crushed and mangled humans," he answered, throwing in a 'thank you' smile.

Turning to Chase, she kissed his nose. "And you, my wonderful Chase, you're the sensible one. Always pointing out the good we've done on each run, how many lives we saved or changed for the better.

"Finally, there's Ray. Don't ever tell him this, but he's been through his own kind of hell on calls and knows just when to gather the three of you as our personal support team: to drag all of us to the nearest bar so we can pour out our feelings, get shit faced and replace a bad day with hugs, kisses, love and laughter…" she turned back to Maverick "…laugh and shed tears over the important stuff, like smashed peas and shredded carrots clogging up the production line."

Wiping a tear from her cheek, Bridget smiled then added, "I hope all you guys have brothers because the other three of us need what Teagan, Aoife and Erin have: three more wonderful men to always be there for us."

"It's been a long day, on two continents and I'm about to fall off of my chair. I desperately need some sleep," Aoife told everyone.

# Chapter 40 – A Sneaky Snake and Food Fight Call?

The following morning came early as Teagan and Aoife reported for duty. Just as they were being welcomed back, the call alarm went off. "Air One, snake bite. Canyon off east end of Ribbon Road, Kearney Mesa. Citizen will direct you in."

"That's us. No rest for the wicked," Aoife said. "Get her cranked up and I'll grab the snake bite kit, bucket and tweezers," she told Teagan.

"Tweezers?" one of the other air nurses said, adding a chuckle.

"Okay, grabbers, pinchers, tongs, snake claw… the pole with the nabber thingy at the end," she said as she ran past the laughing Air Two team in the crew lounge.

"Ribbon Road? What kind of name is that?" Aoife heard Teagan ask as she slipped her helmet on and buckled herself in.

They lifted off, Teagan swung the helicopter around, aimed it west and picked up speed. Nine minutes later they were hovering above a small field, next to a twisty, turny road, bordering a canyon. Below them was a guy franticly waving his arms.

"Well, I see why it's called ribbon road," Teagan said. "Where the hell are we supposed to land?"

"There's a small spot over there." Aoife pointed to the edge of the canyon.

"Are we going to fit?"

Aoife shrugged. "I think so…Maybe?"

"Remind me to kill you if we survive the crash," came back in her helmet.

Laughing, Teagan nursed the chopper over the clear spot then eased the collective down. Just as the skids touched earth, a very small branch flew past the windshield. As she shut the bird down, Teagan said, "Remind me to add tree trimming to the city's call bill."

They both climbed out and Aoife went into the back. She grabbed the snake bite kit and passed it out to Teagan, then grabbed the bucket and snake tongs. "She's over here," the guy yelled frantically as he tried to grab Teagan and drag her into the clearing.

"Stop," she yelled at him. "Calm down, we see her. Just go sit over there. We've got this." she told him, pointing to nowhere in particular.

"He's big and totally pissed," the guy yelled as they turned and started to carefully walk over to the woman, checking every step.

Aoife looked at Teagan. "No snake?" she asked.

"He's behind me," the woman said, not moving anything but her mouth.

"Here snaky, snake, snake!" Aoife called out.

Nothing. No response or movement.

"Speak up," the guy yelled. "I think he's deaf from when she screamed at him."

"If you make me laugh and he bites me again I'm going to castrate you," the woman mumbled.

"In our snake bite class, they said snakes like Celtic music," Aoife said as she pulled her phone out, found an Enya song and hit play. Before the end of the first verse, the snake's head popped up, his tail rattled violently and he let out a loud hiss.

"I think he's a rattler," Aoife said.

"Good guess," the woman said.

"Keep him busy and I'll sneak around behind him," Aoife whispered to Teagan.

"Why are you whispering?" Teagan asked. "He's deaf, remember."

As Aoife started to approach the woman, the snake turned toward her. Instinctively, she crouched down, then duck walked the rest of the way. As she came around the woman, she found herself face to face with the snake… who, she was quite sure was smiling at her. She smiled back, reached out with the tongs, grabbed him and locked the tongs closed. "Got ya!"

Immediately, she realized three things. She'd forgotten the bucket. She's grabbed him too far down his neck and, if they thought he was pissed before, they hadn't seen anything yet.

Panic set in. She stood up. Made three complete turns. Yelled, "Duck!" and let go of the tongs.

The snake, tongs attached, flew over Teagan and the guy next to her and sailed right into the open back door of Air One. The four of them stood staring at Air One until, Teagan snorted, and they all started laughing hysterically.

Engine 36 from the San Diego Fire Department pulled up to find four people on the ground, laughing uncontrollably. Finally, the woman who had been bitten, looked at the fireman and managed to get out, "Can I get a ride with you?"

One fireman looked at the other three and said, "I thought this was a snake bite call?"

"Oh, believe me, this whole call has been snake bitten," Aoife replied as she finished injecting the woman with antivenom.

While hearing the story of what had happened, they all had another good laugh. Afterward, the firemen found the snake, tongs still attached, curled up and asleep on the gurney inside the helicopter.

"I think he's in shock," the one fireman said, carefully lifting the snake with the tongs and putting him in the bucket.

"Yeah, I doubt he'll mess with humans again," said his partner, handing the bucket to Teagan and the tongs to Aoife.

"What are we supposed to do with him?" Teagan asked them.

"Throw him over the ridge into the canyon," one of the firemen said while they loaded the woman onto the gurney. "Think you can manage that?"

"Nope!" Teagan said, handing the bucket back to him.

"I'm applying to the Air Ambulance Group. You guys have all the fun," the fireman said, then he took the bucket and headed for the edge of the canyon.

When they loaded the gurney into Air One, the woman asked one of the firemen again, "Sure I can't get a ride with you?" Turning to Teagan she added, "Nothing against you, they're just a lot cuter and seem to know more about rattlesnakes."

The fireman she'd asked smiled at Aoife and Teagan. "Okay if I ride along?"

"Sure," Teagan said. "You might want to check with her boyfriend or husband over there first though."

"Oh, he's not mine," the woman said. "He was just jogging by when I got bit and screamed."

"Okay, hop on in," Teagan instructed the fireman, then winked at him.

"Think I'll ride up front with you," Aoife said, adding another wink at the fireman as she slid the door closed and the fireman took the woman's hand. Aoife hopped into the copilot seat, she and Teagan smiled at each other, then Teagan eased the collective up and lifted off.

Clicking on her mike, Aoife called in their departure. "Memorial, this is Mercy Air One."

"Go Mercy Air One," came back.

"Roger, in bound with one snake bite victim. Female, twenty-eight years old. Snake was a good-sized rattler. Antivenom administered and victim appears to be responding well. ETA ten minutes. No need to assist. We can bring her down."

"Roger Air One, copy. ETA in ten, no assist needed."

Twelve minutes later Teagan shut Air One down and the fireman helped them ease the woman on the gurney out. "You need a ride back?" Aoife asked the fireman as they headed for the elevator.

"Nope, thanks, but I'll hang around till she's released, then we'll bum an ambo ride back," he said, giving the woman a big smile.

"Got it!" Teagan added a big smile of her own, as they pushed the gurney through the emergency room doors.

\*\*\*

Once the doors to the car park elevator closed on the way back up to the heliport, Teagan and Aoife burst out laughing. "Wow. My guess is those two will be headed for a bar, then one of their beds, before we clock out this afternoon," Teagan said.

"Uh, yeah. I think they were both snake bit, in a good way, as soon as they laid eyes on each other," Aoife added. "Maybe snake charmed would be a better term."

"I'm pretty sure it was your Enya song that did it," Teagan replied.

The two of them changed the linens on the gurney and cleaned out the stretcher bay, readying it for the next call. A call which came before they were even settled back in up front.

"Mercy Air One. Riot at Little Tots Day Care, Bonita Road."

They both looked at each other and laughed. "Can't be the kids. Must be pissed off parents or something," Aofie said as Teagan eased the collective up and they lifted off.

Ten minutes later, a Chula Vista police officer waved them into an empty field across Bonita Road from the day care center. As they loaded their medical gear onto the gurney, the policeman asked, "How many little people can you get in there?" The two of them stared at him as he tried to stifle a laugh. "Today was their karate class and things got a wee bit carried away," he added, while he stopped traffic so they could cross the road.

Carried away was putting it mildly. As they entered the day care center, they stopped and gasped at the mess. Food, toys and chunks of who knew what (some things were best left a mystery) were everywhere. A variety of juices dripped down the walls and off the chins and hair of most of the kids, now up against the wall on one side of the room; orange, apple, cranberry, milk and uh peanut butter (?), with a variety of jams, egg and tuna salads.

The other side of the room appeared to be the vegetarian group. One kid was definitely wearing his salad, while another had a cherry tomato stuck in each ear. Next to him a girl was trying to pry a small, sweat pickle out of her nose.

"Okay! Everybody line up! Single file so we can examine you." Teagan directed the veggie group along the one wall, desperately tried not to snort.

"What did she say?" the kid with cherry tomatoes in his ears asked.

"Line up," pickle girl yelled at him followed by, "Ah choo," as she fired the pickle at the girl in front of her and doused her with pickle juice.

On the other side of the room, Aoife ducked just in time as a bowl of oatmeal sailed past her. "Who threw that?" she yelled as the line of kids, all laughing, pointed at one another. A second later half an egg salad sandwich stuck to the back of her head as chaos broke out again and food, stuffed animals, Legos and puzzle pieces flew everywhere.

"STOP," the policeman yelled. "You're all under arrest! Back against the walls! Now!"

Laughing hysterically, Teagan and Aoife both collapsed to the floor as the kids turned and everything within their reach was directed at the policeman. Ammunition turned from breakfast to lunch as spaghetti, mac and cheese, navy bean soup, grilled cheese, guacamole, tuna salad, hummus, split pea soup, and more 'we're not sure,' flew.

Moments later, SWAT and the CHP arrived; along with Bridget, Kiera and Fae, called out by Mercy Air as back up. Following them were three news vans and dozens of parents who had automatically been alerted by phone of the riot at their kid's school.

It took over an hour to check each kid for injuries. Afterward, Bonita Fire gently hosed them off, one at a time, with a garden hose, before releasing them to their parents. The policeman, however, required more attention since he was allergic to peanuts. So after all the kids were processed, Teagan and Aoife loaded him into Air One for transport to Memorial.

"Memorial, Air One," Aoife got out in between giggles.

"Go Air One."

"Inbound. Twenty-five-year-old male. Allergy. Extensive exposure to peanut butter." She paused for another giggle. "No assist needed but request an isolation bed and that you line the hallway and cubicle with plastic tarps."

After a long pause, the admissions nurse came back. "Is this the policeman from the day care riot?"

"Roger," Aoife answered, tacking on another chuckle.

Another long pause. "Be advised, we'll try and clear a path for you through the news vans but be prepared for more chaos when you land."

"Roger," Aoife said.

"Oh great! My wife and kids are going to be watching this on the news and I'm never going to live this down," the policeman said, as he shook his head and a big glob of peanut butter fell from his ear, while Aoife pulled a Lego out of his hair.

"There is no back way in from the heliport, so I strongly suggest you fake being passed out," Teagan yelled from the pilot's seat.

"Got it," the policeman said, after spitting out a chunk of peanut, then closing his eyes.

Getting in proved to be easier than expected. "Stand back. You don't want to catch what he's got," they yelled as the news people glared as his badly swollen face and arms, then cleared a path, certain he had some kind of terrible, contagious disease.

Cleanup of the helicopter took longer than the run. And, for the next several days, they would keep finding peanut butter, Lego and puzzle pieces, that had somehow worked their way into every nook and cranny of the helicopter. That was on top of the ribbing they took from Bridget, Keira and Fae, as well as everyone at Mercy Air. Even Erin and Ray had gotten wind of the snake and toddler callouts (Thanks Chase and Maverick!) and called while they were all at 57 Degrees to say they were adding 'Snake Enchantment and Toddler Riot Courses' to BA's EMT training sessions. Then they asked if Teagan and Aoife were interested in teaching them.

Once everyone was done kidding them, conversation turned to Erin and Ray and how things were going.

"Great," Ray said. "We were done outlining the courses we think BA might want to offer but now, I guess, we'll need to add two more. Oh, and one of the Fire Brigade's chief officers asked us to add an Emergency Services Driving Course after almost everyone on the truck almost got bounced off on a callout. Seems the country volunteer brigade that he was testing normally drive tractors and don't feel obliged to stay on the roads."

Erin let out a laugh in the background. "Shortest distance, and all that." After another laugh, she added, "Oh, and he wanted extra points for missing a flock of sheep that failed to yield to the flashing lights and siren."

Once everyone quit laughing, Ray jumped back in. "Oh, by the way, we just checked out of the Skyline and brought everything over to our new flat. That's where we're at now."

After describing their flat and where it was, Erin said, "Listen, you've all had a crazy day and we're about to grab something at the pub around the corner, then collapse. So how about if we let you go? We'll catch up with you in a day or two."

Teagan let out a chuckle as she looked at Chase and Maverick. "Crazy doesn't come close to covering our day. We're not sure if we should laugh or cry and I'm sure Chase and Maverick are both thinking 'what the hell have I gotten myself into?' You guys enjoy your dinner at the pub and we'll talk again soon. Stay well and we love you guys!"

As soon as they hung up, she looked around at everybody. "How do you possibly explain today to anybody?"

"Hey, charming a snake, helping a love-struck couple find each other and cleaning up after a food fight is better than our usual day of taping people back together and hosing blood and guts out of our chopper," Aoife reminded her.

Maverick let out a snort. "Are you two listening to yourselves? I can't think of an adjective, or even a group of adjectives, that come close to describing your job. And while the rest of us sit at our desks bored to death, you, all of you, never know what you're going to run into. How many lives you're going to save, or change forever."

He paused, pulled Aoife against him, looked at each of the other women, then back at Aoife. "I'm sure I speak for Chase, and Ray too. I can't possibly think of how I could be prouder of Eff... of all of you... of knowing you and being a part of your lives."

Fae's hand shot up. "Uh, excuse me." Turning to Aoife she asked, "What do you feed this guy?"

All of the sisters were used to teasing each other, especially Fae who had just left the door wide open. "Listen, little Tanker Jock, you might be too young to understand but he came with enough peas and carrots to last a lifetime. I just add me for dessert and he's happy as a clam. Right?" she asked Maverick.

"You got it. She's good at getting me all steamed up. Baste me in some sweet butter and serve me on the half shell..." He paused, kissed Aoife, then added, "... then smear her in-"

"Stop! Stop! Stop! We. Do. Not. Want. To. Know," Kiera yelled.

Just then, someone in an Air Force flight suit came up behind Fae and put a finger to his lips to shush everyone. He gently wrapped his arms around her waist, whispered, "Hi," in her ear. She'd smelled him before he got there... so did the rest of the women.

*Holy shit, he smells good enough to eat*, Teagan, sitting next to Fae thought, as he kissed his way from one side of Fae's neck, across her back to the other side. Fae's face lit up in a gigantic smile as he spun her around, then locked her into an earth-shattering kiss.

Everyone just stared. *Who the hell is this guy?* they all wondered. He was drop dead gorgeous. Tall, olive skin, dark brown hair, hazel eyes sprinkled with gold flecks that lit up the room, and a smile that would make women faint if he directed both at them. Then there was the uniform. No one should ever be allowed to look that good. He was edible! If not edible, then certainly lickable.

"Um… excuse me. What your doing is illegal in public!" Teagan finally said.

After three more slightly toned-down kisses, they finally broke apart. "Oh, this is Matt, my boyfriend," Fae said. "He's an E-3C AWACS pilot. He's about to get discharged and so he's in my class studying for his tanker license, like I am." If possible, her smile got bigger as she stared into his eyes then, tried to suck his tongue out, again.

"Stop that," Teagan said. "I just creamed in my flight suit."

"You're right, they're all crazy. But I love them," Matt said, giving Fae yet another scorcher of a kiss. Fae had warned him about how this meeting was likely to go, so they had practiced the routine they would launch into.

"You two should not be allowed out in public," Kiera said, then looking at Matt added, "Uh, by the way, do you have five brothers?"

"Hey!" Chase and Maverick chimed.

"Sorry, guess we just need two."

"Nope. Two sisters, but no brothers," Matt answered.

"After the dates I've had lately, I can be convinced to switch sides," Bridget whispered to Kiera.

"If they look anything like him... me too," she answered.

Teagan decided to have a little more fun. Hell, if he was going to date Fae, it was only fair he knew what he was getting into. "E-3C AWACS, that's the one with the big flying saucer on the roof, right?" Teagan asked him.

"Yup, that's the one."

"Isn't that the one our grandmothers flew back from California in - just before it became a state?" she asked, scanning the others.

"I see now why you're the way you are," Matt whispered to Fae.

"What the hell does that mean?" she shot back.

"No... no. I meant it in a good way. You're pretty, open minded, intelligent, fun to be with." He paused again. "Oh, I can't forget HOT."

"Aww. Thank you, my handsome knight. The good news is I'm not related to any of them, so the kids should probably turn out okay." That earned her another kiss.

Bridget glared at them, then added, "The bad news is, we're all going to go throw up. Oh, and how long did you two practice this comedy routine?"

"Damn, busted," Fae said.

Digger, who had been sleeping through most of this, stood up, stretched then sauntered over to Matt and put his head in his lap. "Hi, guy," Matt said as he scratched behind his ears. "You been over there guarding and protecting everyone?"

"He's a search and rescue dog, not a watch dog. The only thing he watches and protects is his food dish," Kiera replied.

"You're his handler?" Matt asked.

"More likely the other way around but, yeah, we come as a package."

Scanning everyone, Matt turned serious. "All kidding aside, you're all amazing."

"They are," Chase said. "Between them, I can't tell you how many people they've saved, just since Teag and I have been dating. British Airways and the Heathrow Fire Brigade absolutely love them, and they haven't even met Kiera, Bridget and Fae yet."

Digger let out a howl.

"Oh, I'm sorry Digger, you too."

"Do you think they'll let me take Digger on the plane when we go to London?" Kiera asked Chase.

"I don't see why not. He's easily as well behaved as a therapy dog. Just make sure he's got his 'Search and Rescue' jacket on and you've got all his papers."

"When's the next trip to London?" Bridget asked.

"My guess is Teagan and Aoife will be going back before Maverick and I," Chase replied. "BA is anxious to get their CRM training started. Plus, from what I understand, Ray and Erin have been throwing out all kinds of suggestions for additional training that BA can offer for EMTs and air crews. And that doesn't include Ray's sex trafficking recognition classes. So my guess is, given the interest the two of them are stirring up, all of you will be going to London shortly. Even if it's only to introduce each of you and get started outlining at least some of that training." He stared at Maverick, then asked him, "Care to add to that?"

"Sure. You all should know that we've opened Pandora's box. Turns out, like BA, the seat company we work for has been toying with creating a training division for some time now. Once they got wind of what we're doing with BA, they jumped on it." He paused and looked back at Chase.

"Go ahead and tell them," Chase said. "The offers are probably in their mailboxes right now."

"Okay." Maverick looked at each of them with a big smile. "Don't get mad but Chase and I submitted your bios and CVs, or resumes, to the new VP of training at our company. Not only was he impressed, he's making each of you an offer. But... he wants you as a team. Not because he thinks you can't work on your own but because you each bring something unique to the team plus you already work well together. With you as a team, he thinks we, the company, can offer training that no one else can come close to."

"He can't really expect us to miss out on sneaky snake and tot food fight calls?" Aoife said.

"Funny you should mention that," Chase said. "With all the disruption on flights and abuse flight attendants have been getting lately, that's already been added to the list of possible training subjects. And let's not forget finding snakes, alligators, racoons, fish and who knows what else in the overheads." He paused and added, "Definitely sneaky snake calls; not quite tot food fights, but close especially given the immaturity of passengers lately."

"Uh, any room in all this for tanker jocks?" Fae asked, wrapping her arm around Matt.

"Definitely," Chase replied. "With all the fires in Europe from climate change, training tanker pilots is rapidly moving up on BA's list too. Also the Aussies have already expressed an interest in having Qantas and Australian Airlines work with BA on tanker pilot and crew training."

"Holy shit! Are we in the right place at the right time... or what?" Bridget asked.

Chase smiled at her. "You pretty much hit the nail on the head. COVID opened the eyes of all the major international carriers; that they need to get involved in other areas. Areas that can help carry them through things like pandemics or wars that close off a good part of their route structure."

All of a sudden, a loud ruckus attracted everybody's attention to the back door and Digger took off growling.

"He stole her purse," a guy, next to a girl yelled, pointing at a second guy holding a knife in one hand and a purse in the other.

Digger crouched down a short way from the guy with the knife, growling and ready to launch himself at him any second. "San Diego Sherriff. Put the knife down," Kiera yelled, pointing her gun at the guy.

He turned toward Kiera, Digger tensed and let out another louder growl. "Put the knife down or lose a few fingers," Kiera told him, aiming at his hand.

The guy took a step toward Kiera. Digger's growl got even louder and, before the guy could take a second step, she lowered the barrel and shot him in the foot. "Okay, toes then," she said. The guy screamed, dropped to the floor and the knife skidded under a wine rack. "Down Digger," she commanded.

"Ugh, he was definitely not worth all this paperwork," Kiera murmured as she filled out yet another form explaining why she'd had no choice but to blow the guys toes off. "He's lucky I didn't aim higher or he'd be speaking with a high-pitched voice," she mumbled through a chuckle.

"What are you laughing at?" Bridget asked.

"Nothing," she answered, then burst into a full-blown laugh fit.

"You have an evil mind." Bridget shook her head. "You're wondering why you didn't blow his balls off, aren't you? Like that would have made all the paperwork worth it."

"Did I talk in my sleep?"

"Nope, I'm your sister, remember. I know what you're thinking before you do!" Bridget handed her a glass of wine then clinked hers against it. "To sisters, we're much more than sisters," she toasted.

They both turned to a knock on the door. A second later it opened and Teagan, Chase, Aoife, Maverick, Fae and Matt marched in. Kiera looked over at Bridget. "Why are we the only two without a man in our lives?" she asked.

"Maybe if you'd quit shooting them, they'd hang around longer?" Teagan said.

403

"Hey! I didn't shoot anyone." Bridget said.

"Guilt by association," Aoife answered.

"Ugh, why are you all here again?" Kiera asked?

"To turn in our witness statements and plan the next trip to London?" Chase answered.

"Oh yeah. Sorry, it's been a long day so far, without a lot of sleep last night." Kiera shook her head trying to clear the brain fog. Everybody handed her their witness statements, which she added to the last of her paperwork. "Thank God that's done. Now I get a vacation while they investigate the shooting."

"Perfect, then you're free to join us in London," Teagan said.

"Who all's going?" Kiera asked.

"We're out," Fae replied. "Matt and I have our certification flights over the next couple of weeks."

"I'm out too. We're right in the middle of investigating a major pet smuggling ring," Bridget said. She turned to Kiera. "If you're not taking Digger with you, I could use him."

"I thought about taking him but, if you need him, he's yours," Kiera answered. "What kind of pets are they smuggling?"

"Hamsters and hedgehogs. I even made him an official vest." Bridget pulled a vest out of her backpack. Printed on each side was:

# San Diego Sherriff's Department
# Hamster and Hedgehog Patrol Dog
# Please do not pet me!

Everyone broke out laughing while Digger, tail wagging like a windshield wiper on high, ran over and stuck his head through the opening for his head in the vest. "He's smiling!" Kiera said, then added, "Trader!"

***

Once everyone calmed down, Maverick said, "Guess it's the helo crew: Kiera, Chase and I." Turning to Kiera he added, "Anyone of the male persuasion you'd like to bring along?"

"Ha ha! Very funny smart ass. Do I need to remind you I carry a gun and I know how to use it? Plus the paperwork's all filled out. All I need to do is change the number of perps to two." She looked down at Digger. "I'd sick Digger on you but he's busy making love to his new vest."

# Chapter 43 – London Calling

BA flight 272 landed at Heathrow right on time, despite a late take off thanks to Kiera forgetting to register her weapon beforehand. Adding to her embarrassment, the air marshal on board had requested she join him once they were at altitude and the seat belt sign went off. Everyone else watched as the 6 foot 2 inch, unbelievably good looking marshal waited for her to get her act together and untangle herself from her seatbelt.

"First flight?" he asked as she stood up and started into the aisle but was stopped by the backpack strap wrapped around her left foot. He caught her as she launched herself into his chest. Both hands hanging onto his shirt for dear life, he pulled her and the backpack into the aisle and stood her up. Reaching down, he eased her leg out of the shoulder strap, but as he did, a Tupperware container fell out of one of the side pouches. It hit the floor, the lid popped open and dog food sprayed all over the aisle.

"Is there something else in there I should know about?" he asked, a big smile forming on his face.

"Uh… Sorry, that's for my Hamster and Hedgehog Patrol Dog."

Staring at the backpack he asked, "What is he… a miniature chihuahua? Guess that'd be about the right size for hunting hamsters and hedgehogs."

"No...he... he doesn't hunt them.... he uh... he detects them, then digs where they're at. That's why I named him Digger."

The smile on his face instantly went to shear confusion, while everyone else was snickering and snorting.

"Speaking of digging, I want to see how she digs her way out of this one," Maverick loudly whispered.

Kiera turned, flipped Maverick the bird, then asked the Marshal, "Can we go someplace private?"

Obviously digesting that, his confused look went back to a smile. "Sure, follow me," he said as they headed for the galley in the middle of the plane. Once inside, he looked back at everyone, smiled, then slid the curtain closed.

\*\*\*

Some twenty minutes later, they knew Kiera was back by the crunching sound as she stepped out of the aisle and into her seat.

"Are you okay?" Teagan barely got out in between snickers.

"He took my gun away," she said.

"Smart man," Maverick said.

"Up yours. He's going to return it tonight over dinner at the Pheasant, wherever that is..." then added "...and you're not invited!"

"Wow. First trip and the chihuahua's mom has a date with an air marshal," Chase announced.

"Ha ha. Laugh now but I'll be laughing tomorrow when I tell you all about the wonderful meal we had at the Pheasant. Larry says it's one of the best places to eat by the airport."

"You won't need to tell us because we'll be at the next table," Aoife said. "No way we're going to miss watching you two on your first date." She turned to Teagan. "Remind me when we check in to have the concierge make sure they sit them next to our favorite table."

"Shit," came from the seat behind them.

***

Their trip to the hotel gave them a chance to explain to Kiera how the hopper bus system worked. That, with an Oyster card, would let her get around on her own if she needed to. "Ray and Erin are supposed to meet us at the hotel," Teagan said. "Once we've checked in, we can all walk over to the Pheasant for dinner."

"Is it that close?" Kiera asked.

"Yup. Is Larry supposed to meet you there?" Aoife asked.

"Yeah, or at the hotel if he can get out of the airport soon enough," she answered.

"You two really seemed to hit it off. What was the discussion in the galley all about? Teagan asked.

"He told me my weapon was just an excuse to meet me. He'd seen me in the boarding area, saw I was carrying, and decided to check me out. He said he wanted to make sure 'I was real'. I assured him it was all me, nothing artificial, no Botox inflated parts. That got a big laugh as he tried to explain that wasn't what he'd meant. Next thing I knew, he was asking me to have dinner with him."

The hopper bus pulled into the hotel entrance and Larry, alongside the concierge, was waiting for them. "How the hell did you get here so fast?" Kiera asked him.

"Sorry, I forgot you had to go through customs. If I'd thought about it, I would have had you come with me and bypass all that." He reached down and took her suitcase and backpack. "Got it," he told the concierge, then led her to the front desk.

"Guess you're stuck with me," the concierge said to the rest of them. "Welcome back. How was your trip home?"

"Good… and it's good to be back," Chase replied. "Can you make a reservation for us at the Pheasant?" He looked at the others. "Forty-five minutes?" he asked, and everyone nodded.

"Already taken care of," the concierge replied as Erin and Ray met them in the lobby.

"Uh, so, who's the guy with Kiera?" Erin asked.

"Short story… to be explained over dinner," Aoife replied.

"You do know he's carrying?" Ray added.

"Uh, yeah. So is Kiera, that's part of the story. He was the air marshal on our flight and decided he needed to check out Kiera's weapon… and other parts," Maverick added, joining in.

"Got it!" Erin said, adding a big smile. "Go freshen up and we'll meet you down here."

Twenty minutes later everyone assembled in the lobby for the short walk to the Pheasant. On the way, Larry introduced himself to Ray and Erin and, as he pulled Kiera in closer, explained how she had caught his eye as soon as she walked into the waiting area in San Diego.

After hiking up the stairs, the owner of the Pheasant welcomed them back, then led them to a table toward the back of the upstairs dining area. "What's with the partition?" Teagan asked, nodding toward a folding screen blocking off the back area.

"Oh, private party," the owner said. "They're an older group, celebrating something. We assured them seating you nearby would be okay and you'd be respectful."

"Not a problem," Chase said. "We're all tired from our flight so, if anything, it'll be our snoring that'll disturb them."

The server came and took their drink orders. All they could hear from the party behind the screen was a quiet discussion about something to do with how surprised someone they were waiting for was going to be. "That's neat that they're doing a surprise party for someone," Teagan whispered, just as the server came back with their drinks.

Chase picked up his beer and offered a toast. "To another fantastic trip!"

Suddenly from behind the screen came, "Wait! Wait!"

Someone pulled the screen back and everyone stared at: Aoife's parents, Shawn, CJ, Jessie and Paige. Teagan's parents, Leigh and James. And Erin's parents, Shannon and Bert.

Erin, Aoife and Teagan sat staring with their mouths hanging open. Finally, Teagan recovered enough to ask, "What... what are you doing here?"

"Uh, you need to ask them that," CJ said, nodding back toward their table.

All three of them turned to find Ray, Maverick, and Chase, each kneeling next to them. Each with an open ring box in their hand.

The girls looked at each other. How had none of them seen this coming? Not only had the men gotten together and planned this, but obviously their parents were also in on it.

All three lit up in big smiles, turned to the man kneeling next to them and said, "Yes!"

# Acknowledgements

*A Sisterhood of Heroes* is another collaborative effort between myself and Casey. We've known for a long time how much alike and in sync we are, but our coauthored stories truly let our combined talents shine. And, though unintended, each story quickly takes on a life of its own, so we've learned to just run with them. *A Sisterhood of Heroes* is no exception.

When I finished my first trilogy, *Horses of Tir Na Nog*, Casey immediately suggested that I write a follow-on story about the daughters of the women in the sisterhoods.

That planted a seed. A seed that germinated for five years and finally sprouted during an ambulance ride to the hospital. As my ambulance pulled into the entrance to the Emergency Room, an Air Ambulance helicopter from Mercy Air landed at the heliport. First responders popped into my head and off my story went. Two hours in the MRI chamber later that day, let me rough out several chapters. (Hey, it's not like you've a lot to do while getting MRI'ed.)

Later that day, an email from Casey resulted in suggestions for several more scenes and chapters, and off our story went.

Once again, we learned, supported and complemented each other, via thousands of emails, as chapter lines blurred and soon neither one of us could remember or tell who has written what. All we know is each time we read our story, we love it. Each time we tweaked it, it got better. And when it was finished, neither of us wanted to change a thing.

We believed *Light My Way* brought out the best in both of us and is one of the best stories we would ever write. That is, till *A Sisterhood of Heroes* came along. While a very different story, we think it is as good as *Light My Way* and the two together show the range of our writing.

As before, there really aren't a lot of people to thank.

There is one person though that we can't forget: Kristen Kieffer, creator of Your Write Dream Facebook author group. Not only is that where we met but it's where so many authors, including us, go to learn, ask questions, get support or pour their heart out when writer's block and other doubts set in. Thank you, Kristen, for playing a major role in making us better writers and to love what we write.

Finally, our readers. We, like other writers, often say we write for ourselves, and perhaps we do. But there is still no better thrill then getting a review from a reader who says your story touched their heart or that they loved your characters and your story. Even those who weren't thrilled with it, but take the time let us know why, are still appreciated because they help us become better writers.

So to every one of our readers, thank you for choosing our book to read and please, please leave us a review.

Bob Boze lives in the beautiful South Bay area of San Diego. Casey Fae Hewson lives in sunny Marlborough, on New Zealand's South Island.

Casey and Bob are both published romance and non-fiction authors, editors, speakers and bloggers. Both are avid readers and love writing young adult and contemporary romance fiction, as well as sharing their business expertise.

When Casey's not reading or writing she'll be mountain biking, walking, gardening, travelling and always listening to music. When Bob's not reading or writing he'll be off somewhere roaming the world and sitting with Casey in a pub somewhere, while listening to music and plotting their next book.

Combined, Bob and Casey have over fourteen books and several short stories published, or in work.

Bob's romance novels: *Horses of Tir Na Nog, The Sisterhood, Dreams, The Beach Pool, The Heiress and the Dolphins, Route 66*

His autobiography: *Love is a Pretty Girl With a Cape to Share Your Dreams With.*

Casey's romance novels: *Haven River, Aqua Bay. Misty Springs*

Her business book (under Robyn Bennett): *Minute Taking Madness.*

Their coauthored romance stories: *Light My Way, A Sisterhood of Heroes.*

Their business book: *How Not to Fail in Business Without Really Trying.*

Casey and Bob also offer a variety of writer and business services through their business website, Writing Allsorts. To find out more about the services they offer, go to https://writingallsorts.com/.

From there you can follow the links to their web sites or go directly to https://bobboze.com or https://caseyfaehewson.com to learn more about their books, or connect with them on Facebook, Twitter, Pinterest or Instagram.

Made in the USA
Middletown, DE
01 October 2022